Books by Sally John

FAMILY OF THE HEART SERIES
Between Us Girls

THE BEACH HOUSE SERIES
The Beach House
Castles in the Sand

IN A HEARTBEAT SERIES
In a Heartbeat
Flash Point
Moment of Truth

THE OTHER WAY HOME SERIES
A Journey by Chance
After All These Years
Just to See You Smile
The Winding Road Home

Heaven Help Heidi

SALLY JOHN

HARVEST HOUSE PUBLISHERS
EUGENE, OREGON

Scripture verses are taken from the Jerusalem Bible © 1966 by Darton, Longman & Todd, Ltd., and Doubleday & Company, Inc.

Cover by Garborg Design Works, Savage, Minnesota

Cover photos © PlusOne / Bigstock

The author is represented by the literary agency of Alive Communications, Inc., 7680 Goddard Street, Ste. #200, Colorado Springs, CO 80920. www.alivecommunications.com.

HEAVEN HELP HEIDI
Copyright © 2015 Sally John
Published by Harvest House Publishers
Eugene, Oregon 97402
www.harvesthousepublishers.com

Library of Congress Cataloging-in-Publication Data
    John, Sally, 1951-
    Heaven help Heidi / Sally John.
       pages ; cm
    ISBN 978-0-7369-5468-6 (pbk.)
    ISBN 978-0-7369-5469-3 (eBook)
    I. Title.
    PS3560.O323H434 2015
    813'.54—dc23

                                        2014026847

Printed in the United States of America

      14 15 16 17 18 19 20 21 22 / LB-JH / 10 9 8 7 6 5 4 3 2 1

❧

For
Cindi Cox and Jeff Carlson
Thank you for being there

❧

Acknowledgments

Thank you, readers, for your support and encouragement. I cannot say how often an e-mail, a Facebook post, or a letter from one of you encourages me in my writing.

What do I know about leg injuries, titanium rods, real estate, cars, car racing, sports, trucks, kayaks, and—sometimes—words? Not much. Thank you to family and friends who provided details from personal experience: nephew Matthew John, sister Cindi Cox, Carla and Chester Genack, Elizabeth and Troy Johnson, Tracy and Christopher John. If there are mistakes, these are the people to blame.

Many thanks as always go to the great teams behind this work: editors Kathleen Kerr and Kim Moore, everyone else at Harvest House Publishers; agent Andrea Heinecke, and everyone else at Alive Communications.

Thank you, Tim, for it all.

Residents of the Casa de Vida Cottages

Olivia "Liv" McAlister, owner

Riley and Tasha Baker

Noah and Déja Grey

Sean Keagan

Piper Keyes

Charles Chadwick Rutherford IV

Inez and Louis Templeton

Coco Vizzini

Samantha Whitley

Jasmyn Albright

Beau Jenner, maintenance man

I have taken you by the hand...
Isaiah 42:6

One

Losing control of her car at eighty miles per hour had not been on Heidi Hathaway's to-do list for the first day of February.

Up until the moment she skidded off the freeway, her schedule had been ordinary. After a late lunch meeting, she checked half the items off her list and headed south on the 5 out of Orange County into San Diego, a routine drive that required no extraordinary measures. As usual, she zigzagged around slowpokes. She phoned clients—of course using the hands-free device niftily located on the steering wheel. She drank coffee, changed the radio station from jazz to news and back again, applied lipstick, unclipped her hair and brushed it.

It was a typical scenario for a Southern Californian. As a matter of fact, her friends thought of her as so typical, they said she was a SoCal cliché: blonde, blue-eyed, beach volleyball ace, San Diego State grad with a major in Party Girl, owner of a red convertible.

She didn't mind the teasing, although she had outgrown the party girl phase and for many years had driven a hardtop. Currently her car was a high-end, late-model German beauty, more crimson sparkle than plain old red. She'd chosen the five-door model, better suited to stowing kayak paddles and open-house signs. It was a breeze to maneuver through heavy traffic.

All in all, her life and the forty minutes on the freeway on the first of February were ordinary.

And then they weren't.

The mid-afternoon winter sun dipped at an odd angle. Ocean and sky blurred into one unbroken expanse of hazy blue. The rugged terrain of Camp Pendleton smudged into the color of brown desert camouflage fatigues. A blinding shaft of light sliced beneath the car's visor, penetrating her sunglasses.

A white van sped up on her left and hovered alongside her like a shadow. A semi in front of her reduced speed. A black SUV lingered at her right rear.

She was boxed in.

Except for the small opening on the right, shrinking by the millisecond, just ahead of the SUV.

Her father loved cars. It seemed an odd passion for an egghead of a professor, but it became their common ground from the time she was a little girl. He taught her everything about cars and how to drive. They watched races and paid to drive exotic cars at a track in Las Vegas. He cautioned her to save her competitive streak for selling real estate. The freeway was not a raceway.

The semi in front of her braked.

Her dad's words had never made total sense. If there were six lanes full of vehicles clipping along at high speeds, a little aggression seemed necessary in order to do her part to keep traffic flowing. Getting boxed in was to be avoided. She used all six lanes when necessary, which explained why she was now one lane away from the right shoulder, behind a semi.

Instead of braking, she signaled, sped up, and went for the narrow opening on her right.

And then she had a clear view of red brake lights.

Immediately, dead ahead in front of her.

She had nowhere to go but the shoulder. She torqued the steering wheel and jammed both feet onto the brake pedal. The high-end, late-model crimson beauty hit gravel and spun.

"Help me, God! Help me, God! Help me, God!"

The car flew. It flipped. It bounced. It rolled. Again. And again. And again.

Time ceased to exist. An eternity and a heartbeat melded into one indistinct flow.

Metal crumpled. Glass popped. Air bags burst. Sharp edges sliced and heat seared.

The world vanished.

Two

Along with every other driver around her in the southbound lanes of I-5, Piper Keyes braked. She did not simply slow down; she stopped. Not a good sign for keeping to a schedule.

"Life in Southern California, Pipe," she said aloud to herself. "What are you going to do? Move back to Wisconsin?"

She pooched her lips in a happy-sad smile. The joke was old and private, her favorite Jared-ism.

On the radio a traffic update cut into the Sixties music and she turned it off. Traffic was obvious. She partially lowered the windows of her small sea-green hybrid car. The sun-kissed February ocean air seeped inside. After seven years its warmth in the dead of winter still enchanted her. If she moved back to the Midwest, she would miss it something awful. But then, she'd miss everything.

Oh, right. She imagined her mother's voice asking the obvious. *You'd miss sitting on the highway in the middle of no-man's land?*

Absolutely, Mom, because it's not a highway or no-man's land. It's the Gunnery Sergeant John Basilone Memorial stretch of the I-5 Freeway and it runs through Camp Pendleton, the base where Jared was stationed. I like driving on it and I like sitting on it. I feel close to him here.

And that's a good thing?

What was it about a mother's voice? Darlene's could nag and provoke, encourage and love all at once, even in Piper's imagination. Like any doting mom with a hurt child, she simply wanted her daughter back in the nest, safe and sound and pain free.

Piper's eyes stung. Yes, it was a good thing to feel close to Jared, especially this week, this weepy week. It had begun already, the unavoidable mistiness and tight throat.

The car in front of Piper inched forward all of three feet and stopped again. She followed suit. Ahead she saw creeping vehicles and brake lights, but nothing that explained the jam. Typical. They came and went. In her rearview mirror she glimpsed flashing lights far away. Not typical. It meant something serious had happened.

Sirens wailed now, growing louder. She tensed. Drivers were supposed to move, but getting out of the way was not an option. Emergency vehicles came into view along the shoulder. Police cars, an ambulance, and fire trucks eventually lumbered past, not quite at top speed. The noise of their sirens deafened. She watched as they disappeared in the distance.

Obviously there had been an accident. She wasn't going anywhere soon.

Piper eyed the stack of magazines on the passenger seat. Normally she passed her free time by skimming through photos of famous people. It was her job to know their latest fashion choices. But then, this weepy week did not fall into the category of normal.

She held her breath, keeping the tears at bay. She really did not want to sit there and bawl, though she easily could have.

"Excuse me!"

A shout came from her left and Piper turned toward it.

A guy behind the wheel of a red convertible Corvette, top down, grinned. He pushed up his sunglasses and leaned over his empty passenger seat. "Don't I know you?"

She smiled tightly, shook her head, and waggled her left hand. The diamond caught the sunlight.

He shrugged. "Hey, can't blame a guy for trying."

She pressed the window control and turned away so he wouldn't see the roll of her eyes. Jared would say that she could at the very least blame the guy for being a stereotype, for adding further proof that men who drove red convertibles deserved their bad rap.

In a comic book hero sort of way, her fiancé had been a stereotype. Square jaw, dark brown eyes full of twinkling light when he smiled, broader-than-broad shoulders, muscular but huggable, ruggedly handsome even in pajama-like fatigues. But his persona? Now that didn't fit into any sort of typical guy category.

A horn tooted behind her, startling Piper. She pulled forward another few feet, braked, and folded her hands primly on her lap. The driver back there had no idea who she was messing with. The woman could not imagine the effort it took Piper not to make a disgusted gesture or to scowl in the rearview mirror.

Nuts, nuts, nuts. She muttered the closest thing to profanity that she had in her vocabulary. Jared had thought it cute. She said it was the lingering taste of soap on her tongue.

Maybe she shouldn't be near people right now. She could cancel her next appointment, go home, take some R and R. An emotionally healthy woman would do that. She'd sit in the quiet courtyard, listen to the fountain trickle, and snuggle with Tobi, the landlady's cat.

The mere thought gave Piper the willies.

The willies had nothing to do with her apartment, a cozy cottage in a peaceful complex. They had nothing to do with the people there, least of all Liv, the landlady who lived on the property.

Some called her Mama Liv, but to Piper she was nothing like a Darlene mom with a Darlene voice. Saint Liv fit better. She prayed about everything. Best of all, she had only needed to ask once why Piper sometimes wore the diamond ring on her left hand, sometimes on her right.

"Depends on the week," was all Piper said. Liv never pressed for more.

No, home and the chance of running into Liv or other neighbors did not give her the willies. It was sitting still in the midst of a weepy week that brought them on.

Tearful weeks accompanied Jared's birthday in May, the date of their should-have-been wedding in July, and now, in February, the anniversary of his death. At least they were no longer weepy *months*. At least *life* was no longer one unending crying jag.

She had learned the secret of whirligigging, packing the hours with enough activity to make her spin, round and round. She lost interest in being obnoxiously rude or going on dates with strangers who drove red convertibles.

Her therapist had thought it an unwise system, but she'd retired almost two years ago and Piper never replaced her. The system worked.

She blew out a noisy breath. Glitches were to be expected with any system, though, especially when the unexpected—things like traffic jams— shut it down.

Ask for help, Piper. Her ex-therapist's voice soothed. *You're not in this alone.*

The downside to her Whirligig System was that it did not allow time for making and keeping friends. Even sisters grew distant. There remained only one person to ask for help.

By the time Piper reached the scene of the accident, Darlene's voice coming through the speakerphone had created a bubble inside the car. She yakked about this and that. Piper listened intently to the gossip from Wisconsin, and the world stayed outside.

The *whomp* of a helicopter, the huddles of people, the dented cars, the tow trucks, the lone red car way off the shoulder and pancake flat…they were all blips on a screen already too full of ugliness.

Three

Heidi woke up and immediately wished she hadn't.

Given her can-do attitude toward anything physical, she was not a stranger to pain. Her medical history included a broken collarbone, a broken arm, several cuts deep enough to require stitches on various parts of her body, and a concussion—all before she turned twelve. The injuries were the results of never saying *no* to a dare from her twin brother and his buddies.

After age twelve, Hudson turned to books and she turned to sports. Even without his goading, she was never without a bruise or sprain or ache or pain of some sort.

But this…this was different. Every single nerve ending, inside and out, cried for relief.

"There she is." The calm, disembodied voice belonged to her father.

Heidi heard other muted voices. Faces came into view, blurry and spinning. Her stomach reeled.

"Heidi Ann!" Her mom's voice. "What on earth were you thinking, racing like a chowderhead on that freeway?"

"Rita," her dad chided. "Chowderhead?"

Her mother *tsked*. "This is all your fault, Ethan Hathaway. Forever putting crazy notions in her head about driving. Mark my word, in her mind she was in Vegas, on that racetrack in some extravagant racecar. Am I right or am I right, Heidi?"

She tried to make a silly face. They usually defused Rita's pointless rampages and make her laugh. But Heidi's face felt like a contorted, frozen mess. Her mother ranted on.

"Heidi." That was Val. Her closest friend and business partner said nothing else.

Something was either very good or very bad. Either way, Val would be there with her mom and dad. But so would Hudson. Where was her brother?

Where was *she*? Why the pain? The floating sensation?

What had happened?

"You were in an accident on the freeway." Her dad's voice soothed, in spite of the awful words.

Accident.

"Do you remember it?"

She remembered…bits. Veering the car onto the shoulder. *Off* the freeway. The car…the car flew. Literally. Deafening noises. Pain. Her right leg turned at an unbearable angle. Darkness. Quiet.

She remembered there were voices then, asking her name. Another, a gentler, whispery one. *Take my hand, Heidi. Take my hand.* She was lifted. She screamed. Darkness came again.

She let the disjointed bits of memory go. Sobs gathered in her chest now. They grew and hardened, a solid lump that had nowhere to go. Questions formed, but her tongue refused to take them.

Something was in the way. Something was in the way!

Her father caught her hand midway to her mouth.

"Shh, shh." He leaned close and dabbed a tissue at the corners of her eyes. "It's okay. It's okay. Relax, princess. Just relax."

She saw an image reflected in the lenses of his rimless square glasses. Bandages swathed her head. A huge contraption covered the bottom half of her face.

She whimpered but the sound was drowned by a *swish, whoosh, swish, whoosh*…

A respirator.

"They had to intubate," her dad said softly. "Everything is going to be okay, princess. I promise. Your body's just a little broken…"

❦

What day was it? She smiled. It must be Saturday, a full-on, kick-up-her-heels Saturday. First, she'd present the Fentons' offer on the Ridgewood house. Hands down, a slam dunk. Then there were two open houses—count them, two. Both excellent properties listed with her company. By evening—

"Heidi?" Val loomed close. "Are you awake? For real this time?"

She blinked. "Val—ohh!" She grabbed at her fire-breathing throat and touched something hard.

"Sweetie." Val gently moved Heidi's hand. "Leave the neck brace alone. Here, have some water." She put a straw to Heidi's lips. "They said you'd be really dry. But hey! You're out of ICU and that nasty thing is out of your mouth. Good news, yeah?"

Heidi swallowed, choked, and coughed. Water sprayed.

"Whoops." Val removed the straw. "I'm a lousy nurse. But then you knew that, huh?"

Heidi took hold of the sheet and wiped her face. Her left hand did not move freely. There was an IV in it.

She touched her forehead and felt a thick patch of gauze. And then she saw her right leg.

Suspended.

"You remember that time you had the flu?" Val chattered. "I wouldn't let you stay home, just ordered takeout egg drop soup for you, day and night, delivered to the office. Actually, I think it helped."

"How bad?" Heidi croaked.

"You were really, really bad. High fever, coughing, and—"

She whimpered.

"Okay, okay. This would be worse than the flu."

Get to the point! Get to the point! The shout went no further than her mind.

"Oh, Heidi. Everything's fixable. Everything. Well, not counting the spleen, but honestly, if we can live without one, why do we even have one? You know what I mean? It's one of those things that makes no sense..." Her voice drifted away. Her lips settled into a single line of uneven coral.

Valerie Laughlin was not in a good way. She wouldn't be caught dead with lipstick out of place or her chin-length chestnut hair in need of a brushing. Her close-set eyes almost disappeared beneath puffy lids, their hazel color darker than usual.

Val took a deep breath. "Your mom and dad will be back any minute. They just went downstairs to get some coffee."

Heidi heard the unspoken message. There was more to tell. There was worse to tell. Val was not going to be the one to tell it.

Maybe Heidi did not need to hear it.

She shut her eyes and waited for the magic carpet to swing by again and lift her away.

Four

Piper sat on the beach, her knees up, huddled in a too-large black fleece. Out on the water, a line of surfers in black wetsuits straddled their boards and faced the horizon, waiting. The ocean was flat, a mirror reflecting the gray sky.

She pressed a corner of the soft collar to her nose. The scent was long gone. Jared had not been the type to wear cologne, but the soap he liked with its fresh minty—

"Piper! Good morning."

She lowered the fabric and turned. Jasmyn Albright approached, her dark ponytail swinging. The surfboard she carried made her appear even smaller than she was. She wore a red wetsuit with black panels at the sides.

Piper waved. "Nice suit."

Jasmyn reached her. "It's a little *different*, isn't it?" She grinned and her dimples went deep. "I know this fashionista who taught me that different can work."

Piper smiled at the reference to herself. When Jasmyn's car had been stolen along with a suitcase filled with her clothes, they had done some serious shopping together.

Jasmyn laid down the board and sat beside it. In her mid-thirties, she was also a Midwestern transplant. Wholesome small-town traits oozed from her, things like naiveté and authenticity. What still surprised everyone in the complex was how that demeanor had captured the heart of Keagan, another neighbor, who majored in aloofness.

Jasmyn said, "You're not working today?"

Piper shook her head.

"Are you okay?" Her eyebrows rose. "I'm sorry. I don't mean to pry. It's just that most days you're at work."

If their landlady Liv had ever had a daughter, Jasmyn would have fit the bill. She had the exact same knack for creating instantaneous safe harbors in conversation.

"It's a rough day." Piper paused. The words still took time to form. "It's the anniversary of Jared's death. Four years."

"Oh, Piper." Jasmyn touched her arm. "I'm so sorry."

She nodded. "I had a meltdown at the store yesterday. My boss found me in a dressing room, on the floor hugging a pile of Donna Karan business suits."

"Whoa, I bet those are expensive."

"Too expensive to use as a hankie. Gildy said I better leave and stay away until I had myself under control. And that I was not irreplaceable."

"Did you tell her what was going on?"

"Good grief, no way. We don't bring our personal lives to work. Gildy might not even have one. She's such a stickler for decorum. But I guess that's what makes her the perfect supervisor."

"She sounds impressive."

"She is over-the-top impressive. She looks like photos of some designer from the eighties, like Liz Claiborne with the big round glasses. She's got the smile down pat too, for customers. She personally takes care of the governor's wife. I'm very good at what I do, but some days it's more important that I'm good at kowtowing to Gildy."

"Piper, your fiancé was killed in Afghanistan."

She blew out a breath. "Yeah."

"It's okay to take a day off."

"The job will be there tomorrow, right?"

Jasmyn smiled briefly. "How will you spend the day?"

She shrugged. "My mom and dad already called. Mom will check in again tonight. I'll talk to Jared's parents in Illinois. I'll look at pictures. Not much of a plan."

"But it's a plan. It's a good one. No cemetery visit?"

"That's in Illinois. A VA cemetery near Chicago." She hadn't been there for…a long time.

"Do you want company?"

"Uh, that's sweet. But, honestly, I'm fine alone."

"I totally get it. Does Liv know?"

Piper couldn't help but chuckle.

"Silly question. Will she bring you brownies?"

"Most likely."

"Then I will bring you soup. Chicken noodle. Homemade from Dee Dee's." She mentioned the restaurant where she worked out on the pier and grinned. Piper knew Jasmyn wasn't much of a cook. "Then you're covered. Okay?"

"Okay."

Jasmyn gave her a quick, solid hug and stood. Without another word, she picked up her board and hurried down to the water's edge. She wiped at both of her cheeks, bent to attach the surfboard's strap to her ankle, and waded into the ocean.

Piper wiped her own tears with the sleeve of Jared's jacket. Her throat had closed up, cutting off new thoughts she wanted to tell someone who had not known him.

Maybe she wasn't supposed to speak them. People understood the anniversary of a loved one's death, that it was a sad time, and they might recoil at Piper's realization. She herself had. It was why she had buried her face in Donna Karan business suits.

The thing was, she'd had glimpses of *hope*. Without warning it caught hold of her senses in the perfume of a flower, the song of a bird's chirp, the saltiness of a cracker. She reveled in the awareness of beauty, and for one long moment, there was a subtle weightlessness of her heart.

Like someone free from cancer for years, she dared to think that the future might hold a little less pain, a little less dread. Then the heaviness would barge back inside and the brief respite was over. She was back on autopilot, skimming along the surface of life, making do, going through the motions.

It was simply easier not to feel too deeply because with the hope, the joy, and the beauty came the pain.

The unbearable pain of not being able to share the hope, the joy, the beauty with Jared.

Five

If Heidi could actually climb out of the bed and walk, she would have shot across the room and grabbed the phone from her father's hand.

But of course she wasn't going anywhere on her own, not for a long time, and so she lay there listening to one side of the conversation because her dad disliked speakerphone.

"You know your sister. Endless reserves." He stood just beyond her reach, oblivious to her outstretched arm. "I'll put her on."

It was the third time he had said that.

"Surgery's scheduled for eight o'clock tomorrow...Mmhmm, titanium rod...Yes, sooner would've been better but she had to stabilize. I mean..." His voice lowered as he explained how truly bad she was. Ever since she first woke up, he had been protecting her from the cringe-worthy details.

Her dad was a funky dear, a lit professor who naturally named his twins after old fictional characters and went for the alliteration. Heidi and Hudson Hathaway. Their mother swore she did not recall signing the birth certificates and was only grateful that Ethan had chosen middle names without an *H* initial.

As dear as he was, Heidi's endless reserves were about to hit bottom. "Dad!" she rasped as loudly as her throat allowed.

He nodded. "Yes. Yes...Okay. Love you too, son. Here she is." At last he handed her the phone and winked. "He's in Ecuador! I'll go keep your mom occupied."

Heidi put the phone to her ear. "Hud."

"Hey."

She began to cry, unable to talk.

Her brother inhaled loudly and said nothing.

For several moments they sniffled. It was a twin thing.

She pictured him, his narrow face damp with tears. Hudson resembled their father, except that he wore contact lenses instead of glasses and his thatch of hair was dark brown, not white. Both were six-four and moved like elegant giraffes who could have been dunking basketballs with ease but preferred to curl up with books. Both were sensitive souls.

At last he spoke. "I'm so sorry. And I'm so sorry I didn't know sooner. I thought twins were supposed to get disaster inklings. I got nothing. Tell me about it."

She told him about it, from driving like an idiot to the terrifying crash to the sickening view of her leg in traction. "What's in Ecuador?"

"Llamas."

She smiled and winced. The stitches down the left side of her face pulled.

"This place is gorgeous, Heidi. Put it on your bucket list."

There was no need for him to explain further. He wrote novels and screenplays. He lived most of the time in Baja California, Mexico, but would disappear for weeks at a time, writing and researching somewhere south of the border, often south of the equator. Holidays were not on his radar.

"They say you'll be fit as a fiddle in no time."

"Says the guy who avoids clichés at all cost. Use your own words, Mr. Writer."

"Fresh out of them." He sighed. "Do you want me there tomorrow, Heidi?"

"Of course not. You have work to do and besides, there's no space for you. Mom and Dad are always here. And Val. Friends keep stopping by with flowers. Clients send flowers. The room smells like a funeral home."

He chuckled. "Well, I'll come soon." He paused. "What's the very worst of it?"

"The very worst? There is no very worst. The whole rotten situation is the very worst."

"Okay. How about what could make the rotten situation even worse?"

She shut her eyes. That was an easy one. "I could have hurt someone else."

"Absolutely. That is the biggie—if we don't count the part where you easily could have died. You only *almost* died."

"Are you trying to encourage me?"

"It's my job."

"Usually you're better at it."

"How's this? You caused half a dozen fender benders and a two-hour backup on the freeway."

"It wasn't two."

"Whatever, it could have been *three*. Worse than two. Even more people would've missed appointments, canceled special dates, been late picking up the kids. Think of all those frantic parents and scared little ones and anxious guys with diamonds in their pockets. Whew." He blew out a breath. "Literally there could have been thousands more life-changing opportunities lost forever if it had been three hours rather than two."

"Hud!"

"Another positive is you totaled the car. Isn't that great? You won't have to bother getting estimates and having it repaired. You can just go buy a new one."

She groaned.

"We won't talk about sky-high insurance rates. And, hey! You finally rode in a helicopter."

"That does not count. I was unconscious."

"Nope. It definitely counts. Here's another: With a titanium rod and metal screws inside you, maybe you'll get pat-downs at airport security every single time. Linger on that happy thought for a while."

In the end he had her laughing. But she cried too because laughing made everything hurt more, inside and outside, physically and otherwise.

What had she gotten herself into?

ℒℓ

Heidi awoke to semidarkness, groggy but alert enough to sense someone near the bed. Nurses and their assistants came in around the clock to prod, poke, take notes, and fiddle with equipment. This one fiddled with the IV.

And she began to hum softly.

Heidi relaxed. She recognized the woman. What was her name? M something. Marsha? Martha? Margaret? Margo?

Even in her crabby, woozy state, Heidi had noticed the CNA on other occasions. She was the one who droned like a pesky gnat while she took Heidi's vitals. She called her *baby* and *sugar*, fussed over her, and seemed to work every other single shift. Heidi was unaccustomed to such attention. She did not need it. She wasn't a child. And so she bristled under it.

Slowly, though, she realized how different the other nurse assistants were. They did not make eye contact, intuit her needs, or always deliver what she asked for. Their touch was not warm and gentle. She stopped squirming when M was in the room.

She had meant to tell Hud about M, about how light and peace emanated from her.

About how wacko that sounded.

But Hud fathomed things she did not. He would explain why she felt like a lost child who needed a nightlight and a lullaby in the middle of the night. He would explain why a stranger made her feel safe.

Why had it slipped her mind earlier when she talked with him on the phone? Maybe because since waking up in the hospital, most everything slipped through her mind. Mind? She might as well call that thing inside her head a colander.

"Heidi." M patted her hand. "Heidi. Shh. You need to sleep, baby, not be pop-popping like corn kernels in hot oil. You've got a big day ahead of you, but don't you worry. You'll be just fine."

"I have to call my brother." Heidi's voice rasped, her throat still raw.

"It's one o'clock in the morning, sugar."

"I'll forget to tell him later."

"It'll come to you when you need it. If it's important, then the Lord's still, small voice inside you will remind you. There, there." She gently squeezed her hand. "Just let it go for now. No worrying allowed tonight. That's how you get better. No worrying. Shh. Shh." She hummed again, a rich, melodic sound.

Heidi fought the lullaby's effect, intent on remembering what she wanted to tell Hud about M. He would chide her for not knowing the woman's name. He'd say if M were a client selling a house, Heidi would remember it. She'd say she wouldn't have to. Every name was in her phone.

Where was her phone? *Where was her phone?*

M leaned closer and sang gently, a song Heidi did not recognize. It thrummed inside of her, loosening the anxious thoughts. One by one they seeped through the holes in the colander and she slept like a child.

Six

Piper spooned salsa onto her veggie omelette. Then, as if in slow motion, she set the spoon down and carefully folded her hands on her lap. "I'm hungry."

Seated across the booth table, Liv McAlister spread jam on a piece of toast. "Considering that you have a lovely breakfast before you, you're in luck." She looked up. "Or not?"

"Huh?"

"You sound concerned about being hungry." Saint Liv at her finest, perceiving nuances Piper did not even realize she revealed. "Hunger is a natural phenomenon, you know. It's one reason the species survives."

Piper gave her a fleeting smile. "It was only a few days ago…" She took a deep breath. "Usually my appetite isn't back yet."

Liv nodded. "Four years is a significant anniversary, Piper dear. The pain takes on different expressions. There is no need to feel guilty about the changes."

"I don't want to forget him."

"Oh, honey, you won't forget him. He will only become less constant, and that's a healthy thing."

The words felt like a burst of sunshine in Piper's heart. Yes, having breakfast with Liv had been a good decision.

About once a month the two of them went out for breakfast and a catch-up chat, often on a Monday when Piper's schedule was most open. They did not have a set date, and when Liv had invited her last night, she considered turning her down. Now she was glad she had not.

They sat in Dee Dee's Diner, where Jasmyn worked. It was a retro

1950s restaurant located at the end of the Seaside Village Pier. Large windows lined three sides, providing views of the ocean and people fishing at the railing. Stools at the counter and booths were red vinyl, the floor white and black tiles. Elvis, Pat Boone, and the Everly Brothers had a lot of playtime on the speakers. Malts and fries were the house specialties. The place felt comfortable, comfortable enough to admit hard truths and eat a veggie omelette.

She picked up her fork. "Liv, thank you for understanding."

"My Syd's only been gone for a little over ten years. The thought of him is always a heartbeat away. But." Her blue eyes behind the silver-rimmed glasses seemed focused elsewhere. "But at some point, he stopped greeting me first thing every morning." She blinked and looked directly at Piper. "So to speak."

"How did you feel about that?"

"Oh, dear Lord. I woke up one morning and it was several minutes before my thoughts turned to him. Then I realized this had been happening somewhat frequently. Then I realized the date. It was his birthday! Can you imagine? I tried to justify it by reminding myself I'd spent the previous day crying in anticipation. Well, I just curled up in a fetal position and did not move until suppertime. How could I betray my husband like that?"

Piper heard echoes of her own feelings. Since the day she met Jared Oakes, her first conscious thought had been of him every single morning. Until recently.

She watched Liv sip her tea and gaze out the window. Except for the halo-like fluffy light brown hair streaked with gray, the woman did not appear anything like Piper imagined a saint would. She was more like Julia Child, the chef of TV fame. She was tall, all bones and angles. Liv always dressed comfortably, most often in long skirts and practical sandals. The unpretentious look suited her. Boundlessly compassionate, she paid more attention to others than to herself.

Which explained why in the three years since Piper had moved into the Casa, she had not yet learned much about Syd from her. "How did you two meet?"

Liv smiled and a blush pinked her cheeks. "He was movie-star handsome."

"That's no exaggeration. I've seen his photo in your office."

"We met at a fund-raising event for Balboa Park restorations. By that time I was running my father's real estate company and hobnobbing quite a bit. I was terribly civic-minded."

"I imagine you cut a striking figure."

Liv laughed. "Well, if you're a woman and almost six feet tall, you can't fail at that. But thank you."

"I mean it. It must have been love at first sight for both of you."

"No. Maybe a little intrigued at first sight. I did mention he was movie-star handsome?" She smiled. "He wore a tuxedo. Mm, mm. Let me tell you, he was muckety-muck. I mean, he was highly successful in the San Diego business world. He looked every inch of it too. He had a knack for acquisitions and investments, and he had a smart friend in software development."

"He was well off."

"To put it mildly. That night we met only briefly, through business associates who knew each other. A couple of years later we met again, when he bought a building that was listed with my agency. We became close friends. Eventually we realized we were courting. Finally we married. I was forty-six years old. He was forty-eight."

"Really?"

"Ancient, right?"

She laughed. "How long were you married?"

"Twelve years. He had a heart attack."

"It was sudden?"

Liv nodded. "We had some very good years together. I try not to complain, but they weren't nearly enough."

"That day you didn't get up until suppertime, how did you keep going after that?"

"Well, first I ate a cheese and sausage frittata the size of your face. And you know me, I prayed a lot. Eventually I talked to a wise friend who helped me see that life goes on no matter what. We get hungry. We get tired. We love others. The memories come, we pause, and then we have to let them go or they will bury us." Liv leaned over. "It feels like a betrayal, Piper dear. I know. But it's not. Moving on is how you take care of yourself. And taking care of yourself is a perfectly acceptable way to live. It's another reason the species survives."

Jasmyn appeared at their table, her ponytail swinging, her expression perky above a red-and-white polka-dotted scarf. She was perfect as a waitress at Dee Dee's, although she had once mentioned she wasn't crazy about the poodle skirt and crinoline. At least the bobby socks and saddle shoes were comfortable, she always said. Piper added that with her dark hair, Jasmyn looked great in the red lipstick.

She plopped down now on the bench seat next to Liv, about to speak, and then shook her head. "I'm interrupting."

Liv elbowed her playfully. "Yes, you are. But we don't mind."

Jasmyn eyed Piper. "I'm not so sure."

Piper smiled. "Of course it's all right, Jasmyn. Liv was just telling me how it's not healthy to define myself as a dead soldier's girl."

Jasmyn's eyebrows nearly disappeared into her hairline.

Liv gaped. "Oh, honey…"

Tears stung Piper's eyes. "Jared always zeroed in on the bottom line."

"But it's so harsh."

"Harsh makes it sink in more solidly. And you're right. It is best to move on. To let go."

"You don't want to force it. When you can, take a baby step. Notice that you are hungry and accept that that's okay."

Piper whispered, "My head knows that, but my heart feels guilty."

Jasmyn said, "You know Keagan's fiancée was killed years ago. He—"

"What!" Liv and Piper blurted in unison.

"Oh. You didn't know."

They shook their heads.

"I forget how much he hasn't revealed about himself." She paused. "What *do* you know?"

Piper said, "Zilch except he's quiet, thoughtful, and a little on the intimidating side."

Jasmyn nodded. "Tell me about it. Pack all that into a kiss and you've got Fourth of July fireworks."

Piper and Liv burst into laughter.

"Oh my, honey." Liv wiped at her eyes. "Now what I know about him is that his grandparents raised him back East after his parents died in a car accident when he was twelve. Before he bought the gym a few years ago, he was into software. Although, to tell you the truth, I never believed that one. But Jasmyn, I certainly don't need to hear details. I respect his space."

"It's all right. He doesn't mind if I share some things. Which is what I wanted to say. After his fiancée died, he went totally mucho macho. I suspect he always was to some degree. I mean, he was a DEA agent—"

"DEA?"

"Oh." She smiled crookedly. "Yes, he was an agent and she was too. Kind of makes you wonder why he fell for me. Am I the complete opposite or what?"

"Jasmyn dear, you're exactly what he needed."

"That's what he says. Every once in a while, though, he seems off-kilter. He goes totally noncommunicative. Like he's not sure he can handle going down the beating-heart path again."

Piper swallowed a lump in her throat. "Because to him it feels like he's forgetting her."

Jasmyn reached across the table and laid her hand atop Piper's. "That must be so very scary."

Piper never would have imagined saints also came in petite size and wore saddle shoes and bobby socks.

Seven

Heidi had told her brother there was no *very worst* to her situation. The day she was released from the hospital, she realized that was not true.

She sat near an exit door in a wheelchair. Although there was not a cast on it, her right leg was elevated, sticking nearly straight out. She could not yet bend it further than two degrees. Her neck remained encased in the brace. A pair of crutches lay across the armrests. Under those, on her lap, was a case of meds, all refillable. All the paraphernalia was going home with her.

All temporary, not a *very worst*.

Other vexations were temporary as well. Pain stabbed with every breath she took, compliments of her cracked ribs. She wore old baggy black running shorts and a hoodie, clothes her mother had dug out of a long-forgotten box from Heidi's high school days.

Because her contact lenses were missing and presumed gone for good, she wore her glasses, large squares rimmed in black. She had purchased them as a fashion statement the previous month and soon decided the statement was best left unspoken in public.

Her hair was—She wasn't quite sure what her hair was besides the pits. A portion near her left temple had been shaved, the better for suturing. The remainder hung string-like below her chin. She pulled up the hood.

Two snaggy lines decorated the left side of her face, leftovers from the stitches. One led from the hairline at the temple, the other from below the earlobe. They met where there had been a dimple, forming a jagged sideways V.

Bad, but not a *very worst*.

Val nudged her arm. "Hey, cheer up. You're going to feel fabulous in no time." She sat on a bench next to Heidi, looking her best self again with hair styled, makeup in place, and wearing a black business suit, white blouse, and low heels. In control. Independent.

Heidi nodded, but then she shook her head. "Maybe in six months."

"Oh, it'll be less for you. You're so athletic, not to mention goal-oriented and focused. Think of how far you've come already. You're back on your feet and eating solid food. Nausea is gone."

True. She had graduated from a steady diet of unidentifiable mush and, with the crutches, could walk up a flight of stairs. She had also lived through endless nausea caused by endless triggers.

The memory of her femur breaking while her car somersaulted. She heard it sometimes, although unsure if it was her imagination or if she had really heard it above all the other noise of the car crashing. It sounded like a tree branch snapping.

Other triggers? The fact that a rod had been inserted into the hollowed-out bone of her leg. The anesthesia from two surgeries, one for the spleen, one for the rod. The pain meds and subsequent hallucinatory dreams. The dressing changes. The physical therapy.

Physical therapy. It still made her stomach roil. During the first attempt at standing, she had fainted dead away. Bam. On the floor. She'd slipped right through the hands that had been holding her up.

"You kayak by yourself in the ocean, which means you can survive anything." Val looked through the wall of windows and stood. Not an athlete herself, she had always been easily impressed with Heidi's activities. "There's your dad's car. Let's get this show on the road."

Heidi burst into tears. "I can't do this. I can't do this."

"Oh, Heidi." Val dug into her shoulder bag, pulled out a packet of tissues, and handed her one. "I know the car ride will be crazy scary. Just keep in mind what the doctor said. Take deep breaths. I'll sit in the back with you and we'll breathe together. Okay? I'll jabber, I'll sing, and in forty minutes, you'll be home! You're not going to freak out. You never freak out. You're my rock."

Heidi grabbed the packet of tissues from Val and yanked out a handful. She never freaked out? Well, there was always a first time for everything. No question about it, she was going to spend forty minutes on the floor of her dad's minivan, freaking out.

But that wasn't the worst, not the *very worst*.

The very worst of it—the thing that could not be made any worse—was that for the foreseeable future, she would be living with her parents.

With. Her. Parents.

∂Ωℓ

Heidi survived sixteen days living with Ethan and Rita. They were, hands down, the longest sixteen days of her life.

Her parents' house was a sprawling ranch with a quiet backyard, shaded with several eucalyptus trees. There was no freeway noise or neighbors close by. It should have been a haven.

"I want to go home, Val."

Across the patio table in that quiet backyard, Val looked up from her laptop. "And I want to be a size two and net a million this year. Ain't gonna happen, sugar pie."

There was no need for Val to explain. Heidi's condo had three levels. The first was a garage, half bath, small office. Maneuvering stairs to the living quarters was beyond her ability. She grimaced at the thought of going up and down. Living there, forty-five minutes from her parents, would mean she'd have to drive herself to physical therapy, doctor appointments, the market, and the office—which she planned to do any day now. The only thing holding her back was that she was not yet allowed to drive.

"Heidi, it can't be that bad here."

"You have no idea." She pulled at the tiresome neck brace and ripped it off.

"Your parents are great people."

"Yes, but they're odd. They have odd friends who are here all the time."

Val glanced around the empty yard.

"Okay, okay. Not all the time, obviously. Mom's in her studio half the night, her potter's wheel going round and round, music blaring. Old, old music from the sixties. Three times she forgot to pick me up after therapy. Three times. I sat outside like a little kid left on the school steps. Dad's preoccupied with teaching and writing that book about some dead author. You can't even walk through his office, books and papers are piled so high. I can't anyway, not with crutches."

"And what's your point?"

"They eat hotdogs and chili beans and Oreos. Takeout cheeseburgers and fish and chips are staples. Mom thinks green olives stuffed with garlic is a vegetable."

"I said, what's your point? Your mom's been dressing you for weeks. Doing your laundry. Making you exercise."

Heidi stared at her put-together friend for a long moment. Tears of frustration burned in her eyes. Pulling on sweatpants without her mom's help took Heidi a good fifteen minutes. She still couldn't put on lace-up shoes by herself, let alone tie them, but flip-flops caused her to trip.

Val shut the laptop. "We need to hire Treena. She's already putting in more hours than an intern should, and she's incredibly good at everything. Her class load is light this semester. She'll graduate in May and wants to get her realtor license. As far as I know, she'd like to work with us."

Heidi blinked rapidly.

"Hey." Val reached across the table and squeezed Heidi's hand. "Things will get better, but right now we can't seem to get through a set of new listings. Yesterday you made two phone calls and then napped until bedtime. I know you want to work. It's just too soon. No worries, though. Okay? We'll deal with it."

In reply, Heidi struggled to her feet and thrust the crutches into place. She headed toward the house.

Walking away from Val was her only way to deal with it.

Eight

One month after the accident, Heidi stood on the Seaside Village Pier.

Or rather, she almost stood. She leaned heavily against the splintery railing, her head bowed, her forearms resting on it. She paid no heed to the slimy pieces of fish bait and seagull droppings that now smeared her jacket sleeves. Her arms and legs trembled. Her heart raced and her breath came in snatches. Sweat poured from her, defying the claims of the moisture-wicking fabric. At her feet lay the crutches where they had fallen. Losing her lunch remained a real possibility.

Determined to mark the fourth week of recovery in a spectacular way, she had walked halfway out the long pier. Technically, the splenectomy recovery period was over. Technically, the crutches should be history. Her physical therapists, however, insisted that she should not count on those minimum healing times. She had a lot going on, a *lot*. She needed to pace herself.

No, she thought. She needed to push herself. If she stopped pressing beyond the limits set by those people, she might as well die.

Which, at that very moment, she might be doing anyway. There were all sorts of potentially fatal complications brought on from having a rod for a bone and not having a spleen for bacteria defense. Rapid heart rate? Check. Profuse perspiration? Check.

There were other things. The list of what to watch for filled pages and pages. They haunted her—

"Heidi?"

She turned and saw a pretty young woman wearing big sunglasses. Her light brown hair was chin-length and held off her face with a wide navy blue headband.

"I'm Piper. From Tellmann's?"

Heidi blinked. Piper was the personal shopper who could make a gorilla look elegant, or an average-looking athlete-slash-real-estate-agent appear cover-photo ready for *Inside San Diego*. "H-hi."

"Are you all right?"

"Uh, no. Not exactly."

"Want to sit down? There's a bench over here…" Deftly, she slipped the crutches into place at Heidi's elbows. "Good to go."

They took small, slow steps until at last they reached a molded concrete bench set in a small section of the pier that jutted out. They sat facing the ocean.

"Here." Piper opened a plastic water bottle and gave it to her. "Drink."

Heidi closed her eyes and focused on breathing and swallowing. "Thank you."

"Sure. If you don't mind me asking, what happened?"

"Car accident." She gave her a small smile and recapped the bottle. "I flew off the freeway. My fault. Fender benders but no one else got hurt." She still clung to that. If others had been hurt…

Piper asked for medical details.

Heidi briefly explained what had been broken, fixed, and replaced. She gave a *Reader's Digest* version of life with the 'rents. She griped about being unable to drive or work. Her irksome tone reminded her of nails on a chalkboard, but it had become normal and she couldn't retune it. "Sorry. I'm having a rough day." *Like every day.*

"No, I'm the one who's sorry." Piper was soft-spoken and personable. She had an eye for fashion, but it was the way she cared for customers that made her so good at her job. "How awful for you."

Heidi nodded and wiped a corner of her sleeve at her sweaty brow. Her stomach felt unsure of what to do with the water she had drunk. Worse, though, was the sudden attack of the uglies. Sweet Piper was traffic-stopping beautiful. Great skin, perfectly proportioned features, big green eyes behind her designer sunglasses.

Heidi had never been overly concerned about her looks until Val insisted the shorts and sports bras had to go. The SoCal beach persona did not play well in the big leagues and that's where they were headed with their firm, SunView Property Management Agency.

So Heidi went shopping. She met Piper at Tellmann's, and the saleswoman took her from ho-hum to super stylish career woman. Besides landing on the local magazine cover, her image appeared regularly with Val's in ads and even on billboards. It received attention, business and otherwise.

Now it seemed that image belonged to a stranger. Heidi had lost too much weight, sported a scar, limped, and could not have clothed herself in a decent blouse and skirt without taking a heavy-duty pain pill or asking her mom to button and zip. At least she had classy new prescription sunglasses.

She sighed and touched the bill of the black cap on her head. "Like my new style?"

Piper's smile held nothing but compassion. "Bad hair day?"

"You have no idea." Because of the shaved side of her head, she'd had all of her hair cut short. Really short. Short as the bristles on a hairbrush.

"Actually, I recognized you from the jacket."

She glanced down at the silky black fabric with baby blue piping and its matching pants. "This generic thing?"

Piper laughed. "Galleta is hardly generic and it's adorable. I distinctly remember someone else trying on this same outfit and I was thinking, 'If she only had Heidi Hathaway's shoulders, it might work.'"

Heidi smiled and felt ooey-gooey.

And then she felt weird and flustered.

The ooey-gooey phenomenon had begun with Margaret. That was M's name, the CNA in the hospital. The woman touched a chord inside Heidi and it had been resounding ever since, deeply. Too deeply for words. She had not been able to tell Hud about it yet.

She blamed the drugs that were still part of her regimen. She hoped when that changed, the other would go away too. It was becoming an issue.

The problem was, Heidi Hathaway did not do ooey-gooey. She played beach volleyball, kayaked, and sold real estate. She did not notice things like how wholesome Piper seemed. She did not notice how sitting next to her was like being close to a fountain and getting splashed with a permeating sense of goodness.

No, she did not notice those things.

Piper chatted away, probably trying to keep Heidi's mind occupied while she recovered from her too-long trek because that was the sort of thing that kind, wholesome people did.

Although they had never socialized, they enjoyed an easy rapport and had swapped personal tidbits through the years. Heidi knew that Piper was from the Midwest, and that her fiancé had died overseas, in the military. A saleswoman herself, Heidi had always admired Piper's professionalism. Somehow she pulled it off and seemed a genuinely nice person at the same time. But then she only sold *clothing*.

Heidi cringed. She hadn't always been that snooty, had she? Maybe she had. Maybe hiding it had been easier back when her appearance was admired and her work was successful and she did not walk with crutches.

Eventually the uglies slunk off into the shadows. Her heartbeat and stomach calmed. She checked her watch. "I should go. My mom is supposed to pick me up in an hour. It'll take me that long to hobble back to the street."

Walking the pier had been her father's idea. Knowing what the ocean meant to his kayaking daughter, he had declared that the drive to it—nearly an hour each way from their house—was worth it. Getting her back on the water, so to speak, was a priority.

The physical therapist had gone ballistic when they mentioned the plan. He warned them in no uncertain terms not to take the risk. Of course that only challenged Heidi and her dad to try anyway.

Three times they had ambled down the sloped ramp to where the wooden pier itself began. They'd sat on a bench for a while and headed back up to the street. Today Ethan had dropped her off, unable to stay.

"I'll hobble with you, Heidi."

"You don't have to. I'm sure you have other things to do. I'll be fine."

"Right. Shall I call the ambulance now or after you keel over?"

Heidi smiled or grimaced. They often seemed one and the same. "Thanks for the water and keeping me company. I-I'm good now. You go on."

"Uh-uh. You just went white as a sheet. I'll be right back. Don't go anywhere." She hurried off.

Don't go anywhere. As if she had a choice.

Her heart pounded again, echoing in her head. More than anything—worse than the pain, the limp, the scars—worse than all that was the helplessness. There wasn't a thing she could do about that because the truth was, she was absolutely, without a doubt, flat-out helpless.

Nine

Piper loved her Seaside Village community. Within minutes of Heidi turning white as a sheet and nearly fainting, the bait shop guy had called the lifeguards who drove their pickup out onto the pier and took her vitals. They gave them a ride up to the street where senior police volunteers bundled them into their cruiser and drove them the four blocks to the Casa de Vida.

Piper knew all those people by name and they knew her by name. They were like the extended family of the more closely knit group who lived at the Casa.

Of course she suggested they wait for Heidi's mother at the Casa rather than on a sidewalk bench. Now they slowly walked from the cruiser toward the front gate.

Heidi stopped and read the sign spelled out in pretty tiles on the wall. "Casa de Vida. House of Life. What is this place? It looks like a secret hideaway."

The exterior of the Casa always caught the attention of passersby. A twelve-foot-high, off-white adobe wall ran most of the block and was covered with hot pink bougainvillea. Tops of palm trees from the other side were visible. The privacy gate was made of thick wood and stained a deep brown.

"It's an apartment complex made up of a dozen attached bungalows."

"A complex of bungalows?" She removed her sunglasses and stuck them atop her cap. "And you rent one? I've never seen anything like this."

Wait until you see the inside. Piper did not want to hype the place too much. She adored everything about it, but who knew? Heidi had told her in the past about her condo. It sounded sleek and contemporary, nothing at all like the cozy 1927 vintage Casa.

Heidi continued gazing at the exterior. Being a Realtor, she probably saw a lot more than Piper ever did.

What Piper noticed was how much the woman had changed from the last time they'd seen each other at the store. Heidi had never been gaunt, hesitant, negative, forgetful, or disheveled. Her injuries—the V-shaped scar on her left cheek, the limping gait, the stories of her spleen and leg—made Piper want to cry.

They made her want to gather her into the Casa de Vida fold.

She blamed it on the turning point at breakfast with Liv and Jasmyn. Since then she had become more at ease with what she called her *Jared lapses*. He wasn't always right there in the front part of her mind. She was settling into that reality and—even more surprising—she was becoming more aware of others' pain.

"Let's go inside." Piper entered the code on the lock, pushed the gate open, and walked through it into the courtyard.

First came the lush sight of colors upon colors. Green trees, bushes, and wide leaves of tropical plants. Flowers in every shade. Bright red umbrellas open over patio tables. Next came the floral fragrance and the sounds of birdsong, trickling fountain, and wind chimes. The air was thick enough to feel and taste.

Beside her, Heidi gasped.

Piper smiled. Her friend was hooked.

"Oh my goodness. It's like a magical kingdom. Where are the—Oh! They're tucked away. Like little seaside cottages."

Piper studied the site that never grew old. The cottages, or bungalows, ringed the courtyard, each nearly hidden behind foliage. They shared side walls. Their roofs were flat, the exterior walls white, and each front door was painted a different bright color and set back in alcoves.

Heidi grinned at her. "Which fairy tale are we in?"

"I guess my landlady's. She owns and manages it and lives here. Oh, there she is, behind the fountain." Piper waved to her.

Liv straightened, a watering can in her hand, and smiled. She wore a straw sunhat and gardening gloves. "Hello!" She set down the can and walked over to them, or rather sashayed. It was a familiar sight in the courtyard, as if she heard music while tending her plants.

"Liv, this is Heidi Hathaway and she needs a home without stairs."
Piper nearly bubbled over with excitement.

Heidi said, "What? No, I don't. A home? Not really."

"Just temporarily."

Liv's smile was gone. She pointed to the crutches. "Did you get hurt?"

"Car accident. I'm living with my parents until I can drive again and
live in my multilevel condo. The crutches will go any day now. I don't need
them all the time like at first…" Her voice trailed off.

"Hm."

Piper said, "But it's not the best situation. I get it, Heidi. I could never
ever live with my parents again. And this place is perfect. One-story cottages. Wonderful neighbors. The downtown is a short, flat walk away."

"I'm really fine."

Piper resisted pointing out the obvious ways she was so not okay. "Liv,
can we at least show her Cottage Three? It's empty and clean and ready."

"Well, I'm a little busy at the moment."

"Please, please. I can do it."

Liv took off a glove and pulled a hankie from a pocket of her khakis. She wiped her brow with it. "Uh, Jasmyn is in the office. Maybe she
could—"

"I'll get her." Piper practically jogged away.

Thoroughly confused.

What was up with Liv? She wasn't the landlady Piper had counted on
greeting them. No matter what the situation, that woman smiled and
talked. She welcomed everyone and immediately shook hands and said,
Hi, I'm Olivia—call me Liv—McAlister. She was never *busy*.

Piper had seen time and again how the woman worked graciously with
whatever was thrown at her.

Weird. Maybe saints took days off. She hoped Saint Jasmyn was in
residence.

Piper found her in the office, behind the big desk, working on the
computer. She was Liv's right-hand woman, an unofficial assistant.

"Piper, hi." She grinned.

"Hi. I brought home a stray."

The grin did not fade.

Whew.

Jasmyn nodded at Liv's RagaMuffin curled up on one of the pink floral chairs. "A cat friend for Tobi?"

"A woman friend for us."

"A woman! Really and truly?"

"Yes. Liv said we can—"

"Show her Number Three! On it." She pulled open a drawer, took out a key, and did a pump fist. "It's my first time."

Piper laughed. "Her name is Heidi and she says she doesn't want to move."

"But you think…?"

"She has no idea how healing this place is."

"And she's like we were when we first arrived."

"Mm-hmm. Hurting and oh-so-needy."

Ten

If the woman had worn a sandwich board sign that declared she offered peace, comfort, and wisdom to all those in need, the offer would not have been any clearer than it was.

Just like Margaret at the hospital.

What was it with these women?

Or what was it with Heidi? Before the accident, would she have picked up on such a thing?

The ooey-gooey sense overwhelmed her again, the second time within an hour or so. It was over the top. She needed to sit down. "I need to sit…" She turned and stubbed a toe on a flagstone.

The woman—what was her name?—grasped her arm and steadied her. "Let's sit right there."

She shuffled to a nearby wrought-iron patio table, leaned the crutches against it, and plopped onto a padded chair. "I'm sorry, so sorry. I'm intruding and—I didn't catch your name?"

"Olivia. Would you like some water or tea?"

"No. Thank you. Piper and the lifeguards gave me water." She dug in the large bag hanging crosswise from her shoulder, pulled out a bottle, and unscrewed the lid. "I simply overdid it today."

"Pushed yourself too far?"

Heidi nodded, gulping water and trying to blink discreetly in an attempt to focus on the woman. As with Piper, goodness splashed all over her. This time, though, she was getting soaked. Even her eyes were wet, literally.

Was she crying? But she was awash in safety and joy even.

"Are you sure I can't get something for you?"

"I'm…" She fanned herself. "I'm…" Happy. Hopeful. Safe. Lost. Confused. *Feeling.* "I'm…"

"Not yourself?"

"Exactly." She blinked and met the baby blues behind the glasses. "Your place is absolutely delightful." *Delightful?* Since when did she say *delightful?* "Beautiful."

"Thank you. It is a bit of a gem hidden in the middle of Seaside."

"Prime property. I imagine developers have knocked on your door, offering you a lot of money."

Olivia cocked her head.

"Oh good grief." Heidi winced. "That was rude. I'm so sorry." Again she was sorry, so sorry. "I'm a real estate agent. It seems I can't help but go there."

"That's perfectly understandable. I've seen your picture around. Sun-View is the agency, right?"

"Uh, yes. That's the one. You recognized me? Yikes. I didn't think I resembled any of those photos. Piper was the one who coached me into dressing like a businesswoman. Wearing makeup. Combing my hair." She pointed at her face. "Not this."

"Your name is easy to remember."

"Oh, that. Yes, that's my father's doing. The alliteration."

"Ah."

"My mother is into painting and pottery. They live out in Poway. I told you what I do. I'm successful. Single. Basically easy to get along with. Unless you try to gouge my client. And why am I telling you all this? I sound like I want you to think I'd make a good renter, but I don't need a place to live. Just a mix-up of signals with Piper, I guess."

Olivia gave her a small smile.

Heidi drank more water from the bottle to stop her magpie impersonation. The truth was, except when she had been with Margaret at the hospital, she hadn't felt safe since the accident. Not safe in this bone-deep, permeating sense of safety.

Before the accident she had lived life in a safety zone of well-being, embracing the adventure of all life offered. Forging ahead, full bore. That all went away in the flick of a steering wheel…

Olivia stood. "Here come Jasmyn and Piper. They'll show you the cottage. At the least, you'll satisfy your real estate agent's curiosity."

"I guess that's true. I am curious to see the interior. I appreciate—"

"It was nice meeting you, Heidi Hathaway."

Heidi watched Olivia glide away and nod as she passed Piper and a small, dark-haired woman.

Piper introduced Heidi to Jasmyn Albright, a bubbly woman probably close to her own age, instantly likeable.

Again with the emotional response. She hoped this craziness would go away sooner rather than later.

The three of them walked amid the fairyland foliage, through a bright orange door—Jasmyn called it *tangerine*—and into Cottage Three.

Heidi found herself gaping again, as she had when she first entered the courtyard. "This is…indescribable."

Jasmyn grinned. "Isn't it though? Here, come and look in the kitchen."

She could see the kitchen from where she stood because the place was super small, but the coziness begged her to explore. Walls were pale yellows, hardwood floors gleamed, simple furnishings provided the basics.

The floor plan consisted of an L-shaped area, living room at the bottom and galley kitchen along the stem. French doors at the far wall opened onto a tiny patio. Back at the bottom of the L, interior French doors opened into the bedroom. The bathroom was located just inside. Towels hung on the bar and a pretty bottle of liquid hand soap sat on the pedestal sink.

Heidi said, "Wow. I usually don't care for old-fashioned and homey, but this cottage is wonderful. And it's furnished. Anyone could move right in."

"The night I first arrived last year," Jasmyn said, "I needed a place to stay. All the neighbors pitched in with a chair, a lamp, and a rollaway. When Liv redid this cottage, she decided to include the basics, just in case of another emergency."

Piper said, "Or in case someone needs a temporary place and doesn't want to move furniture in." She winked.

"Well, it's great, but, Piper, I'm really not looking for a new home."

"Maybe it's looking for you."

"I'd never lease, though. It's my number-one rule. Financially, for me, it's not smart." And it smacked of her parents' lifestyle, a thing to be avoided at all cost.

"The train station is three blocks away. If you're not driving yet, you could take the train to your office."

"Plus," Jasmyn said, "everything you need is within walking distance. Groceries, coffee shop, the beach."

"And," Piper added, "you have the perfect next-door neighbors. I'm in Four and Chad—he's a total loveable puppy—is in Two. What else is there?"

"My condo? I'd have to make two payments."

Jasmyn frowned. "I see your point. If it helps, Liv is open to short-term and month-to-month. Her rent is reasonable." She gave her the details.

"Reasonable? That's crazy dirt cheap."

"I know, right?"

Heidi's phone dinged in her pocket. She glanced at it, surprised to see a text from her mom already. "My mom's waiting out front."

As they made their way back through the courtyard, Heidi's steps grew heavy.

She did not want to leave the Casa de Vida.

That feeling was truly crazier than the cheap rent.

Eleven

Hands on her hips, feet flat on the floor, Heidi surveyed her parents' messy living room. Her mother called it the *Early Lived-In Period*. Heidi called it chaotic. Books, newspapers, shoes, and clothes littered the couch and chairs and floor.

Maybe she should rethink the Casa de Vida. Two weeks after seeing it, she was still dazzled by it and Piper, Jasmyn, and Olivia.

But lease? *Nah*. And anyway, as soon as she could get behind the wheel of a car again, she'd move back to her condo. It'd take her about a nano-second to pack up.

She shut her eyes to block out *Early Chaos* and exhaled slowly. Leaning to one side, she stretched her muscles beyond their comfort zone. Her body was like the sprawling room before her, out of shape and unbalanced. Although she walked without the crutches now, she still limped. Only slightly, but enough to make her suspect the right leg was shorter than the left by a zillioneth of an inch or so. The doctor said it was her imagination.

Whatever.

Her midsection protested the stretch. A wave of nausea flowed through her, and she broke out in a cold sweat. She sank onto the overstuffed arm-chair, put her head between her knees, and moaned.

It wasn't the first time. Nor the second…

But it seemed worse. No, not seemed. It was definitely worse. She had finished six weeks of physical therapy with flying colors. The crutches were history. On her pier walk last week with her dad, she had made it from the parking lot to the bait shop and back, no problem. She could manage it alone; she was sure of it.

But this…this…She hated to admit it, but this creeping discomfort involved more than coping with physical issues. It had to do with being alone.

Her parents were spending her dad's spring break week with friends in Phoenix. They had suggested hiring a nurse to stay with Heidi. Of course she pooh-poohed that idea. *Remember?* she had said. *I live alone?*

Then her mother pointed out that she hadn't spent a night alone in two months. Life had changed.

Temporarily, her father offered.

Heidi had exchanged a look with her mother. The man tended to dwell in fiction. Her life, with the limp and heavy-duty pain pills and fear of riding in cars, had changed forever.

Odd as her folks were, their presence kept her mind occupied and off other things. Maybe Val could come over. No. She and her husband were attending some party tonight.

Heidi leaned back in the chair and took her phone from the end table. It was the same model with the same turquoise cover as the old one, but it was new. As were her handbag and laptop. Totaling the car had totaled countless odds and ends.

Fortunately she had been able to retrieve the phone data from the cloud. She scrolled through her restored contacts now. Most friends were in the same category as Val. They had partners. They had a life.

Actually—despite the number of cards and flowers they'd sent—Heidi sensed that all these people were more *acquaintances* than *friends*. When was the last time she had lingered with anyone over coffee or dinner just for fun? She did not play. She worked. She spent time with clients. Some would say she had no life, but she loved her nonlife…if that was what it was.

Had loved. How could she love what was no more?

She scrolled back to the beginning again. This time the first name caught her attention: Adam. He was Val's younger brother, Heidi's age. He was the reason she and Val had met in the first place.

As college freshmen, Heidi and Adam met in English 101, both on the fast track to failing the class. Which they proceeded to do. Although they had nothing else in common and were never attracted romantically, they were best friends for the next four years. They managed to graduate and credited each other for that accomplishment. After, they drifted apart. Adam traveled overseas for several years. She went into business with Val.

When he returned to the States, they were both a far cry from the wild college kids they'd once known. Occasionally they met up, usually through Val, the common denominator. But their special link remained. The instant-friend spark always ignited, no matter how much time had passed between meetings.

Her finger hesitated over his number. He had a steady girlfriend who had never warmed to Heidi. He worked long hours at his own business. He would be busy. She shouldn't bother him…

Her chest ached with every shallow breath. Pincers gripped her lungs. What had they called each other back in college? *Best buds.* That was it. She touched the cell phone screen.

⟳

Adam entered through the kitchen door, smiling and carrying a potted plant full of mini yellow and red peppers. The guy owned an organic farm. Of course he would bring a plant. He set it on the counter.

Heidi greeted him. "Hey."

He wrapped her in a hug.

Nearly as tall as he was, Heidi rested her cheek against his soft flannel shirt and breathed more easily than she had since her parents had left.

"Hey, yourself." Stepping back, he ruffled her short, short hair. "Nice."

"You lie."

"It'll grow, but overall you look a hundred times better."

"Than what?"

"Than you did in the hospital."

She gave him a puzzled look.

"You don't remember."

"Ohhh." She moaned. "Really?"

"Yep. I stopped by twice."

"Drugs."

"How many times have I told you to just say no?" He shook his head in mock dismay. "I'll get the soup."

Within minutes, she was sitting at the kitchen table, comforted by his familiar soft tenor as he made small talk. She watched him stir a pot of vegetable soup and broil garlic bread. He'd agreed to come over only if he could cook dinner for her. He was all too familiar with her parents and their dietary habits.

Adam resembled his sister, though his chestnut hair was thicker and more reddish than Val's, his face a little wider, like their dad's. His hazel eyes were more green than brown-flecked. He had a mellow, earthy demeanor that had matured into confidence. The goofy, confused college kid had found himself, and that person was a genuinely nice guy.

She wondered why she hadn't called her old friend sooner.

He carried two bowls to the table. "This is a great kitchen. Big. Country-ish."

"I never noticed."

He laughed and his grin crinkled his face. "That's 'cuz you're a businesswoman, Heidi Hathaway. See no domesticity. Hear no domesticity. Spoons? Napkins?" Not waiting for a reply, he opened drawers until he found what he wanted, brought them over with a plate of bread, and sat across from her. "What?"

"Thank you for coming."

"Thanks for finally asking."

"You have a life. Why would you want to hang out with an invalid?"

"Hm. Val never mentioned you changed your middle name to 'Victim.' FYI, I think the shelf life of that identity is three and a half months. Time's about up."

"Maybe your shelf life as friend has expired."

"Ha, ha."

Heidi picked up her spoon and waited for Adam to do his thing. Years ago, somewhere the other side of the world, he had acquired the habit of pausing to give silent thanks to—as he put it—the God who created dirt and seeds.

He bowed his head; his long lashes swept his cheeks. And then he looked at her and smiled. "How's your appetite?"

"It came back when I smelled your soup. I take it everything is from your farm?"

"Not the chicken broth." He winked. "Veggies and herbs, yes."

They ate, conversing as if in the middle of an ongoing conversation. It had always been like that with them. They didn't so much as catch up with each other as step into the everyday stream of their lives.

He said, "Val says you can walk most of the Seaside Village Pier."

"Only about half of it without keeling over, which is what I did last month." She told him about the adventure, making light of it, but he didn't smile.

"Heidi, how did you get home?"

"Short version, this girl took me to her apartment complex and tried to convince me to rent one. It really was an amazing place, this grouping of bungalows around a private courtyard."

"You'd never rent, though."

"Nope, never." She hesitated.

"Aha! There's a definite 'but' in your tone."

"It's too weird."

He burst into laughter. "If I had a nickel for every time I heard you say that."

"I'm serious, Adam. This is way, way weird. Beyond weird."

He drew his hand down in front of his face, pretending to wipe away the smile that kept tugging at his lips. "Okay, I'm ready now." His nose twitched. He repeated the hand motion. "Okay, now."

It was the best she was going to get. The two of them had been sharing weird observations since they both received an F++ on their first English 101 papers. Who gets an F++? They wondered.

She shouldn't have said anything, but if she were honest, she was ready to pop with the story. There was no one else to tell except Hud. But when her brother had visited, the opportunity never arose. Their parents were around and—

"Heidi?"

"Uh, the thing is…since the accident, I've been…I've not been myself. I've been…"

"Sandra Bullock?"

"No." She chuckled. "I've been feeling…feeling…"

"I bet you have. The pain must be excruciating."

"Adam."

He grinned and then turned serious. "Okay, I'm listening. You've been feeling what?"

"Feeling…" She sighed. "Off-kilter. I'm so stinking needy. Like you said, Victim is my new middle name."

"Hey, I was teasing."

"But it's true. And people pick up on that. They've been unbelievably kind and I've been unbelievably…" She swallowed. "Responsive."

"You do realize the trauma you went through was huge."

"I guess."

"No one expects you to bounce back overnight."

Except maybe for Val. "You know I've never been an ooey-gooey person, but something snapped at the accident. Besides my leg. When you're all scrunched up inside a scrunched-up car off the side of the freeway, there's not a whole lot you can do. And when someone says 'take my hand' and holds your head and promises you're going to be all right, there's not a whole lot you can do either." She blew out a noisy breath. "Except feel ooey-gooey grateful."

"That was the something that snapped?"

She nodded. "Adam, am I a cold-hearted, self-centered career woman?" Her voice caught. "That's a dumb question. Don't answer."

"It's not dumb."

"I already know the answer. It was dumb to ask it."

"Heidi, what I've always seen is a focused woman. First it was on the court or sand or water. Then it was business. To others, that sometimes looks cold-hearted and self-centered."

"'Focused' is a nicer way of putting it."

"You're not unlikeable, Heidi. You're not a horrible person. You are who you are. That's neither right nor wrong. Does the ooey-gooey bother you?"

"To no end. I don't know what to do with it."

"Simply feel it."

"But…" But feeling it meant blubbering and wordlessness and— "Depending on others. It means depending on others."

"For what?"

"I don't know. To emote with?"

He smiled. "You liked the apartment complex?"

"I loved it. I felt good and safe there."

"Which is why you're considering renting."

"I am not considering it."

"Almost considering, then. Do you feel ooey-gooey around me?"

"Why else would I have called you? But you don't count. You're in a different category altogether."

"Hm."

"Hm."

They stared at each other in silence for a long moment.

"Man," he said, "I don't know what to say. You've gone from cold-hearted career woman to an emoting, sensitive wacko. You win the award for experiencing the weirdest event in our ongoing contest."

"Thanks." She rolled her eyes. "Don't tell anyone."

"I won't. But seriously, there is a valid explanation. You've lost your identity."

"What?"

"Val says you're not working much yet. That must be doing a number on you. Work was your life. You loved every twenty-four/seven inch of it."

She shrugged, trying to appear nonchalant. He was so right-on, though, she wanted to cry.

"Your PPP factor is down to zilch."

"PPP factor?"

"Possessions, power, prestige. Your PPP factor is kaput."

She opened her mouth to disagree and closed it.

"You still have possessions, but not the important ones. The car is gone. You can't live in your condo."

"My kayak sits in storage. Where does the power come in?"

"You can't drive. To you, that's the epitome of powerlessness."

"Yeah. And I can barely walk down the block or dress myself."

He nodded. "And the third one, prestige. What makes you feel admired and respected?"

She whispered, "Work."

"Yeah."

"I never would have thought my identity was wrapped up in those things." Tears sprang to her eyes. "I don't know who I am anymore. So maybe those things are who I am. Or was. Or will be?"

"If you want. You're a fighter. You'll get back to it or ahead to whatever is best for you."

"Good grief, I sound like an angst-ridden college kid searching for her identity."

"The good news is you're thirty-five. It won't take nearly so long this time to slog through and find it." He smiled. "How about a game of Scrabble?"

"No. Help me figure this out."

"No. You need to step away from it."

"No, I—"

"Hush." He stood and began clearing the table. "Stepping away *is* how we figure it out. Trust me. Been there, done that."

Struggling to rein in emotions that insisted on running amok, she watched him load the dishwasher.

She should have called her old friend sooner. He ranked right up there with Margaret and Olivia for making her feel safe. She wondered why she had never noticed before.

Twelve

Heidi gripped the dashboard of Val's SUV. For thirty minutes she had strained against the seat belt to keep hold of it.

From the driver's seat, Val sighed.

Heidi said, "I can't help it."

"I know." She drove into the parking lot of a strip mall that housed several storefronts, including their own SunView Property Management Agency. "The question is…" Val swung into a space, turned off the engine, and turned to her. "What are you going to do about it?"

"Adam said he'd take me driving someday. Soon." She winced at the thought. She so did not want to get behind the wheel of a car. Sitting in a passenger seat still took every ounce of courage she had.

Val rolled her eyes. She was in full Monday-morning battle gear. During the whole drive, Heidi had listened to her one-sided conversations on the phone. Val was not in the mood for a coddling session, a thing Heidi would have welcomed.

Yes, she was totally out of her PPPs.

"Val, I'm sorry you had to pick me up. If my parents had been back in town—"

"Not a problem. Helping you figure out transportation is not a big deal. What is a big deal though—well, I'm wondering if you should be at the office yet. Your inability to focus created issues last week."

"Which I will fix today." She had spent three half-days at work the previous week and yes, added more work than she finished. "Honestly, I am feeling better."

"The doctor said you might need a year to completely recover. One.

Full. Year. You're nowhere near the end zone. I keep saying, we can work with that. You don't need to come in yet. Treena is doing great. So stay home. Take up knitting. Lease your condo. Go to a spa."

"Whoa, back up! Lease my condo? Are you nuts?"

Val held up a hand, traffic cop style. "Hear me out, sweetie."

"I'll live on the ground floor and hire a full-time limo before I give up my place."

Val simply looked at her. She did not have to say anything.

Heidi had barely made it through the weekend without falling apart. Adam had helped tremendously Saturday evening. But…she had slept worse than normal for three nights, she had not eaten aside from his soup, she had not spoken to a neighbor, she had not gotten online, she had not showered yesterday…

There was no way she was ready to be alone. *I'll live on the ground floor…* The fear in her voice thundered above its silly bravado.

Val said, "Do you want to hear the numbers first or the potential plan?"

Heidi frowned.

"I'll give you the numbers. Between the market and your absence, it's been a lousy few months for us."

"How lousy?"

Val tapped her manicured, French-tipped fingernail on the console between them, stalling. "We have enough to pay rent and staff salaries." She gave her specific figures. "For now. If we forego our usual take. It's just another tough season, like we've been through before. We put on our big girl pants and work smart."

"Val, it's never been 'if we forego our usual take' bad. What does Craig say?" Craig was Val's husband and their CPA who owned a small accounting firm.

"That it's really that bad."

"This didn't just happen yesterday. Why didn't you say something sooner?"

"Heidi, come on. Why do you think?"

The accident.

Her chest tightened as her mind raced down a dozen rabbit trails. Val had a husband with a good income. Val was an excellent agent and administrator. She would work her tail off while Craig paid their mortgage and bought groceries.

None of those things were true about Heidi. Her small savings would not carry her for long. Her parents never had any extra money. Not that she would ask them—

"Hey." Val touched her arm. "I'm not blaming you. You know that, right? This is on both of us. If you'd been on board these past months, it still might have been almost this bad. The January figures…" She shook her head.

"Okay." Panic set in. How was she supposed to make ends meet?

"Okay. Here's an idea. I met a couple on Friday. Lovely people from England. Here for six months or so, for his work. I took them around this weekend to our rental properties and nothing fit. Not even close. What they want, Heidi, is what you have."

"Oh, Val." She groaned the words.

"They can pay more than your mortgage. It would tide you over nicely." She slumped back in the seat.

"If you say yes, we'll show it to them today."

"All my stuff—"

"That's why we have a crew. They'll clean *and* pack up your personal things. Closet. Drawers. Desk. If the storage unit at the complex isn't large enough, you can put things at my house. I've got more extra space than your parents." She paused. "So what do you think?"

What did she think? That there was not another option.

⁂

As the Thompsons—the lovely couple from England—strolled arm-in-arm down the walkway toward the street, Heidi shut the front door of her condo.

Her just-leased condo.

Val had been right. Walter and Penelope were lovely people. Mr. Darcy and Elizabeth Bennett in the flesh—the A&E version anyway. She'd watched that one ages ago with her father after he finally gave up getting her to read *Pride and Prejudice*. Like the characters, the Thompsons were prim and proper and witty. Heidi immediately trusted that they would respect her home and her things. All it needed, they said, was a teapot.

Heidi hobbled into the small room located off the entry, her home office. She had made too many trips up and down the two flights of stairs and once unintentionally bounded down a step. She was in pain.

Sinking into the recliner next to her desk, she thought of the pain pills in her handbag in the kitchen, up on the second level. She hadn't wanted to take one before meeting the Thompsons because she wanted a clear head when she met them.

Her cell rang in her jacket pocket, a jazzy tune she had assigned to Val. "Hi, Val."

"Well?"

"Well, yes. We did it. Month-to-month through December."

"Heidi, that's wonderful! I'd whoop and holler but I know this is unbearably hard for you. Keep in mind it is a good thing in the long run. Truly."

Rather than say *whatever*, Heidi kept silent.

"You'll get back in your home in no time. I'll pick you up in forty-five. Okay?"

"Perfect."

Forty-five minutes of bawling seemed plenty long enough.

She propped up the footrest and soaked in her space one last time.

There was a half-bathroom off the office. Through the other door she could see the entryway, a door to the laundry room that led to the garage, the staircase up to the other rooms. The master bedroom and balcony were on the top floor with views of canyons, wide open sky, and, in the distance, a ribbon of ocean.

Everything about the condo was contemporary. Lots of black and white with silver accents. Geometric designs. Nothing rounded or floral. Everything had its place and nothing was out of its place. Nothing approached a bright color like tangerine.

Tangerine. The door of Casa de Vida, cottage number three. Its door and window boxes and the two Adirondack chairs that sat in front.

She glanced around her office. Her sterile, functional office. Since when did color and cozy speak to her?

The tears came then, tears of frustration, regret, fear, pain, and longing. Her life was like a wild mustang, racing uncontrollably out of sight to nowhere. She got that.

But what she could not understand was why in the world she had ended up in such an appalling situation.

Thirteen

Thursday evening, Heidi's parents arrived home. She met them at the door, oddly relieved to see them and hug them long and hard.

As far back as she could remember, that didn't happen. It was a first.

On the way home they had picked up KFC—original recipe, complete with mashed potatoes, gravy, biscuits, and chocolate chip cake—and now the three of them sat at the kitchen table, eating and catching up. As her father gnawed on the last chicken leg, Heidi delivered her news about the Thompsons.

Ethan's face reddened as if a bone stuck in his throat.

Rita smiled, but her eyes did not crease.

Ethan coughed twice. "Heidi, isn't this too soon to make such a major decision?"

"We thought," Rita added, "that after another month or so of exercise, you'd be moving back home, toughing it out."

"Recovering as you've always recovered, ahead of the doctor's schedule."

"Being your typical independent self."

"I thought we'd go driving next weekend. Perhaps in the desert to get you started, away from traffic."

Heidi looked back and forth between them. "What's going on?"

Her parents looked at each other.

She had never seen them both at a loss for words.

"Heidi." Her father reached across the table and took her hand. "I'm afraid we have some news that…well…that doesn't quite harmonize with yours. We, uh, we've made a major decision ourselves and quite honestly, we did not factor you into it."

Rita said, "We haven't factored her in since she was nine. We haven't needed to." She turned to Heidi, her eyes filling. Her voice grew husky. "You've rolled with the punches. You did laundry and homework, saved money from babysitting and always worked. Went to college. None of which we told you to do. You were a pistol, but aside from athletic injuries, you were never a worry to us."

"What is it?" Heidi sputtered.

After another exchanged glance, they apparently agreed that Ethan would explain. "I'm overdue for a sabbatical. There is interest in my book from a major publisher. I need to give it my undivided attention. Therefore"—he squeezed her hand and let go—"we're letting this house go and moving to Phoenix. In six weeks."

Late Friday afternoon, Heidi sat at her desk at the office, fragments from the bombshell her parents dropped the night before still warm on her lap.

What were they thinking?

They weren't. They never did. They made decisions based on the direction of the wind. She swore they did. Which way is it blowing today? Out of the west? Let's move east then.

But they had never moved out of state.

Val appeared in the doorway. "You okay?"

"Sure."

"Thatta girl. Way to hang in there." She continued on her way.

It was the umpteenth time she had checked on Heidi since bringing her to work that morning, the umpteenth time Heidi replied *sure* in hopes that it would come true.

"Val!" she called out.

Her friend returned. "Yeah?"

"I have to go with the cozy cottage."

Val began to speak and then she simply nodded. They had discussed Heidi's options ad nauseam. Breaking the contract with the Thompsons only guaranteed messy issues on every front and the real possibility that she could not pay her bills.

"Will you close the door, please?"

Val gave her a thumbs-up, backed out, and shut the door.

Their agency, SunView Property Management Agency, not only sold real estate, it offered full-service property management. Owners paid Sun-View to be landlords. Some properties were vacation rentals, beach condos, and houses that few people could afford to live in full-time. Some were regular homes, long-term rentals scattered about the county.

Through the years Val and Heidi had created a niche for themselves in that side of the business, mainly by keeping an excellent staff. Compared to making a sale, it was humdrum. But it was steady and the database presented a long list of possibilities for Heidi to choose from for a rental. She had spent most of the previous night and all day poring over it. Not one of them fit her needs. Not one came anywhere near reasonable cost, no stairs, centrally located, month-to-month.

She scrolled through the contacts on her phone. Piper had entered her own number and the main number of the Casa de Vida. Just in case.

Against every fiber of her being, Heidi had reached *just in case*.

"Casa de Vida." The voice belonged to the woman who wore the invisible sandwich board sign that mutely declared she offered peace, comfort, and wisdom to all who came within three feet of her.

"Hello. Olivia? This is Heidi Hathaway. Piper introduced us last month."

"Yes. I remember."

"Um, my circumstances have changed since then. Drastically. I know I insisted that I was not looking for a place, but now I am. Is your cottage still available?"

A silent moment stretched for so long, Heidi wondered if she'd lost the connection.

Olivia cleared her throat. "Well, it is vacant."

Heidi waited for more. It did not come. The woman was making her beg for it. Which, by now, she was ready to do. "Does vacant mean available? I'd like to lease it. Jasmyn said you'd do a month-to-month. The thing is, I've rented out my condo and my parents are moving, which means I have to move out of their house. I can't find a more suitable place than yours."

"Typically, I need to sit on a decision for a while."

Heidi blurted, "I'm happy to pay more than Jasmyn mentioned."

She cringed. She had done the math; she could pay more with what the Thompsons were paying her, but it would be tight.

"The money is not it. I just prefer time to think and pray about it."

Heidi tilted the phone away from her mouth and exhaled loudly.

"Let's say twenty-four hours. Is that acceptable?"

"Yes. Thank you. Fine. Shall I call you—"

"I'll call you. Goodbye."

"Bye."

The woman prayed about tenants? That was a new one. A little weird. But no weirder than Heidi knowing a safe harbor when she saw one and being willing to beg for it.

Fourteen

Liv parked her minivan in a beach parking lot forty minutes south of Seaside Village. She cut the engine and shook her hands to unclench the fingers.

Since her heart attack last fall, freeway driving unnerved her. She avoided it as much as possible. But dodging it today was not an alternative. There was another route, side roads that would have taken her days to maneuver on a Friday afternoon. At least it would have felt like days.

She needed to talk to him now if not sooner.

Liv climbed out of the van and headed to the boardwalk, a wide sidewalk bordered by a low wall and the beach on one side, homes on the other. The area was crowded, more than usual due to young people on spring break. Inline roller skaters, joggers, and bicyclists whizzed by. It would be a long trek.

Eventually she reached the multilevel beach house, out of breath and ready to burst into tears.

Julian was waiting, as she knew he would be, perched on the low stone wall that separated his patio from the boardwalk. He rose, smiling. A bit more gray colored his curly hair than last time she'd seen him. His eyes twinkled behind his rimless glasses.

"Livvie McAlister." He embraced her. His deep voice rumbled in her ear against his chest, its familiar Scottish accent a comfort. "Welcome."

Welcome. How she needed to hear that word.

Liv had many friends and acquaintances she could have called for support. She had a close circle she referred to as her top people when she was in need of serious prayer, a simple e-mail away. But for this…For this there was only him.

They made small talk, sat on his patio in padded chairs back a ways from the boardwalk, and he served iced tea. Remaining outdoors was her choice. She figured that with all the people strolling and rushing by, she was less likely to wind up a huddled, weepy figure on the floor. Not that Julian would have minded. It was simply not what she wanted to do.

Again. Once a day was enough.

"So." Julian looked at her. "You said you needed a sounding board."

"I've done something dreadful."

He simply nodded, not refuting her statement with an inane comment. She knew he would respond honestly.

Which explained why she had called him. That and the fact that they shared history. Long ago, he had been an associate of Syd's. He was much younger than her husband, but he was smart. Syd had already made his fortune in mergers and acquisitions. But because of Julian's software business acumen and their friendship, Syd had amassed another fortune.

"I have a potential new renter. You may recognize her name. Heidi Hathaway."

"Of SunView Properties?"

She nodded. The company managed the beach house vacation rental next door to Julian's house.

He let out a low whistle. "Small world."

"Yes, well, it seems to be a big, big problem for me."

He tilted his head. "Do you know Heidi Hathaway?"

She shook her head. And then she began to weep, quietly. There went that hope of not crying in public. She used a paper napkin to dab at her eyes.

"Livvie, you and Syd were there for me when I was at the bottom."

She nodded. They had been there to see Julian reel from his own divorce and estrangement from his children.

"Without you, I never could have accepted who I was—God's beloved—despite what I'd done to hurt others. You're losing sight of that truth for yourself."

Again she nodded. "It's just so much easier when the hurt I've committed against others is not in my face."

"Ah, but every now and then, unless it's in the face, we lose sight of its significance. Of how thoroughly, unconditionally, we are His beloved."

"I'm no spring chicken. I understand. Do I really need reminders?"

"Apparently you do."

She cried for a while, drank tea, and sat quietly with her old friend. Julian understood that she was not seeking answers. Instead, he gave her the strength to sit in her dark space and breathe.

Late that night, Keagan appeared at Liv's office door. "Hi."

"Did I leave the gate open?"

"Do you think you might have?" He sat in a chair the other side of the desk. "Mind if I sit?"

Since Keagan had first arrived at the Casa some years ago, she considered him angel-like...and not in the warm fuzzy feminine version. He was serious, strong, and scary, exactly what one needed in an angel. Whenever she was preoccupied and inadvertently left the gate open at night, he shut it. When she had suffered the heart attack, he found her in a timely fashion. When she struggled with a decision, he offered insight.

He said, "If you might have left it open, then something's up."

She sighed. "Heidi Hathaway is what's up."

"Why don't you think she fits in here?"

"I didn't say..."

"You didn't have to."

"She fits fine. I'm a little nervous about making another mistake with Cottage Three."

Her glaring mistake had been twofold. She had leased Three to the grandson of a friend without praying or even giving it a second thought. How could a go-ahead be any more obvious than to have a friend ask a favor? Also, Keagan had been out of town. If he had run a background check, they would have known that the boy was bad news. In the end, gang members seriously beat him in the cottage and the police came.

Keagan's laser beam eyes narrowed. "You're nervous of repeating that mistake? To quote a friend of mine, *applesauce*."

Somehow, the angel tripped her trigger. It was the closest she'd ever come to feeling anger toward him. She felt heat rise in her chest, but tried to make light of it. "That's my word. You're not allowed to use it. Especially when I mean what I say. I am skittish about this one."

He gazed at her for another long moment and stood. "Okay. We're here if you need anything." He left.

We're here. Sean Keagan never used to say *we*. He and Jasmyn were that close.

Their blossoming love was delightful to watch, but also bittersweet. How soon would they marry and move out of the Casa? There was no question in her mind that they would. They weren't simply head over heels in love, they were deeply contented.

Like she and Syd had been. Not inexperienced twenty-somethings, they had been around the block. They knew—as she and Syd had known—when it was right.

She only wished she could be as certain with Heidi Hathaway, one way or the other.

✑

"Livvie, lease the cottage to Heidi. It's the right thing to do."

Liv bolted upright in bed. The room was pitch dark. Her heart pounded.

Was she having another heart attack?

"Lord…"

It's the right thing to do.

The voice reverberated so distinctly she wondered if it was really in a dream. Syd's voice sounded as it had in real life. His tone laced with care and attention. His words concise. His viewpoint wise.

Suddenly, a brand new thought presented itself. Poof. It was like the surprise lily, suddenly *there* where, a blink of an eye before, there had been only a bare patch of dirt. Why hadn't she realized it before?

Heidi Hathaway should not pay for your mistakes.

"Okay, okay. I get it. I get it."

Liv reached for her glasses and her cell. Young people never minded receiving texts in the middle of the night, did they?

She entered a message. "I'll e-mail the lease to you. Liv."

She backspaced and keyed in *Olivia*. She hadn't even properly introduced herself to the girl yet. That would have to change.

Fifteen

Ten days after deciding the cottage at the Casa de Vida was her only port in a storm, Heidi moved into it on a Monday. She hoped by Tuesday that life would be better than the preceding ten days which had been one long stretch of tears, disbelief, regret, and more than a smidgen of anger.

She truly needed to lose the attitude. As Val had told her last night on the phone, it was unbecoming.

From Heidi's point of view, it produced headaches.

Heidi rode with her parents in their old van, her mother's vehicle for hauling artwork and, at times, her potter's wheel. It was plenty large enough to hold Heidi's one suitcase, laptop, and French press coffeemaker. That was about all she was bringing with her.

Rita parked in the alley, next to the back gate of the complex. Before they'd climbed out, Jasmyn, the assistant, appeared and greeted them with her warm smile and the keys. Ethan and Rita instantly fell in love with the woman. The three of them acted as if they were long-lost friends.

The same happened with Piper, who welcomed them into the court-yard. And with Beau, the bear-sized maintenance man who offered to help carry things.

Others stopped to say hello. Sam, a totally put-together woman in a black suit who kissed Beau on his cheek before rushing off. Chad, a seriously hot young guy. Inez and Louie, an older couple. Coco, an even older woman with rosy cheeks and bobbed blonde hair, sitting in a wheelchair. Noah, a tall, skinny forty-something with a disgruntled teenage girl in tow.

The same connection happened with each and every one, even the teenager.

Heidi was not surprised. Her parents related to strangers at the drop of a hat. She had the feeling that Casa tenants were of the same ilk. On another day she would have been right there with her parents, but passing out business cards, *connecting* on a different level.

No, on another day, she would not even be there. Not even close by.

As she unlocked her tangerine front door, her father whispered in her ear, "You're in good hands, princess."

Inside the cottage, her mother continued the oohing and aahing she'd begun in the courtyard. Every now and then she smacked her hands together once. "Oh!" Smack. "This is adorable. Look at that woodwork. Look at the archways, the rounded corners on this wall. Oh!" Smack. "The curlicues up there." She pointed above the kitchen cabinets. "Oh!" Smack. "Back there. More French doors." She strode to them.

Jasmyn followed and the three of them went outside to the postage stamp of a patio.

Piper said, "Heidi, not to be nosy, but I only see one suitcase and one hanging bag. Where are all your clothes?"

"I've been living in sweats and shorts for months. I even wear my 'sports suits' to the office." She sank onto a recliner, wiggled around in it, and put up the footrest. "Nice size. Not too big, not too small. Just right. Goldilocks would approve."

Piper chuckled. "I hope that means you do. Most of the furniture in here is used, from other residents, but that piece is new. For some reason, Liv insisted on buying a comfortable chair and a good mattress. I think we told you that she's never furnished a cottage before."

"Is she around?"

"No, she's out. So aren't you, like, tired of wearing sweats?"

Heidi smiled.

Piper shrugged. "Clothing is my life."

"My regular clothes are at my friend Val's. I had to move personal things out of my condo last week because the renters wanted in immediately. They'd been living in a motel for a month."

"So aren't you tired of wearing sweats?"

Heidi laughed. Maybe she was in good hands. Maybe the friendly attitude was contagious.

Later that day, after she had found a home for her sweats in the closet, she and her parents ate pizza at the small dining table on plates that did not belong to her.

Rita said, "Everything is nicely done, Heidi. These porcelain dishes." She held a slice of pizza and turned the yellow plate upside down. "Made in the USA. Six place settings. Excellent. You'll be comfortable here without your things for a while."

She nodded, appreciating her mother's encouragement, but the panic was setting in.

Ethan said, "Do you want to come home for the night?"

Heidi took a few shaky breaths. *Home.* As in that condo where the Thompsons from England now lived? Or her parents' house? "N-no. I might as well start now."

Her father did not hide emotion well. Sadness and guilt—things he had admitted to her over and over during the past two weeks—drew his mouth down. His eyes sagged, their creases more pronounced.

Heidi pushed back her chair, went over and hugged him. "I'll be okay, Dad. What doesn't kill me makes me stronger, right?" It was a favorite line of his.

She felt his head nod against hers.

Somehow, she made it through their goodbyes.

$$\mathcal{SLe}$$

Late that night, when Heidi finally convinced herself to give sleep a try, she went to bed, leaving a nightlight on in the bathroom and a lamp on in the living room. She snuggled against the new mattress—its firmness just right. Again with the Goldilocks routine.

She felt the soft zillion-count threads of the peach colored sheet and downy, pale yellow comforter. She had dried her face with a thick, pale green towel with a tag that read *Tellmann's Exclusive.*

Despite the used furniture—*gently* used—the cottage was well appointed, unlike most furnished rentals Heidi had seen. Although she herself had not grown up surrounded by such things, Val taught her to recognize it. Val, from a wealthy but broken home, would appreciate the place.

Exhausted, Heidi closed her eyes. She had not had a good, restful, un-drugged sleep since January thirty-first, the night before the accident. She doubted that would change in an unfamiliar cottage.

Her eyes opened. Adrenaline surged through her and she threw back the covers. Nope, it was not going to change.

And so she walked out to the living room and peered through the curtains into the courtyard aglow in twinkle lights.

The night would be long, but at least now she would not disturb her parents as she prowled about.

Sixteen

Late Monday evening, Piper returned home from work, ready to drop. Tidying up the Tellmann's women's department after a three-day sale was not for lightweights. But worry turned her steps toward Liv's office.

Where she found Jasmyn seated behind the large desk.

"Piper, hi. Come on in. I was just closing up shop."

"Where's Liv?"

"On a retreat."

Piper sat in one of the two overstuffed chairs. "A retreat. What does that mean?"

"She says she goes now and then to reboot."

"There must be a lot of time in between the now and then. I've lived here for three years and as far as I know, she's never gone on a retreat. With her church?"

"No. She went alone. She was evasive about it though. You know how she can answer a question without answering it and keep on talking. She asked me to take over for a few days. I mean totally over."

"It's not like her to avoid a newcomer."

Jasmyn clicked on the keyboard for a moment before looking up. "I've only been here for eight months, but...I've noticed she seems distant."

"I thought she would have called a 'let's make Heidi feel at home' meeting by now, before she moved in." Whenever a new renter was expected, Liv held a Casa meeting. Residents would eat her lasagna and brainstorm about how to make that person feel welcome.

"Yeah. I was surprised that she hadn't made a casserole and brownies for her."

"At least Heidi doesn't know what she's missing. She still refers to her as 'Olivia' because that's how Liv introduced herself. Obviously Heidi never got the 'Olivia call me Liv' talk. What does Keagan think?" Out of everyone at the Casa, he was closest to her.

As if on cue, the man opened the door and walked in. "Hi, ladies."

Piper looked at Jasmyn. "How does he do that?"

She smiled and blushed.

Keagan kissed the top of Jasmyn's head.

Seeing him openly affectionate made Piper smile. He had always been friendly enough and helpful, but totally inscrutable. He was a martial arts teacher and fit the persona to a T.

"What's up?" He walked back around the desk and sat. An orangutan would not have been more out of place in the pink floral office.

Piper said, "What's up with Liv?"

"Why do you ask?"

"Sean." Jasmyn's unusual use of his first name added a somber tone. "She's acting really strange." She glanced at Piper. "It's not just how she's been with Heidi. There's been a definite—I don't know how to say it. Lack of—of—oh…"

Piper said, "Lack of what?"

"Joy." Jasmyn winced.

Piper understood the wince. Saint Liv without her joy was not Liv. She was nowhere near Liv. It was inconceivable.

But it was exactly what Piper had glimpsed as well.

Jasmyn said, "The energy is all wrong here. It's like her prayers are missing."

Piper blinked. Only Jasmyn would catch on to something like that.

They both turned to Keagan.

He shrugged.

The women peppered him with questions. "What if she had a car accident? Should we call the hospitals? The police? The highway patrol?"

"I'm her ICE contact, so if there were an emergency—"

"Where is she?"

He blew out a loud breath. "On that, ladies, I don't have a clue."

Seventeen

Liv was a mess.

She should have told Heidi Hathaway about…about things. Now it was too late. The girl would be moved in by now.

Why had Liv thought she could get away with staying mum? True, the situation was temporary. Heidi wished she did not have to live at the Casa. She made that quite evident. She had no other choice, though. Six months max and she would be out of there. Liv could stay even-keeled that long, communicating on shallow levels.

Good heavens. She didn't even keep a shallow type of relationship with the postman or the trash collector.

But explaining things to Heidi would most likely have caused the girl to change her mind about living at the Casa. And she desperately needed to live at the Casa.

And so Liv had kept quiet.

But…she was a mess.

Because this morning she had realized that the others would come at some point. Heidi's friends. They would visit and the jig would be up. Liv's truth would come out.

How more unfair could Liv be? How much lower could she sink?

She was thoroughly ashamed of herself.

So ashamed she had treated herself to three days away in the desert, in an out-of-the-way blip in the road called Anza Palms, a place only campers, hikers, and golfers cared about.

She sat in a large suite at the Inn. The season was past, which meant the rates were ocean-floor low and the temperatures suitable for frying eggs on the sidewalk.

She and Syd had honeymooned at the Inn, the only resort in Anza Palms. Even the sweet memories, though, did not soothe her.

She phoned Julian, the second time in two weeks. Apparently she was getting the hang of asking for help, an activity she still avoided, even after sixty-plus years. Sixty-plus-plus...

Her old friend answered his phone. "Livvie. Hello."

Once again she sank into his calm voice. She told him where she was. He remembered that she and Syd had honeymooned there.

"Exactly," she said.

For a moment, he was quiet. "You have regrets."

"We fell in love. While he was still technically married. It was wrong, Julian. It was just plain wrong."

"Yes. It damaged you and others on a deep level. Wounds and scars irrevocably change the interior landscape, but..." He paused. "Life goes on."

"I am so ashamed." She began to weep quietly.

Julian did not speak.

At last she recovered. "I've never said that to another human being."

"Confession is good for the soul. I'm safe for you because of our history together. If it's any consolation, Liv, you two weren't a couple until after he was divorced."

Well, the area remained gray. "Let's talk in whole truths, Julian. They were separated when we met, not divorced."

"That is true. It was at the fund-raising gala for Balboa Park. We both met you that night."

"Through friends of friends."

"The three of us spoke for maybe ten minutes. Hardly a cause for shame."

"He and I *flirted*."

"For ten minutes. Did it lead to anything?"

"N-no. Not directly. But—"

"You looked stunning in that holly red dress, by the way."

"Thank you. As I was about to say, there was a spark."

"Livvie, come now. What line did you cross?"

"Making eyes."

"You hold yourself to impossible standards. It wasn't until a real estate deal brought you together that you became friends, right? Even then it was casual. Now and then. Unless you both hid a romantic relationship from me, that's all you were for a long, long time."

"Our friendship was what you saw."

Syd's long, drawn-out divorce robbed him of any desire to enter another romantic relationship. Although she adored him, she respected his healing time and never pressed for more. In time, he noticed her in a different way and things changed between them. The ink wasn't quite dry on the papers though, and that still haunted her.

Standards were meant to be high, weren't they? Otherwise there would be nothing to shoot for.

She voiced her earlier thought. "It's a gray area. Besides, there is the admonition that marriage is for life."

He sighed. "In a perfect world it would be for life."

They had discussed such matters before, with Syd. Julian had pursued money as if it were a mistress and abandoned his family. Once Syd became aware of his own marital trouble, he focused on fixing his marriage, but it had been a one-sided effort. His wife had moved on emotionally long before.

It was all iffy in the timing, all overlapping situations, all bordered in gray.

"Liv, you know there are no pat answers. But there is your Abba who loves you and wants the best for you. Living in past mire is not a requirement for God's love."

"But the mire has plopped itself on my doorstep."

"Heidi Hathaway's connection to Syd's children."

Liv closed her eyes. Yes, Syd's children, Valerie Engstrom-Laughlin and Adam Engstrom. The apples of his eye. "Heidi is Valerie's business partner. I imagine she knows Adam as well. The thing is…" She opened her eyes. "I haven't told Heidi who I am."

"Ah. She didn't recognize your name?"

"I guess not." Liv had not taken Syd's last name, Engstrom. Her maiden name, McAlister, was well established by her father decades before she took over his business, McAlister Realty. "Syd called me Livvie, but to the kids I was always just the Battleaxe. It could be she's never even heard my name. Heidi won't want to live at the Casa, not if she's good friends with Valerie."

"You need to tell her."

"Yes, I do."

"Liv, think of it. What an amazing opportunity to force a meeting with Valerie and Adam. Perhaps they're ready to forgive you. They simply haven't known how to take the first step."

She had longed for that. Time and again, though, they had refused to have anything to do with her.

She had always given Syd a wide space when it came to his children. He had a relationship with them that did not include her. He attended the significant events of their lives without her. The situation hurt both her and Syd, but they refused to strain things further with Valerie and Adam, to complicate their lives more than they already were by forcing Liv on them.

After his death, there had been no one to promote her cause to the young people. At Syd's memorial service, they ignored her completely. She sent them condolence cards and many of his personal items, things he had wanted them to have. They had not replied, not even with a thank-you note…or a hateful one for that matter.

Julian said, "They're older now and have most likely discovered that forgiving you is for the good of their own souls."

She smiled. "You are hopelessly optimistic."

"I learned that from you. All right, then. Get over yourself already. This is not about you."

No, it was not about her. Of course she wanted to be accepted and understood. Even liked by them. But her ego wasn't the point.

Syd's children were the point. Had Heidi shown up on her doorstep in order to bring Valerie and Adam into her life again?

The answer was obvious. God always brought people to the Casa for Liv to love on…and to learn from.

Eighteen

Tuesday morning, Heidi felt like the new kid in school. The pit in her stomach reminded her of childhood, when so often her family moved and she *was* the new kid in school, on the block. At the Casa de Vida.

She missed waking up in her beautiful condo. Going for a run. Zipping to the office. Working, working, working. Blowing off steam paddling her kayak or spiking a volleyball.

After coffee, a few bites of toast, and several deep, rib-aching breaths in her cozy, old-fashioned cottage, she headed across the courtyard to the office. The flagstones were pretty but—if her stubbed toes were any indication—a little uneven in places. It would be easy to trip and fall flat on her backside.

Fear barreled through her. Then fear about being fearful unleashed another wave.

"Oh, what am I doing?" She stood still and forced a few more deep breaths, hoping not to lose her breakfast all over those pretty flagstones.

She made it to the office, located in another cottage, one that also housed the communal laundry room. Its door was ajar and she went inside.

"Good morning, Heidi." Jasmyn greeted her from behind the desk. "Thanks for stopping in." She had asked her to sign some paper about rules and regulations. "I'm sorry I forgot to include these when I e-mailed the lease."

"No problem." A week ago she had signed the lease online. In her mind, there had been no reason to see the place again.

"How was the first night in your new home?"

"Fine." Her smile went up and down. What was it that made small talk impossible with this woman? "Actually, I didn't sleep very well, but I haven't since the accident."

"Of course you haven't. Last year I lost my house in a tornado in Illinois. I didn't sleep for months and months. What you've been through seems a hundred times worse. I mean you were physically injured, not just emotionally and mentally. But trust me, the Casa is a safe, healing place. Let me get those papers for you to sign." She went to a filing cabinet. "Liv said she was sorry to miss your move-in day."

"No problem." Heidi looked around the feminine décor, a large oak desk in the middle of a pink floral sea. "You call her Liv?'"

"Yes. She usually goes by that." She rummaged in a drawer.

Heidi noticed framed photos on the side wall and walked over to them. And found herself gazing at Val and Adam's dad.

What?

She had met him a handful of times. His classic good looks—tall, dark, and handsome—were revealed in this photo, styled like an old movie star. It was an eight-by-ten, black-and-white glossy. His expression was nothing less than a thousand-watt smile. There was an inscription across the bottom: *Best wishes. Sydney Engstrom.*

Jasmyn said, "Isn't he handsome? I heard he was a great guy."

"Oh?" She swallowed and turned, unsure what to say.

"He died about ten years ago."

"Who was he?"

"Liv's husband. She never took his name, I think because she had been established for such a long time in business as McAlister. Hey, she was in real estate too, just like you."

"Really?" Yes, really. Heidi actually knew that much. She had been unaware of the name, though. Years and years ago Val had told her that the Battleaxe—Val's sole name for the woman her dad had taken up with—had been a big deal agent back in the day. That fact alone could have explained her friend's unbalanced approach to being successful in the same field.

"They married late in life. I think they had twelve years together. Not many, but it sounds as if they were very happy. Liv didn't move in here at the Casa until after he was gone."

"Hm." She accepted a pen from Jasmyn and bent over the desk to read the papers. The words blurred. She imagined the hurt on the faces of her friends when she told them she was leasing a cottage from the Battleaxe.

꙳

At the office of SunView Property Management Agency, Heidi sat in an armchair beside her desk, her right leg propped up on another one, and wondered how much more she could handle in one morning.

She was running on fumes. The gas tank had been all but drained. No sleep. The information about her landlady, Olivia McAlister a.k.a. Battleaxe. Getting to the office. Piper had driven her and she was a cautious driver, even taking surface roads for Heidi's sake instead of the freeway, but…But Heidi and cars were not yet on a first-name basis. Sitting upright for the short drive had been a struggle.

The biggest issue of all though was whether or not she should tell Val and Adam about the landlady.

Sooner or later Val would want to see her new place. What if she ran into the owner? Val had met her father's second wife. Even all these years later, she would most likely recognize the tall woman before she heard her name.

"Heidi."

She jerked and peered over her shoulder.

Treena stood in the doorway. She was a twenty-something college student, a friendly, cute rah-rah type who would do well in sales. "You know, you could be suffering from PTSD." She tucked her perfectly bobbed black hair behind an ear, revealing a large silver hoop.

"PTSD?"

"Post Traumatic Stress Disorder."

"I know what it stands for. I wasn't in a war."

"Car accidents cause it too. It's your thousand-yard stare that makes me wonder. You've been sitting there looking at nothing for an hour." She shrugged. "I mean, after what you've been through, it's a possibility. Maybe you don't need to spend the whole day here yet. For the sake of your health, you could leave. I'm just saying."

Heidi nearly snapped at her to keep her *just saying* to herself, but the words *don't need to spend the whole day here* zinged. No, she did not have to stay. She could leave. Nothing was keeping her there.

Except for the fact that she did not have a car.

"Let me know if you need anything." Treena left.

Heidi slowly got to her feet and went into Val's office next to hers.

Val looked up from her computer. "Hey."

"I have to go home."

"Okay."

"I need a ride."

"Treena's available." She winked. "It's in the job description for paid intern."

"I—I…I don't want to ride with her."

Val leaned back in her chair. "Heidi."

"She drives like I do. Did."

"Cab."

"Oh goodness no. I wouldn't know what I was getting into until it was too late."

"We can't keep this up, sugar-pie."

"She thinks I have PTSD."

"Maybe she's right. You should tell your doctor."

Heidi's chest hurt. Was it PTSD or the fact that she did not want to tell her best friend that she was paying rent to the enemy?

Val stood. "I'll tell Treena to drive slow."

"You don't want to see my place?"

"Some other time. You know what's on my plate for today." She stopped talking abruptly.

Oh no. Val must have researched the Casa de Vida and found Olivia McAlister's name—

"Heidi, I want to see it. I truly do. But I can't. Not yet. You said it's quaint and, honestly…" She wiped at the corner of her eye. "You are so *not* quaint. I almost cry every time I see you limp and now I have to imagine you renting a quaint cottage?"

Heidi sank into a chair. "It's well done, though. Nicely appointed." She did not mentioned some of it was *used* appointed. "I'm okay."

"No, you're not. But we can't make you all better in one fell swoop today." She sniffed and wiped the corner of her other eye. "We simply have to live through it. I'll let Treena know."

She nodded. No way was she telling Val about living with the woman who had ripped Syd Engstrom away from his family.

Nineteen

The day after returning from the desert, Liv rose earlier than usual. She felt like a child, shoveling peas into her mouth in order to get the nasty taste over and done with before enjoying the rest of the mashed potatoes and gravy.

Confessing to Heidi Hathaway was going to be the worst taste of the day. Why wait?

Liv made her rounds in semidarkness. *Her rounds.* Syd had coined the term. When he was alive, they lived elsewhere, in a pleasant house not far away. Most days she would visit the Casa at some point and make her rounds.

She strolled through the courtyard now, pausing before each front door to offer a prayer for the residents within. As she faced the tangerine door of Cottage Three, her pause stretched into a linger.

"Abba, I'm sorry." Again. How many times had she said that over the last few days? "Give me gracious words to explain the situation to her. Give her wisdom to decide what's next. And heal her broken body. Her heart is probably a bit of a mess too."

A short while later, as the darkness lifted, Liv sat in the holly red Adirondack outside her cottage, Number Ten, and drank tea. Residents left, getting on with their day.

Jasmyn stopped by first—breakfast shift at the restaurant began bright and early—and planted a kiss on Liv's cheek. "Welcome back!" In reply to Liv's question about Heidi, she said that yes, she had moved in and had been around the evening before.

Samantha, the busy engineer, went out of her way to greet Liv, a thing she never used to do before Jasmyn befriended her and she fell in love with Beau.

Piper blew her a kiss as she hurried toward the front gate. Chadwick—cheeky Chadwick, the perennial student—hurried along behind Piper and waved gaily.

Riley smiled, striding toward the back gate. Her little nine-year-old Tasha made a beeline to Liv and gave her a big hug. "Bye-bye, Miss Liv."

Noah, the stork—he was quite tall and gangly—did not glance her way. Music would be filling his head without the benefit of some gadgetry hanging on his belt or from his ears. He was gifted that way.

Eyes glued to Heidi's door, Liv hesitated to leave her post. She would have liked more tea, but absolutely could not bear the thought of missing the girl.

By nine o'clock, Liv had a mental list of options. Call her. Knock on the door. Phone her office and ask if she was working today. Write her a note. Let it go.

Nothing struck her as proper landlady behavior.

The day moved at a snail's pace. Liv spent much of it hovering in the courtyard, pulling weeds. By eleven o'clock, she tossed aside the proper landlady decorum and knocked on Heidi's door. Several times. She phoned. Again. And again.

There was no answer.

By noon she was at her wits' end. Had she made a mistake? Should she not have rented to Heidi? How on earth had she not told Heidi that she was Syd's widow? How could she be sixty-plus-something and still behave so foolishly?

She phoned Keagan, who heard the tears in her voice and hurried home from the gym he owned, a few blocks away.

He met her at the fountain. "You're sure she's here?"

"Jasmyn said she saw her last night. I haven't seen her come out. I might have missed her, but—Oh, Sean. I'm so worried."

"My understanding is that she's not working full time yet. There are all sorts of reasons why she's not answering your knock or call. You could be flashing back to last year's fiasco in Number Three."

She sank onto the narrow edge of the fountain, the nearest seat. It was true. She could be feeling last year's nightmare more than she cared to admit. "I feel like I'm losing my footing."

He knelt before her and removed his sunglasses. The laser-like blue gaze held her, reminding her that Sean Michael Keagan had been her rock for a long time. "This is why you have me and Jasmyn around. Take a deep breath."

She wondered if anyone had ever said *no* to him.

"Now what has ruffled your mother-hen feathers? You typically give us space, even the new ones."

Well, she was not about to spill the beans to anyone, not even Keagan, before she had spoken to Heidi. "Maybe it's the memory of that last boy who lived there."

"We know that Heidi is recovering from a bad accident. It could be she sleeps a lot, like Jasmyn did when she first got here."

"The accident! Her poor body. Oh, Sean, something is wrong. I just know it." She grasped his shoulder and stood. "Come. We have to check on her."

Liv hurried toward Heidi's door, taking the large ring of keys from her pocket.

Keagan followed. "You're sure."

"Give it a good knock."

He banged on the door. They waited a moment. Liv heard a faint noise.

Keagan said, "She's coughing."

Liv unlocked the door and went inside. "Heidi! It's me. Liv." She hurried through the living room through the open French doors into the bedroom.

Even from the doorway Liv could see that the poor girl burned with fever. She was tangled in the bedclothes and moaning, her hair damp, her face flushed.

"Heidi." Liv bent over her and smoothed back hair from her face. She was hot to the touch but wore sweats, as if she were chilled. "Can you hear me?"

Her eyes fluttered open. "I'm sorry." A coughing fit overwhelmed her and she curled into a fetal position.

"Oh, honey."

Keagan stood beside her. "She had her spleen removed, right?"

Liv nodded, dread in the pit of her stomach. There could be serious complications.

"We have to get her to the ER. Ambulance or your van?"

Heidi gasped between coughs, "Van. No ambulance. Please."

He unwound blankets from her legs, scooped her up, and headed out the door.

∿

Liv sat in a chair beside Heidi's bed in the ER and held the girl's hand. In the flurry of nurses and doctors attending to her, Liv had lost track of time. She only knew that Heidi had been given fluids, antibiotics, and tests. Most importantly, she knew that Heidi did not have OSPI, serious infections that people without spleens sometimes developed.

And died from.

Thank You, Abba.

Heidi smiled at her. "Hey, I'm okay." Her voice was weak and her skin pallid, but the fever was gone and she was sitting propped up in the bed. "I knew this could happen. I just didn't realize how fast and how sick I can get sick. What'd they call this? Upper respiratory infection?"

"Something like that. If Keagan hadn't suspected..."

"If you hadn't barged into my cottage, uninvited. Do you do that often?"

"Oh, dear. No. This was a first."

"I'm glad you did and brought Keagan with. I thought he was a little scrawny, but whew. He's a powerhouse in disguise. Is he spoken for?"

Liv laughed. "Yes, he is. Jasmyn."

"Really?"

"But we can borrow him anytime. Inez calls him our resident knight. By the way, a nurse told me that you could wear a bracelet so that medical people know about your spleen. Or lack of."

She grimaced. "I have one in a box somewhere. I thought if I ignored the truth, it would go away. But I'm never going to get better."

"Honey, you will get better. You'll be different is all. Germs will have a heyday and you simply must keep an eye on them." She squeezed her hand and let go. "Now, I really think we should call your parents." Throughout the ordeal, Heidi had begged her not to.

"They'll feel guilty and want to drag me home. I can't go back there. The cottage is...it feels like home already."

"They need to know what happened."

"I'll tell them later. Liv, I promise if I feel the least bit sick again, I will get help immediately. I had no clue how fast it happens, but now I do."

"All right."

Heidi locked eyes with her. "Is it okay if I call you Liv?"

She sighed. Somehow the girl knew. "I prefer it over Battleaxe."

"Yeah, I imagine so."

"How…?"

"I saw Syd's picture in your office."

"Of course. Heidi, I apologize for not saying something sooner. It's a part of my past that still hurts, and I'm afraid I couldn't own up to it."

"I thought you probably needed the rent." A tiny smile played at the corners of her mouth.

Liv had the sensation of an iceberg melting in her chest. *Abba, You brought her to me, didn't You?* "No, I was simply being a foolish old woman. I was ready to tell you this morning. That's why I was aware that you hadn't come out of the cottage yet. Then, when you didn't answer my knock or phone call, I became concerned."

"If you had told me sooner, you wouldn't have been watching for me. I might have laid there for a long time."

"Or not moved into the Casa at all." She sighed again. "I recognized you right off as Valerie's partner. Since Syd died, I've followed her career and Adam's from afar. They were the apples of his eye. Did you know Syd?"

"I saw him a few times. Adam and I met in college. He introduced me to Val. Syd showed up now and then. He sometimes showed up at Adam's gigs, in those unbelievable dives." He had played guitar in a band.

"You weren't at the memorial service, were you?"

"No. Our business was growing and we didn't have anyone to cover for both of us, so I had to work. Otherwise I would have been there. Syd seemed like a really nice guy. Their mom, Cathy, always put him down. Sometimes it would get so bad, I'd have to leave. My parents aren't anything like that."

Liv nodded. The woman had cheated on Syd and blamed it on him. His workaholic lifestyle had pushed her away. Liv tried not to judge. She had not walked in Cathy's shoes. But the toxic overdose she had given her children about their father upset Liv.

As in most cases, both people contributed to the demise of their marriage, although Syd always took full responsibility. His life in those early days was making money.

But all that was not the point of explaining things to Heidi. She touched the girl's arm. "I realize they blame me. Your living at the Casa will cause problems. I should have thought this all through the minute we met."

"I have to tell them." Her expression was soft.

"Yes. All I can offer is a refund and free rent until you find another place. I can help with that. I have friends who—"

"No! No. I don't want to move. The Casa, the cottage—I wasn't exaggerating when I said it felt like home. I want to stay."

"But…"

"Yeah. I'll see how it goes with them."

"And I'll pray. That's what I do, about everything. Some people think I'm an odd duck. Or worse." She shrugged. "Now do you want to move out?"

"Nope."

"All right. Let's start over." She put out her hand. "Hi. I'm Olivia, call me Liv, McAlister. I was married to Syd Engstrom, your business partner's father."

Heidi smiled and shook her hand. "It's so nice to meet you."

⁂

Later that evening, Liv gathered three people on a need-to-know basis. Jasmyn, Keagan, and Piper needed to know.

They sat in her living room, she in her recliner, the women on the couch, Keagan in a chair. Tobi, her RagaMuffin cat, snuggled on Piper's lap and stared at Liv as if she were offended that she had not yet been clued in.

Jasmyn said, "Heidi is totally, absolutely, really fine all alone in her cottage?"

Liv smiled at Jasmyn's string of adverbs. It was the way she spoke. "She is totally, absolutely, really fine all alone." Liv had just finished telling them about the hospital visit and bringing Heidi home. "I have something else to discuss."

The three of them exchanged glances. No, all four of them did.

Piper nudged Jasmyn, who said, "We've been concerned."

Liv's heart melted all over again. These young people were family. "You have?"

"For goodness sake, Liv, you didn't tell Heidi to call you Liv. You didn't call a Casa meeting before she moved in to tell us how to make her feel at home. You weren't here when she moved in. You haven't baked her a casserole or even a small pan of brownies."

Liv blinked a few times.

Piper said, "All of that is so unlike you."

Keagan's eyebrows rose, almost imperceptibly.

"Well…I've been preoccupied." She took one deep breath and exhaled. "Syd had two children. One of them is Heidi's business partner, Valerie Laughlin. The other is Heidi's good friend from college, Adam Engstrom."

There was a long pause and another exchange of glances. Not even Keagan knew that Syd had children.

Keagan said, "You're a stepmother."

Liv could not stop the cringe in time. "Technically. We never had anything to do with each other. Or rather, they with me. I tried, but they were sixteen and thirteen when we married. I respected their distance. Syd interacted. I worked." *And their mother needed a scapegoat.*

Jasmyn said, "Is this going to be a problem for Heidi?"

"I'm afraid it could be. Syd's children always rejected me. They'll be hurt by Heidi living here. I've offered to help her find another place, but she says she wants to stay. I should have told her right off the bat. I knew she was Valerie's partner. It's all my fault."

Piper leaned forward. "All?"

Jasmyn's eyes widened.

Liv understood the question. "Not all, but enough to be ashamed. Syd and I became acquainted through business at the time of their separation. Later we were, um, close friends, before the divorce was finalized. Anyway, I just wanted you to know what's going on."

Piper cleared her throat and sat back, hugging Tobi. "I don't mean to make light of it, but I'm glad you're not perfect."

"You thought I was perfect?"

She nodded. "You're Saint Liv. I thought if you knew things about me, you'd be horrified."

"Oh, Piper dear. Never, never ever believe that. We all make mistakes. Do things we're ashamed of. Even when we're old enough to know better."

"But you're so—so…" She shrugged.

Jasmyn said, "Beautiful and wise and loving."

Piper pointed at Jasmyn. "Yeah, what she said."

Liv said, "You girls are awfully kind and sweet."

Keagan said, "What about me?"

She smiled.

He winked.

Twice now, since they met many years ago, she had seen him wink.

"You're courageous, Liv," he said, "as well as beautiful, wise, and loving. I appreciate your telling us."

"Okay, maybe you're sweet too."

Jasmyn said, "What did Heidi say?"

"That the Casa feels like home."

Piper giggled. "It's what they all say."

Jasmyn walked over, bent down, and hugged Liv. "It's time for a potluck for the newcomer."

"But what if she leaves?"

"Olivia McAlister." She tilted her head back and looked at Liv. "Aren't you praying that she stays?"

Liv thought about it for a long moment. If Heidi stayed…Valerie would either disown her partner or…or visit the Casa. "You're talking nigh on a miracle."

Jasmyn laughed. "So?"

So. So indeed.

Twenty

The infection laid Heidi low for days on end. She could not remember ever having been so sick. Nor could she remember hearing a lecture like the one the doctor had given her before she left the ER.

What? he had said. *You moved?* His voice had risen in disbelief, nearly screeching. *You moved? Literally, as in taken your belongings from one home to another? Do you know how many stress points you racked up on that alone? You're going to the office? You walk how far? Please don't tell me you're driving.*

Okay, okay. She got it now. Pushing herself beyond reasonable limits was doing more harm than good.

But stir-crazy was stir-crazy. By Saturday, when her dad suggested they go car browsing, she could not stay home any longer. She told him yes. Later, en route to the dealership, between coughing fits and clutching at her ribs, she told him about her week. Most of it. The ER, yes. The specifics of Liv finding her almost delirious and Keagan carrying her to the van, no.

Ethan glanced over at her. "So I should turn around and take you home."

"Dad, I feel better today."

"Your cough—"

"It comes and goes. A little outing won't hurt. I'm on antibiotics and I am just sitting here." And glad not to be freaking out. She trusted her father's driving. Not an ambulance driver's, nor Treena's, nor her own.

"The spleen thing…you would have gotten sick anyway?"

"Probably. Any germ passing by hitches a ride in my body. The doctor said I need to incorporate balance, though, and not put more stress on the immune system. It would help if I didn't push myself."

Ethan chuckled. "And you told him 'in your dreams.'"

She smiled. "I only thought it."

"That answer right there tells me exactly how sick you were."

She heard the worry in his tone and knew he was doubting his own choices about moving away. "Hey, Dad."

"Hmm?"

"Don't put your life on hold for me. Contrary to what things seem, I am not some delicate hothouse orchid."

He held out his hand and she squeezed it. "But you are my princess."

"Always."

Heidi and Ethan hung out for a while at their favorite car dealership, sitting in the latest models, choosing which ones they liked best and least, thoroughly enjoying themselves.

After a time Ethan put an arm around her shoulders. "It's too soon to buy, isn't it?"

She nodded. "Even if it were my left leg that was injured…" Driving again was not simply a physical thing. She could not envision herself getting behind the wheel of a car without crawling under it.

"Whenever you're ready, I'll be here and we'll shop. Okay?"

"Okay."

"Hey, let's swing by Adam's place. It's just around the corner and your mother is craving his squash blossoms."

"Mom's craving a vegetable?"

"Not the squash part, just the blossoms. She'll stuff them with goat cheese and walnuts and create an edible work of art."

"Let me guess. You're going to the Duncans for dinner." They were the only friends her mother tried to impress with culinary skills.

He laughed.

It was good to hear the laugh and to think of her parents living their own life. She did not want them hovering over her. Despite the illness and ER visit, she already felt so much more comfortable at the Casa than she had in their house. Liv helped, of course. Heidi was hooked on her, or rather the comfort she felt in her presence. She had referred to herself as an odd duck, but—hands down—she had nothing on Ethan and Rita's oddity.

Olivia McAlister, a.k.a. the Battleaxe.

Heidi walked with her dad to his car and groaned to herself. She was meeting Val later, at a coffee shop, to tell her about Liv. Now she might see Adam, but she would have to pretend all was well. She preferred not to open that conversation with him first.

Adam's Garden was located in one of the rural areas that truly was around the corner from civilization. There was the sprawling city and then presto, around a bend there was country.

Ethan pulled into the Garden gravel parking lot. It was full of cars. Eucalyptus trees surrounded it. Hills rose in the distance. The sky was bluer than it was back around that bend.

"Dad, I need to sit a bit." Her leg ached. She coughed. Two good excuses to stay put and miss running into Adam.

"Sure. I'll get the veggies."

Heidi watched him walk away. The stillness seeped through the open window and enveloped her. The absence of city noise reminded her how loud life was elsewhere.

Adam had not started out as an earthy type guy. After he came back from overseas, when his father died, he was a somber version of his old self.

While Adam was gone, Syd purchased the small, organic farm for his son without ever telling him. Syd died and Adam came home to a surprise. His dad's will stipulated that Adam would own the farm only after he worked it for three years. Then he would be free to run it or sell it. That was his inheritance.

It was a wise move on Syd's part. He knew his son better than Heidi would have guessed. Adam fell in love with the work.

After three years he renamed it and turned so-so profits into comfortable ones. He added vegetables, hired more staff, kept the roadside stand open seven days a week, and sold at farmers markets and high-end restaurants. He also turned an old outbuilding into a small café, The Grounds.

Over time he grew into a centered, happy, earthy type guy.

Heidi noticed a tall wispy woman enter the café. She recognized her. Maisie was Adam's long-time girlfriend, a baker who provided goodies for the shop. She seemed a natural for the scene in her chunky sandals and swishing colorful maxi skirt, her long curly hair tied back with a scarf.

Heidi had met Maisie a few times and thought she was a good fit not only for the farm scene but for Adam as well. Val's take was that he should keep looking. But she was his sister. No girl was good enough.

The sound of steps on the gravel drew her attention to the driver's side open window. Adam peered inside. "There you are."

So much for avoiding him. "Hi."

"Hi." He grinned. "I saw your dad. We decided I'd take you home. Okay with that?"

"Uh, I guess. Why?"

"My booth at the farmers market in Seaside is running low on butter lettuce. Since you live there and your dad lives way the other direction—Actually..." His smile became a straight line. "Actually, I want to talk to you."

Oh no. He knew about Liv.

"I'll get my truck. Be right back." Adam tapped the door and strode off.

Heidi watched him. He greeted everyone he passed. In his brown cap, blue jeans, boots, and distressed gold T-shirt, he resembled every other guy working the farm. That was Adam, low-key and friendly.

She really hated the thought of introducing Olivia McAlister back into his life.

༄

After Heidi had told her dad goodbye, Adam drove them to the farmers market—apparently a weekly affair—a few blocks from the Casa and delivered his lettuce. Now they sat in his pickup across the street from the Casa. He had yet to say anything that warranted his phrase *I want to talk to you.*

"This place looks interesting." He studied the Casa through the windshield. "You like living here so far?"

So far she had spent four days in bed. "I do. It's quiet and the neighbors don't seem to be around a lot. Val feels bad for me because the cottage is not my style."

He removed his cap and finger-combed his thick hair. "That's Val. You're in a different space, though, after what happened. Styles change when needs change. All sorts of things change when needs change."

"Mm-hmm."

"Heidi, I, um, the thing is, Maisie and I…we're having issues."

"Oh." There it was, the reason he wanted to talk to her, why a friend would seek out a friend. They'd been in this territory before. "Adam, I'm sorry. Are you okay?"

"I'm not sure how I am. In a major funk. How do you stop thinking about someone who's been in your head for years?"

Head? Maybe Val had been right about Maisie not being the one. "Head? Is that a guy's way of saying heart?"

He studied her now, his hazel green eyes intense. "She hates farming."

Heidi's brows went up.

"We thought it was no big deal." He shrugged. "Young love. Whad-dya gonna do?"

"She hates farming?"

"She hates farming, the farm, and everything related to it except the café."

"And you love it all."

"Yeah. Sometimes I think I'd be more lost without it than without her. So…" He shrugged. "Anyway, when I saw your dad well, I, um, I missed you. I missed talking with you, like the old days. That night at your house was good." He flashed a self-deprecating smile. "Best bud."

She chuckled at the nickname. They had been the best of buds. Like eating comfort food, they found respite in each other's company during their challenging college years. "That's exactly why I called you."

"I'm glad you did." He paused. "I've wondered why you and I grew apart. I guess there are obvious reasons."

"You think?" She added a snarky tone. "As in you left the country for years on end."

"I came back, but you'd gone all career woman on me, all about the PPPs, power, prestige, and possessions. Too busy for the old best bud."

"Well! You started planting and had your nose buried in a hole all the time."

"How would you know?"

"I just did. Then you took up with Maisie."

"And you with what's-his-name."

"That was his name."

He laughed.

She tried to laugh, but something wasn't funny. "We were good platonic friends, Adam."

He winced. "Yeah. Or something." He muttered the words and faced the windshield. "Anyway, thanks for listening. It helps like it always did. I should get going."

His sudden shift of gears puzzled her. The Maisie thing had him off his game, but Heidi couldn't let the Liv thing wait. If she didn't tell him now, later would be worse. "Do you have one more minute? Something's come up."

He turned to her. "What's wrong? Did the doctor tell you—"

"No, it's not that. Adam, you know my landlady. She's…she's Olivia McAlister."

For a long moment there was no recognition in his eyes. For him and Val and their mother, the Battleaxe did not have a real name. If they had ever mentioned it to Heidi, she didn't remember it.

She waited. She simply could not refer to Liv as the Battleaxe, not in jest, not to jog his memory.

The light dawned and with it came a flash of anger. "You have got to be kidding."

"I just found out a few days ago. She's really not what you think—"

"Give it a rest, Heidi." He stuck his cap back on his head and he started the engine. "I'll never want to talk to that woman. You know that. You've always known that."

"But she's kind and good and—"

"Did you tell Val?"

"Not yet, but—"

"You seriously think this woman is good? Unbelievable." He reached across her and yanked the handle, pushing open the passenger door. "You've been snookered just like Dad was."

Heidi's entire body tensed and she pointed a finger at him. She couldn't help it. Sometimes even best buds caused discomfort. Lashing out was the only release. "You need to cool off and grow up, Engstrom."

"And you need to get your finger out of my face."

She did just that and slid from the truck, landing too hard on her right leg. Pain shot through her, but it was nothing compared to the sudden ache in her heart.

Twenty-One

Liv watched Adam Engstrom's pickup roar away from the curb and Heidi limp toward her, muttering to herself.

Apparently, something had gone awry between the two.

She had just opened the gate and spotted the logo on its door as the truck sped off. The bouquet of colorful vegetables tied together with lettering underneath—*Adam's Garden, Organic Herbs and Vegetables*—told her whose it was.

Heidi reached her and blew out an exasperated breath. "He is totally unreasonable. I mean how can you make an adolescent vow and still think it's valid at age thirty-five? What an idiotic way to live. Honestly, even I realized that leasing was a necessity, even though I've sworn since I was a kid that I'd never do it. You'd think by now he'd be mature enough to move on. Get over it already."

Liv gave her a sad smile. It went without saying that Heidi had told Adam that the Battleaxe was her landlady. "Honey, if Adam allowed me into his life, he'd feel disloyal to his mother. He'd feel that his adolescent vow was all wrong. Two things that no one welcomes with open arms."

Heidi did not reply for a moment. "That would be a little more involved than renting versus buying."

"A little."

"But he doesn't know you, Liv. He should give you a chance."

"That's for him to decide."

"He once told me his dad said you were not the cause of the divorce. I don't think he believed him because, like I told you, his mother constantly told him otherwise."

"And as a mere child he was forced to choose between them."

"Well, he should get over it. Cathy has been happily remarried for years and years. I need to sit down."

They went into the courtyard and sat on a bench just inside the gate. Heidi propped her leg on it, grimacing.

Liv said, "May I get something for you?"

She shook her head. "Answers for Val and Adam?"

Liv had those, but she wouldn't say them out loud. Cathy's adultery had not been revealed to anyone except Syd. He had eventually told Liv because he told her everything. His ex-wife married the man within six months after the divorce. It turned out that he was a decent stepfather to the children, a solace to a large degree.

But blaming their mother now for her contribution to the split would not help Valerie and Adam accept Liv.

"Heidi, I'm the Battleaxe, or rather the scapegoat, and that's all right. It helps them deal with the hurts. It doesn't impact my day-to-day."

"Scapegoat? Maybe you've worn that costume long enough."

She smiled to herself. As if she could simply chuck it. Young people were a breath of fresh air, even when their ideas were utter nonsense.

"I hadn't meant to tell Adam today. My father and I stopped at the Garden and ran into him. He wanted to talk about, um, some personal things." She glanced at Liv. "Issues with his girlfriend."

"Do you mind my asking…Were you two an item?"

"No. We were always just friends. We never went out." She glanced at her watch. "I have to go. I'm meeting Val at the coffee shop in an hour. She wanted to talk business."

"Heidi dear, I am terribly sorry you're the one who's suffering now. If you'd like, I can evict you. Then you can blame it all on me."

"You can't evict me. I could sue you."

She chuckled. "I bet you wouldn't."

"No." Heidi went quiet, her bright blue eyes unfocused.

Liv thought the cheek scar gave the girl's face an unexpected quality. What was still a pleasant appearance—that of a confident, healthy athlete—now had the additional hint of vulnerability. The combination was lovely. She doubted Heidi had any idea.

"Liv, Adam really needs to get to know you. If there's any way I can make that happen, I will."

She stared at her, taken aback at the declaration, but even more so at the obvious similarity between the girl and herself as a young woman.

What a curious thing.

Twenty-Two

Piper sat in the quiet courtyard and wondered if she had just lost her job. After yet another run-in with her supervisor, Gildy, she had skedaddled from the store. On a Saturday afternoon. A Saturday afternoon!

Her father would say she had been doing her own thing on the job for some time now, behaving as if rules did not apply to her. There was a good likelihood that today's action had sealed her fate. Gildy would be crazy not to fire her.

She scrolled through the contacts on her phone. Her dad would not be her first call.

As a personal shopper, she was given a lot of leeway with her schedule. But she was also a sales associate and worked on the floor whenever necessary. Saturdays were necessary. Leaving that day had been completely irresponsible.

Since the anniversary of Jared's death, she had been experiencing hope. Large doses of hope, the kind that entire cultures must cling to in order to survive. It led her to engage less with whirligigging and—strangely enough—to demonstrate more kindness toward Gildy.

The woman did not take kindly to kindness. She rebuffed Piper's bubbly demeanor and all Piper could do in return was smile. Taking her supervisor seriously had become a thing of the past. Gildy's threats, frowns, and *tsk*ing mattered no more. Piper loved the shoppers and the clients and the work. Gildy could fuss all she wanted. Piper refused to shut down again.

Her father would remind her that she had bills to pay.

By now she should have been a manager with Gildy working for her. But a year of grieving through self-destructive means had changed that course. Missing work and showing up with a hangover on a regular basis guaranteed that upper management lost its interest in her career.

At least she had kept a job with Tellmann's. At least she eventually got her head straightened out and made some progress. At least she still loved her work and it still made her happy. When Jared died, so did her desire to be top dog. She had been content with the status quo, grateful to be able to make ends meet and coast through the rest of life.

Now, though, something had begun to itch and she wanted to scratch. Which explained why she was scrolling through her contacts.

An acquaintance had offered her a job some time ago at a boutique in an exclusive area. It seemed a possibility. Less pay, most likely, but—

The chimes from the front gate rang out their Westminster tune. It was a pretty sound that Piper had first thought overkill in the age of the cell phone. Delivery people and visitors could always call when they arrived at the locked gate. Besides that, each cottage still had its own intercom. But old-fashioned Liv kept it and, like right now, it was being used.

She went to the solid wood gate in the twelve-foot wall. Much of the time the gate stood wide open to everyone. Not bothering to peer through the peephole, she pulled it open and looked up into the face of a stranger, a tall, slender stranger with unruly dark brown hair and an expression of—of—

Of whatever it was she was feeling.

He said, "Uh, hi."

Two syllables delivered deeply and softly put Piper in a stupor.

"Is this the Casa de Vida?"

More deep, soft syllables. The Spanish name of the place spoken like Inez spoke them, lightening off the tip of the tongue. The resident, an older woman from Mexico, had tried to teach Piper—

"The sign here says it is." He pointed at the wall where the name of the complex was spelled out in tiles.

She nodded, her face hot.

They stood there. Speechless. Blinking at each other. Slipping into a space that had been created solely for them. In that long, silent moment, Piper knew in her bones that once they became accustomed to each other's presence, that space would feel like home.

She knew because it had happened to her once before. With Jared.

She swallowed. "Hi."

He smiled. His narrow face creased and his eyes shone a baby blue. "Hi."

She recognized him then. "Are you—"

"Are you—"

"Hud?"

"Piper?"

She smiled. "You look just like your dad with Heidi's eyes."

"You look just like Heidi described, only…" His Adam's apple moved above the open, white button-down collar of his shirt. A rosy tint colored his neck.

What hadn't already melted within her did so now. She wasn't going to ask *only what.* She got the drift.

He smiled, a slow, spellbinding appearance, and put out his hand. "Nice to meet you."

She shook his hand. The goosebumps prickled then. And the butterflies flapped their wings.

"Heidi's not answering her phone or her buzzer. Is she here?"

"I…I…I don't know. Good grief, where are my manners?" *Where's my head?* "Come inside." She backed away and shut the gate behind him. "I only came home a few minutes ago. I haven't seen her today."

As he looked around the courtyard, he whistled a note of appreciation. "Heidi said this place was like a Shangri-La, but I could not have imagined this."

"My mom calls it a Garden of Eden without the zoo."

"Does she live here too?"

"Wisconsin. Do you want to knock on Heidi's door? It's the—"

"Tangerine one." He glanced around at the ring of bungalows. "There."

Piper watched him lope past a tall bird of paradise to the door with the small wrought-iron curlicue attached to it, shaped in a three. He wore jeans that were at least thirty-six inches in length. His wrinkled shirt was tucked into them, its sleeves rolled partially up his forearms. A large mocha-colored messenger bag draped from a shoulder. He was rugged but…but without the rough edges.

He knocked a few times and called out his sister's name. There was no response. He turned and shrugged.

"You're welcome to wait here."

"Is that all right?"

"Of course." She gestured toward one of the tables. They sat under its red umbrella. "Can I get you something? Water? Iced tea?"

"I'm fine, thanks."

Fine and then some. He was nice looking, his face narrow with the trendy facial hair, more than five o'clock shadow but less than beard. His shoulders were wide.

He thumped his bag onto the flagstones and pulled a phone from his pocket. "I'll try her cell again."

Piper's heart pounded. She was instantly transported back to sixth grade, the year she thought Jimmy Peters hung the moon and the stars. She never exchanged two words with the boy, although she hoped with every fiber of her being that one day her name would be Piper Peters.

"You don't have to keep me company." He smiled, the phone at his ear. "You probably have something else to do?"

She shook her head.

"Me neither." He turned off the phone and set it on the table.

They fell silent again, not quite making eye contact, stealing glances at each other. She smiled. He smiled. It should have seemed awkward…but it wasn't.

Discreetly, with her hands under the table, she moved the diamond ring from her left hand to the right. "Is Heidi expecting you?"

"No. I have to be in L.A. tomorrow and thought I'd swing by to see how she's doing. I just drove up from Mexico."

"She said you live there." That explained his native-like accent.

"Yeah. I went down to Baja to do some research about ten years ago and stayed. I like the slower pace. It's good for me, for writing. Have you been?"

She shook her head.

"Would you like to visit?" His sudden lopsided grin gave him a boyish look. "That sounded a little forward."

She laughed.

He laughed.

All of her earlier concerns went *whoosh* out of her head. Old job. New job. No job. Gildy. The acquaintance with the job offer in her contact list. What did they matter?

If Hud Hathaway invited her to fly off to the moon, she would say yes.

Twenty-Three

Heidi drank iced green tea at a table in a neighborhood coffee shop called Jitters. Piper had pointed it out to her one day as they drove through the small downtown area of Seaside Village. As her friend had promised, the town offered everything within four blocks of the Casa.

She had planned to walk the four blocks, but considering the doctor's lecture and the disturbing talk with Adam—not to mention the jolting jump from his truck—she asked Jasmyn for a ride instead. Of course the woman hadn't minded a bit, but Heidi had. She hated that she could not take care of herself.

Waiting for Val now, she looked around the large room of tables and couches. Typical of the beach culture, the ocean decor was casual. Surfboards decorated the walls alongside photos of Seaside and original artwork made by locals. All sorts of people filled the seats: gray-haired tourists, poets with their Macs, teens, surfer dudes in cutoff jeans, T-shirts, and flip-flops, and people in business casual talking over legal pads.

Val entered, wearing her own business casual, a black pencil skirt and white blouse, briefcase in hand.

Heidi waved her over, pointing to the lidded to-go cup. It had sat there for ten minutes, but Val wouldn't mind its temperature as long as it was black coffee.

She slid into a chair across from her and grinned. "You've really got the hang of this new style of yours. What's it called? 'Something the cat dragged in'?"

"Thanks." She touched the neck of her old blue T-shirt that sported a large volleyball. "It took me hours to pull it together. You don't think the hair is overkill?"

Val laughed. "It's growing, sugar-pie."

"I'm not so sure." She held a few strands straight up from the top of her head. "I think it's almost at two inches?"

"Almost. It's trendy."

"That's me." The banter drained what little energy she'd bundled together for their meeting. Her relationship with Val was solid, business-wise and friend-wise.

Val sipped her coffee. "Mm. Cute place and good coffee. I'm impressed." She jumped into a description of that day's open houses and how well Treena was doing.

Heidi interrupted. "Val, I have something to tell you."

"What's wrong? Are you all right?"

"Yes, it's not that. It's a weird thing about where I live. I—"

"I knew it wasn't right for you. Oh, Heidi. I tried talking Craig into giving up his home office. I'll just tell him it can't be helped. You need—"

"Val, my landlady is someone you know. Olivia McAlister."

Her friend turned a few shades of red that grew brighter and brighter. "No way."

"I found out on Tuesday. I didn't know how to tell you. Then I got sick and—well, this is the first chance."

"She's the one who took you to the hospital?" Her face could have lit up a city block.

Heidi nodded. "Dad and I stopped at Adam's today, and I told him."

"How did he take it?"

"I think I lost a friend. Val, I don't want this to come between any of us. She really is a nice woman."

"She broke up our family."

"Years ago. You're grown up now. You might want to revisit things."

"You know what? That doesn't matter. Look, it's not your fault. You can live wherever you want and be nice to her if you want. But I probably won't ever want to see your quaint little cottage."

Heidi bit her lip.

Val gathered her things. "There's a lot going on that I've been protecting you from. Okay? Things are worse financially than I let on. Much worse. And, as long as I'm being completely honest, Craig and I aren't getting along. So your little tidbit is a little too much to digest right now. I'm going to go now before I pop." She stood and walked off before Heidi could say a word.

Heidi looked at the to-go cup of coffee on the table. Val never left behind a to-go cup of coffee.

Twenty-Four

Following the aroma of coffee, her eyes at half-mast, Heidi shuffled from her bedroom to the kitchen. As she poured a cup, she heard voices and noticed the French doors stood open. Without her glasses on, she saw only two blurry figures seated outside on her back patio.

The events of the previous day rushed at her.

Adam. Val. The awful talks with them. Hud's surprise presence in the courtyard when she arrived home. Feeling ill again and going to bed before dinner, totally missing out on her brother's visit.

She sipped coffee, waited for a caffeine jumpstart, and pondered as she did every morning a list that had not existed before the accident. Where were her glasses? Should she try the contacts? Did she need a pain pill? No, *when* would she need one? And which one? Would her ribs hurt less today when she took a deep breath or coughed? Was her scar less red? Had her hair grown enough to entirely cover the shaved patch?

"Hey." Hud stood in the doorway. "Good morning, squirt."

She gave him a halfhearted smile. All she had these days were halves. Halfhearted, half-mast, half breaths, half steps…

He took the cup from her hand and gave her a hug. "Come outside. Piper and I bought scones for you."

She blinked up at him.

He shrugged and made a wry face.

Well, *that* was interesting. Hud and Piper.

Outside, Piper smiled. "Morning, Heidi. Did you sleep well?"

"Either that or I died." She winced. "That wasn't funny."

"No, it wasn't." Hud guided her onto a chair, handed her a cup, and ducked back inside to grab a chair from the kitchen table.

The patio was tinier than tiny, with a bistro style table and two chairs. But it was private. The complex's back wall was twelve feet high; eucalyptus trees towered over it from the other side. Neatly closing in the area were tall fences and, to the right, a windowless wall of Piper's cottage.

"At least you slept well," Piper said. "That's a start, right?"

"Definitely." It was the first undisturbed rest she'd had since— since…Yeah, since then.

Piper lifted a napkin and revealed a basket of scones. "We walked to Jitters. Hud said cranberry-orange is your favorite, but there's blueberry too."

Hud set a small plate in front of her and handed her a napkin.

A linen napkin, like the one on the basket, brightly colored like the doors on all the cottages. A swirl of orange, red, blue, green. The plate a bright tangerine.

She looked at the mug in her hand. It matched the plate.

Her eyes stung. She hadn't noticed the details yet. She'd been too ill. She'd been self-absorbed. She'd been angry at circumstances that had forced her to leave her home and live at this place.

"Heidi?" Hud leaned forward.

"Everything is so pretty." She used the napkin to wipe her eyes. "They still think she's the Battleaxe."

"Adam and Val will come around sooner or later."

Piper said, "All they need to do is meet Liv."

Heidi nodded. Late yesterday, after Val had left the coffee shop, she remained seated, too upset to get up and walk the few blocks home. Out of nowhere, Keagan appeared. Liv had sent him. With few words, he bundled her into a minivan, drove her to the Casa, unlocked the back gate for her, and was gone before she could thank him.

She had entered the courtyard where Hud and Piper sat laughing, heads close together. Like his parents, Hud had the Hathaway effect, able to take up with a stranger as if in the middle of a conversation. But when he invited Piper into Heidi's cottage, Heidi resisted. She needed alone time with her brother, to tell him personal things.

Sweet Piper said, "Of course. And by the way, I hope with my whole heart you don't have to move. Liv told me about her stepchildren."

Heidi had pulled Piper inside then. She knew about Val and Adam? That made her new friend practically family.

Not up to playing hostess, Heidi had given them a short version of her conversations with Adam and Val and gone straight to bed.

Emotion flooded her now. Liv's pretty things and her obvious care for others, Piper's steady attention, and Hud's surprise visit all rolled into one cloudburst of such beauty, she thought she might drown in it.

ꝏ

Heidi watched her brother pack up his few things. "You sure travel light."

He rolled up the sleeping bag he'd used on the couch. "Sorry I have to leave so soon."

"I'm just glad you stopped by. This meeting is a big deal, huh?"

"The biggest." He zipped shut his backpack and sat on the couch. "Do you believe it?"

"Your dream come true."

They grinned at each other. Hud had been writing screenplays since he was five years old. Heidi and neighbor kids acted them out.

He skipped college, went to Mexico, and wrote suspense novels. The fourth one hit the top-ten bestseller list a few years ago and now was being made into a movie. He had written the screenplay.

He said, "I could still get you a walk-on part."

"Yeah, right. With or without the crutches?"

"You might want to stop feeling sorry for yourself."

"Be quiet. I like doing it. I think I'll move to Hollywood, start an acting career, make new friends. The crutches and the scar could be my trademark. Maybe I'll use the neck brace too."

"Heidi, you've got a whole complex here of potential friends. Dad was impressed with everyone he met."

She smiled. "You were too, weren't you?"

His eyebrows went up and down. "Man, she is beautiful. Every which way."

"What happened? I went to sleep while you two were talking out here, and then I woke up and you were still talking."

"She went home for a while. I invited her down to Baja. She said yes."

"No way."

"It was a joke, but…I don't know. It's like we've known each other forever. If I didn't have this meeting to get to…" He shrugged.

Heidi stared at him. His heart had been broken once, a prerequisite, he said, for writing well. After that, he never had another serious relationship. He would have told her if he had. And he seldom blushed or stumbled over words like he was now.

"She is beautiful."

"Hauntingly beautiful." He raised his hands and let them drop on his knees. "Did you know she wants to be a photographer?"

"Really?"

"That's her 'impossible dream,' as she put it. She packed her camera away the day Jared was killed and hasn't picked it up since. When they told her the news, she was photographing military families on base at a soccer tournament."

"How sad. But she likes her work at the store."

"Yes and no. She walked out yesterday, something about her supervisor being difficult." He paused. "She doesn't complain, does she?"

Heidi smiled. "No."

"And she's thinking of working in a boutique."

"My, my, I didn't know any of that stuff."

"You've been preoccupied."

"With complaining."

He smiled. "Anyway, what are you going to do about Adam and Val?"

"Find a new place to live."

"Heidi, this is perfect here. And it's temporary. If they can't handle—"

"I think Liv is permanent, my relationship with her."

"What?"

She took a deep breath and began to explain how safe she felt at the Casa. How Liv exuded peace and every other adjective that was related to *good*. "But that's probably my fever brain talking, or the pain meds. Val is my lifeline, personally and business-wise. Adam used to be, and now that he and Maisie are having serious issues—"

"Serious issues? Curious. After how many years?"

"A lot. Anyway, hurting them is not an option. If I stay even temporarily here, up close with Liv, it will deepen the rift between us. If I move,

I can still visit Liv, but it won't be an everyday situation for them to deal with."

He studied her for a long moment. "It's like with Piper. I think if I swing by here on my way home later this week…or if I call or text her…or if she came to visit…" He shrugged. "My life would never be the same." He stood abruptly. "I have to go, squirt. And, rift or no rift with Val and Adam, I think you should get outside and spend time with your neighbors."

Twenty-Five

As she walked from the street toward the Casa's front gate, Liv turned and waved to her friend Flo as she drove away in her little electric car. Liv was all for taking care of the natural resources the good Lord had given, but heavens to Betsy. That go-kart was for the birds. Next week, she would drive herself and Flo to church in her minivan.

She turned back and studied the front wall of the complex, noting where the bougainvillea needed trimming. The handyman, Beau, was great at everything she threw his way: plumbing, wiring, construction, maintenance, and repairs. When it came to Southwestern plants, though, the Tennessean did not have an eye for detail.

How she loved her home and everyone in it, but she was more than grateful for the friend and church that offered her an escape. A tad too much drama had surrounded life at home lately.

Yesterday, after seeing Adam roar off in his truck and sending Heidi off to meet Valerie at the coffee shop, she took a long, hard nap on her couch. At dinnertime, her cat Tobi roused her. They ate tuna sandwiches in the bedroom and watched an old movie. She kept the lights off, her phone on, and prayed no one would need her, at least not until morning. If she'd had the energy, she might have hightailed it back out to the desert inn.

The gate opened now and Heidi emerged with a young man. From the way they carried their long limbs, Liv assumed this was the twin, Hudson. He was a fine specimen of an elusive expat who wrote books, dressed in khakis and a button-down shirt, a bag slung over one shoulder.

Heidi spotted her and smiled. They walked to each other. "Liv, this is my brother, Hud."

He smiled and shook her hand. "The landlady extraordinaire."

"Oh, my." He was a charmer. She felt herself blushing. "And you're the writer extraordinaire. I enjoyed *Silver Heart* very much."

"Thank you."

Heidi said, "You didn't mention that you read his work."

"Only the one, so far. After you told me your brother was a writer, naturally I Googled him. You know, purchasing an eBook takes less than thirty seconds."

Hudson laughed. "Your support is much appreciated."

Heidi elbowed him. "Liv, half the Casa has hard copies. You don't have to buy any more. You can borrow. Though I doubt Riley will loan hers. She is starstruck and Hud signed them."

"Half the Casa?"

Hudson said, "Riley and three others. And I think Noah's copies are e-versions."

"Four readers right here. Plus me now. Isn't that delightful?" Liv grinned. "Did you meet everyone then?"

"Almost."

Heidi said, "He'll be back in a couple weeks."

"Right. I have to go now." He hugged Heidi and shook Liv's hand again. "Thank you so much for giving her a safe place." His eyes held hers.

Liv smiled. She adored genuineness. "My pleasure." *I hope she stays.*

They said their goodbyes and watched him walk down the street.

"He parked about two blocks away," Heidi said.

"Parking can be an issue here."

"Well, not for me." She gave Liv a large, phony grin. "Did that sound like a complaint? Hud says I should quit complaining. I just meant I don't have a car. Ha, ha. No parking issues for me."

Liv smiled and patted her arm. "You complain all you need to. I just won't listen. But tell me about Valerie."

Heidi's shoulders sagged and she groaned. "She won't be visiting anytime soon."

"I'm so sorry."

"I'll give her time and then we'll talk some more. She is a reasonable person. She can be, anyway."

"Like her father." She sighed. "My offer still stands. Free rent until you find another place, and I can help you with that."

"I sincerely hope you don't have to."

"Me too, Heidi. Me too." Her mouth twitched. "Because I'd like to get to know Hudson Hathaway. He is a charmer, isn't he?"

Heidi laughed.

Twenty-Six

Piper whirligigged her way through Sunday. The default mode had kicked in that morning as she said goodbye to Hud.

Evening fell now. She sat in her car, parked down the street from the Casa, and replayed it. Over and over and over.

The goodbye had been…weird and wonderful. She wanted to comb her fingers through his thick hair and kiss his beautifully shaped lips. She wanted to hug his broad shoulders and get lost in his embrace. From the wistful gaze on his face, she assumed he was dealing with similar thoughts.

It all sat there between them for one eternal moment.

Then she smiled and gave him a little wave. He did the same. She walked away from Heidi's cottage.

And got busier than busy.

She went to church. Having grown up attending with her parents and five siblings, she still went regularly. The old ways comforted her. The candles, the familiar words, the bread and wine.

Strange that she could whirligig in such a setting, but she did.

Liv once told her that God worked in people even when they weren't paying attention. The Creator of the Universe, as she sometimes referred to God, absorbed fears and guilt, pouring love and goodness into the spaces they left behind.

Piper certainly hoped so, because she had no clue what to do with the mess churning inside of her.

After church she went to work at the store, glad that it was Gildy's day off. The two associates who had most likely noticed Piper's abrupt absence the previous day only looked at her in a knowing way. There was no need for them all to gossip. They were basically in the same boat when it came to their boss.

After leaving the store, she went to the gym and worked out until at last there was not one spark left inside of her to energize a whirligig.

She had told Hud almost everything about herself. She had listened to his stories. They covered the biggies: family, significant others, broken hearts, work, regrets, and dreams. Virtual strangers catching each other up on entire lifetimes.

She held back in one area, only because it was brand new. The words had not formed yet to explain that love was knocking. The thought of opening that door again had sent her into the tailspin.

Opening it meant it might close. After Jared's death, when it closed with a slam and she lost her grip on life, her parents had come to visit. Her dad stayed for a week, her mother for seven more. Darlene nursed her back to sanity and found Saint Liv.

They met in Ralph's grocery store over a display of fresh corn on the cob. The women struck up a conversation. Darlene, having grown up in central Illinois, naturally knew corn. While Piper stood off to one side inspecting tomatoes, her mother showed the tall stranger how to inspect the kernels and choose the most tender, most flavorful cobs. She explained how best to cook it: Cover the corn with water, bring it to a boil, turn off the heat, put the lid on the pot, let it set for ten minutes.

She also gave Liv the whole history of the Keyes family up to Jared's death. Liv described Cottage Four at the Casa de Vida, a mile from where they stood. A saint emerged and Darlene could go back home.

But she was still Piper's first call.

She picked up her phone. Darlene answered on the first ring.

"Mommy, I met someone."

After a comforting talk with her mom, Piper walked home. She entered the courtyard, embracing its luscious nighttime atmosphere. Patio lights were strung in trees and solar lamps softly lit the paths. The fountain trickled. Jasmine was in full bloom and its heady perfume soothed her.

Chad sat in the shadows outside his cottage, Number Two, his face lit by his cell phone. "Hi."

"Hi." Suddenly desperate for company, she sat in his other Adirondack. "Mind if I join you?"

He chuckled and set his phone down.

Charles Chadwick Rutherford IV was about twenty-five, a perpetual college student who spent much of his time on a surfboard. His looks were exquisite, from wavy brown hair to hazel eyes to rakish grin to a body created to wear tuxedos. He could have modeled for Polo—clothing and cologne—made a fortune, and paid back the vast amount his father must have already spent on keeping him in toys, school, and housing.

He was also a loveable puppy who made no secret of his adoration of Piper. Time and again she let him down gently. *Dinner at Mr. A's? A Padres game? Wicked in Los Angeles? You are a sweetheart, Chad, but I have other plans. A long weekend in New York? A week in Hawaii? Truthfully, Chad, my heart is just not there, you know? Jared was my one and only.*

Chad said, "Heidi came out today."

"Great."

"She walked her brother to the gate, so some of us met him. Wow, I had no idea she was related to *that* Hathaway."

"You knew who he was?"

"Yeah. Didn't you? Hudson Hathaway is a bestselling author. I've read his books. So have Noah and Louie and Riley. We were all ga-ga until we heard about his Hollywood gig. Then we drooled. Seriously. All over his Tevas. Riley got her copies and had him sign them. I'm starting a Casa fan club."

She laughed. "He seemed so down-to-earth."

"You met him then?"

"Yeah." *Yes. Yes. I met him and I don't understand what happened to my one and only, to my heart that had no capacity for another.*

"You don't read thrillers, so he probably wasn't such a big deal for you."

She bit her tongue to keep from bursting into laughter.

"I'm sure Louie would loan you a copy." His phone rang. "Pizza delivery kid at the gate. Want some?"

"Sounds good."

He gave her an odd look and answered his phone. "Be right there." He clicked it off. "My place or yours?"

"How about right here?"

"Works for me."

He strode off to the gate.

Piper's heart boomed. She was sure Chad would hear it. *Not such a big deal? Oh, Hudson Hathaway was an incredibly huge deal. Was she ga-ga over him? Check. Drooling. Check.*

A few minutes later, the box between them on a low table, they ate a garden pizza from paper plates and drank root beer. Light spilled out from his bay window and open front door. He entertained her with stories about one of his business professors.

The food worked its natural wonder, fueling her mind and body. She hadn't eaten since that morning's scone.

"Piper, how did you meet Jared?"

His question stunned her. Despite his flair for audacity, Chad could be sensitive. He had never asked for details before now.

He said, "Was that too impertinent?"

"Not at all. You really want to hear it?"

"I wouldn't have asked if I didn't."

In a flash Piper saw the scene from eight years ago. In another flash she saw the scene set yesterday at the gate. They were separate, distinct…and the same. She closed her eyes for a few seconds. Jared. Hud. First sight.

"Piper?"

She looked at him. "Gathering my wits."

He smiled.

"I was at O'Hare Airport, on my way to New York to train at our store there. A huge ice storm hit and the airport shut down. I was walking around, trying not to panic. The storm was so bad, the city was basically shut down too. I couldn't go home. I finally found a seat in an area that wasn't too crowded. I sat down and then…" She took a deep breath. The memory of her first glance of Jared David Oakes still jolted her. "And then I saw this guy in desert fatigues leaning against a wall. He noticed me at the same time."

Chad leaned forward. "And then what?"

"That was it."

"Nah."

"Yeah. We stared at each other. He was with a few other Marines and one of them nudged him. He walked over, got down on one knee, and said 'Will you marry me?'"

Chad blinked.

She shrugged. "We talked all night. By the time he walked me to my boarding gate, I said 'Maybe.'"

"That's crazy."

"I know. But I also knew he was the one, and not just because he was the best-looking guy I had ever seen in my life."

"Was he a better-looking guy than me?"

"Sorry, Chad. No contest."

"Ouch."

She laughed.

Late that night, Piper sat cross-legged on her bedroom floor in front of the closet, surrounded by shoes, clothes, shoeboxes stuffed with photos, six cameras, camera bags, camera lenses, and a tripod.

She clenched her hands, opened them, and kneaded them. Touching the cameras after all these years actually made her fingers ache.

She loved taking photographs. The six cameras ranged from the simplest point-and-shoot—a gift from her dad when she was nine—to the exquisite Nikon worth thousands.

Jared had given that one to her on the first anniversary of the day they had met. Her hobby became a passionate pursuit. Their friends, all military personnel, paid her to do family shoots. She captured life on the base and newspapers published a few poignant photos of servicemen and women saying goodbye to family or reuniting with them after serving overseas.

Then Jared died. Friends were transferred to other bases or stopped calling because she had pushed them away. The camera was stuffed in a box shoved to the back of the closet, never to see the light of day.

Piper did not know why she brought it out now. Unpacking it, though, seemed a fitting end to a very strange day.

Twenty-Seven

Heidi thanked Jasmyn for the ride to work and stepped out of her car. The taste of humble pie was growing less tart. If she wanted to get to the office, she needed a ride.

And she wanted very much to get to the office. She had given her sick body a week to recover. Two weeks were out of the question, no matter how loudly that ER doctor had insisted. No matter how bad the coughing fits could get. Also she had given Val four days to cool off. Even four and a half were out of the question.

Last night, a short while after telling Piper her plans to return to work, she was ambushed by Piper, Jasmyn, and Sam. They insisted she was not ready for a cab or the train. They would drive her.

Her hackles had gone up, but only briefly. Hud's words had resounded. *You might want to stop feeling sorry for yourself.* Honestly, that attitude was not helping her move forward. She had swallowed one more lump of pride and thanked her new friends.

Friends. Wow. Did she actually consider them friends?

Maybe. Maybe.

Heidi unlocked the front door of SunView Properties, strode through the front office, unoccupied at six-thirty in the morning, and headed down the hall to Val's door. It stood ajar and she rapped on it. "Val?"

"Heidi! Come in."

She pushed the door open and went inside. "Hi." She sat across the desk from Val.

"I didn't expect you already. I thought the doctor said two weeks."

"Totally beyond my realm of capability. I feel fine."

Val smiled. "You look fine. I think your hair has reached the earlobes."

Heidi yanked on a strand. "If these waves would straighten out, it might be. I don't know where they came from."

"Hud's hair is wavy."

"Mm-hmm. Val, I—"

"Don't worry about it."

"Which? My Olivia McAlister connection or you and Craig?"

She shook her head. "Neither. We have work to do, sugar-pie."

"Val—"

"Seriously, Heidi, it does not matter. None of it. We're playing a major game of catch-up here. I figure you can—"

"The other stuff does matter, Val. I can't breathe because the elephant in the room is taking up too much air. I know you won't come right out and tell me to move, but I will. If you can't stop in my home for a cup of coffee because you're afraid of running into Liv, then I'm not going to live there."

Val bit her lower lip. Her breath came in short puffs. She shook her head.

"It's okay, Val. I told her I might leave. She understands. She even offered to help me find a place."

"She understands?"

"Yes. She's not the ogre you've always imagined. She truly is not." She studied her friend's face, wondering how far to press. Liv was a lovely, gracious woman. Stating that, however, might be going overboard. "We all make mistakes."

"But my mother—"

"This is about you, Val, not your mother. You're almost forty years old. I'm—"

"Thanks for adding a couple of years."

"Just rounding up to make my point. Which is, you're not a kid anymore who hides behind her mom's take on the world. I'm not saying you should become good friends with Liv or even be nice to her. I am saying that for your own sake, you need to let go of the hatred."

"She broke apart our family."

"Did she really? Was it all her fault?" The words slipped out before Heidi could edit them. She was busy doing more math in her head. Besides Val's age, there were other numbers to consider. Jasmyn had said

Liv and Syd were married for twelve years. He'd been dead for ten. That equaled twenty-two years.

Which meant Adam was thirteen when they married.

When his mother Cathy married his stepdad, he was eleven.

Val said, "Yes, it was her fault, all her fault. Mom never wanted a divorce. Gunther was a lifesaver. If they hadn't married, things would have been a whole lot worse."

"Your stepdad is a good man. They've been married a long time."

"Twenty-four years."

Heidi did not pursue the math angle with Val. Maybe Liv and Syd were together a long time *before* they got married. Maybe Cathy met Gunther and married him on the spot. Maybe it was indeed all Liv's fault.

Heidi felt a stab of guilt. "Anyway, do you want my opinion?"

"That feisty tone says you are feeling better."

"Yes, but we need to move quickly. Give me some work to do before my naptime."

Val's smile wouldn't hold. "All right, what's your opinion?"

"You needed to blame someone. Nobody wants to blame their own parents."

"Oh, I blamed Dad plenty."

"Yes, but you didn't shut him out completely."

"No. Only his wife, who—thank goodness—at least knew how to take the hint and make herself scarce. And now you're living with her. I still can't believe it. That has to be one of the weirdest things I have ever heard in my life."

Heidi thought she might have one better. "Let me tell you about Liv's sandwich board."

"What?"

"It's like she's got comfort written all over her. I'm not kidding. It oozes from her. I feel, well, I feel comforted around her. She's different. Honestly, I can see why your dad loved her."

"Heidi." Val's eyes were opened wide. "You make that woman sound like your long-lost fairy godmother or something."

"I'm sorry. I probably exaggerated." She hadn't. She hated walking on eggshells, but she saw no other way to smooth things over with Val. "I just wanted you to see that she's a human being."

"In your world, maybe. She'll never be in mine nor Adam's. So no, I will not be coming over to your quaint cottage for coffee. Seeing the Battleaxe would bring up way too many awful memories. Even the thought that I might see her makes me sick to my stomach."

It was the hatred that made her feel sick.

"But honestly, Heidi, if you like it there so much and you think she's a nice person, don't change a thing." Val's voice had been steadily rising. "I won't hold it against you. We can still work together." She brushed her fingers under one eye, then the other. "Actually, I have something in mind for you today." She sniffed and rummaged through a pile of papers. "A new client—what did I do with that sheet? Oh…"

Heidi heard a muttered curse and saw near panic on Val's face as she shoved papers all around her desk. It seemed an overreaction to the Liv situation. She leaned over the desk and placed her hands on top of Val's. "Hey, you're stressing out. Listen, I'm back. I can carry my load again." Now that was an exaggeration, but she was willing to go at it hard. "Okay?"

Val nodded vigorously and then she burst into tears. "You-you c-can live with me," she blubbered.

"What did you say?"

She pulled her hands out from under Heidi's and covered her face. "Oh! I'm living my mother's life!"

Heidi felt as if she had been punched in the stomach. Living Cathy's life meant only one thing. She stood and shut the door. "What's going on with you and Craig?"

Val buried her face in her arms on the desk and sobbed.

Heidi rubbed her friend's shoulders and murmured silly things. "It's okay. I'm here. Cry it out, hon. Just cry it all out."

Heidi was surprised and yet not completely. Craig Laughlin was a quiet accountant, passionate about numbers. He could have figured out her math questions in a heartbeat. When it came to taking care of the agency's finances, Craig was smart. He had steered them along a steady course.

He and Val were opposites. Aside from the age-old attraction theory, it was a mystery how they ever got together and stayed together for seven years. The upside was that they complemented each other at times. He calmed her, and she unearthed his social side.

But they'd always been consumed with their separate careers, and truthfully, Val was a handful. Her personality sometimes wore on Heidi, who was secretly relieved when Craig nixed the idea that she could move in with them while she recovered.

Val mumbled something.

"What?"

She raised her head. "I think he's having an affair."

"Oh, Val. Not Craig. He's crazy about you. He's a solid guy—"

"Who slept on the couch last night because he came home so late and didn't want to disturb me. Who has done that three times this month. Who canceled our annual April sixteenth day-after-tax-day dinner celebration. Who gave away our tickets for one of the Padres games, which we never do without discussing it. Who hasn't kissed me goodbye three mornings straight. And who"—she took a few jagged breaths—"who last month went away overnight, said there was a work-related thing in L.A., but I found out there wasn't one."

The logical explanations Heidi began concocting fizzled with each new scenario. "Last month?"

"There was other stuff before last month. Little things I didn't notice until I put all this together."

"I wish you'd told me."

"Right. You have a foreign object in your thigh and an empty space in your belly and you get sick at the drop of a hat. You have enough going on."

"Well, I'm here now. Did you talk to him?"

She shook her head.

"You have to ask him what's going on. Don't you?" How would she know? She'd never been in a long-term relationship.

"No! No. I don't want to. I'm afraid to find out. I don't want to live my mother's life." She cried again.

Heidi leaned over and hugged her friend. She had no answers for her. Silly soothing remarks seemed pointless in the face of such sadness.

Liv would comfort Val, offer wisdom, and pray. It was an odd thought, out of the blue, but no way would Val receive good things from the Battleaxe.

God, whoever or whatever you are, we need help.

Heidi began to weep, from empathy for Val and from the sudden realization that she had cried out for help as she flew off the freeway. And she had not died when circumstances said she should have.

Yes, the timing of everything had worked in her favor. The medics and even the helicopter pilot and the accident site all worked in her favor too.

But maybe there was more going on. Maybe, when she let go as she had to while lying scrunched up in her scrunched-up car, maybe then Whoever or Whatever sometimes opened paths that led to hope and healing.

It wasn't like she had anywhere else to turn.

Twenty-Eight

Heidi settled into a daily routine. With her whole being she hoped that it would not last much longer.

She'd been at it for all of ten days.

"I'm not going to make it. I am not going to make it," she muttered to herself, seated at her office desk, chin in hands. What had her brother texted the other day? *"I think I can. I think I can." Repeat often.*

Whatever.

Her ribs still hurt when she moved a certain way. That certain way changed by the hour. They stabbed when she coughed. Her leg ached, deep inside. It was an incomparable pain that lived deep inside the echo of that tree branch snapping. She limped. That week, at the three-month mark, she went to the doctor. He said she limped because she imagined that she should. Give it another three months.

Her hair—Best not to dwell on that topic. The scar—Ditto. She shampooed the hair and ran a comb through it. She applied sunscreen and eye shadow. End of morning prep time.

One of her three new best friends drove her to work every day. They took turns without complaint. Piper, Jasmyn, Sam, Piper, Sam, Jasmyn. Their schedules varied. They allowed her to take a cab home only because they had their own lives to tend to. She considered the train, but tackling the distance between the station and the Casa was more than she could handle yet, physically and emotionally. Val did not offer, and she did not ask.

Her daily to-do list included calling Adam two times. Two times ten equaled twenty. It was overkill but she didn't care. He had yet to call back.

She and Val worked a little differently than they had in the pre-accident, pre-Craig-gone-weird days. The biggest change was, of course, the transportation thing again. Val was out of the office most of the time. Heidi did office-y stuff, hers and Val's. She talked to clients on the phone and tried to get a feel for houses via online photos.

That was pathetic.

The other difference was that Val clung to sanity by her neatly mani-cured fingernails. Although Heidi asked her once a day how things were going with Craig, Val only shook her head.

Other than that Heidi avoided talking about Craig. She totally avoided the subject of Liv, which was tricky. She talked business.

Two smart, mature women worked in the office. Cynthia and Dawn carried the load cheerfully and pretended Heidi was in charge. Treena, the intern Val hired, spent more time now doing what Heidi wanted to do, going out and about with clients and networking in the community.

At lunchtime, Heidi ordered takeout, two servings. She ate one at lunch and took the other home for dinner.

Her stamina lagged. She cut her days short, went home to her quaint little cottage, and vegged out, watching more television than she had in her entire life. At seven o'clock every evening her father called. They chat-ted. He asked if she wanted to get behind the wheel yet. They could drive along the Strand, five miles per hour. She said no. Did she want to ride up to Orange County and back, make her first run on the freeway past the site? *No!* No. He was more of a dear than ever.

Then she ate her takeout and fell asleep watching the nine o'clock news.

It was a routine she would gladly throw out the window if she had the choice.

Her cell phone rang now. She read Jasmyn's name on the display. All three new best friends were already in her "Favorites" contact list along with Liv. The thought struck her that in three months her world had been turned upside down, shaken out, turned right side up, and filled with totally unfamiliar people and places and situations.

"Hello, Jasmyn."

"Hi. I'll just keep you a minute. Liv and I are planning a Casa potluck for tonight. Do you think you can come? You don't have to bring any-thing."

"But it's a potluck."

"Yes, but you're the guest of honor. If you can come?"

"Let me check my calendar. Hm. I am a little busy. Television and take-out Chinese. Bed by nine."

Jasmyn snickered.

Heidi laughed. She was about to throw her routine out the window. "But why am I the guest of honor?"

"You're the new kid on the block."

New kid on the block. New kid at school. She sure could not recall ever being a guest of honor as a kid.

Instead of a pit in the stomach, she felt a lump in her throat.

Evidently a Casa potluck meant a lot of food and a lot of people in the courtyard. The evening was mild for springtime at the coast. The sky was not yet dark, but all the twinkle lights were aglow, strung in the jacaranda branches, around palm tree trunks and various shrubbery.

Heidi sat at a rectangular table, happier than she had been for a long while. She met or re-met all the residents and gradually began to put names to faces. Liv insisted she invite her parents. The love fest began between those three the minute they met, as Heidi had known it would. She wasn't even embarrassed that they brought the Colonel's chicken, their contribution to the potluck.

A hint of sadness came, though, when she thought of Val.

That afternoon, Ethan and Rita had picked Heidi up at the office. Although they knew of Val's connection to Liv and would not have mentioned the potluck to her, Heidi was thankful her friend was not around to see them leave. It would have felt like a deception.

Maybe she *should* move from the Casa.

Heidi had broached the subject one more time last week. Val insisted that she stay put. She herself had enough to be concerned about between business and Craig. She could not add to her load by being responsible for upsetting Heidi's life even further by telling her to relocate. The Casa was temporary. Besides, they probably didn't have time to have coffee these days. Later, when life calmed down and Heidi had moved home, they would have coffee at her condo.

Heidi had not mentioned her sense of permanency about the Casa as she had to Hud. That rash statement had been a spur of the moment emotional blip with her brother. She was not a cottage leasing type person at all. She missed her condo with its sleek lines and private entrance and private little courtyard.

Then why was she so happy at that moment, surrounded by strangers and 1920s architecture?

"So how is your brother?" the woman seated next to her asked. Riley? Yes, Riley.

"Fine, I guess. I don't hear much from him." She smiled. "Is he really a big deal?"

"Yes, he is." She laughed.

Riley had long blonde hair just like Heidi used to have. She was a single mom with a distinct fragile air about her. It had been humorous to see her so excited last week to meet Hud. Her daughter, Tasha, nine or ten years old, was a sweetheart who hugged Heidi whenever she saw her.

"Riley, do you mind if I ask why you live here?"

"It seems strange, doesn't it? Tasha is the only kid around. But my work is close by. With her Down syndrome, she has special needs. The best facilities and school I could find are all in the area. And there's Liv. Well, everyone at the Casa makes it a safe home for us, but Liv…" She shrugged. "You know."

Heidi nodded. Yes, she knew.

A shrill whistle drew their attention to the food table where a grinning Piper lowered her fingers from her mouth. People laughed in surprise. "Blame it on having three brothers," she said. "Okay, listen up. Beau here is trying to get our attention. The guy is way too soft-spoken."

Everyone laughed as the gentle giant's cheeks turned pink. Sam stood beside him looking even redder.

Beau said, "Thank y'all." His Tennessee accent seemed more pronounced. "I, uh, we, uh, that is, well." He glanced at Sam and clasped her hand. "We don't want to take the spotlight off our guest of honor, but Sammi and I—"

People whooped and applauded. Chad slapped Beau on the back. Jasmyn ran over and threw her arms around Sam. Tears streamed down Liv's cheeks as she hurried toward them. From her wheelchair, Coco pumped a fist in the air and shouted, "Yesss!"

Heidi turned to Riley. "What just happened?"

She grinned. "I think Beau and Sam are engaged. Excuse me." She went to Coco and pushed her chair over to the couple.

Heidi's mom slid into Riley's vacated chair and her dad sat on her other side. The three of them watched the residents gather around the couple, everyone clearly excited about the announcement. Heidi rehearsed their names, committing them to memory. Beau, Sam, Liv, Jasmyn, Riley, Tasha, Coco, Noah, Louie, Inez, Piper, and Keagan.

Suddenly, she felt overwhelmed with more goodness than her heart could contain. There was absolutely nothing in her experience to compare it to.

Her mother touched her arm. "Wasn't that beautiful?"

Heidi could not have agreed more.

Twenty-Nine

Piper flicked the turn signal and glanced over at Heidi in the passenger seat. "Freeway okay with you?"

Facing the windshield, her arms crossed tightly over her midsection, her lips a grim line, Heidi nodded vigorously. "Great."

"We're running a little late, so I thought…"

"Yeah."

Piper turned onto the freeway ramp and eased into early morning traffic. Typically she took surface streets when she drove Heidi. They were still her friend's preferred route.

"I think I can. I think I can."

Piper smiled at Heidi's mantra. "And remember to breathe."

Heidi did so, deeply and noisily. "Hey, I've got a new exercise. Riley showed me."

Piper glanced over and saw Heidi stretch out her arms.

"Keep your eyes on the road. I'll show you later. But what you do now is cross your wrists, like this. Clasp your hands and fold your arms back, into your chest. Voila. I am soothed."

"Let me know if you're not."

"You are a fine driver, Piper. I can push myself to exercise and work, but this car and freeway business still throws me for a loop. I guess I should thank you for nudging me along."

"Anytime."

"Are you okay?"

"Sure."

"Sure?"

The question hovered while Piper changed lanes. She feared saying things out loud. They might fall apart in the air. Their truth might turn to ash and she'd have to once again take two steps back after going three wondrous ones forward.

"Piper, we're spending a lot of time together. I can tell you're subdued today."

She shrugged and took her own deep breath. "It's Jared's birthday. He would have been thirty years old."

"I'm sorry."

She nodded and forged ahead. "Actually, subdued is good. The first birthday, just a few months after he died, I got drunk with his buddies. The second one was a repeat. There wasn't much downtime in between the two. Things were pretty ugly for a while. My mom decided enough was enough, so she came out for the third one and kept me sane. Then she happened to meet Liv in the grocery store, and before you knew it, they had me moved into the Casa. By Jared's third, I was good at keeping very, very busy. I only cried during the lulls. Only missed a week of work instead of two. And now here I am at the fourth."

Heidi reached over and touched her arm.

"I cried last night, but not all night." She lifted her sunglasses briefly. "See? No puffy eyes. This morning I called his mom and managed not to blubber. And I am going into work."

"Progress."

"Progress. It still hurts, but in a different way. I can't explain it."

"How is his mom?"

"She and his dad—honestly, I don't know. They have another son and a daughter and three grandkids. We never really connected. Jared used to apologize for their attitude. He was their oldest, their golden boy. They're Chicago old money. No girl would have been good enough for him, but I didn't even come close. A Catholic girl who didn't go to college? Whose dad was a high school shop teacher and whose mom was a third grade teacher? No way."

"But you still call them?"

"Twice a year and I send Christmas cards. It's the right thing to do."

"You are a good person, Piper Keyes. How could anyone not like you?"

She laughed.

Heidi remained silent as Piper headed toward an exit ramp. Once they slowed for a stoplight, she blew out another noisy breath. "All right. That wasn't too awful. The conversation helped, I think. It kept my mind occupied. Thanks. What are you doing after work?"

"Keeping my mind occupied." *Whirligigging.* "I signed up for a photography class. It starts next week, but I have to buy some things."

"Maybe you could squeeze in dinner with a friend too? Not exactly a celebration, but a recognition of Jared's day?"

Piper smiled. "I might be able to squeeze that in." *I wonder if that friend's brother is in town again?* She held the impulsive wish close to her heart and waited for the tidal wave of guilt to hit.

But it didn't come.

I'm sorry, Jared. I am sorry.

She apologized not from guilt this time, but from a sadness that would always be with her. She was moving on and he was not going with her.

⁊ℓℓ

Piper made it through the workday without a fussy exchange with Gildy. That was progress too.

Early evening she waited in the courtyard for Heidi, snapping pictures. She was never without her favorite camera these days. The heft of it in her hands and the challenge of framing a shot gave her a joy she hadn't known for a long time.

Little Tasha posed for her beside every plant, stone, and table. Their giggles must have carried because soon others joined them. It took a few minutes, but Piper finally caught on that they were all going to dinner with her and Heidi. Tasha, Riley, Coco, Liv, Inez, Sam, and Jasmyn.

Heidi spoke quietly to her. "I hope this is appropriate? I mentioned to Jasmyn why we were getting together. Things sort of mushroomed after that."

Piper grinned. "It's absolutely, totally appropriate." She mimicked Jasmyn who she assumed spearheaded the gathering. It was what Jasmyn, a.k.a. Liv-in-the-making, did so well.

A family outing. Piper instantly warmed to the idea.

With Riley pushing Coco in her wheelchair, they walked a few blocks to a restaurant, a casual place with a large rooftop dining area. They all piled into the elevator.

Jasmyn, naturally, knew the manager. No matter that it was a last-minute, busy Friday night reservation: The woman ushered them to a round table with the best view of the setting sun. Propane heaters and umbrellas made for a cozy setting.

Piper had thought she might need to try out Heidi's new exercise with her arms in order to soothe herself, but she was—surprisingly—relaxed.

Until the waitress said, "Are you all celebrating something?"

The entire group exchanged glances until Heidi spoke up. "Life."

Jasmyn added, "New beginnings."

Inez said in her Hispanic inflection, "Beautiful love."

Riley and Tasha looked at each other and shouted in unison, "Piper!"

Sam said, "Saying yes to the unknown future."

Coco said, "Us girls."

Liv smiled. "Joy in the morning."

"Jared." Piper spoke softly, but distinctly. "We're celebrating Jared Oakes."

And then they did, with food and conversation, laughter and tears, stories of the past and hopes for the days ahead.

✺

By the time the women parted ways in the courtyard, Piper was telling Heidi about her hope to quit Tellmann's. Shivering in the evening air, they gravitated into Heidi's cottage and sat on the plaid couch that had originally belonged to Inez. She passed it on to Jasmyn, who used it for a short time. Inez did not buy junk, nor did she keep the same décor for long. The thing still appeared new and was quite comfy.

Heidi said, "Hud mentioned something about a boutique."

They had talked about her? Piper hoped the warmth she felt would not turn into a blush. "Yeah. He was, um, easy to talk to. I haven't told anyone about this. My dad will have a fit."

"Want to trade dads for a while? Mine will say go for it."

"That was Hud's advice. I think what I need is my dad's practical voice without the conniption fit."

"That would be me." Heidi grinned. "I'm nothing like my brother or my dad who do not understand the concept of *practical*. And since the accident, I don't have energy to throw conniption fits. Tell me about the boutique."

"Oh, Heidi. You're the first person I thought of when this came up. You have your own business. You're successful at it. I want to be you."

She laughed. "Not as successful as you think, but I'm happy to tell you what I've learned."

"Thanks. This acquaintance, Stella, owns a boutique in Rancho Sierra."

"Ooh."

"Exactly. Upscale. She's had the place for years. The clientele is what you would imagine. They're not going anywhere if she sells. Early in April, Stella asked if I'd like to work for her. We've batted the idea around some. Then a few weeks ago she turned sixty and suddenly realized she wants to do other things with her life. She asked if I'd like to buy the shop. Otherwise she'll put it up for sale or have a going-out-of-business sale."

"Wow."

"She'd stay on for a while, until I got grounded."

"It's an enormous step."

"Heidi, I'm so ready for an enormous step. I'm beyond ready to move forward. I'm meeting with her at the shop tomorrow, before it opens. Just to explore what we could do. I haven't even been there for ages."

"What's it called?"

"Stella's."

"Well, that's the first thing you'll want to change." She grinned. "This is so exciting for you. Okay, no conniption fit, but I have a word of caution: It will be your life. It will be your entire life. Twenty-four/seven does not begin to describe it."

Piper swallowed. "Can I ask you a huge favor?"

"Of course."

"Will you go with me tomorrow?"

She hesitated for a beat. "You want my opinion on the shop?"

"Yes."

"Um, well, okay. Does Stella own the building?"

"No, she leases the space."

Heidi smiled. "Good. Then I won't be thinking about getting her to sell it through us at SunView."

"Heidi."

"Kidding. Sort of. It's like you with clothes. I go straight for the real estate jugular."

She tried to keep her expression neutral, but she felt her forehead crease.

"Piper, don't look so worried. You are a good person, like I said earlier. You are also amazingly good at helping women get in touch with their femininity."

"I sell clothes."

"You sell more than that. Trust me. When my friend Val told me to tone down the sporty persona, I thought we would never make it as partners. I was an athlete. If you hadn't remade me, I wouldn't have found the confidence to relate to people about their real estate needs."

Piper stared at her.

She laughed and the powder blue eyes that hadn't sparkled in a long time lit up. "It's true. And I would love to check out Stella's and dream some big dreams with you."

Piper smiled, but her brow did not smooth out. A sudden attack of qualms hit her. Why now? She had been fine talking with Stella, imagining a new beginning.

But…she looked into that other pair of powder blue eyes.

Things had changed.

Thirty

Early Saturday morning, Heidi found Liv sitting in one of two red Adirondacks in front of her red front door. Or, as Piper had once corrected her, *holly* red.

"Good morning, Miss Heidi. Have a seat."

"Good morning, Miss Liv." She sat in the other holly red chair, a low wicker table between them.

"Care for some tea? I happen to have another cup right here."

She smiled as Liv poured hearty English tea from a pretty floral pot into a porcelain cup. "Thank you."

They had done this a few times now. Heidi's sleep schedule had not found a routine. As she became more comfortable outside her cottage, she roamed the courtyard at all hours and discovered that Liv did the same.

Heidi was growing more comfortable with Liv's perspective. Despite the offsetting business about Val and Adam, she deserved the nicknames *mama* and *saint*.

They chatted about the special dinner for Piper the previous night.

"Speaking of Piper, we're going out today."

"To the boutique. Yes, she told me about that. I'm so glad you're going with her. She needs someone with your experience to lend an ear and offer wise advice."

"I'm not sure. This is different from a real estate agency."

"But you know all about the headaches and the joys of owning your own business."

"You think that's enough?"

Liv nodded. "She has the technical experts to advise her on other

137

matters. The market. The financial side. Et cetera, et cetera. But you'll be her reality expert."

"Like telling her she won't have another life?"

"Exactly."

"Did you love it?"

"I adored every little thing about it. I take it you do too?"

"Yeah." Heidi thought it strange that she and Liv could be two peas in a pod. The woman lived on a different plane from most people. "You'll be praying?"

Liv grinned like a little girl at Disneyland.

Heidi might as well give her the whole day to pray about. "The boutique is near Adam's Garden. And I'm wondering if I should stop in. You know, since I can't drive, it'd be a good opportunity. He's not returning my calls and, well, I'd like to see him in person."

"Oh, that's wonderful! Lord, have mercy. I pray that Adam's heart softens toward you again. And I pray that you and Piper are given wisdom about the boutique."

"Amen." She leaned back in her chair and sipped tea, overwhelmed with a sense of peace.

And she thought *her* parents were odd.

⌇⌇

Eucalyptus trees towered over the quiet community of Rancho Sierra. Like Adam's Garden, it sat tucked away, a surprise appearance around a bend in a winding, hilly two-lane highway. Freeways, beaches, tourists, and fast food restaurants were nonexistent.

Gates blocked driveways of large estates. Acres of foliage camouflaged the houses. The town itself was an understated two blocks of shops, galleries, and offices, each with its own discreet sign.

Stella's boutique was located there, near the corner of the first block heading east.

Heidi stepped out of Piper's car, parked just beyond it at the curb. "Ideal location."

Piper locked the car and joined her on the sidewalk. "It is."

"I forgot how beautiful this place is. And quiet." She inhaled. "And fragrant."

"Have you sold anything here?"

She shook her head. "Nope. Val and I call this the real estate of fresh seafood served on a bed of rice with capers and a drizzle of Béarnaise sauce on top. We deal in the meat and potatoes variety."

They strolled along the litter-free sidewalk, past hanging flower baskets, past large pots brimming with more flowers, past people who smiled and said hello.

Piper whispered, "Movie stars live here."

Heidi whispered back, "So I've heard. Producers and directors too."

"Baseball and football players."

"The owner of a Canadian hockey team."

"Really?"

"Second home."

"And CEOs."

"And friends of people in high places."

Piper grinned. "Regular people too."

"Maybe a few." Heidi winked and opened the door to Stella's.

A bell tinkled softly and they stepped into a glossy designer magazine spread.

"Isn't it lovely?" Piper said. "I've shopped here for clients when they needed something specific that Tellmann's didn't have."

Heidi had never set foot in the place. One glance told her that Stella did not carry real sportswear. Everything was elegant and displayed elegantly. Besides clothing there were shoes, accessories, jewelry, lingerie, and gifts. It was a one-stop shop for women who majored in looking fashionable and apparently—Heidi deduced from the price tag on a handbag—minored in budgeting.

Her mind raced. The merchandise had to be worth a fortune. What would it cost to insure? Another fortune. And the overhead for running a business in Rancho Sierra? Rent had to be sky high.

She was out of her league. She knew real estate, not retail. About all she could offer Piper was moral support.

A woman approached, smiling broadly at them. "Piper." Of course she looked the part with fluffy shoulder-length bleached blonde hair, flawless makeup, and a slender physique. She wore a lavender silk dress that swished when she walked. Piper had said she was sixty, though she could have passed for fifty. Somehow her creamy skin had missed contact with the California sun. Even from a distance her perfume was pleasant, not overpowering.

"Stella." They hugged briefly. "This is my friend, Heidi Hathaway."

They shook hands.

"Heidi Hathaway! From SunView Properties?"

"Have we met?"

"No." She had a wonderful smile and her eyes were bright and attentive. "I've seen the ads and that magazine cover. You and Val Laughlin are striking. When I have a young customer in need of a career look, I use you two for a model."

"Thank you. Piper is totally responsible for anything striking about my look. She is not responsible for this today, however." Heidi slipped a hand into a pocket of her capris and felt suddenly gauche. "I was in a car accident."

"I'm so sorry. Is that why…" She touched her own cheek, referring to Heidi's scar.

"Yes."

"Oh, honey. How awful. Are you all right now?"

"Doing better, thank you."

"Well, it's a pleasure to meet you. I'm glad Piper brought you along. You certainly know all about running your own business. Shall we talk, ladies?"

They talked. Heidi was impressed with how much legwork Piper had done. An attorney, an accountant, and a local Chamber of Commerce member had given her good insights into buying the shop. Stella showed her the books. Before they talked specifics, Piper asked for a week to think about the big picture.

Back in the car, Heidi complimented her.

Piper smiled. "What do you think? Overall?"

"It's a perfect fit. Your age is a major plus. Her clientele is aging and the younger women think the shop is for older women."

"I agree."

"I liked Stella very much, but you're sharper and a tad more personable."

She stared at her.

"I'm not exaggerating. I don't understand retail, but the numbers seemed positive."

"They did. That's the stuff I have to study more."

"And then you have to ask the big question."

"Do I want this to be my life?"

"Exactly."

"Do you regret what you've done?"

"Only the accident. I've loved every minute of the work. The twenty-four/seven aspect suited me. You cannot imagine how much I miss it."

"Was there a downside?"

Before the accident she would have said no. But now she knew better. People had sent flowers to the hospital, but when it came down to wanting to invite a friend over to spend the evening with her, she had no one except Adam—and he had not been anywhere near current.

"Yeah," she said. "There wasn't time to maintain friendships."

Piper gave her a soft smile. "It was a tradeoff."

"There's more, Piper." She thought of what she had asked Adam that night. "I turned into a cold-hearted, self-centered woman. That's how I beat out the competition. Honestly, though, I was probably halfway there because I'd always been about being competitive and winning in sports." She shrugged. "But you're different. You're nowhere near cold-hearted and self-centered. And this business is different. The shop is a destination. It's not really in competition with the big stores."

"Heidi, you're not cold-hearted and self-centered."

"Oh yes, I am. The accident put it on hiatus, but it's lurking."

"Well, I disagree." She started the engine. "Thank you for coming today."

"You're welcome. I want to ask a favor. Do you mind making a stop at Adam's Garden on the way back? It's just around the bend."

"You want to buy food? Are you cooking tonight?"

She smiled. "No. I need to…mend a friendship."

"See? What did I just say about no cold heart?"

Heidi hoped Adam, her other friend, was as blind as Piper.

Thirty-One

Heidi watched Piper's mouth form a large O and stay open. "Piper, you're going to catch flies."

"Wow! Adam from Adam's Garden is Liv's Adam? And yours?"

"We met in college." She'd already told her that. "Piper, I'm not getting out of the car until you lose the starstruck face."

"His produce is like the holy grail for chefs. Every one of them interviewed in all the magazines mentions it."

"Every chef?"

"Every single one."

Heidi smiled at her friend's serious tone.

"And *West Coast Cuisine* did a feature article on the garden. I think there was a full-page photo of Adam. If it's the one I remember, he's handsome. Which I suppose he would be considering his dad's 'movie star' looks, as Liv puts it."

Heidi vaguely remembered the article from a few years ago. Val had shown it to her, and Heidi sent him a congratulatory note. It had been a boost to his reputation. "You really are impressed."

"If I cared about cooking, I'd be even more impressed."

Heidi pointed at the stack of magazines on the backseat. "I figured those were only about fashion."

"Oh, I read anything that has photos. Pictures of people shopping for produce and eating in restaurants are great examples of current trends in clothing and hairstyles." She smiled. "This guy is a big deal. And you two are friends?"

"Yes." She hoped. "Okay, are you over the initial OMG reaction?"

"Yep, I am ready to go. But you don't want me hanging with you while you talk to him. What shall I do?"

"Buy veggies?"

Piper giggled and peered through the windshield. "Great idea since I am such a fanatic about cooking. I suppose I could get some things for Liv and Noah. Is that a café over there?"

"He added it about a year ago."

"I'll get a coffee too." She looked at her. "Don't worry about me, Heidi. Take your time."

She nodded, suddenly too nervous to even say *thanks*.

"I'll say a prayer that Adam will get over being upset with you." She gave a thumbs-up.

Heidi nodded again and returned the gesture.

ℓℓℓ

As Piper strode off toward the café, Heidi stood beside the car and second-guessed her decision to speak to Adam face to face.

Several moments passed before she thought of calming herself with a deep breath and folding her arms against her chest. She was sure she looked odd to some people, but she was growing accustomed to that.

Odd. Could she echo Val's wail and say she was living her mother's life?

She smiled to herself. At least she had her own oddities and not her mom's. The facial scar and limp and hairdo with its patch above one ear that still looked more shaved than not were all her very own. What were a few deep breaths and a self hug?

As she relaxed, people bustled about here and there, paying her no attention. Adam's place was popular. Because preparing gourmet food had never been on her to-do list, she had visited only a handful of times. There had been the grand opening. The opening of the café, the Grounds. Now and then with Val or with her dad. Once with her mom, who gave Adam a pot she had thrown for him on her own wheel. It sat now off to the right, near the entrance to the café, a tall, narrow, glazed reddish orange creation that blended in perfectly with the rustic surroundings. It really was one of her mother's best.

To the left of the parking lot was the market. Canopies shielded rows of tables full of produce. Staff members wore brown caps or wide-brimmed hats and the trademark distressed gold-colored tees or polos.

Directly ahead, in the center, pathways led to the public gardens. They displayed samples of the produce that grew in the private fields beyond.

Around and over it all towered the ubiquitous eucalyptus. The whole area smelled like the trees and pungent herbs, a combination of sweet and dry and earthy.

She'd never noticed how lovely the place was. It reminded her of…of Liv's Casa.

She wouldn't be sharing *that* information with Adam.

If she could find him.

A tiny office sat beside the gardens. His house was tucked back further, hidden from view by trees and bushes. Like the café, the office and house were refurbished outbuildings, part of the original farm, built of dark shingles.

Heidi headed toward the center. Adam could be anywhere. Should she ask a staff member to contact him? No. She'd been contacting him for days on end.

The path was well-trodden dirt with signs of a recent raking. Everything was meticulously kept, again like the Casa. There were small signs beside many of the plants. Common names and Latin ones were written in Adam's neatly drawn print. His attention to detail no doubt led to the success of the Garden. Val was the same way when it came to business. It made all the difference—

"Heidi."

At the sound of Adam's voice behind her, she stopped and turned. Neither of them moved. Neither of them smiled.

And she realized what had happened between them. Their growing apart had been less about his travels or her career or her boyfriend or his girlfriend…and more about how they themselves had changed.

Their college camaraderie had been based on having fun, getting by in classes, keeping each other company when they skipped class, empathizing over crazy parents, pushing each other to graduate despite their best efforts to achieve the opposite. They'd basically spent those four years inside a private biosphere.

They graduated from college and the biosphere decomposed. It was as if they had reached the future that they always pretended was not going to happen and discovered it did not hold space for each other. There was no space for camaraderie in the seriousness of adulthood.

Why was that?

Adam approached her, a half smile in place. "Hi."

"You never write, you never call."

"Sorry about that." He pursed his lips and his shoulders sagged. "I mean it. I really am sorry about that. Honestly, it was just easier to avoid you."

"Easier than…?"

"Easier than a lot of things." He tilted his head toward the office. "Let's talk inside. If you have time?"

Why else was she there if she didn't have the time? Agitated, she spun on her heel, turning too quickly for the left leg to catch up to the right.

Adam caught her by the hand mid-stumble and held on as they walked. "You okay?"

"Happens all the time." Dread swept through her. It did happen all the time. At least often enough to frighten her. Something wasn't right, but she chose the automatic response. "I'm fine."

"Says Pollyanna."

"Touché. All right, I admit that it upsets me."

"You're still in the early part of recovery, aren't you? Nowhere near the full year I heard was necessary."

"True."

"I hear a 'but.'"

"It doesn't matter."

"Of course it matters."

She didn't want to talk about her leg and how unbalanced she felt.

He said, "What does the doctor say?"

She limped along beside him. *Limped.* It was how she walked. It didn't matter. She wasn't a runway model. "He says to give it time."

"Sounds reasonable."

"That's me."

He chuckled, squeezed her hand, and let go. "That's you."

The office door was ajar. They entered a square, windowed room. It contained a counter, a desk, and a table with a coffeepot.

"Can I get you something to drink? Coffee? Water?"

She sat on one of two hard chairs off to the side of the counter while he poured himself a cup of coffee. "No, thanks. And thanks for not ducking down another path."

"I tried." He wasn't teasing. "Got about three feet." He sat beside her. "I am so sorry for pushing you out of my truck."

"You didn't exactly push me. I slid out on my own."

"It was close enough and it was despicable behavior. It scared me. How could I be like that to you of all people? I was so ashamed, but I was angry too. You'd brought Livvie McAlister back into my life." He took a breath. "You're welcome to tell me again to grow up."

"Grow up."

"Hey, I'm working on that." He smiled. "Remember M.J. from school?"

A tall African-American came to mind. "The funny guy who had us believing he was named after his second cousin Michael Jordan."

"Yeah. Mitchell Jamal Camden is a high school counselor now. We've stayed in touch, get together once in a while. Since that day I pushed you, we've met a few times—and not to play basketball."

She blinked. Adam had asked for help? Adam never asked for help. He was like her in that way.

"He's pretty good with adults, especially when they're stuck in adolescence. He's helping me sort through some things. I didn't take your calls or call you back because I was too ashamed. You remind me of my idiotic behavior that day and Livvie reminds me of how stupid I was years ago."

"So we're like goads for you?"

He chuckled. "Cattle prods. Who wants that?" He shook his head. "I blamed her for taking away my dad and then I chose to live overseas, away from him, missing out on the last years of his life that I could have spent with him."

"You were young and confused."

"That reasoning might have worked for back then, but not today. My parents' divorce broke something inside of me. It's such an obvious cliché, you'd think I would have seen it and gotten over it ages ago."

"I don't think things work that way."

"No, they don't. In my child's mind, I wasn't good enough to keep Mom and Dad happy and together. Ergo, I wasn't good enough for much at all."

"Your travels brought you to a new understanding of yourself, though. Right?"

"Definitely. God became real. I had a deep sense of being loved and knew such peace. When Dad died, I finally was able to receive his acceptance through his gift of this farm. I was doing great until a couple weeks ago when you started the goading."

"You're welcome."

He lowered his eyes. "The divorce wasn't Livvie's fault."

"I would guess that one person alone is never at fault."

He looked at her. "I mean, Dad told me it was not because of her. He said he was totally responsible. When Val and I were little, he worked all the time. He preferred to work all the time, especially after he met Julian. He was almost young enough to be Dad's son, but he was a genius for making money. The situation killed my mother's love for Dad. Livvie was not in the picture until years later, and for years after they were only good friends."

"Then why...?"

"Gotta blame somebody. There were the usual extenuating circumstances. Mom and Dad married young. They came from divorced homes. They had nothing but big dreams to make money. He fell in love with making money and she fell in love with spending it. The rest is history."

"I'm sorry."

"Do you know how fortunate you are? Wacky as Ethan and Rita are, they were always a solid entity."

She nodded. "I never wanted to be like them and I hated how they moved us around all the time, but I never felt unaccepted or unloved."

"I asked Dad once about Livvie. That's what he called her. I've been practicing it. I didn't think you'd appreciate me referring to your landlady as Battleaxe." His hazel green eyes softened. "Like I said, M.J. is helping me work through some junk."

"That sounds really good." *Okay.* "What were you saying? Something about asking your dad about Liv?"

"Liv?"

"That's what she usually goes by."

He nodded. "'Livvie' was probably Dad's special name for her. I believe he really did love her. Anyway, I asked him what was it like to be friends with a woman for years and not intend to court her. He said, 'It's like you and Heidi Hathaway. You were always there for each other.' Curious, huh?"

If Heidi were in her right mind rather than in the throes of the crash's aftermath, she would not have noticed a tickle in her throat.

Not have noticed? It would not have happened in the first place. "Yeah. Curious."

He gazed at her for a long moment. Something shifted in his expression. He swallowed, blinked, and changed the subject.

Maybe the gaze and the shifting expression were only in her imagination. She hoped not, though. She sincerely hoped not.

And that was the most curious thing of all.

Thirty-Two

Piper shook Adam Engstrom's hand and smiled. Although the famous farmer did not resemble his dad's photograph, he had his own intriguing features going. His greenish eyes were the clearest she'd ever seen. There was something about them that made her think he knew deep secrets about life. It probably came from growing it.

They stood outside the café, in shade provided by wisteria that laced the overhead pergola. The whole place—what she had seen of it anyway—was lovely and peaceful.

She told him as much and he grinned like a happy little kid.

"Did you get back to the garden area?" he asked.

"Not yet." She glanced at Heidi, whose brows went up. "Oops. Another time. Heidi needs to get to the office ASAP."

"I understand. My sister would make a great drill sergeant." He elbowed Heidi and she nudged him back.

"Thanks, Adam." The sudden somber expression on Heidi's face appeared to say that she was grateful for more than the three long-stemmed sunflowers she held.

"Thank you."

Piper hoped the little exchange and those flowers meant their discussion had gone well.

A curly-haired woman came up behind Adam and laid a hand on his arm. "Excuse me, Adam." She gave what could only be construed as a fake smile, her small face masklike. "Hello, Heidi."

"Hi, Maisie. How are you?"

"Fine, thanks. Adam, there's a problem with the espresso machine."

"Again? I'll be right there." He rolled his eyes. "What does a coffee shop have to do with growing vegetables? See you, Heidi. Nice meeting you, Piper." He gave a little wave and walked off with Maisie, his hand at the small of her back.

Piper whispered, "Who's the hippie?"

"Girlfriend."

They walked toward the parking lot, Piper carrying one cloth bag full of green goodies and another of breads. "I saw her in the coffee shop earlier."

"She bakes and delivers her stuff here."

"She makes a great Americano. I gathered she was pitching in because they were shorthanded. I bought some of her bread for Liv and Noah."

"Nice."

They reached the car and got inside.

Piper started the engine and backed out of their spot. "How'd it go?"

Heidi sighed in a satisfied way. "Really well. He apologized for having an issue with Liv. I don't think he's ready to meet her, but we're cool."

"I'm glad to hear that."

"Me too. I didn't know if he'd even want to meet you. I mentioned that you lived at the Casa too, but he didn't hesitate."

"He seems like a really good guy."

"He is."

They rode in silence, out onto the highway and along for a mile or so before Piper said, "She wasn't nice to you."

"Who would that be?" Heidi chuckled. "Maisie has always been threatened by me, I think because I've known Adam for a lot longer than she has."

Piper plunged ahead because the nagging voice in her head wouldn't stop. "I saw the way she looked at him and I saw the way he looked at you with those angel eyes of his."

"Angel eyes?"

"Yeah. Beautiful and otherworldly. It's like they can see straight into your heart." She glanced at her friend. "But when he looked at you, there was even more. She *should* be threatened."

Heidi blinked several times, facing straight ahead, the chuckle long gone. "The last time I saw him, he said they had issues because she detests farming. Maybe she's rethinking that attitude. The way she touched his arm…his hand at her back."

Exactly. "But—"

"But no matter. Hey, my brother is coming to town on Tuesday."

A wave of heat flushed through Piper and she knew her face must be red. "Oh?"

"I saw the way he looked at you, the way you looked at him."

"Shut up. You did not. You were too exhausted to see anything but the insides of your eyelids."

Heidi laughed. "He'll be around all week to help Mom and Dad pack up. And look at that." She pointed out her side window. "You just missed the freeway ramp."

With the thought of Hudson Hathaway back in town, Piper figured she might miss more than freeway ramps. Things like appointments, words, sleep…

"By the way," Heidi said, "he does not have a Maisie in his life."

Piper sighed to herself, not sure if that was good news or bad.

Thirty-Three

Liv fretted.

How in the world did mothers do it? Carry this *awareness* of children day in and day out for years and years and years and years, from babyhood on into adulthood?

Having never been a mother, she'd always found the idea incomprehensible. As a young woman, she had somehow been graced with the absence of a ticking biological clock. There had been no special man, but plenty of friends. Work, community, and church were her life and she adored it all. She needed nothing else.

Then she met Syd too late to start a family. They were happy and content, despite the shared sadness that she was not a stepmother or even a friend to his children.

When Syd died and she moved into the Casa with Tobi the cat, she felt the first inklings of a *mama hormone,* or whatever it was. She had no control over it. The people who lived in her little complex, no matter their age, were her *children.* She fussed over them, loved on them, and prayed for them every day. She baked goodies and cooked for them. She cleaned the courtyard like it was their shared family room. She probably would have done laundry for them but stopped short of offering. There were only so many hours in a day.

Things leapt to another level when she met Jasmyn Albright. Suddenly Liv ached for a daughter, specifically the motherless girl from Illinois. In turn, Jasmyn longed for a mother figure. Their relationship settled into something as close to an adopted family as possible.

Liv stood now in the center of the courtyard, Tobi at her feet. It was near midnight. The fountain was off. Some of the patio lights still glowed. Solar lights lit walkways. She wrapped her sweater more tightly across her chest and gazed up at the few stars visible between the trees.

She did not know why she fretted at times. Perhaps she took her self-appointed mothering role too seriously. Perhaps she was just getting too old to mother full-time. Or perhaps the Spirit agitated her spirit so that she would spend more time in prayer because there were needs she did not know about that needed to be brought to the throne of grace.

Well, she was too keyed up to sleep or admit she was silly or old. She would go with the last choice.

She glanced around her beloved Casa de Vida. Most of the cottages were dark. Piper's lights were on. She was the night owl. Light came from the Templetons'. They seldom turned off all the lamps. Dim light showed through the blinds of Riley's, Jasmyn's, and Coco's. They burned night-lights.

Her mind raced but her bones were weary. Sitting, however, was out of the question at this hour. The chairs were damp with the night's coastal air.

"Let's make our rounds, Tobi."

The cat meowed in agreement. Night strolling was her favorite.

Ne

As usual, Liv went in numerical order.

Keagan's bungalow was Number One, the first inside the front gate, appropriate for a sentinel. She paused, as she would at each, a fair distance from the door set back in an alcove, not wanting her murmuring to disturb anyone.

Sean Keagan. She thought of Jasmyn's account of his lost fiancée, of his demanding work with the DEA. They were things Liv had imagined colored his past and, naturally, his present.

"Lord, have mercy. Christ, have mercy."

She paused, imagining the Keagan of recent months, the man who tenderly spoke in Jasmyn's ear, who laughed with her as Liv had never heard him laugh in eight years. Once she had seen them kiss, a lingering exchange at sunset down on the beach, arms around each other. They didn't know she was on the sidewalk, up above.

"The sternness is gone from his countenance, Abba. Give him courage to love Jasmyn well, to move forward in their relationship. Thank You."

Liv moved a few steps to face Cottage Two and smiled. "Chadwick. Lord, have mercy. Christ, have mercy. Is he calming, Abba? I think so. Thank You for his sobriety. For his silliness and teasing that reminds all of us to walk with a bit more lightheartedness. For telling his heart that he is Your beloved. Help him to ace his finals this coming week."

No reason not to ask the Creator of the moon for the moon.

Cottage Three. Liv sighed. "Oh, Abba, where do I begin? Thank You for bringing Heidi into my life. Bless her, bless her, bless her. Finish the healing in her body and mind. Give her large interior spaces for resting and receiving. Heal any rift between her and Valerie and Adam."

Valerie and Adam? No. She would not go down that road tonight.

Cottage Four. "Piper."

Liv thought of the girl's recent challenge, passing the fourth anniversary of her fiancé's death and his birthday. Now she wondered about changing jobs. "Abba, she'll need wise counsel. Protect her heart too, protect her from shutting down, from fears of moving on out of the hurtful places."

Cottage Five. "Noah and sometimes Déja."

What did she know about the stork-like, fuddy-duddy who was a gifted pianist and chef? About the teenager with multi piercings who wore a lot of black? "Well, You know what I always pray. Help him figure it out. Protect her while he's occupied with it."

It referred to everything about the man's life. There was a disconnect somewhere. He worked hard at several things—megachurch pianist, pianist for theater productions, sous-chef at the local upscale restaurant. He and Déja seemed to get along, although his daughter lived with him only part time. Was he divorced or separated? Liv was unsure. She had seen his wife, Karis, occasionally in her car, when she would drop off Déja. She'd smile and wave at Liv. He was nice too, if a bit distant. He enjoyed sharing his scrumptious culinary creations with his neighbors.

Liv remained silent for a long moment, waiting for a word on how to pray differently. None came. "If he's floundering, give him firm footing."

Cottage Six. "Sweet Riley. Sweet Tasha. Hold them close. Hold them tight. Give them ears to hear the songs You sing over them without ceasing."

Riley's story was a sad one. She had been married. Six months after Tasha's birth, Drew Baker confessed he did not want to spend his life with a special needs child and he moved out. Although he supported his family financially, he never visited. As far as Liv knew, he never called. He remarried.

But Riley was strong and Tasha was a treasure and, in many ways, more intelligent than her father.

"Just my humble opinion, Lord."

Cottage Seven.

Liv nearly sank onto a damp chair and wept tears of joy. Since Jasmyn's arrival late last summer and her influence, Samantha had shed her cold career woman persona like a molting snake did its skin. She was funny and caring and now...*Oh*. Liv sighed. And now she was in love with Beau Jenner.

"Lord, she's come a long, long way. Keep her going. When the past reaches out to steal the beauty she has found, halt it in its tracks. Give her courage to be her true self, to enjoy being an engineer and a wife." *Hm.* "And a mom?"

Samantha and Beau were young enough to start a family. Beau was a sweet man from Tennessee, an orphan without siblings, who would care for them through thick and thin. Samantha, though, carried major baggage. She had a mother, but to Liv it sounded as if she had never been mothered, nowhere near in a healthy manner. She had a stepfather who had always ignored her and half brothers much younger than herself. She had grown up in poverty on a reservation in Arizona.

Those were a few points in the negative column.

"But I've seen the miracles, Abba. Thank You. Thank You for their future—Oh!"

Liv sat this time, smack down onto a wicker patio chair, instantly sopping her backside.

Samantha and Beau would not want to live at the Casa. Would they?

No. Without a doubt, no.

Liv simply could not imagine them doing so. Although Samantha rented one of the two-bedrooms, Beau was literally too large of a man to live inside a beach cottage built in 1927. He practically had to walk sideways through the interior doors and duck his head. His apartment was in another community, a newer—much newer—place. One that accommodated his size. They would go there. Besides that, Samantha kept an office at home. She needed an extra bedroom.

They would move out of the Casa.

"Oh, Abba. Really?"

Tobi meowed at her feet, cocking her head, asking a question.

"Or are you telling me to quit feeling sorry for myself?" Liv smiled sadly. "All right. Birds must fly from the nest." She wiggled out of the seat and pulled at the back of her skirt. "And, ew, wet clothes are for the birds."

She stepped past the walkway that led between Samantha and the Templeton cottages to the back gate and she paused near Cottage Eight. "Such joy here, Abba!"

Louie and Inez were in their eighties. They had been married forever. Liv should probably consider herself more a daughter than a mother to them. The lines blurred at times. Either way she loved caring for them. Louie was a retired Navy man. Inez had been born in Mexico and had actually worked for Liv's father as a housekeeper at the Casa when Liv was a girl.

"Bless them, their children, their grandchildren, and their great-grandchildren. Amen."

Liv turned. Cottage Nine was split in two, housing the office on one side, the laundry on the other. Cottage Ten was hers. Eleven was Jasmyn's.

"Thank You." Sometimes Liv's heart was too full to say anything else.

And lastly, Cottage Twelve. "Coco. Sweet dreams, dear lady."

The woman was of indeterminate age, a dancer in films from the 1950s, who sometimes could not remember Liv's name. She had a nephew and a niece who each came once a week to visit and take her out to do errands. Riley, Piper, and Jasmyn pitched in where needed.

"Bless them, Lord. Give us all wisdom on how to best take care of Coco."

She hoped they would not have to move her to a home. So far, she did not always need the wheelchair and was able to generally take care of herself.

Liv turned slowly, taking in the small homes one more time, embracing the people in them one more time in her heart.

"O Lord our God, accept the fervent prayers of Your people. In the multitude of Your mercies, look with compassion upon us, for You are gracious, O lover of souls."

Now Liv was ready to stop fretting.

Thirty-Four

Tuesday evening, as a bright orange ball of a sun floated above the ocean, Piper pulled into the first parking space she came to between the Casa and the pier. Grabbing her camera off the passenger seat, she got out of the car, crossed the street, and raced half a block and onto the ramp leading down to the pier.

The sun kissed the water and she stopped at the railing to photograph the—how had Jared described it? The everyday, mind-blowing event.

She peered through the lens of the very nice camera and clicked, clicked, clicked, clicked. There was such satisfaction in recording the moments. In capturing the essence of the world turning, of life moving forward.

She continued snapping pictures after the sun disappeared, catching its reflection in a subtle glow just above the horizon.

"What's it look like from where you are, Jared?" she whispered. "Is it still everyday and mind-blowing?"

They had talked of life after death. Given his profession, it was an unavoidable topic. Maybe they believed that something amazingly wonderful came after because of what he did. Death was continuously in their face. Even on base, danger surrounded him. Guns, explosives, war games with live ammo, helicopters that crashed, wildfires.

Of course something amazingly wonderful came after.

She lowered the camera. Of course there was no proof, but it gave her hope instead of despair. She had done despair. Functioning was a hit-or-miss affair.

As night fell, she hugged the camera to herself and stood there, suspended between day and night. Between light and dark. Between past and future.

How long could she linger in between?

Bottom line, Pipe? Jared's question.

As long as she needed to linger in between.

The sodium lights along the pier gleamed. Piper raised the camera again and caught their slow brightening.

"For you, J."

Piper entered the Casa courtyard. She'd left the car parked a few blocks away. Sometimes, especially in the busy summers, it would be the only choice. Tonight, though, she could have found a spot right out front of the Casa. Instead she chose to wait for the sunset, walk back to the car, gather her things, and stroll three blocks.

She was procrastinating.

Because it was Tuesday.

Because Hudson Hathaway was due in town.

Because she was suspended in between.

"Piper!" Heidi appeared on the other side of the fountain. "There you are."

Within moments Piper's hesitation flittered away and she was walking into Liv's cottage where some of the others had gathered. Heidi, Jasmyn, Keagan, Riley, Tasha, Chad…Hud. There was, she figured, safety in numbers.

She melted at the sight of him, like a sixth grader with a crush on Jimmy Peters. When he turned to greet her, the tongue-tied reaction struck both of them again. He gave her his slow, spellbinding smile.

Her ears felt on fire. She bumped Jasmyn's outstretched hand, knocking the plate she was carrying along with its slice of rhubarb pie halfway across the living room.

There was a flurry of activity to clean it up and cut and deliver another piece to her.

As if she could chew and swallow.

Hud knelt beside her to scrape rhubarb from the rug. He said, "Hi."

"Hi."

Their arms touched. She tingled. Textbook case. What happened to safety in numbers?

She sat for almost an hour, listening to the chatter about his work. He seemed uncomfortable with the attention, but graciously responded to questions about his books and the making of a movie.

Chad said, "What's it like being famous?"

Hud blushed. "I don't know. I stay home and write."

"Except when you're meeting with movie producers."

"Well, yeah."

There was laughter and teasing. Liv bustled. Heidi and her famous brother fit in. Piper participated. To some degree. A little.

When she at last excused herself, the others did as well.

In the courtyard, Heidi and Hud strolled on either side of her.

Heidi said, "Hud, are you going to Mom and Dad's?"

"Nah. It's late. Okay if I crash on your couch?"

"Sure, but I'm crashing right now. So goodnight. 'Night, Piper." She entered her cottage, but Hud did not follow.

"She's not back to par yet. It's weird seeing her tire out like that. It's only nine o'clock."

"I remember her being high energy whenever she came into the store."

"The Energizer Bunny."

"That was her. One time she drove up after an open house in San Diego and then she went to meet clients for dinner and then she was showing them a house or two."

"And probably driving past six more." He shook his head. "It's going to be a long year for her."

"She's making progress. She's definitely more settled than when I first ran into her."

"Has she said anything to you about driving? Or riding past the accident site?"

"No."

"I don't want her to give up. Those are major milestones that the old Heidi would have been on top of by now. The old Heidi also would not be wearing glasses."

"The old Heidi is gone. For good." The awful words echoed in her head. "I'm sorry. I shouldn't have said that."

"My guess is that you speak from experience."

She reined in emotions that had been bouncing wildly inside of her since she stepped into Liv's cottage and saw him. They'd gone from school-girl crush to being angry at Jared all over again for dying to wanting to hang out in Mexico with a stranger to—

"You want to go to the coffee shop where we bought the scones?"

That would do for now.

꙼

Piper and Hud sat on stools at a counter against the window and drank tea. Jitters was a sprawling shop with a front and a back room. A popular gathering place any time of the year, it was packed that mid-May evening with the first wave of summer tourists. Almost every chair, stool, and couch space was occupied. The hum of conversations muffled the ambient music.

By now Piper and Hud were reacclimated to each other and able to speak in complete sentences. It had only taken about an hour at Liv's in the so-called safety of numbers.

She had told him about her visit with Heidi to Stella's Boutique. "But Gildy has muddied the waters." Piper crossed her legs, careful to avoid his long leg situated so close to hers. "She's being *nice*."

Hud chuckled. "That's too bad."

"It is. I'd rather give my two weeks' notice without feeling bad."

"Are you ready to quit?"

"Not quite. I have appointments with a loan officer and a lawyer. There's still a lot to do before I know if I can or want to move ahead with things." She smiled. "Guess what I did yesterday."

His powder blue eyes shone. "Went skydiving."

"No."

"Hot-air balloon ride."

"No. FYI, the only thing I do that involves heights is ride the escalator to the third floor at the store."

"Okay. You trained for a marathon."

"I don't run. Or jog."

"Hm. So much I don't know about you." He winked. "You caught a thirty-pound halibut off the pier. Got a speeding ticket. Got a haircut.

Found a hundred bucks. Had lunch in Paris with Tellmann's CEO. Was named best personal shopper of the year by the *L.A. Times*. Stop me if I'm getting close. Signed on the Princess of Wales as a client."

"Close." She grinned.

"No."

"No, not really close. It was only the governor's wife. And she's Gildy's client, not mine. But I, by myself—because Gildy gave the job to me—helped Mrs. Governor choose a dress for her to wear to her niece's wedding."

"That's huge." His voice was sincere.

She smiled. "You're sweet. It's not *New York Times* bestseller huge. It's not 'oh they're making a movie from one of my books and I wrote the screenplay' huge."

"Hey, don't downplay it. That's like comparing apples to rocks. Personally taking care of the governor's wife's fashion needs is a major accomplishment in your world. Congratulations, Piper Keyes."

"Thanks." She grinned.

"You're welcome. Why did Gildy have you do it?"

"I have no clue. Like I said, she's just being *nice*."

"Is she grooming you to take over for her?"

"Not a chance."

"If she were always this nice, would you stay with Tellmann's?"

"I wonder?" Piper shrugged. "I'd have more time for photography. Which, by the way, I've begun."

"Get out of town."

"Really. I started a class, one night a week, and I've been taking pictures like crazy."

"That's great."

"It is. Enough about me. What's new with you?"

"Besides what you heard at the inquisition at Liv's?"

"I guess you famous people have to put up with that sort of thing."
He laughed.

"I have something to confess. I haven't read your books."

"Not one?"
She shook her head.

"Geesh. I am so utterly offended. I can't believe I'm even sitting here talking to you."

"What if I read one and I don't like it?"

"Then you'll have to read another."

She dropped her teasing tone. "Seriously, Hud, I'm sorry I haven't. Louie loaned me a copy of *Silver Heart*, but…" She stopped short of trying to explain why she hadn't read it. Twice she had peeked inside. Both times words blurred and she touched the print and the whole experience felt alive with Hudson Hathaway. She wasn't ready to get that close to him. Not yet. Maybe not ever.

"But…" he echoed, "let me guess. You don't read suspense thrillers. You prefer biographies."

She stared at him. "How did you know that?"

"You're too wholesome to soak your brain in violence."

She opened her mouth and closed it.

He chuckled. "I'm not saying my readers aren't moral, decent people. Some like to fight evil vicariously and my stories provide that opportunity."

"But I'm not wholesome. Seriously, I'm not."

He squeezed her hand on the counter and let go. "Yeah, you are, Piper. The word doesn't mean perfect. It's who you are. You can't help it."

"Is that good?"

"It's not good or bad or in between. It just is."

"*Wholesome.* It sounds sickly sweet and phony. It sounds like a disease nobody would wish on their worst enemy."

His laugh started deep in his throat and grew until his shoulders shook and tears seeped from the corners of his eyes.

"It does, Hud. It sounds awful."

"I never was good with words." He still laughed.

She punched his arm. "Come on. Seriously."

"Ouch." He rubbed his arm. "Say, how about those Padres?"

"Padres? Who cares? I'm a diehard Cubs fan."

"Really? You like baseball?"

"Hello. I lived in Chicago. In *Wrigleyville*."

"Wow. Is that like close to the field?"

She rolled her eyes dramatically. "Do you like baseball?"

"Yep."

"So we have something in common."

He smiled.

She smiled. She wanted to smooth back a lock of his dark brown hair from his forehead, but she resisted.

Hud would go home to Mexico and be lost in his work. She would buy a boutique and be lost in her work. They were now-and-then friends who might run into each other, who might enjoy each other's company for an evening.

No reason for emotions to bounce wildly.

Thirty-Five

Hud had lied to Piper.

He watched her now from the corner of his sister's cottage. A light affixed above her door cast a glow on her as she unlocked the door, opened it, turned and waved at him, stepped inside.

The door clicked shut.

Not one to put too fine a romantic twist on things, he nevertheless imagined something inside of him clicked shut too.

"She's a beauty, isn't she?" The voice came from behind him.

Hud turned to see Chad emerge from the direction of his cottage the other side of Heidi's. He stepped over to meet him, further away from Number Four. "Out of my league."

"Nah." Chad's super-white, super-straight teeth flashed in the dim light. "Man, with a reputation like yours, you must get any chick you want."

"'Chick' being the operative word."

"I hear you. Piper is most definitely not a chick."

No, she was wholesome. Which was what Hud had lied about. It was a good thing. It was goodness itself—not phony, not sickly sweet, not of her own doing. Add to that her ethereal beauty and she was unreachable. Brick walls were inherently built between her and guys like him. The bricks could be scaled, but he lacked the climbing gear.

He said, "To set the record straight, I'm basically a hermit living south of the border. I was almost engaged once." He shrugged.

"But now you write bestsellers and make trips to Hollywood. They have parties and groupies for people like you."

"I shudder at the thought."

Chad laughed. "Anyway, she is *not* out of your league. Trust me. I've been crazy in love with her for three years now. I'm finally catching on that she'd never fall for me." He placed his hand over his heart. Although he teased, there was a catch in his voice. He cleared his throat. "I'm not Mr. Macho Marine. I have not succeeded at anything important. Although I am an excellent surfer."

Hud smiled. "And I am an excellent teller of vicious tales."

"Vicious. Hmm, yeah, I see your point. But you know, even though she looks like one, she's not a fragile, wilting flower."

"There's definitely a vulnerability about her."

"Yeah. The death of a fiancé has that effect."

Hud recalled Piper's earlier statement, about the old Heidi being gone for good. Obviously she had been talking about herself, about the loss of the old Piper when Jared died. "It's something she may not ever get over."

Chad shrugged. "I still say you're selling yourself short, buddy. Well, good luck with the movie and everything. See you around."

"Thanks."

Hud let himself into his sister's cottage, Chad's words echoing in his head.

Was it possible Piper could…? No. The fiancé ordeal aside, even the distance between his home and hers aside, they were too, too different.

Thirty-Six

Heidi scooted close to her brother, nudging his arm up over her shoulders, and slipped hers behind his waist. They stood on their parents' driveway and waved until Ethan and Rita's minivan disappeared around a corner, U-Haul in tow.

"They're never coming back, are they, Hud?"

"With them, you never want to say never."

"I guess that's true. But this move out of state is their biggest ever. It feels different, somehow."

He squeezed her shoulders and let go. "What happened to the sister who said, at age ten, that she could not wait to leave home?"

"You have to ask what happened?"

"No, I'm sorry. I don't. Maybe I just wanted to remind you that you're still you, Super Squirt, able to leap tall buildings in a single bound."

She smiled at the old nickname. "Right. Crutches might help with the bounding. I need to sit down."

They went to the low concrete slab in front of the door and sat on it, the best choice despite the late morning sun. The outdoor furniture was gone and the yard was a water conservationist's Utopia—all gravel with a few barrel and beavertail cactus plants.

"It's so hot here inland. Why would they go to a place that's even hotter? I bet it's a hundred-fifty degrees in Phoenix today."

He poked her with his elbow. "Are you about done grousing? Because I have some major grousing to do."

"What would that be? You have to figure out what to do with all your money?"

166

"You really are in a bad mood. Wait. Is it more than that? Do you need money?"

She bit her lip and leaned over to study the scar below her shorts, just above her knee. It was about two inches long, made when the surgeon inserted a screw to hold the rod in place. She was getting used to scars. The one on her hip, where the rod had been pounded through, was about four inches. There was another surgical incision on her abdomen. A myriad of reddish lines, all shapes and sizes, dotted her arms. She scarcely noticed the V on her cheek anymore.

"Do you need money, Heidi?"

"Not yet."

"It's that bad?"

"Getting there." She straightened her back. "I think Craig is moving out. Val dropped hints, but she won't really talk about it. If it's not business-related, she clams up."

"He wouldn't hurt her by doing something shady with your finances, would he?"

"Craig Laughlin? No. It's just her coping mechanism that doesn't help matters. And, too, the overall disconnect. It's like he's a step or two removed from the agency and it'd be better to have him involved on a daily basis. Which he might do if I ask him. How is it possible that he can cheat on his wife and still be a good guy?"

"We men are complex creatures."

She snickered. "Mm-hmm. See a pretty face and your common sense flies right out the window. Can't get any more complex than that."

He sighed dramatically. "That's what I wanted to talk about."

"Oh boy. Here it comes. You're infatuated with Piper."

"Does it show?"

"Let's see. You've been in town four nights, supposedly to help Mom and Dad pack. You've slept on my couch every night. You've taken Piper out to dinner twice, once after a movie, and to Jitters once. Mom was thrilled you were here at the house last night to eat pizza. Yes, I'd say it shows."

"I think I'm falling in love."

"Hud, seriously? You just met her. She's beautiful. Every guy falls in love with her. I myself never had that problem with guys."

"You've had plenty of boyfriends. And you are beautiful, Heidi."

"I used to be medium okay. Piper's in her own special class. Pretty and feminine." She chuckled. "I don't know why we get along."

"Because she's genuine, too. Caring."

"She is. And I will be forever grateful that she took me to the Casa. You know she's crazy about you too. Oh, look at that. You're blushing."

"Hot sun." He gave her a crooked grin. "I disagree, but either way it doesn't matter. She lives here, I live there. She wants to buy her own store here. I'm a hermit. She's a social butterfly who shopped with the governor's wife."

Heidi smiled. Piper had told her about that event.

"And still," Hud went on, "I ask myself the impossible: How do I court her? She's in love with a superhero. I only write about superheroes. Why would I even consider courting her?"

"Because there's always hope when it comes to love. Think about this. She moved here from Chicago not knowing anyone but Jared. That proves she has a spirit of adventure, which is right up your alley. Who's to say she wouldn't love you and tweak her plans? Don't write yourself out of this story, Hud."

He turned to her, his eyes wide.

She burst out laughing. "I don't know why she'd love you. You look exactly like Dad."

He smiled. "Good-looking dude, our dad."

They chuckled for a few moments, not speaking.

Then Heidi pressed her palms against her eyes. "I miss them."

"Me too." He placed a hand atop her head on the still too-short hair. "What do you want to do, Squirt?"

"I don't want to go to that open house."

"Then don't. Didn't you say the intern was overseeing it?"

"Treena. Yes. She can handle it." Heidi took a deep breath and exhaled. "You know what I want to do?"

He shook his head.

"Ride past the site." She met his questioning eyes and nodded.

⁂

Hud was a good driver, although not in the same way Heidi considered herself and their father good drivers. Hud would never make one lap around a racetrack in a Lamborghini Aventador LP700 without careening out of control.

Which meant he had no inclination to rule the freeway. She felt safe in his substantial SUV, an Explorer. At least as safe as she could feel at this point.

They had picked up I-5 in Oceanside and driven twenty minutes or so north through Camp Pendleton. Traffic moved steadily. It wasn't rush-hour thick, not middle-of-the-night light. Just regular. Like that day. That Day.

She thought of the photograph her dad had shown her once, while she was still in the hospital, when she was stupefied enough to want to see it and foggy enough not to remember it clearly. In it the German-made crimson beauty was unrecognizable, an accordion squeezed into colorless layers. She never asked to see the picture again. Her father never offered to show it.

Hud took an exit into San Clemente now and turned into a gas station. She would have asked if he needed gas, but her voice seemed out of commission. Hud parked off to the side, not near a pump, shut down the engine, and turned to her, sliding his sunglasses atop his head.

"How you doing?"

She nodded.

He watched her.

She watched him and wondered—not for the first time—if they had comforted each other, sightless, in the womb.

"Try a deep breath."

She nodded again and tried. Her chest trembled with the effort. "Oh, why did I do this?"

"Because you're ready."

"No, not why did I ask you to bring me here. I mean why did I drive like an idiot and fly off the freeway and hurt myself?"

"It was an accident. There is no 'why' to it."

"I was happy. I was fine. Why did I hurt myself, Hud?" Her voice rose. "Don't I like myself? Do I feel guilty about something? Was I subconsciously punishing myself?"

He rubbed her shoulder. "It was an accident. All the best NASCAR guys have accidents. Le Mans drivers. Indy 500. You think all those people race in order to punish themselves?"

"I don't know."

"They don't. They do it because they are a brick shy of a full load."

In spite of every nerve afire with tension, Heidi laughed.

"Like you and Dad." He chuckled. "You got all the looks. I got all the brains."

"You're blathering."

"Is it helping?"

"No." She smiled. "A little."

"All right then. Let's do it." He squeezed her shoulder. "You might get a leg cramp if you keep braking like that."

She had one in her calf already, but her right foot moved by no choice of hers, slamming again and again against the floorboard.

They were soon merging into the southbound traffic.

While Heidi held herself tightly and braked, Hud spoke in his soothing tones. The landscape rushed by her side window. Browns, greens, a ribbon of ocean. She couldn't look straight ahead. She did not want a sense of driving herself.

He said, "I'm going to stay here in the slow lane, okay? Did Dad tell you he's been past it? I've seen it, of course, coming back from L.A."

"How can you tell the spot? You can't see anything, can you?" A fresh wave of panic bubbled in her throat. "The car's not there, is it? Is the vegetation torn up or—"

"The car was towed that day. Vegetation is all grown back or popped back into place. You know how hardy this coastal stuff is. Dad wasn't ready to come out here until all evidence was gone. He asked the highway patrol for the coordinates. But neither of us would have needed that. It's fairly obvious where it happened." He gestured toward the right. "Watch closely."

"Then I'd have to keep my eyes open."

"Just watch. In ten minutes this will all be over. You don't want to miss it. Once you get through this, you're home free. You will have faced the lion. He will slink away, tail between his legs."

She spotted a steep drop off.

And a guardrail over a river.

And terrain dotted with huge, jagged rocks.

And a barbed wire fence.

A gorge.

A sudden rocky upslope.

"Hud." She couldn't tear her eyes away. "I don't remember ever notic-ing…"

"Me neither."

"If I…"

"If you'd gone off at any other spot…"

Horror filled her. "I wouldn't have lived through it."

"No, I don't think so."

"Where—" Then she saw where. She saw The Spot. The place where she had all but thrown her life away.

The sight imprinted itself on her mind, a branding iron of wide open brown desert camouflage, bright blue sky, and in between light skipping off the ocean. Light brighter than sunshine.

Sensations thrust their way through her. Flying. Flipping. Bouncing. Rolling. The sound of shattering glass, crunching metal, her voice scream-ing, her bone snapping. Snapping. Snapping. The crack of it echoed over and over.

Heidi burst into tears.

But the light, the light brighter than sunshine, remained, consum-ing all the rest.

She felt the car stop, felt her safety belt loosen, felt Hud's arms come around her. He held her close as she cried and cried.

Thirty-Seven

Sometimes adding fuel to the fire helped it burn out faster.

Loneliness was Liv's fire. The fuel? Watching the sunset from the pier alongside lovey-dovey couples getting their romantic fix.

She sighed, rather loudly, as she stood at the railing that faced northwest. No one would hear her between the wind and the talkative crowd of gawkers and passersby. She sighed again.

It wasn't a pity party. It was more like an intense delving into an emotion. She figured that it hit because of recent developments with Heidi, Valerie, and Adam. Syd was all over them.

I miss him, Lord! I miss him so much.

"It never goes away, does it?" The voice belonged to a stranger nearby, a woman probably about her age with silver hair, wearing a dark blue fleece and jeans. "The emptiness." She smiled at Liv, sadly and knowingly, and turned back toward the ocean.

"No, it doesn't, not completely." *Oh dear.* Had she spoken aloud?

They exchanged no more words, two widows in silent communion with each other.

As sunsets went, it was a mediocre one. The overcast sky on the horizon nipped it early and stole away the faded yellow ball before it could turn brilliant, liquid orange.

But a sunset was a sunset. People whistled, clapped, cheered, and kissed. Liv sensed the energy of the Almighty surge through her, quenching the fire of loneliness, leaving her drained and yet somehow filled at the same time.

She turned away from the railing and caught sight of a familiar couple, down a ways, nearer Dee Dee's Diner at the end of the pier. Keagan and Jasmyn.

Oh. Oh, my.

The thing about public displays of affection was they were both public and private. Typically she averted her eyes, giving people their space. But this was Jasmyn, her surrogate daughter, and Keagan, the man Jasmyn loved and who loved her. The couple Liv adored. She did not avert her eyes.

Keagan's hands were on either side of Jasmyn's sweet face. Their kiss was heartbreakingly tender.

Then Keagan reached into his jacket pocket. Liv noticed there were people near them and now a few of them clapped. Jasmyn tilted her head, clearly embarrassed although her grin was as big as all outdoors. Keagan handed her a small box and she lifted its lid.

Oh, my.

Liv saw no more through her tears. She walked away, heading home, blinking and dabbing her eyes, laughing and smiling and thanking God.

"Liv." Jasmyn embraced her, squeezing tightly. "You silly goose. Why didn't you meet us on the pier?"

Keagan hugged her next. "Really, Liv, you didn't need to give us our space."

She laughed. "Applesauce. Of course I needed to give you your space. Sit." They sat on her couch, holding hands, as she sat in the recliner. "I'm always around you two."

He winked. "Not always."

"Well, okay." She made a shooing gesture and grinned. "I am tickled to pieces. Congratulations. Did I already say that?"

"Twice, but who's counting?" Jasmyn held a hand out to Tobi, who jumped on her lap and immediately purred loudly. Her ring—a beautiful setting of diamonds and a large sapphire that matched her eyes—sparkled.

"Listen to that. Tobi's happy too." Liv felt her own purr shift into a low gear. She feared to ask what came next. Did they have a date? Where would they go? She changed the subject. "Can I get you some tea?"

Keagan said, "No, thanks. We just wanted to tell you first."

"And ask you a favor." Jasmyn looked at him and he gave a slight nod. "Well, Sam has hinted that she and Beau might find a bigger apartment when they get married."

Liv's shoulder's sagged. "I assumed they would. Her office space…"

"And his size."

"And, too, there isn't much privacy at the Casa. Every time you walk out the door, you're in the courtyard with a neighbor or two. I can understand that you young couples would want something different. The Casa is good for singles and old—"

"Liv." Jasmyn dumped Tobi onto Keagan's lap and moved to the floor beside the recliner. She touched Liv's arm. "We don't want to go anywhere. We just want first dibs on Sam's bungalow."

Liv stilled her right hand that she realized was kneading her chest. "Don't be silly. You'll need—"

"To live here." Keagan used his assertive tone.

She gazed at her two young friends. "But…"

"But nothing." Jasmyn shook her head adamantly. "Your assistant manager lives on the premises. Your guardian angel slash knight in shining armor does too. We love you, Liv."

Well, she loved them too. Maybe she could find her voice later to tell them.

Thirty-Eight

"Piper, it felt angelic." Heidi's eyes were wide, her blonde hair halo-like in the café's dim lighting.

Piper would have teased her about Adam's angel eyes, but the subject matter was too serious. Her friend had just described an incredible sight of an otherworldly brilliance on the ocean off the freeway.

Heidi leaned back in her chair, her expression radiant. "And then all the rest was gone. Poof."

"All the rest?"

"The accident. The horror of it. The details of it. Hud pulled into the rest stop along there and I cried, but it was like crying things out, all the toxic fears." She pointed at her leg. "All the anger over this."

"It was healing."

"Exactly. I imagine I'll feel it again, now and then, but now I know none of it can hold power over me anymore."

"That's wonderful. Do you think you're okay with driving on the freeway now?"

"I'm all right with *riding*. We did it twice, up and back down. The second time was much, much easier."

"Wow. You've got to tell Liv."

"I will. She'll appreciate the weirdness of it, won't she?"

Piper laughed. "The otherworldly brilliance? Oh yeah."

They sat in the café at Adam's Garden. The Grounds was a mix of state-of-the-art coffee bar and French country décor with some California gold rush thrown in. Images of roosters and sunflowers were everywhere. Sepia photos of miners and people panning at streams were everywhere else.

175

Signs—*Order Here, Pick Up Here, Guys, Gals*—were lettered on boards in a kindergartener's style.

The square tables were solid wood with ladder-back chairs and lit chunky candles set in antique lanterns. Red-and-white checked curtains hung at the windows. Large blue lanterns hung from the paneled ceiling of dark wood and thick beams.

A bar and stools straight out of a Western lined one side. Behind it was a wall of shelves and a huge mirror, filled with coffee-and-tea-related items: mugs, teapots, bottles of flavored syrups.

"Interesting décor."

Heidi grinned. "Italian Renaissance in the bathroom."

"I noticed when we were here last Saturday."

They exchanged a look, brows raised.

"Adam and Val's mom, Cathy, is an interior decorator."

"It's eclectic."

"And you're diplomatic. It's horrid. If he ever had to list it…" She shook her head.

Piper smiled.

Hud headed toward them, weaving his way around the crowded tables. Piper wondered again why she was there. Earlier, Heidi had phoned her at work and invited her to join them at the café that night to hear Adam's band. Without the slightest hesitation and with too much enthusiasm, she had said she would meet them there.

She met them, spent the first ten minutes gyrating through her *Jimmy Peters hangs the moon* emotional dance and faking a manner that said she was cool, that she had it all together.

Hud set a small tray on the table and unloaded iced teas and a plate of nachos smothered in cheese and jalapenos.

Heidi said, "Nachos? Seriously?"

"What'd you expect? Crudités and hummus? The jalapenos are organic." He sat. "Piper, thanks for offering to take Heidi home with you."

"It's so out of my way, but you're welcome."

He gave her his slow smile.

Hot cheese and spicy peppers would refocus her attention from this intriguing man who had more influence over her emotions than he should. She shoved a chip into her mouth and chewed.

He was leaving tonight, heading up to Los Angeles. Evidently Sunday mornings did not prevent movie people from scheduling meetings. She was glad and not so glad. Tonight was the fourth evening out of the past five that they'd seen each other. First was the late-night Jitters time. The next night they'd gone out to Dee Dee's Diner on the pier and ate hamburgers, fries, and malts and walked on the beach after. The next night they'd gone to a silly movie, a rom-com—light on the romance, heavy on the comedy—and then ate sushi at a small place next to the theater.

They talked about everything under the sun. She enjoyed herself more than she had in years. Four years to be exact. And she wished he wasn't leaving again. But grateful too. They were at platonic, where they had to stay given their living situations. Yet…Yet…In the middle of the past four nights she had woken and felt the loneliness like a boulder on her chest.

She could fall in love with the guy in a heartbeat.

Like she had Jared.

Which was why she knew it was for real. She had been there, done that.

The lights dimmed. Hud and Heidi, on either side of her, stopped a conversation Piper had not heard one word of. At the back end of the room, Adam and two other guys in jeans and white shirts sat on stools behind microphones. Adam and one of them held acoustic guitars, the third was at a keyboard. Without a word, they began playing.

The music was mellow and emotional. Downright romantic. Piper held her breath for a long time and simply felt the music. After a bit, Adam sang, his voice low and engaging.

In her peripheral vision, Piper watched Heidi. Her friend's expression was still peaceful. No, not quite. It was beyond peaceful, as if the changes of earlier in the day were still going on, clearing out old things and—maybe now—receiving new. Maybe she could see herself as warmhearted, not cold.

Talk about platonic relationships. Heidi had told Piper that was all she and Adam ever had between them, despite Maisie's suspicions. Piper wondered if they might glide on into something different, though. Even before the events of today, Heidi was certainly not the same person she had been before the accident.

As Piper had told Hud, the old Heidi was gone forever. Like with Piper, she viewed life through a pair of lenses she never would have chosen for herself. Everything was seen as a before or an after. The two never met.

Hushed voices drew her attention back to Heidi, who was in animated conversation with a dark-haired woman. Piper recognized Val, Heidi's partner, from photos.

She was clearly agitated and her voice grated in a harsh whisper. "What do you care, Heidi? You left me too. Left me high and dry."

Heidi struggled to get out of her chair. Standing always took her some effort, especially when her chair was scooted under a table, like now.

Hud stood, stepped near Val, and spoke so quietly Piper could not hear the words.

Suddenly Adam's voice came through the speakers, saying it was time for a short break and they would be back in a bit. He made a beeline for their table.

Val burst into tears and she resisted Adam's arms around her, but he held fast and moved her toward the door. Heidi and Hud followed. Piper caught a few curious glances thrown her direction, grabbed her bag and Heidi's, and soon found the four of them outside, around the corner of the café in a secluded spot.

Adam held his sister's arms. "You've been drinking."

"Tell me something I don't know." Val slurred the words. Mascara streaked her face.

Heidi said, "Did you drive yourself here?"

"You think I have chauffeurs at my beck and call like you do?"

Hud sidestepped over to Piper and whispered, "Uh-oh."

"Val." Heidi's voice trembled. "Let's go home."

"Yeah, right. I told you, I am not stepping a foot inside your *quaint little cottage* at the Casa de Battleaxe," she sneered. "I wouldn't even put my little finger on that big wall. What is that all about anyway? That wall? It makes it look like some secret place that only certain people can know about. If that isn't the most self-centered, dumbest—"

"Val, I'll come to your house. Hud can drive us. I'll spend the night and we can sort things out tomorrow."

"Let me sort it out for you right now. You abandoned me. Craig abandoned me. What's to sort out?"

"Let it go for tonight, hon. Let it go."

Val wailed and Adam pulled her into a hug.

Piper looked to Hud for an explanation.

"Her husband moved out."

"Today?" she mouthed.

He nodded.

Val pushed Adam away and put a finger very close to Heidi's face. "I don't need you or Craig. Just go your merry way like you've been doing for the past four months. Get all snuggle bunny with the Battleaxe. You know, that hurts worse than Craig hooking up with some floozy. At least he has an excuse. He's an idiot and I'm too good for him. But you were my *friend* and you went off and found, of all people, that woman to be friends with. How dare you!" She whipped around to Piper. "And who are you?"

A blast of alcohol-laced air struck Piper.

"You're that girl from Tellmann's, aren't you? And you're one of them, too. One of the Battleaxe's minions. What do you think you're doing here?"

"I'm just—"

"Leaving." Hud put an arm around Piper and stepped between her and Val. "Heidi, come on."

"I have to stay. Val needs me."

Val barked a laugh. "I don't think so, Hathaway. I haven't needed you for a long time." She turned and teetered down the path.

"Hud, I'm staying."

Adam said, "No, Heidi, you're not. It shouldn't matter, you and Olivia McAlister, but it does. Somehow, it just does." He hurried after his sister and disappeared in the shadows.

Piper was shaking. Hud kept his arm around her and pulled Heidi in close with his other. Huddling together, they walked to the parking lot.

Heidi cried openly. "I didn't mean to. I didn't mean to. How…? Why…?"

"Shh, shh," Hud soothed.

They reached Piper's car. She handed Heidi's bag to her and dug into her own for the key.

"Are you all right to drive?" Hud asked. "I'll take Heidi and follow you."

She nodded and fumbled with the key fob, hitting the *lock* button several times.

He took it from her, unlocked the door, and opened it.

Instead of getting in, she turned where she needed to be, into him. He wrapped his arms around her and she held on to him.

"I'm sorry you had to hear that."

"Me too." Her voice was muffled against his shirt.

The closeness of him warmed and scared her. It was familiar. He was familiar. He was a stranger but familiar. And safe.

How could that be?

ѕℓℓℓ

Darkness had fallen by the time Piper drove into a parking space at the curb across the street from the Casa. Hud parked behind her. His big black SUV behind her the whole way had been a comfort.

The three of them walked through the gate and into the courtyard. Piper remembered a curious thing Val had said. "I didn't think Val had ever been here, but she mentioned the wall."

Heidi said, "I'm sure she's driven past it a time or two. She's the type to check into any kind of property, especially if it belongs to her dad's wife." They stopped near Heidi's cottage. She hugged Piper. "I'm sorry."

"It's not your fault. I had a good time until, you know."

Heidi smiled. "It was fun, wasn't it? We probably won't do it again."

"Probably not."

"I have to go to sleep and forget all about this."

"Remember the good stuff, though. You had an amazing day on the freeway, Heidi."

"Yeah, I guess I did. Thanks." She hugged her brother. "And thank you for that amazing ride."

"Mm-hmm." He kissed the top of her head and let go.

"You won't stay?"

"No. Unless…"

"Nope, I don't need you. I've got Piper next door. Chad on the other side. Liv across the courtyard." She went to her door and unlocked it. "I've got Jasmyn, Keagan, Riley, Noah, Inez, Louis, Coco, little Tasha, Sam, and maybe even Beau because I bet he's hanging at Sam's. Night, you two."

Hud chuckled as his sister shut her door. "Piper, I don't know where she would have been after a scene like that if she didn't have you all here."

"But…" She hesitated. "Maybe it wouldn't have been so bad if I hadn't introduced her to Liv."

He shook his head. "Don't go there. Trust me, Val was in a bad way tonight."

"Obviously."

"She would have lashed out at Heidi if only for being in an accident that's left her unable to give a hundred percent at the office. Business is slow. Val's marriage is on the rocks. Craig moved out tonight. From what Heidi told me, it's been coming for a while. He admitted to having an affair. Heidi is a convenient scapegoat at Val's lowest point. Her problems are all Heidi's fault. We all do it when we can't handle reality."

"Kind of like Jared's death. That covers a lot of things."

"I'm sure it does. A death would be the deepest of hurts."

"I should say it *covered* a lot of things. Past tense."

Shadows hid his eyes, but he faced her, and she felt their warmth. "Going out without a scapegoat is a scary thing."

"I'm thinking more along the lines of healthy."

"That too."

Talking to him was—to quote her dad—like falling off a log. She wished it wouldn't bruise like falling off a log did, but she suspected it would. Relationships tended to do that, platonic or otherwise.

She said, "Do you have a scapegoat?"

"Nothing like yours. I was never hurt so deeply. There was a girlfriend who decided she no longer loved me because basically I was a self-absorbed idiot."

She smushed her lips to keep from laughing.

"You can laugh. I was that. I am that. I am because she spoke it into being. I blame her for making me one."

"That's why you live by yourself in Mexico and write bestsellers."

"Correct. It's what self-absorbed idiots do. And I blame my dad for why I write suspense. When I was growing up he drilled into me that the classics are the only fiction worth reading. I went the total opposite direction."

"You're a rebel too, then."

"I am."

"It all sounds positive to me."

"Aside from the self-absorbed hermit persona."

"Yeah. But you can always change the downside. Make healthy choices."

"You're not teasing now, are you?"

She smiled. "If the shoe fits…But I should read one of your books before I say anything else."

"You still haven't read one?"

"I'm going inside right now to read *Silver Heart.*"

He smiled. "Goodnight, Piper."

"Night." *When will I see you again?*

She watched him walk to the gate, turn and wave, and close it behind himself. Apparently he could not hear the question her heart shouted.

Thirty-Nine

By Monday morning, after the Saturday night brouhaha, Heidi's appetite returned. She sat in a booth at Dee Dee's Diner at the end of the pier with Liv and Piper and watched Jasmyn set a plate before her. It held a stack of buckwheat pancakes topped with a pile of fresh strawberries and a dollop of whipped cream. Four strips of bacon were on the side.

Jasmyn smiled. "We'll get you back to your healthy weight in no time."

Piper said, "Should we talk about fat, cholesterol, empty calories, and worthless carbs?"

Liv laughed. "Lack of fiber?"

Heidi reached for the pitcher of syrup. "Give me a break, girls."

They ate and chatted. Jasmyn joined them in between serving other customers, conspicuously flashing her engagement ring. The news had spread through the Casa yesterday like a wind-whipped leaf around the courtyard. Inez's laughter had drawn Heidi outdoors where she had actually spotted Keagan in the middle of a blush.

Heidi admitted to herself that she basked in the comfort of their new, yet solid, friendship. The thought of facing Val at the office was not a happy one. She would cling to the encouragement these Casa ladies so generously offered.

"Heidi, dear," Liv said, "when will we see your brother again?"

Twin blossoms appeared on Piper's cheeks.

Heidi could not hold in the chuckle.

Piper looked downright alarmed. "What's so funny?"

"Sugar rush." Heidi blinked at a rash of sudden tears. Piper and Hud? How beautiful was that? *He's crazy about you too.* It wasn't something you

183

admitted without permission. "Um, I don't know when he'll be back. He's never been regular about visiting but now that he has people to see in Hollywood, who knows?"

Piper pulled at the neck of her striped knit shirt as if she were hot. "He told me they're talking about a sequel already."

Heidi shoved a bite into her mouth. *Really?* He hadn't told her that.

"My, my." Liv was suitably impressed. "They haven't begun filming the first one yet."

"The idea came out as they tweaked the screenplay. They saw where they could start storylines with the hero that could be followed in another story. He'd have to write a new story since he doesn't have a book sequel." She smiled. "You know how that goes."

Liv laughed. "Yes. It happens all the time with my friends. Are they filming in Mexico?"

Piper's smile faded. "Mm-hmm."

"Oh." Liv sighed. "I guess once that starts, we won't see much of him."

Heidi swallowed. "Baja isn't that far. It's where he lives and drives here from."

Liv turned to Piper. "How are the boutique plans coming?"

"They're okay."

"You're having doubts, Piper dear. Do you want to talk about it?"

"The financial side of things looks just fine. It looks great, actually. The loan will probably be approved. It's the commitment that I'm coming to terms with."

"Understandable. It's huge."

"Yeah. Heidi said it will be my life. So I've been pondering what that means. Does it mean I can't go to Wisconsin for Christmas? Or bop down to Mexico or wherever or even keep up with photography as a hobby?"

Mexico? She had really said it. She skimmed over the word, but she had said it.

"Maybe I'm still not ready to commit, even after four years."

Not ready to commit? That left Hud out of the picture. Poor girl didn't know up from down. Heidi had no idea what to say.

However, Saint Liv spoke up. "You'll know when it's time. If Stella can't wait, then you have your answer there." She paused, her kind eyes twinkly behind her glasses. "And any other commitment will make you hesitate. That's not bad. You've been through so much. Give yourself a lot of leeway."

Piper nodded.

Heidi nodded with her. She wanted to call Hud right then and there and tell him to get a clue already.

Jasmyn slid onto the bench seat next to Heidi. "I have a five-minute break. Tell me quick, what can I do to help you this week? Work? Doctor? Hair salon?"

"You're making fun of my hair."

"Never." She pointed to her dark hair wrapped in a tight bun with pencils stuck through it.

They all laughed. Jasmyn was a sparkplug.

Heidi said, "There's only work on the calendar. Thank you. Needing a ride might be nearing an end." She exchanged a glance with Piper who smiled. "Hud took me past the accident site on Saturday." She told them about the experience in glowing terms. There were no other kind of terms to describe it.

"Wow," Jasmyn said.

Liv yanked a napkin from the dispenser and dabbed at her eyes. The woman seemed to have nothing to say, but her expression affirmed to Heidi that something beyond words had indeed happened out on the freeway.

Heidi thanked Piper for the ride and climbed from her friend's car stopped in front of the agency. During the ride over from Seaside Village, they had not mentioned Hud's name. Heidi worried she would make a middle-school declaration like *Hud loves you. Do you want to go out?* She assumed that Piper worried she might reveal what she was trying so hard to keep secret, that she cared for Hud but she also feared having her heart broken again.

Heidi stepped into the office. Cynthia and Dawn greeted her with smiles and waves, both of them on the phone. So far, so good.

She went down the short hall, heart pounding and a prayer on her lips. Yes, a prayer. After Saturday, she accepted the notion that there was Another at work around her and probably within her, and that He or She was on her side. A word or two—*Help, I can't do this*—comforted her.

It was Saint Liv's influence. Praying seemed the same as breathing to the woman.

"God," Heidi whispered now, "help Val."

She peered through Val's open door and tapped on it.

Her friend looked up from her desk. The hangover that she undoubtedly endured after Saturday night was still evident on her pale, haggard face. Her attempt at a smile was borderline smirk and wince. "I'm a pill."

"You are and I love you anyway." She went inside and sat. "I'm here, Val. You can go home and rest."

She shook her head. "It's better to keep busy. And"—her voice caught—"Craig's at the house, getting more of his things."

Heidi began to rise from the chair.

Val stilled her with a raised hand. "No hugs. I've cried my eyes out and I'm done."

"But you need to talk about it. Stop protecting me. You've kept me in the dark and carried this burden too long by yourself."

"I'm more concerned about our lagging business."

"Val, seriously? This is your *marriage*."

"And it's a no-brainer. He cheated. I'm out."

"Won't you work on it? See a counselor?"

"Nope."

"I'm sorry."

"Me too. And I'm sorry for taking it out on you the other night."

"I'm sorry I hurt the agency by driving like a lunatic." She wanted to tell Val about the healing experience on the freeway, but she couldn't find the words to explain it.

There was a wall between them. Had it always been there?

"Heidi, accidents happen. Like I kept telling you, we'll get through this. It's not like it is with me and Craig."

"I—"

The intercom on Val's phone beeped. "Val, there's a gentleman here to see you."

"About?" Val replied.

"A rental."

Val rolled her eyes.

Before Val said something snarky that Heidi knew was on the tip of her tongue, Heidi said, "Send him back."

Cynthia typically would have taken care of him, but Heidi trusted the woman. She knew what she was doing. She wouldn't pass him along without good reason.

The good reason appeared at the door at Dawn's elbow. "Go on in, sir."

"Thank you," he murmured in a deep voice.

Some people filled a room when they entered it. He was like that. His personality or his spirit or his whatever simply took over the air. He wore sand-colored dress slacks and a white shirt that draped elegantly. Its sleeves were folded partway up his forearms, the collar open. Heidi imagined a sport coat and tie were in his car.

Val stood, gaping. "Julian?"

The man smiled and extended his hand. "Val, nice to see you again." He turned to Heidi. "You must be Heidi Hathaway."

James Bond came to mind, the Sean Connery version of British elegance. "Hi." She shook his hand, taking in the brown curly hair streaked with gray, the calm brown eyes behind rimless glasses. "Have a seat."

He sat.

Val said, "Julian was my dad's business partner. How are you?"

"Fine, thank you. Although I feel a bit awkward."

Heidi could not imagine such a put-together man feeling awkward.

"I've been using your agency for years to manage a vacation beach house I rent out. Since you first opened for business, actually. Nine years."

"You have?" Val was surprised. "Why did you never tell me?"

"It was a practical decision. If your agency did not do well, I would simply take my business elsewhere. By not telling you, there were no hurt feelings. By the way, your staff has done a remarkable job for me all these years. I couldn't be happier."

"That's good to hear."

"Also, I haven't dealt directly with your people. An assistant does that for me. I've kept my identity a secret from renters simply because I live next door to the house. I didn't care to be personally available to vacationers. I enjoy their company, which I doubt I could do if they informed me of leaky faucets and whatnot."

"For nine years?" Val still sounded astonished.

"My name isn't on any paperwork. It's under a corporation. The previous owner, Faith Fontaine, lived in the house for fifty years. She had no family and left it to me in her will. She was a lovely lady, quite elderly when I moved in next door."

Heidi said, "On the boardwalk in Mission Beach."

"You know it?"

"In the early days I worked closely with Cynthia and Dawn to set up our system. I vaguely remember the story about an elderly owner because her place was in tiptop shape. We usually avoided those old places." And now she lived in one. "But hers was different. I never would have guessed we still have it."

"Well, you do and it's usually occupied."

Heidi grinned. "Thank you for making us money."

He chuckled.

Val exclaimed, "Nine years! You could have said something. We wouldn't have told anyone."

Julian nodded. "I've made things awkward. The truth is, I didn't want to upset you. I was your father's friend. Your mother was not a fan. When he passed away, I saw no personal role for me in your life. Perhaps that was foolish on my part, but it is what it is."

"No, it makes sense. Mom grudgingly gave dinner parties for Dad's associates, but she made it clear that she was not a happy camper. I don't understand how she thought he could make a lot of money—which she loved spending—by being at home."

He smiled in a sad way. "You were the apple of his eye, you know. You and Adam. We kept our fingers crossed about Adam, but Syd knew beyond a shadow of a doubt that you would succeed, specifically in the business world. You have the same drive he did."

"I missed the lesson that workaholism is detrimental to a marriage." Her face puckered.

"I'm sorry." He paused. "Actually, that's why I'm here."

"Why?" Tears glistened now. "You can't know about my marriage."

"I can only assume from what you've just uttered that you've adopted the work ethic your dad and I followed. It annihilates marriage. It killed mine and his. I hope yours is salvageable. Val, Livvie McAlister did not tear apart your family."

Heidi gawked at him. Val wept quietly and pressed a tissue to her eyes.

Julian went on. "She's not a saint, but she comes close. She deserves, at the least, the benefit of the doubt. When I heard that Heidi had moved into the Casa, I realized there were ties between us all that shouldn't be ignored." He stood. "Well, that's a bit for you to sort out. It has been a pleasure indeed to see you again, Val, after all these years, and to meet you, Heidi. Take care, ladies."

Before they could reply, he was out the door.

Heidi and Val stared at each other. Inwardly, Heidi cheered. Outwardly, she had nothing to say.

Val sniffed and balled up the tissue. "'Benefit of the doubt?' In his dreams. He always was an odd duck. Moving right along." She looked down at her laptop and clicked away on the keyboard.

Despite Val's tears, Heidi feared her friend was turning into an ice queen.

Forty

"Julian, you didn't." Liv sank into her recliner, cell phone in hand.

"I did."

"Why?"

"Livvie, you know why." He exhaled loudly. "I couldn't let the lie go on any longer."

"Oh, Julian, you're not still angry at Cathy for blaming me?"

"No. I simply sensed that with Heidi moving into the Casa, old emotions would surface for Val. It was time to give her a release valve."

Liv rolled her eyes. "A release valve?"

"Yes. A new perspective that might give her a way out of the confusion. And, quite honestly, it was time I touched base with Syd's child. She's so much like he was in his younger days."

"Will you ambush Adam too?"

"Livvie." His tone chided in a teasing way. "No, I won't. Adam is fine."

"What do you mean, 'Adam is fine'?"

"He cultivates the earth. That tells me he's in touch with truth. He'll work through any remaining anger that may have manifested itself."

"Well, I have nothing to say to that. I'm flummoxed."

He chuckled. "I thoroughly enjoyed telling Val and Heidi and the other two women, Cynthia and Dawn, about my little arrangement with Faith's house. I certainly hope Val doesn't decide to spill the beans to everyone who rents it. That would ruin all my fun."

He laughed some more. Liv failed to see the humor. Her hope was that the encounter would not widen the rift between Val and Heidi.

When it came to meddling, Julian was way ahead of her.

190

That evening, Heidi knocked on Liv's door. "Come inside, dear."

"I don't want to be a pest."

Liv pulled on her arm and shut the door behind her. "Pests crawl on the ground. Have a seat. May I get you some tea?"

"No, thank you." She sat on the edge of the couch, her poor broken body straight as a ramrod.

Liv wished she could throw her arms around the girl and convince her that it was all right to let down that iron guard of hers. Casa people did not bite. Although she had loosened up some, Heidi still retreated when it came to heart-to-heart connections. A spontaneous hug at this point was out of the question.

Instead, Liv smiled. "I talked to Julian."

Heidi smiled and her entire demeanor changed.

Julian's impact was like that.

"Is he for real? I've never met such a—a gentleman. It's an old-fashioned word, but it's the only one that comes to mind."

"Yes, he is for real. It's not just the Scottish accent. He's genuinely wise and gracious."

"He spoke highly of you. You must be good friends."

"We go way back, although we don't see each other often. I met him the night I met Syd. They were already fast friends and business partners." She paused. "I hope Valerie wasn't upset by his visit."

"Valerie and upset are synonyms. I shouldn't say that. She has one of those personalities that gets things done. It can be difficult on those around her." Her shoulders rose with a deep intake of breath and then she exhaled. "But Julian's timing was impeccable. Let me back up. Saturday night, Piper, Hud and I were at Adam's Garden. His band was playing— I would have invited you—"

"No worries, dear. We wouldn't want to foist me on Adam."

"Anyway, Val showed up. She'd been drinking and was not in a good way."

Oh, no.

"She doesn't do that regularly. She told us that her husband admitted to having an affair and he moved out. Then…" Heidi took another breath. "I'm going to hyperventilate."

"It's all right, dear. Take your time."

"Val laid into me. She said I had abandoned her too. That she doesn't need me. Adam told me to leave. Oh, it was awful. Poor Piper heard it all. Hud got us home. So, today Val and I more or less made up, but she really won't let me in. Into her heart. She's all business."

Liv couldn't help but smile inside. She hoped Heidi heard her own words as she described a woman whose heart was held tightly shut.

"Then, out of the blue this morning, Julian appears, walking right into the middle of us talking more or less around this mess."

"And that was impeccable timing?"

"Yes. He, in my opinion, told her exactly what she needed to hear."

"Really? He phoned earlier and told me what he said. I wasn't so sure it was helpful."

"I'm sure it was, Liv. She wouldn't have heard those things from me. He was calling her out on how she's hurting herself."

"What was her response after he left?"

Heidi pressed her lips together, raised her hands, and let them fall on her lap. "Ice queen. Right after he left, we worked on real estate. We worked hard. I don't know what will melt her."

"Perhaps it's too soon. But how is this affecting you?"

"Me?"

"Have you thought about you?"

Heidi was quiet for a long moment, her eyes unfocused. Then she scooted back on the couch, melded into its cushions, and looked at Liv. "If I hadn't had the accident, if I hadn't met you and Piper and Jasmyn…Then Val would be Ice Queen One and I'd be Ice Queen Two."

Liv could have done a back handspring. The girl knew. She *knew*. "But now, because you've had the accident…?"

"Oh, a lot of things now." Her nose wrinkled as if she'd tasted something bitter.

Like kale, maybe. She'd get used to it. *Lord, let her get used to the changes.*

"Mostly now, though, I feel bad for Val. I want to help her but I don't know how. We're the best of friends and I don't know how."

"For goodness sake, child, your accident wasn't quite four months ago. That's not long for such a serious situation. You can't dismiss that. You help her by taking care of yourself. You simply must take care of you, Heidi. For example, you look like you should be in bed. Did you eat dinner?"

"Yes, Mama Liv. And I will go to bed as soon as I go home."

"Good." Liv chuckled. "I hope I don't scare you away, but I have to ask it. Should you be working at all?"

"I have to. Business is slow. We need me pulling my weight."

"And what happens if you get sick again? Or simply too run down? How about working smarter? Is there a way to do that?"

Heidi shrugged. "I feel okay. Compared to four months ago, I feel great."

"Compared to six months ago?"

"Point taken. I have a doctor's appointment on Thursday. I'll ask him what he thinks."

"Good idea."

"I need a ride. Asking Val is out of the question. Piper is busy. Big Memorial Day sale at the store. Jasmyn can't get off work. The holiday weekend starts early and will be extra busy. Sam and Beau are going to Arizona."

Samantha had told Liv about the trip. She had even asked Liv to pray about it. Beau was going to visit the Navajo Reservation where she grew up and meet her family. Samantha was shaking in her boots at the prospect. Beau would love the big outdoors as Samantha did, but her mother, step-father, and half brothers? They were so dysfunctional, he could easily call off the engagement. Naturally, Liv had soothed her fears to some extent.

Heidi said, "The thought of a taxi ride all the way to my doctor with an unknown driver makes me want to throw up. I should carry a paper bag."

"Or you could ask me, dear."

"I hadn't thought…" Heidi's eyebrows rose. "I'm still getting used to asking for help. Are you available? Would you mind? Will you give me a ride?"

"Yes, no, and of course. This is a way to take care of yourself too, Heidi. Let others know what you need. Okay?"

"I'll…I'll try."

From the panicky expression on her face, Liv figured that for Heidi the prospect of trying to let others into her heart terrified her. She probably felt like she stood on a cliff with all ten toes wiggling over the edge.

Cliff jumping and kale eating. Heidi was in for a treat.

Forty-One

Late Thursday afternoon, after her checkup with the doctor, Heidi swallowed a pain pill with a full glass of water. Although she knew it by heart, she read the prescription label on the bottle. Two pills were allowed. They were heavy-duty, stronger than she needed. Since the end of physical therapy, she had cut way back.

If she wanted to get hooked, she'd actually have to work at it by taking a lot all the time. That would lead to telling whoppers in order to have more prescribed. *Oops, that last bottle was almost full and I threw it in the trash on garbage pickup day. The pain is still at a twelve out of ten, like most of the day.*

She glanced at the clock on the range. Four forty-nine. Almost five. If she took another, would she sleep from five to five or be up at, say, two-thirty? Four would knock her out for sure, at least for a while. She knew that. She'd done it twice. Once during the first week at her parents' home, once during the first week in the quaint little cottage. They made her itchy and antsy. What would three do?

Have you thought about you? Liv's words came to her.

It seemed like that was all she thought about, poor Heidi Hathaway. Except for her left big toe, every single centimeter of her body hurt, inside and out. They didn't ache, they cried out in pain. She had no stamina for work. She had no stamina for germs.

And those were just the physical manifestations. She couldn't drive. She could scarcely sit still while riding on the freeway. She couldn't sleep. She was afraid to put contact lenses into her eyes. She was afraid of stubbing that left big toe, for Pete's sake.

Things weren't right between her and Val, and she knew their relationship would never be the same no matter how well they got along at the office. Things weren't right between her and Adam. At least Val was polite and talked with her, if only mostly about business.

Heidi had no idea how to fix those things.

Her parents were long gone. Her parents had *abandoned* her. Her brother was absent and often unreachable. Strangers lived in her beautiful home with all of her *stuff*. She had left too much there. Photos, artwork, favorite pillows, favorite mugs, Hud's books and others.

If she didn't seriously exercise soon, she was going to explode. Strolling did not cut it. She longed to kayak. She longed to play volleyball on the beach or hop on a surfboard. She'd even welcome a jog at the water's edge.

But her leg wasn't ready. Not that it would ever be ready for most of the sports she had engaged in…

Heidi swallowed a second pill and set her glasses on the kitchen countertop. She went through the galley kitchen into the living room, lay on the fairly comfortable plaid couch snug against one wall, and folded a too-soft bed pillow under her head.

She was tired of thinking about herself.

But Liv hadn't meant it in that way. *You simply must take care of you, Heidi.*

"I am, Liv. I ate crackers before I took the pills and now I'm going to rest and pretend like my life isn't falling apart."

But her mind raced.

Ice Queen Two might be the best route to take yet.

The doctor she saw that afternoon—a different one this time, a woman—had released her to drive. She said things were healing nicely. When Heidi found Liv in the waiting room, she said, "Give me your van keys."

Liv had whooped. Outside in the parking lot she dug in her handbag and pulled out the red coiled bracelet that held something like three hundred keys. "Here you go."

"I was teasing."

"Applesauce. The doctor said you are fine to drive."

"Yes, she did. But she was talking about my leg and my reflexes, not my head."

"Heidi, dear, that's an easy one." She held the back of her hand to her forehead. "I feel faint. It must be the heat. You're going to have to drive us home."

Heidi had smiled. "Nice try, but…" She shook her head. "Not there yet, Liv. Besides, by now traffic is picking up and there's no good way around that one stretch of the 52. I'm too shaky."

Liv had narrowed her eyes. "After my heart attack, I refused to drive, just like you're doing. One excuse after another. Finally Jasmyn all but shoved me into the driver's seat of the van."

"She's a tough little thing."

"Mm-hmm. Then she climbed in the passenger seat and ordered me to drive around the block. I was shaking so hard I could scarcely keep my hands on the steering wheel."

"She's brave too."

"Yes, she is. Stubborn too. I did it."

Heidi had sighed.

Liv took the keys back and headed to the driver's side. "I am none of the above. You'll be ready when you're ready."

Now, as palm tree shadows danced on her living room ceiling, Heidi wondered if that would ever, ever happen.

The doctor had told her more…

After thanking Liv and turning down the offer to take home a casserole the woman had in her freezer, Heidi had gone out the front gate to the mailbox. It was a large square with slots that opened to eleven separate compartments. She unlocked hers, took out the mail, and opened two envelopes. Then she reentered the courtyard and went inside Cottage Three.

There really was no other place she'd rather be. If one had to fall apart, it was best to do it in a pretty, peaceful, cozy setting.

Inside the one envelope was a medical bill. She thought she had good coverage.

Had thought. Past tense. Paying the five figures noted in bold font at the bottom of the twelfth and last page was inconceivable.

Inside the second envelope was a short typed note from Walter and Jane Thompson, the couple who lived in her condo with a month-to-month lease who had said they needed the home until December.

Until now. Something had come up. They would, unfortunately and with immense regret, be moving out June thirtieth.

Which meant Heidi could move home. If she drove. If she had a car. If she had money to meet the big mortgage payment. If she wanted to leave the pretty, peaceful, cozy Casa de Vida, the House of Life.

The doctor had told her more…

No. She wasn't thinking about that right now. Heidi was going to take care of Heidi.

The freeway ride with Hud felt like a long, long time ago. It had been a pinprick of light on a black canvas.

She picked up the phone from the floor, turned off the ringer, and laid it back down. She covered herself with the beautiful quilt handmade by Inez and closed her eyes.

Forty-Two

Piper unhooked the connecting cord between her camera and her laptop. All two hundred photographs were downloaded.

Seated at her kitchen table, she had watched the process. Photos appeared lickety-split on the screen.

The first ones were from four years ago.

Jared mid-laugh in the ocean, his arms raised, a wave crashing about him, water droplets caught mid-splash. Jared eating a taco. Jared gazing at her, one corner of his mouth creased, his eyes at half-mast. Jared sliding across home plate. Jared rock climbing. Jared through the bus window, giving her a thumbs-up but not smiling.

Until tonight, she had never looked at them. When checking her new photos on the camera, she never went back far enough to see Jared's face.

She had also avoided the next batch, the ones of families at a kids' soccer tournament. Not many dads were in the pictures because they were overseas, some of them in Jared's unit. It was the day she learned he had been killed in a foreign town with an unpronounceable name.

What if she had lost them? How stupid of her not to have taken better care of them. She worked quickly now saving them in a file, connecting to an online service, uploading them, ordering four-by-six-inch copies. Only after she hit "Submit Order" did she breathe easily.

She rubbed her face. It had been a long day at the store, the first of five. Funny how any holiday called for a Biggest Sale of the Year. Would she do that at her own boutique? A Biggest Sale of the Year seemed out of place at Stella's in Rancho Sierra. Lowest Prices Ever just wouldn't blend in with the upscale shops.

198

What was she going to do about that situation?

The phone rang and she picked it up from the tabletop. It was a strange number, a string of—Was it Hud?

"Hello?"

"Piper, it's Hud. Hi."

"Hi."

"Sorry, it's eleven-thirty. But if I remember correctly, you said you were a night owl."

She smiled. "I was awake."

"It's good to hear your voice."

"Easy for you to say. You're a hermit who says he talks to no one for days at a time."

"Come on. I wouldn't say that to just anyone." He chuckled. "I'm calling about Heidi."

She grimaced. *Admit it, Pipe. Your heart just sank.* A little. Only a little.

"She's not answering her phone. Do you know if she's home?"

"I can knock on her door."

"Would you mind?"

"On my way." She slipped on a pair of sandals and headed out the front door.

"She had a doctor's appointment today and I expected to hear from her by now."

"Liv took her. I'm knocking now." When there was no answer, Piper hit the door harder with the side of her hand. "Lights are off. Maybe she's asleep, Hud."

"It's not even midnight."

"But you know how easily she tires. Hang on. I'm walking over to Liv's. She's a night owl too. So how is life in Mexico?"

"Uh—honestly, I'm kind of missing the States."

Piper nearly tripped rounding the fountain. "Oh?"

"Yeah." His tone was excited. "I had such a good time at Adam's the other night. I've never been kicked out of a café before. Maybe next time I'm in town we could try getting thrown out of that coffee shop down the street from you."

She laughed.

"I'm still sorry about you being stuck in the middle of that mess."

"I'm fine."

"Good. Heidi told me the other day that she and Val made up. What's new with you?"

"Mmm, I had tamales for dinner. Inez gave them to me."

"I really enjoyed talking with her. Her Spanish is pretty good."

Piper laughed again. Inez was Mexican.

"What else?" he said.

She told him about the sale at the store. Like he'd be interested.

"Anything on the boutique decision?"

"Not yet."

"What do you do this late at night?"

Piper lingered by the jacaranda tree, taking her time getting across the courtyard. Hud's voice in her ear mesmerized her.

She said, "Tonight I was transferring photos from the camera to the laptop. Some of them have been in there a while. Some for four years." She told him about her photos of Jared.

"Piper, that sounds like a huge step."

"I guess it was."

"You okay?"

"I panicked for a few minutes, thinking about how easily they could have been lost or deleted. But now…it feels like I finished something." She covered the remainder of the courtyard. "I'm just about at Liv's. Hold on."

She knocked on Liv's door.

"Coming!" Liv opened it and Piper told her what was going on. She held out her hand for the phone. "Hudson. It's Liv. Heidi was doing just fine when we came home. The doctor released her to drive. I tried to give her the keys but she said she wasn't ready…The doctor also said everything is healing nicely, right on schedule." She laughed. "Well, yeah, right on the medical schedule, still too slow for a Heidi schedule…Yes, I'm quite certain she is at home. I was in the courtyard much of the evening, as were others…Do you want me to unlock her door and check on her?…All right. Nice talking to you. Here's Piper." She gave her the phone and waved goodnight.

"Hey."

"Hey." Piper headed back toward her cottage, Hud's voice once again in her ear. "I bet she's just sound asleep."

"I'm sure that's it. But you'll keep an ear open?"

"Of course. I'm taking her to the office in the morning. I'll tell her you called."

"Thanks."

"Call again anytime." She winced. Too forward. Too forward.

"Mm-hmm. Or you call me. Now that you've got my number."

"Mm-hmm."

"Mm-hmm. Night, Piper Keyes."

"Night."

Boutique? What boutique?

Forty-Three

Heidi slept soundly on the couch until five-thirty and awoke with a start. She felt no pain, no aches, no woe is me.

The euphoria lasted only a split second, long enough for her to pull on running shorts and get one arm through a T-shirt. *Running* shorts? In her dreams. *Enough with the whine.* She pressed on.

Not wanting to carry keys, she didn't bother locking her door. She strode through the courtyard blanketed in semidarkness and dense marine air. Near the front gate, Keagan emerged from his bungalow, dressed in sweat pants, T-shirt, and running shoes. He was a spare man, not much taller than her, but she knew from personal experience how strong he was.

They greeted each other in quiet voices and walked together out to the sidewalk.

He said, "Headed to the beach?"

"Is there any other place?"

"Not when you live in Seaside." He strolled beside her.

"Don't let me hold you up," she said. "You're probably out for a run."

"No worries. What's your fastest time to the end of the pier and back?"

"Fastest time. Right. I've only *strolled* to the end a few times, eaten at Dee Dee's or sat on a bench, and *strolled* back. I don't time it."

"Do you have a goal?"

"Goal?" She wanted to bawl.

"For when you'll start timing it."

"Goals aren't for people who stroll." She heard her tone. "I'm whining. My brother says I need to stop. There's a goal for me."

"Maybe a physical goal would help."

"I suppose I could think about setting one now. I had my four-month checkup yesterday. The doc basically said…" The doc said a lot. She had said too much. Way too much. "Uh, she said to go for it."

"For 'it'?"

"Sweat."

He smiled. "I bet you miss that. Jasmyn told me you're an athlete."

"Was."

"You still qualify."

She shook her head. "Nope. 'Athlete' is ancient history for me."

"An athlete is simply a person who's skilled in physical exercise. You'll get back to it."

She squirmed inside. Keagan was like a brick wall that could talk. There was no getting around his questions and not a lot of emotional feedback to respond to. "I haven't mastered strolling. That's not even on the spectrum, is it?"

"Sure it is. And here you are, working at it."

"Whoopee."

"You're selling yourself short, Heidi. There are plenty of other forms of exercise you could engage in now."

"But nothing high-impact. I can't play volleyball." She winced. It was the first time she had said that out loud. Her stomach flip-flopped. The loss of one of her greatest joys hurt. But what hurt worse was the image of diving for a ball or crashing into a teammate, of coming down on a gym floor or even the sand with her leg at a wrong angle beneath her. Which not only could but most likely would because of what the doctor said…

She swallowed. "I can't run or jump or—"

"What *can* you do? Not can't."

What in the world did Jasmyn see in this guy? "What can I do. Um, let's see. Yoga. Yuck. Walk. Ho-hum. Dance. No way. Bike. Mm, maybe."

"You're whining."

And wondering how to disengage from the conversation.

Except for an occasional dog walker, not many people were out and about. They passed between a large resort and a parking lot and then crossed a street where the concrete ramp that led out to the pier met the sidewalk. At her first downward footstep, she instinctively slowed.

Keagan kept pace with her. "Have you considered circuit training at a gym?"

Her mind flashed to high school. Dull, indoor activity. She thought of her mom's foray into exercise by joining a popular club where older women without a competitive streak gingerly engaged with machines. Weights and cycles and elliptical trainers and rowers—"Rowers?"

"Why not? Get yourself in shape so you can kayak again. Jasmyn said you liked it."

Liked it? It was another of her great joys. In recent years, it had probably ranked at the very top. With her crazy work schedule, grabbing her paddle from the car and her kayak from storage at the harbor had become easier than scheduling three friends to meet her at the beach for a game.

Why had she lumped kayaking in with all the other sad losses? That was easy to answer. Her life was one big sad loss. What didn't get lumped into that? The minute she tried to separate issues, she factored in tiredness, germs, work priority, lack of car, and—of course—the leg. Everything rolled right back into one big miserable glob.

At the ramp's end, Keagan turned to continue down its other section, to the beach below, and stopped alongside the railing.

She stopped with him, letting the sound, sight, and scent of the ocean fill her. Waves lapped lazily. It wasn't a good morning for surfers.

He said, "I'm sure you realize this, but your muscle tone and stamina will come back. You're starting from scratch."

"I've never had to start from scratch. Muscle tone and stamina were always there. I walked when I was ten months old. I could serve a volleyball when I was seven. I hit free throws at eight. I surfed with a long board at nine. I was a junior beach lifeguard and swam around this pier all the time. In high school I played point guard, first base, sweeper, and ran cross country."

He gave her a little smile. "Welcome to the regular world."

She sighed. "I don't like it."

"You'll adjust. Let me know what you decide. Seaside Gym offers discounts to Casa residents."

"I'll think about it, thanks. You own the gym, right?"

"Co-own." He gestured toward the pier. "It's all yours, Heidi. Aim for Dee Dee's."

She eyed the long, long path of rough-hewn railroad ties. Fishermen and women dotted the railings. The gray mist remained, but the lamps were off. Too early for its sign to be lit, the Diner was a vague outline far, far down the path.

It was an intimidating path of warped and chipped timber, each rugged board a monster's hand ready to grab a foot and yank it. Sidewalks weren't any better. Sand was the worst.

"Heidi, you're an athlete. Despite your natural gifts, you know what it is to push your body to its limits. Why are you hesitating to do that now?" The brick wall spoke again and her own brick wall crumbled.

"The doctor said…" She pressed her lips together.

"If you say it out loud, some of the debilitating power it has over you might go away."

She met his eyes. Usually masked behind sunglasses, they were a laser beam of royal blue that conveyed a hope she no longer possessed. It filled her with trust. "The doctor measured my legs."

He tilted his head and his faced softened as if he knew what she was going to say.

She squeezed her eyes shut briefly. Regret and fear and anger spit out the words. "The surgeon missed it by a hair."

"The limp."

"Not going away."

"I'm sorry."

The devastation she had held at arm's length struck her with the force of a six-foot wave. It knocked the breath from her. She covered her face with her hands and sobbed. Life as she knew it was over. Totally gone. Kaput.

She sank down onto the concrete and curled up, arms over her head, her face against her knees. Why had so much been taken from her? Adam had called it power, prestige, and possessions. She called it her real self. Who was she with a limp and a future without hard exercise that soothed and energized?

Heidi sensed Keagan sit down beside her. His arm came around her shoulders.

And she cried harder.

They sat together like that, quiet except for her occasional gulps. After a while, a calm settled inside of her and she tiptoed around a new thought. Who was the real Heidi Hathaway? Maybe the woman who sat there. Who just sat there.

She wiped her face with the sleeve of her T-shirt. "Sorry."

"Don't be." He lowered his arm and handed her a small packet of tissues.

She couldn't help but smile. He was so not the type to carry tissues in the pocket of his sweats. "Really?"

He actually rolled his eyes. "They're Jasmyn's."

She pulled out a wad and blew her nose. "I guess I hadn't cried yet. Over any of it."

"Tears are cleansing." He gazed off toward the ocean for a moment and then turned again to her. "Your coordination is off. Are you afraid of falling?"

"No. I'm just so tired of my feet fumbling like they don't know where the stupid ground is right beneath them."

"Well, get over it. Life goes on. It'll take practice and a lot of sweat." He crooked his thumb toward the pier. "Start there. You can do it."

"What if I can't?"

"Then call me."

"I didn't bring my phone."

"That's a good sign. Subconsciously you didn't think you would need it." He smiled and held up his hand for a high five. "I'll swing by and check on you."

She slapped his hand. If she had any money, she'd forget the gym and hire him as a personal trainer. Maybe therapist too.

Forty-Four

Heidi sat at her desk and smiled. She felt no inclination whatsoever to whine. Endorphins, the aftermath of sweating, might have done the trick alone, but she was riding on much more.

Keagan—who would have thought?—had encouraged her to accept the limp and walk the pier. Piper—so down-to-earth in spite of her ethereal beauty—had driven her to the office and encouraged her to call Adam.

Accepting the limp as a part of her everyday life loomed so far outside the realm of possibility, she was inclined to not even consider it. The mere thought made her want to sit down and cry. But she had already done that and Keagan basically told her to get up.

She had gotten up and she had walked the pier, out and back. There had been no thirty-minute break or keeling over. Toe stubbing had been held at only five times.

Maybe…just maybe…

The exhilaration had carried over into the office. She attacked several projects and signed on two new clients. She searched the database and came up with potential renters for her condo.

And now, finger poised above the phone's "send" icon, she looked at Adam's name and number.

What had Piper said in the car? "He's your friend. Why wouldn't you call him?"

"Because it'll sound like a date?"

"So?"

"So…so, I don't know."

"Is it a date?"

"Not if he's still with Maisie."

"Then it's his choice." Piper had braked at a stoplight and looked at her. "What if it were up to you, though?"

Heidi still wasn't sure. Adam Engstrom was not the boy he was in college. She was not the same girl. She wasn't even the same girl of five months ago. She had lost more than she cared to ponder at the moment, but on the other hand, she had gained a new perspective.

One that noticed the peace at Adam's Garden and a mysterious inner light in his hazel green eyes and a loneliness in her own heart.

She touched the icon.

He was probably busy on a Friday at lunchtime. She'd leave a voicemail—

"Heidi?"

"Hi."

"Is Val okay?" There was an edge of panic in his voice.

"She's fine. She has some showings this afternoon and isn't here."

He exhaled loudly. "I just thought…"

"I never write, I never call. You figured it must be an emergency."

"I'm sorry."

"Don't be. Under the circumstances—"

"I mean I'm sorry for Saturday night, for being short with you and for not calling."

She opened her mouth to say *no problem*, but sensed that would make light of his sincere apology. And besides, it had been a problem. "Thank you."

"I would have gotten around to calling."

"Yeah, right. When? Christmas?"

He chuckled, catching on to her snarkiness as he always had. "New Year's for sure."

"Thank goodness I wasn't holding my breath."

"Yes. And thank you for being there for Val."

"Of course. I'm not exactly up to par—"

"But you're present. She needs you. Did she tell you Mom and Gunther just extended their trip?"

"No."

"Staying another month in Italy. She could use some mom time, but that's not happening. You're the next best thing."

"What is it with parental abandonment these days?" She told him about telling Ethan and Rita goodbye, making light of the miles between them.

"But admit it, Heidi, you miss them in a way."

"I do. Especially now, when I'm feeling like a lost little girl." *Whoops.* Had she really said that? "That's an exaggeration, but with the accident and all…" *Rats.*

"Feelings aren't right or wrong. You can feel like a lost little girl." He paused. "Even though we both know you've never felt that in your entire life."

She laughed. "Exactly. I'm not sure what to do with it."

"Do something that makes you feel found."

She blinked. Adam, like Keagan had done earlier, zeroed in on her deepest fears and needs. "Actually, that's why I called. There is something, but I can't tackle it alone." She hesitated.

"You don't need to second-guess yourself, hon."

Hon? The tickling was doing its thing in her throat.

"I know there's been a lot of water over the dam, but this is still me."

It was indeed still him. Adam, her old friend who had tackled the hard things with her up until they went their separate ways and forgot how to connect in that old intuitive way. New pathways needed to be cleared between them. She could tell him. She had to tell him. "I want to go kayaking."

"When?"

Just like that. *When?*

She said, "Now."

Adam picked her up at the office mid-afternoon.

Earlier in the day, clinging to the slender thread of hope Keagan had offered during their walk, Heidi had packed beach towels and her sun-blocking capris and long-sleeved shirt that kept her warmer on the water than a bathing suit. She carried it all in a large bag out to the parking lot where she spotted Adam walking her direction.

Years ago, he had been a Southern California cliché himself. Sun-bleached hair, broad, bronze shoulders, cute. Always wearing shorts, shirts, and flip-flops. Always smiling.

She noticed now that he had matured into a man, more handsome than cute, his muscles more solidly defined. His smile was less constant but somehow more genuine.

He wore long navy blue swim trunks, a plain white T-shirt, and sunglasses. He must have had a haircut because the reddish chestnut did not flip out as it had last week. He greeted her with a smile.

And a paddle. With translucent red blades on each end. Red. From a distance she could make out a symbol on them. It belonged to an expensive brand.

He shrugged. "I didn't send flowers to the hospital."

"Oh, Adam." She handed her bag to him and took the gift. "This is exquisite." She ran her hand along the pewter gray shaft, admiring the nifty button release that would break it down into two sections. She studied the asymmetrical blades. "Wow. This doesn't even weigh two pounds. Wow. Did I already say that? Mine wasn't this nice. Not even close." She looked up at him. "Thank you. You shouldn't have. Seriously."

"Seriously, I wanted to."

"How did you know mine was gone?"

"I asked your dad a while ago. You never left home without it back in college. I figured it was in the car that day. Come on, let me show you what else I bought."

What else he bought? He must have left the farm right after they talked and gone shopping.

As they walked toward the front end of his truck, she noticed a small red flag flapping on a pole behind it. "What is that?"

He only smiled.

They walked around the truck. The tailgate was open and protruding from it, with flags attached for traffic safety, was a long bumblebee yellow kayak.

"Adam!"

"I've always wanted one."

"You have not." She laughed and went over to examine it. "This is gorgeous. What is it? Eighteen, nineteen feet? And three hatches. You could go to Fiji in it." She spotted the brand. "Good grief. This is rated number one." It would have cost a small fortune.

"It was the only tandem sea kayak the store had. Since yours seats one, we needed it today." He shrugged.

She stared at him. "But I said we would rent one."

"But the rental place makes you stay in the harbor."

"But that's okay."

"But it's not real kayaking. You've always said that."

"But I don't think I'm ready."

"Enough with the buts." He tousled her hair. "We don't have to go out in the ocean. By the way, I bought life vests too."

Another thing she had lost in the accident.

"Is it okay if I store the kayak with yours when we're done?"

Suddenly unable to speak, she nodded.

Adam was not a kayaker. He was not a surfer. He wasn't all that crazy about wading in lapping waves on the beach.

He was, evidently, one really good friend.

ole

Heidi sat in the front cockpit of the kayak, stiffer than its hull, the paddle across her lap. They'd been in the water for two minutes. "Adam, I can't."

"Are you kidding me?" he shouted dramatically from behind her. "After all the money I spent?"

"Not funny."

He chuckled. "Remember the first time you took me out? Now that was funny, after the fact. I bet I looked just like you do now. All bug-eyed and shaking in your boots. Or flip-flops."

She looked over her shoulder and frowned at him.

"Face forward and put your paddle in the water." The sun glinted off his glasses.

She turned back around and did as he said.

"There you go. It's a nice kayak, isn't it? Nice day too. At this rate, maybe we'll see the sunset from here at the dock. Don't forget to breathe."

His soft tenor was familiar, comforting. It carried the past into the present. She almost felt at home.

The water in the harbor was calm. Docked boats and yachts lined most of the shore on three of its four sides. A small fishing boat passed them. Two big sea lions barked from a dock. With the Memorial Day weekend already underway, the shop and restaurant area was packed with people.

She fell into a rhythm, dipping the paddle right, left, right, left. The kayak was larger than hers and had rudders. The maneuvering nuances intrigued her, but her arms tired easily. She took frequent breaks.

Behind her, Adam more than pulled his weight, covering for her lack of strength and steering. Although they'd kayaked often during college, he hadn't been out in years. "Like riding a bike. Muscle memory."

She wished she had some muscle with a memory.

They skimmed along, out to the more open area where a jetty separated the harbor from the open ocean. Spray soared above the divide from a wave crashing on its other side. Seagulls cawed. The late afternoon sun warmed her face. The breeze sang in her ears. The perfume of brine saturated her with a sense of life.

As it always did.

"Heidi, what do you think?"

She eyed the opening twenty yards out and saw the whitecaps just beyond. A small sailboat floated through the gap toward the open water. A solo kayaker paddled his way in, nodding in their direction as if to say *Go.*

Go. Go for it. You can do it. I think I can. I think I can.

She wanted to. Oh, how she wanted to.

She looked over her shoulder at Adam. His crooked smile told her he knew. It told her that he had her back.

As he always had.

Forty-Five

Piper met her old friend at the food court in the mall during her lunch break.

Zoey had short, curly hair the color of a shiny penny, bright green eyes, a freckled nose, and a laugh that made strangers at nearby tables smile. She pointed at her round dome of a tummy. "After four, she's our 'oops' baby."

Awash in indecipherable emotions, Piper began to reach over the table and hesitated. "May I?"

"Of course." Zoey took her hand and placed it on her stomach. "There. Feel that? It's her foot. She's stretching."

The tiny hard lump filled Piper with awe. Of course she had been around pregnant friends before, but this was different. She was in uncharted territory here. "I feel like a dam just opened inside of me."

A slow smile spread across Zoey's face. "Those are 'I want to be a mommy' hormones."

"You made that up."

"It happens, Piper. Tick tock, tick tock."

She removed her hand. "Will it stop?"

"Only one way to stop it."

Piper made a funny face, but something inside her shifted. Suddenly she felt a huge void and her entire being ached.

"Is there someone?" Zoey shrugged. "Not that you can't technically do it alone these days, but it's easier to partner up on this venture."

"No. Yes. No. Kind of."

Zoey laughed. "That's wonderful."

"I'm…scared."

"After Jared, you have every reason to be scared out of your wits." She laid her hands atop the rounded dome and studied Piper. "But it's not simply the fear of losing someone again, is it? You're afraid of leaving Jared behind."

Piper nodded. "I am doing better, though. I can almost admit I'm sort of attracted to this other guy."

"'Almost and sort of.'" Zoey smiled. "Piper Keyes, has anyone ever told you that Jared Oakes loved you in a way most people can't love others? Seriously. It was subtle, but a few of us wives noticed. Lucy, Calli, and I. The word we came up with was *agape*, the church's idea of how God loves us. There wasn't one clingy, codependent, jealous, or 'me' bone in Jared's body."

"That's a bit much."

"Believe me, we rolled our eyes plenty. Even in our first years of marriage, our husbands never resembled him. They loved us, sure. They would do anything for us. But if things went haywire, they'd be out the door and looking for a new girl. Case in point, Lucy and Theo. Jared wouldn't have done that. No matter what."

"What are you saying?"

"I'm saying he was all about your well-being. If he could sit down here right now in his flesh and blood, he'd say he'll always live in your heart. And then he'd give you his blessing to fall in love with someone else."

Images of Jared flashed in her mind. At a party. A picnic. A ball game. In serious dialogue with others. Talking with his mother on the phone. In every instance, his eyelids would close slowly, his lashes sweeping down like an airborne feather. After a second or two, they rose again and his eyes found her.

Without fail, whatever else was going on, he remained present to her. Lovingly, wildly, completely present.

Her friend's words struck home. "Thank you. I've missed you, Zoey. I'm sorry for not keeping in closer touch."

"No worries. We're here now and you have photos for me."

"Yes, I do." Piper pushed her half-eaten salad to the side and pulled a large manila envelope from her bag. She slid out a stack of pictures, different sizes, some in color, some in black and white.

"Oh, these are magnificent." Zoey oohed in hushed tones. Smiling, she went through the photos. "The kids are three, six, eight, and ten. Soccer stars." She looked up. "Piper, I am so glad you still had these. How much can I pay you for all of them?"

"Nothing. I uploaded them online. I'll e-mail you the link, so if you want more you can order some. Will you send me Lucy and Calli's information? And anyone else you recognize in those pictures."

"Definitely. I'm still in touch with a lot of the wives. We're all scattered around the country now." Her eyes were damp. "That day…"

"Yeah. That day."

Piper and Zoey were quiet, sharing the memory of a day that was more precious and more heartbreaking than any day had a right to be.

Forty-Six

Twilight fell as Heidi and Adam walked through the harbor parking lot, a huge area filled with cars, campers, and boats on trailers. The evening air was wet and chilly. They laughed and shivered in their damp clothes. Her bag was slung over his shoulder. They'd left the life vests in the storage unit with the kayak, but carried their paddles, broken down into halves.

"Whoo!" she yelled for the third time, thrusting her arm skyward. "We did it!"

"You did it."

"I never would have done it without you, so thanks."

"You keep saying 'whoo' and 'thanks.'"

"Did I say I love my paddle?"

"Yep. Where did we park the truck?"

"No clue. Whoo!" She kicked up her right leg, too late realizing it wasn't a wise thing to do.

Adam caught her before she fell. "You okay?"

"Yeah." She leaned sideways against him and glared down at her feet.

"Heidi Hathaway, what did you say?"

"I said 'yeah.'"

"After that."

"Nothing."

"To quote your dad: Only lazy people use those words."

She straightened up and faced him. "They don't work anymore, Adam. My legs."

"I know."

"How do you know?"

"I just know." He wrapped his arms around her, his paddle at her back, hers at his.

If she hadn't spent the past couple of hours gliding across the ocean, watching dolphins play and pelicans dive and anchovies run and the sun set, she would have burst into tears. Again.

She spoke into his shirt. "The doctor said they're not exactly…even."

He tightened his hold on her. After a long moment, he said, "You'll adjust."

She nodded.

"Anything I can do?"

Don't leave me again. The thought took her by surprise. She pushed away from him and chose other words. "Take me kayaking again?"

"For sure. How about dinner now?"

She wanted to go home and put on casual clothes, but again switched directions. Inviting him to the Casa was shaky ground. Likewise was asking him where he stood with Maisie. "Dinner sounds great. I'll go in the restroom over there and change. Do you have anything else to wear?"

He handed her the bag that held her work clothes. "In the truck. I'll wait—"

A horn blasted as a car drove straight at them, its headlights centered on them. It screeched to a halt, and Val jumped out, yelling. "Where have you two been? I've been calling and calling."

Adam looked at Heidi, his expression mirroring hers with wide eyes, raised brows, and dropped jaw. In unison, they whispered, "Jiggers! It's the cops!" They snickered quietly.

Their silly expression had come from an old movie they'd watched. It burst from them the night cops had shown up for real—or rather, campus security. The uniformed man found the two of them inside the school library after hours. True, they had hidden in the stacks at closing time, but their motive was pure. They weren't finished with the reference books they needed for papers due at nine the next morning and were hard at work when he appeared. At least they hadn't stolen the books.

After that, whenever things turned messy—a bad date, a bad grade, any disappointment—they declared the cops were on the way. The giggles helped.

Val's heels clicked determinedly against the asphalt, growing louder with each click toward them. From her obvious distress, Heidi wasn't sure the giggles would help this time, though. Her friend's hair was disheveled, her skirt wrinkled, her blouse out of the waistband. But she wasn't like she had been the night at Adam's place. Her voice was sober, deadly sober.

She reached them, hands on her hips. "One of you could have told me where you were! I've been phoning both of you for hours and hours."

"Val," Adam said, "what's wrong?"

"You leave your farm and tell no one where you're going? Absolutely no one? And you, Heidi, you walk out the office without a word or even a note to Cynthia or Dawn about where you're going?"

Heidi started to protest. She had always come and gone at will, especially during the past weeks. The ladies had their own work to do and when she had left that afternoon, Dawn was at lunch and Cynthia was talking to clients in the conference room. Everybody had everybody's phone numbers. Not that that helped when her cell was locked up in Adam's truck.

Val didn't slow her tirade to hear a response anyway. "I had to track down what's her name!" She made a wild gesture with her arm. "At Tellmann's."

"Piper?"

"She said you went kayaking. She knew. Since when are you kayaking? Since when are you two doing anything together?"

Adam touched her arm. "Val, slow down. What's happened?"

The stream of words abruptly stopped and Val began to cry. "Heidi, it's all gone. It's all gone!"

"What's gone?"

"The money. The agency's money. Our money."

"What do you mean?"

"What do you mean, what do I mean?" She cried harder. Mascara ran down her cheeks. "Our money is gone, Heidi. It's gone. We have a thousand dollars in the bank. A thousand. That's it."

Heidi stared at her business partner.

Val wailed, "And I can't find Craig!"

Forty-Seven

Still dazed from Val's news, Heidi could not remember how she convinced Val and Adam to go to her cottage, but there they were, drinking coffee and talking in circles.

They had probably agreed to go to her place because the Casa was near the harbor. Val was in no shape to get back in Friday night freeway traffic to go home, and Adam's teeth chattered with cold. The prospect of running into Liv McAlister paled in comparison to everything else that was going on.

Still, things were awkward. Her friends' comments about her home were kind enough, but stilted. At Heidi's insistence, Adam had showered first and changed into jeans and a sweatshirt. Afterward, she showered quickly, wondering what they were doing in her kitchen and hoping Liv wouldn't knock on the door.

Using Heidi's laptop, Val scrolled through their account on the bank's website. They were at a loss as to what had happened. It was, as she had said, at only a thousand dollars.

"Val, Craig would not have stolen the money."

"You want to bet on that? And he wouldn't have cheated on me either." She leaned toward her, making very close eye contact. "Who else do you think could get into our bank account?"

"It must be a mistake."

"On a Friday night, with the banks closed until Tuesday because of Memorial Day, and Craig nowhere to be found."

"Where would he go? Why would he go?"

Adam nudged the girls aside and made his own search. "Okay, look at this. Here's a withdrawal. Here's another. And another. They're transfers."

"To where?" Val practically shouted.

"I can't figure it out. I'd call my CPA but that would be Craig."

"You better check your account."

Adam shook his head. "He doesn't get into my account."

"Doesn't he have to—"

"Val, you're married to the guy. He's a little more involved with your business than mine." He exhaled. "I'm hungry."

Heidi opened a cupboard, pulled out a box of Wheat Thins, and handed it to him. "Takeout?"

He nodded and dug into the box. "My treat."

Forty-Eight

Something was going on at Heidi's.

From across the courtyard, Liv noticed a man open the front gate, receive a large bag—probably carryout and, from the aroma, probably Chinese—and go into Heidi's cottage.

There was enough of a familiarity about him that cautioned Liv to stay in the shadows rather than call out a hello and sashay over to speak to him as she normally would have done. As she watched, his identity unfolded to her.

Adam Engstrom. Syd's youngest.

Hm.

She had been right not to insert herself into the situation. Until Heidi gave her the go-ahead sign, she thought it best to avoid Adam and Valerie. Any first step taken toward reconciliation had to be theirs. The fact that Adam was actually at the Casa, actually in the vicinity of the Battleaxe, might indicate he'd dipped his big toe into the sea.

"Lord, we could use a Red Sea scenario any day now. Wide, dry path."

Liv went inside her cottage. It was laid out similarly to all eleven of them, L-shaped living room and galley kitchen. Off the living room, through an archway, hers had a square hall with doors to the bathroom, a linen cabinet in the wall, and the bedroom. Corners were rounded in the old fashioned way. Although she would take Syd and their large house back in a heartbeat, she adored her snug bungalow.

She had gone a bit overboard with the feminine décor. Ruffles, floral, lace, cross-stitch and embroidery were everywhere, most of it in shades of pink. Oils and watercolors painted by local artists filled the walls.

Knickknacks consisted of gifts: Lladros from Syd, Iowa's Isabel Blooms from Jasmyn, shells and rocks from Tasha, Mexican pottery from Inez, candles and vases from friends.

When she moved from her house ten years ago, she brought with her as much furniture as she could stuff into the three rooms. Couch, chairs, recliner, dining table that opened out to seat eight, hutch, queen-size bed, end tables, nightstands, lamps, and dishes. There was not a bare corner anywhere.

Yes, one's first impression was of clutter. But she and Tobi liked it. Most importantly, many residents could, at the same time, find a place to sit and eat. The young ones didn't mind the floor or the bay window seat.

She went into the bedroom now, to the low dresser she and Syd had shared. Atop, on a doily in an eight-by-ten pearled frame, was her favorite photo of him. Unlike his funny movie star pose that she kept on the office wall, this photo captured him unawares. Sky and a hillside of leafy green plants were in the background. Turned slightly sideways, he appeared to be looking at them, a small smile on his lips.

Liv had taken it at Adam's Garden, years and years before it was Adam's Garden. That day Syd had bought it for Adam, for when he returned from overseas. Or for when Syd died.

Her husband had known what would speak to his son, even though his son could not hear the words Syd spoke to him until his father had been long gone.

"Syd, he's here."

She sat on a frilly vanity stool and had herself a good cry.

Forty-Nine

Adam shut the door to Heidi's cottage—and to a whole lot of female hysteria—and walked out into the cool night air.

"Whew."

He glanced around the courtyard and gave himself a moment to let the noise in his head dissipate. His sister was absolutely bonkers. Not that he blamed her. He simply couldn't watch it any longer.

Heidi was holding her own, level-headed as usual. Even in their ridiculously carefree days of college she had a practical streak a mile wide, which probably saved them both from a heap of trouble. They'd not been arrested or in an accident or robbed. Or worse. And they had managed to graduate.

But he saw the deep concern in her furrowed brow and sad eyes. Too much had been thrown at her in recent months.

The night's quiet seeped into him. It was not the fathomless silence of the farm. He could hear distant freeway traffic, train whistle, and sirens. But it was enough to induce stillness.

He walked a path lit by solar lamps, toward the sound of a gentle trickle, and came to a fountain. It welcomed him to sit and—as a favorite writer of his put it—entertain silence in his heart and listen for God's voice.

If there was a spot of ground available, Adam avoided chairs. He sank cross-legged onto the flagstones, still warm from the day's sun. Behind him the fountain sang. He inhaled alyssum, eucalyptus, jasmine, soil, sea air, and a hint of pine.

Heidi came to mind. Naturally.

The essence of his friend was fading away. Living in this little safe

223

harbor had helped to an extent. Still, though, he saw a vacancy in her eyes. The accident had ripped into her soul and it was leaking.

The accident had also brought her back into his life.

One day at the hospital, he had sat in her room and watched her sleep, her body broken and sprouting tubes. He went home and dug a shallow thirty-foot ditch for furrow irrigation and told Maisie he needed space.

Adam closed his eyes and stopped the train of thought.

Kayaking had been a good gift to Heidi and to himself. His purchase had been outrageous, but worth it. To get her out there again on the ocean had pumped new life into her.

And that…that was everything.

He had sat behind her in the kayak and read her body language. She'd lost too much weight. Her healthy athlete's build was gone along with her long blonde hair. She didn't paddle hard or often. Her weakness was obvious. Even her strong voice was unsure. He'd noticed her slight limp. Getting into the kayak and paddling were accomplished at the speed of sap dripping from a tree.

He had been patient and persistent. True to form, she hadn't quit.

That day a few weeks ago when anger blindsided him, he had been overcome with joy at seeing her at the farm with her dad. He felt transported back to college, relaxed in her presence, wanting to spend time with her.

She wasn't ready to consider the two of them reconnecting. She had so much else to deal with, all that soul leaking. Despite his outrage at the appearance of Livvie McAlister at the gate, the timing could not have been better. It shut him up before he'd made a fool of himself.

He wondered if he would have a chance to speak again.

After a time he opened his eyes. A light from an open doorway drew his attention. He could make out a figure inside. A tall woman. A very tall woman.

His father had been a large man. Adam never had caught up to his height or breadth.

In appearance and every other which way, Syd and Livvie had made a striking couple.

Adam stood and walked to the open doorway. Through it he spotted a desk. She sat behind it. He knocked gently on the door.

Livvie looked up. After a brief hesitation she smiled tenderly. "There you are."

He winced. Attempts at a deep breath failed. His throat ached. At last he whispered, "Yes, here I am."

Fifty

Heidi cleared the table of Chinese takeout containers, noisily crumpling things to muffle the sound of Val crying her eyes out in the bathroom.

Completely on autopilot, she stuffed everything into the trash can, made another pot of coffee, and thought about kayaking with Adam earlier. A remnant of euphoria remained. Kind of like a jet's vapor trail in the sky long after it was out of sight.

There was a knock on the door. Adam must have locked it on his way outside to get some fresh air. More likely he went to get away from the two crazy women.

Heidi wondered how long it would take for the truth to sink into her. She and Val were in deep trouble. It didn't matter tonight what or how it happened. They might have to call the police to find Craig and report stolen money.

Jiggers, it's the cops.

She groaned and opened the door. "Piper!"

"Oh, good!" Her eyes were wide and full of concern. "You're okay. I am so, so sorry I told Val you were kayaking with Adam and that you probably went from Seaside Harbor. Heidi, I really don't break confidences, but she was unbelievably upset."

"No worries. She needed to find me. She's here now."

Piper slapped a hand over her mouth.

Heidi smiled. The girl was so refreshing. Hud really should get off the starting block and get serious about her. "She's in the bathroom. We're having some major business issues."

"I'm sorry. Can I do anything?"

Heidi shook her head. "I'd ask you to make us dinner but we had take-out."

"You could have asked Liv. Seriously, she always has casseroles tucked away—ohmygosh. Val is here. As in *here*? At the Casa? At Liv's place?"

"Hard to believe, I know. Adam is too. He's out for a walk."

"Does Liv know?"

"We haven't seen her. Probably best to keep it that way for now."

"It sounds like you have enough else going on. Call me if you need anything, okay? Please."

"Thanks."

"Sure." She turned and then she turned back. "How was the kayaking?"

Heidi's tension instantly drained and she smiled. "It was simply amazing."

Piper gave her a thumbs-up and a huge grin.

As she walked away, Heidi's mind raced back to the mess they were in. She should let her parents know. Not yet. No reason to disrupt their night. They could wait until tomorrow. Hud— "Piper." She stepped outside. "There is something you might do for me."

"What?"

"Would you mind calling Hud? Tell him...um...tell him..." Why keep it a secret? SunView Property Management Agency would be a headline by tomorrow. "Tell him someone wiped out our bank account."

Piper walked promptly back over to her and wrapped her in a tight hug.

Autopilot mode turned itself off and for the second time that day, Heidi burst into tears.

Fifty-One

Liv wanted to embrace Adam, Syd's own flesh and blood. Two things kept her seated behind the desk. One, her legs wobbled like crazy. She couldn't trust them to hold her up. And two, there were way too many conflicting emotions parading across the young man's face.

"Have a seat, Adam."

"Uh, thanks." He glanced around the office and chose the stuffed chair in the corner.

Having the desk between them simply would not do. Liv put her palms on it and pushed herself to her feet. "Well, this is awkward."

"About as awkward as it can get."

Smiling, she kept a hand on the desk for support as she shuffled round it and went for the chair across the lamp table from his. "I was talking about my empty kitchenette." She gestured toward the back of the room. "I have no tea or cookies to offer you. What were you talking about?"

He smiled then.

She saw his father's eyes and thought her heart might burst with joy and sadness and everything in between.

"Cookies," he said. "I was talking about cookies. I can do without tea but Dad said your chocolate chip macadamia nut were incomparable."

She laughed, long and hard.

He joined her.

After a bit, he said, "I don't know where to begin."

"How about…" She paused. "How about we just begin?"

"All right." He nodded. "All right, but I want to say two things. I know it wasn't your fault. And I know he loved you with his whole being."

Liv sat back in her chair, speechless, her throat wobbly as her legs.

"Let's make it three things." He inhaled one deep breath and exhaled. "I also know that you loved him, Livvie. That you loved him dearly."

If he added a fourth thing, she would end up on the floor, a wobbling mass of gelatin.

Fifty-Two

Heidi heard the front door open and left the kitchen table to meet Adam as he reentered the cottage. He had been gone a long time.

"Adam. Val's on the phone with—"

"We talked." His smile was goofy, the kind he'd typically shrug after and say *beats me*.

She waited for him to say it.

Instead, though, he stepped close to her, pulled her into a hug, and held her fast without a word. She slipped her arms around him and smelled the night air in his shirt.

Through the years, they had hugged frequently, as friends do. In greeting, in saying goodbye, in laughter, in turmoil. Even in pretending they were a couple in order to deter another guy or girl from making unwanted advances.

This wasn't one of those hugs. Heidi wasn't sure what it was…except more.

He had talked? To whom? Slowly it dawned on her: Liv. He and Liv had talked.

Adam whispered *thank you* into her hair and let go.

"You talked and it was good." Heidi smiled.

"Nah, it wasn't good. It was stupendous." He shrugged. "Beats me."

She chuckled.

He looked toward the kitchen. "Is she yelling at Craig?"

"Yeah. All I gather is that he's been with Treena."

"Oh, geeze. 'Been with,' as in 'been with,' as in not just tonight?"

"She's the one. I didn't catch for how long. Tonight he took her to the airport and had his phone turned off this whole time."

Val charged through the kitchen, shouting into the phone. "I said get over there now! You have no choice." She punched a finger against her phone and grabbed her handbag off of a chair. "Come on. He's meeting us at the house."

Exhaustion pulled at every nerve in Heidi's body. "We can't do anything tonight, can we? Let's start fresh in the morning—"

"Where is your head, Hathaway? Our account has been drained. We. Have. No. Money. Our CPA swears he did not touch it. If he can't find it, as of tomorrow morning we are out of business."

"Val, there are all sorts of safety measures in place. The bank wouldn't—"

"And you know this, how? Pack your pjs. It's going to be a long night."

Adam said, "Val, are you calm enough to drive?"

"I'm fine."

"I'll bring Heidi. You go ahead."

Val left in a huff.

Adam's brows rose. "Probably not a good time to introduce her to Livvie. Are you okay to go?"

She wasn't, but she couldn't abandon Val tonight.

⟲

Craig Laughlin resembled a little boy, a genuinely nice one. He had a small face, neatly trimmed blonde hair, a quiet demeanor, and not one malicious bone in his body. Heidi had asked him once if he'd ever owned a dog named Lassie. He had said no and blushed.

Tonight he looked haggard.

In Adam's truck on the ride over, Heidi wondered aloud how in the world Treena had ripped such integrity from Craig. "And don't say because he's a male. That excuse is so overused. Craig is—was—oh, he still is—a sincerely good guy. Cheating on Val simply would not have been an option for him."

"There's no easy explanation, Heidi. But Treena couldn't seduce him if he didn't give her permission."

"That just stinks. He didn't steal the money too, did he?"

Adam had reached over for her hand and given it a squeeze.

At Val and Craig's house, the four of them crowded into the bedroom used for a home office. Craig preferred the desktop computer and easy access to papers and reference books rather than working in their more spacious kitchen on a laptop.

Like every other room in the house, it was professionally decorated by Val and Adam's mother. Fortunately, Val had worked closely with her mom, going for resale value rather than the outlandish statement Cathy produced at Adam's café. Colors were neutral, lighting bright, chairs comfortable.

Heidi missed the tranquility that the Laughlin home had offered in past days.

At the moment Craig was scrolling through the accounts exactly like they had done at the cottage, over and over again, expressing disbelief over and over again.

Craig said, "I don't understand this."

Seated on the leather loveseat beside Adam, legs curled beneath her, Heidi fought to keep her eyes open. She felt almost sick to her stomach, a combination of exhaustion and dread. Sleep would help. That ER doctor would reiterate the effects of stress on her spleenless body. Liv would remind her that this was not how she should take care of herself.

But what else could she do?

She wore sweats and had packed a change of clothing and a few other items. If she spent the night, then Adam wouldn't have to backtrack to take her home. She'd ride with Val to the office. Or the bank?

She would go to bed, but the trouble was that Val's guest bed was a small hide-a-bed which they now sat on. Although the house was large and lovely, it had only two bedrooms, this office and the master bedroom. Maybe she could go downstairs to the couch in the family room. Just lay her head down…

Val poked Craig's shoulder. "Did you move the money?"

"For the hundredth time, Val, no, I did not move the money. I had no idea this happened. No idea."

"Then do something. Do your magic." Her voice had softened to a dull butter knife. "You're the accountant. Find it."

He worked at the computer. After what felt like an eon, he sat back in the ergonomic desk chair, took his hands off the ergonomic keyboard, clasped them on his lap, and murmured something.

"What?"

"Hundreds of thousands of dollars disappears…" He whispered and gulped several times. "In the Caymans. I can't pick up another trail. The final transfer occurred around five o'clock tonight."

The three of them stared at the back of Craig's head.

At last he swiveled around. He'd gone from haggard to someone in need of CPR. "Treena took it. Embezzled it. Stole it. I'm sorry, Val. I'm sorry, Heidi. I…I showed her a little bit of what I do for your agency. She wanted to learn everything about the business. I showed her some banking stuff, basic stuff anyone who does online banking would know. But she acted like she didn't know. I explained the separate accounts to her. How we keep aside money for taxes, for insurance, for salaries. Your savings." His face reddened. "Stupid, stupid ego. She played me. Somehow, she hacked her way inside. Somehow, maybe, she figured out the passwords."

Val's tone hit razor sharp again and she swore loudly.

Heidi scrunched further down, laid her head on the couch's wide arm, and smelled its leather.

Val screeched, "Where is she, Craig? Where was she going?"

"New York City. To visit family."

"She doesn't have family in New York City!"

He swiveled back around. "I have to make some phone calls."

Heidi closed her eyes.

Fifty-Three

After Heidi's tearful breakdown, Piper had gone home and phoned Hud. When he didn't answer, she left a voicemail. "Hi, it's Piper. Um, Heidi asked me to call. Long story short—Actually, I don't know the long version. Anyway, uh, they're missing money. She and Val. She said their bank account was drained. Isn't that awful? She's upset. Who wouldn't be? She'll call when she knows more. And, uh, well I guess that's it. Bye."

Now, a couple of hours later, Heidi had called from Adam's truck and asked her to phone Hud again and Liv, to let them know she was all right and would be at Val's working with her and her husband. She'd probably spend the night there.

Piper cringed at the thought of her nervous voice earlier and gave herself a verbal shake. "You sounded like some gaga teenager. Get a grip, Pipe. You talked to the guy last night. He's an acquaintance. No big deal."

Right. Piper could almost hear her friend Zoey laughing her contagious laugh…stating with utmost faith that Jared would give her his blessing to fall in love…

"Honestly, it's a simple phone call. You're passing on a message. It's nothing to do with liking the guy. In that way."

And what way would that be? Puppy love. Crush. Head over heels.

Yep. The last one.

"Nuts, nuts, nuts!"

She grabbed her cell and called Liv. "I hope you're awake."

The woman's low chuckled filled her ear. "I am now."

"I'm sorry."

"And I'm joking. What's going on?"

"Heidi asked me to call you. She's probably going to spend the night at Val's. Something has come up." Heidi had said she could tell Liv about the missing money, so she proceeded to do that.

"Oh my. That's terrible. Are you all right?"

"Me?"

"You sound a bit off."

"I'm fine. A little tired."

"And?"

The woman had heard an *and*. Uncanny.

"Piper dear, you can tell me to mind my own business."

"Why would I do that?" She couldn't help but laugh. It ended in a whimper. "Bottom line, I have to call Hud and give him the news and I have…I have feelings for him and…and now I've told you so maybe I can call him and act like I don't."

"Why would you want to act like you don't?"

"I don't want to encourage him. Neither do I want to scare him away."

Liv laughed. "Clear as mud. I'm sure you'll hit just the right balance. Goodnight, dear."

Piper paced through her bungalow twice and then, standing in the middle of the living room, she phoned Hud again.

"Piper. Hi. I just listened to your voicemail. Is she okay?"

"As much as she can be. There's nothing new to report really." She explained about Heidi going to Val's. "She wanted me to tell Liv that she might not be home tonight."

"I didn't know the Casa was a girls' boarding school." There was a grin in his voice. "I'm glad you two have a mother hen keeping watch over you."

"So is my mom."

"I should call Heidi."

"Things sound a little crazy for her. When I stopped in her place, Val was crying in the bathroom and Heidi cried when I hugged her. I think she was just limiting her phone calls. She's so exhausted. Did you know Adam took her kayaking today?"

"Really? No kidding?" He laughed. "That's fantastic. Yeah, I bet she is wiped out. Good old Adam. I guess that means they're on speaking terms again."

"She called him."

"Good for her. Well, between you, Liv, and him, she's in good hands. So how was your day?"

Besides mommy hormones and crying in the food court it was… "Interesting. Remember I told you last night about the old photos I found on my camera?"

"Yes. Soccer tournament on the base."

"Before work I met an old friend for lunch at the mall. She was there that day with her four kids. I had pictures for her. She loved them."

"She's a military wife?"

"Was. Her husband is an insurance agent now. They live in Orange County. Not too far from the mall."

"Do you see her often? Or others from back then?"

"No. We've drifted apart. Most are out of the service and don't live close by. And, um, well that's the way it is."

"I imagine you were a tight group. Wives and girlfriends. Husbands and boyfriends?"

"There were two husbands. Their wives served with Jared." Her stomach ached. She sat in a chair and bent forward. "I sort of went off the deep end when it all happened. I…I couldn't stand to be around those women. Life went on for them. Not for me. I drank with some of the guys at bars near the base. Eventually I went my own way. That sounds so…I don't know what. Nothing good anyway."

"It sounds like pain. Don't beat yourself up for acting out on it."

Piper shut her eyes and simply breathed for a few moments. She straightened back up. "So how was your day?"

"More emotional than yours."

She recognized the tease in his tone. "No way."

"Yes. My good guy tracked the bad guy down to Puerto Vallarta. Turns out it was a trap."

"Yikes. Then what happened?"

While Hud told the story in his soothing tone, she slumped down in the chair and swung her legs over the arm.

Ending the day with his voice in her ear could easily become habit-forming.

Fifty-Four

Heidi awoke with a start and realized her face was mashed against upholstery. The racket of a coffee bean grinder reverberated through her.

She groaned and rolled over. New day, different couch. What was up with that? She was on Val's sofa this time, in a family room, at one end of a large open area that encompassed it, the kitchen, and dining area.

"Yo, Heidi!" Val called from behind the counter where she poured ground beans into a coffeemaker. "Time to get a move on. We have to get to Craig's office ASAP."

Sunlight streamed through a wall of windows. The morning mists of *May gray* and *June gloom* did not typically linger where Val lived and where Heidi's condo was, far inland from Seaside Village. The sun burned them off early. It was an odd thing to notice, but she suddenly missed overcast skies, salty scents, and quaint cottages.

She pulled a blanket over her face and felt a vague tickling sensation. Or was it bubbling? Or sheer joy? She resisted the urge to giggle. There was absolutely no reason to smile, let alone giggle. Her life careened out of control on the freeway almost four months ago and last night it flew into one more rollover. Why...

Oh right. Last night. Yesterday. Adam.

Talking, laughing, kayaking, riding in his truck, eating at her place. It was all so familiar and comfortable. Like old times.

She blinked under the blanket. There had been the hug after he talked with Liv. And then later, much later in the middle of the night, there had

237

been his arm around her, steering her down the stairs and onto the sofa. He had found a pillow for her. He had covered her with the blanket. He had…kissed her forehead, whispered goodnight, and promised to see her later.

Not like old times. More like a whole brand new world.

Had she imagined the kiss?

"Hathaway, wake up!"

"I'm awake." She lowered the blanket and sat. "What did I miss?"

Val walked over and handed her a cup of coffee. "My threat to sue Craig's firm?"

"Val, come on. That wouldn't help."

She yanked the blanket off the end of the couch and sat. She wore charcoal gray slacks and jacket with a peach silk shell, pearls, and black pumps, her *get out of my way, I mean business* outfit. "It would help channel this anger. I have never been so mad."

"I hadn't noticed." Heidi sipped her coffee.

"We have appointments. Craig and some investigator at his office. A lawyer at the lawyer's office."

"I only brought chinos and a T-shirt with me."

Val glared. Her eyes were clear, their hazel color enhanced by perfectly applied eye shadow and liner. Her perfectly applied foundation did not even crease. Not one chestnut hair strayed from its perfectly styled place.

"It's a nice T-shirt. No logo."

"Find something in my closet. You've lost enough weight to fit into my skirts, I'm sure. Or call that Piper woman. Couldn't she go inside your quaint cottage and find a suit and run it over here?"

"First off she doesn't have a key and she works—"

"Whatever. Did you bring makeup? You might think about covering up the scar. Soften it a little. I have some great stuff in the vanity drawer. And if you can get by without those weird glasses—well, I know you can't see without them. Weren't you going to get contacts again?"

Val was on a roll. Heidi let her get to the end of the litany of criticisms before she said, "What about Cynthia and Dawn? Did you tell them?"

"Not much. Only that Treena embezzled every last penny."

"Was it every last penny?"

"I don't know. We'll meet them at the office later. Cynthia offered to cover the Belson open house. Dawn said she'll stay available for whatever we need."

"Val, what exactly do we need?"

"A miracle. Go get dressed. Please."

A miracle?

Heidi mentally composed her own to-do list. Calling the woman who prayed about everything filled the number-one slot.

Fifty-Five

Liv never needed much of an excuse to throw a picnic in the Casa court-yard. The sky was blue? *Inez, do you have time to make tamales? Noah, that yummy taco casserole of yours would be great. Chadwick, we always need snacks. Riley, your strawberry cake is the best dessert ever.*

Official holidays, though, brought with them the added sense of a turning point, a watershed moment so to speak.

Memorial Day marked the beginning of summer, weeks before the longest day of the year in June. Lifeguards went back on duty. Multitudes of tourists began their festive assault on Seaside Village. Desert and ocean weather collided, producing overcast mornings and warming afternoon temps. Outdoor concerts and theater began.

Liv sat at one of the tables now, admiring her and little Tasha's hand-iwork. They had decorated the courtyard with festive tablecloths, succulents in pots as centerpieces, and strings of Japanese lanterns around the center. Colorful plasticware and napkins were stacked at one end of the long table where, at the moment, food was being organized by Déja. The teen had taken a sudden, most likely passing interest in her father's gourmet skills and eagerly volunteered to pitch in.

Not everyone had arrived yet. Piper was still at the store. Jasmyn and Keagan were at the gym, closing it up early. Beau was at home, fixing his Granny Mibs' Best Doggone Ever Potato Salad.

Just returned that afternoon from Arizona, Samantha sat now beside Liv, her dark eyes shining. She had let her thick black hair grow out a bit and the new style softened her stoic engineer demeanor. "Liv, how did he do it? How did Beau take my messy memories of growing up on the rez and turn them into treasures?"

Chuckling, Liv leaned over and gave the young woman a quick hug. "Samantha, there is no answer to that except that's just Beau."

"I know," she whispered. "And he loves me."

"Yes, he does."

"He even had my mother doting on him. I doubt she'll come to the wedding, but she said she might."

"May I ask, did you decide on a date?"

"You may ask." She smiled and offered no more information.

Before falling in love with Beau Jenner, Samantha had never been one to tease others. Liv grinned. "All right, I will. Did you decide on a date?"

"Yes, we did decide." Again, she abruptly stopped talking.

"What is the date?"

Samantha's face shone like a rising sun. "July thirtieth. We really, really want to do it here, in the courtyard. Would you mind?"

Liv laughed. "Goodness, what a splendid idea. I would love for you to get married here. I think that will be a first for the Casa."

"It'll be small. Beau's pastor will do the ceremony. Jasmyn's my maid of honor. Keagan is best man. Tasha is flower girl. You know Beau has no family and I don't, not to speak of anyway. We're inviting my boss and his family, a few of Beau's friends, and everyone from the Casa, of course. Jojo's Catering will do the food."

"No potluck?" Liv chuckled. "And what about a honeymoon?"

"British Columbia. Trees and wilderness."

"Perfect. How long?"

"Two weeks." She leaned in close to Liv. "I never imagined I would be part of a family like yours here. I never imagined I would get married."

Liv patted her cheek. "I did, dear."

Samantha's dark eyes glistened with tears, a rare sight. "I know."

"And I am tickled to pieces for you and Beau. Even if you have to move."

"You intuit everything, don't you?"

"I just pay close attention to those I care about."

"We were strangers that day in Jitters when you told me about your vacant Cottage Seven."

"What can I say? Sometimes I get nudged to care about a stranger."

Samantha grinned. "Thank you."

"Thank the One who nudges."

"Amen." She straightened. "You haven't asked where we'll live after we get married."

"You'll leave the Casa. It's what naturally comes next for you two."

"It is. I don't like it, but I would like even less not living with Beau. He just doesn't fit well inside these old bungalows."

"That's the truth. Whenever I see him duck his head to get through a doorway, I think of a bear and I want to get the breakables out of his way." She spotted Beau walking toward them, all six-foot-five, two-hundred plus pounds of him. "Speaking of the bear."

He stopped beside Samantha's chair. "What bear? Are you talking about me?"

"Do you know another bear?" Samantha took hold of his hand. "I was telling Liv our plans."

He knelt and slipped an arm over Samantha's shoulders. "Miss Liv, I am truly sorry for stealing her away from the Casa."

"I appreciate that, Beau. I'll miss her like the dickens, but it's the appropriate next step for you two. Will you live in your apartment?"

They told her no, they'd found a house to lease, available September first, six blocks away. Until then, they would live in Number Seven.

Beau added, "I'll wear a helmet. That way when I hit my head on a doorjamb, I won't get bruised."

Samantha laughed, totally enamored with her guy.

Liv could speak altruistic words until she was blue in the face, but her emotions roared with selfishness. When she heard now that she would have the entire summer to grow accustomed to the idea of Samantha leaving and that their new home was a mere six blocks away, her heart expanded.

Beau and Samantha set off to help Déja with the food table. Liv gave her own "Martha" self a time-out and simply sat, "Mary" style.

One of the enjoyable features of a potluck was that it gave everyone an opportunity to touch base with everyone else. Given the proximity of their living arrangements, it seemed they would all run into each other often, but that was not the case.

For a few minutes, she simply watched conversations form, a living and breathing organism of community. Not for the first time, she thanked God that they all got along. Samantha used to be standoffish. Chadwick used to get on everyone's nerves. Noah used to allow little Tasha to get on his nerves. Louie still had no patience for Coco and her wheelchair, probably because he feared he'd be confined to one in the future.

Liv chuckled to herself. What would she do if these people snipped and groused and gossiped? She'd probably not hold potlucks.

Heidi slid into the empty seat beside her. "May I have an audience with the queen?"

"Oh, dear. Is that what I act like?"

"Yes, but a benevolent one. Wise too." She winked. "You won him over."

Liv sighed. "Truly?"

"Yes, truly, truly."

"Well." She smiled. "Well. My goodness. I don't know what else to say."

Heidi laughed.

They hadn't seen each other for days. They hadn't had a chance to revel together in the aftermath of that red-letter moment when Adam knocked on her office door Friday night.

But Piper and Heidi had kept her in the loop. Late Friday night, Piper had told her that Heidi was spending the night at Val's because of a business emergency. Saturday morning, Heidi phoned and said that apparently someone had wiped out the agency's bank account.

Liv assumed the girls had kept her informed because she was a mother figure to them and would worry about a long absence. Much as she tried to downplay that Mama Liv role, they picked up on it and, fortunately, did not seem to begrudge her for it. Now she wondered if they would add *queen* to her list of nicknames. She hoped not.

Heidi said, "Adam plans to be here today."

Liv put a hand on her chest. It took a moment for her to find her voice. "Oh, my. Here for a potluck. Oh, my."

Heidi nodded. "Major surprise, huh? He's changed since the other night when you two talked. I can't explain it. It's like something has been settled inside of him."

"I gather that he's decided to stop letting childhood pain define him. He's forgiving me, his dad, and, I hope, his mother. A deep wound has begun to heal. That releases him to move forward."

Heidi grew quiet, her eyes focused on something unseen.

Liv assumed she followed a train of thought that needed attention. She waited.

At last Heidi made eye contact. "Apparently Treena, our recently hired intern, fooled all of us and stole the money. Of course I'm angry at her and scared about what comes next, but somehow it doesn't feel personal. Professionals will work on the mess. Val and I will work on redefining business. It's the other that feels personal."

"The other?"

"The accident. I'm redefining who I am."

"That is rather personal."

"But whose fault is it? Who do I blame? Who must I forgive in order to release myself to move on like Adam has?"

"Who *do* you blame?"

"Me, myself, and I." Her face sort of folded in on itself. "I feel so stupid. So reckless. So clueless. So selfish. So ugly. So unlovable. And to top it off, the accident led to the agency fiasco. If I'd been there, pulling my weight, Treena could not have gotten away with this."

"Heidi, dear, forgiving ourselves can be the hardest of all."

"What if I had killed or maimed other drivers or passengers? A little kid?"

Liv reached over and squeezed Heidi's hand. "Shh, shh. You didn't. That did not happen. Yes, it could have. Yes, you caused a terrible thing as it is. You changed your life forever, robbed yourself of abilities. You were absent from work and maybe that led to an opening for Treena to do her awful deed, although honestly, she could have still—"

"No. Not with me there." Tears trickled down Heidi's cheeks.

"Well, the important thing is, you've accepted that you were responsible for the accident. You'll pay for it every time your leg aches or your car insurance premium comes due. But where does it say that you have to carry the guilt around?"

Heidi blotted her cheeks with a napkin.

"Dear one, God has already forgiven you. There's no reason for you not to forgive yourself."

"I remember hearing that in Sunday school when I was a kid. But…" She shrugged.

"But you find it hard to trust. Jesus showed us through His life and death that God is love. That He accepts and forgives us, no matter what we've done or haven't done. He welcomes us all into His presence."

"Even me?"

"Even you."

"I feel like…I'm not sure. Since the accident I seem to keep bumping into something bigger than me. It happens with you. With Piper. Jasmyn. Keagan. And Adam too." She paused. "It started before I met you, though. There was a nurse in the hospital. And before that, at the scene. The medic who kept talking to me made me feel so calm." Her breath caught, as if a new thought had just struck. "It's like whispers of love from all of you."

"They *are* whispers of love, Heidi. All that bumping is into Someone, the Spirit of Christ."

"He loves me?"

"He's wild about you."

"Really?"

"Really."

"How do I…?" She tilted her head, her forehead creased. "How…?"

"How do you live out of being cherished by God?"

"Yeah."

"Pay attention to the bumpings. Let yourself receive what Jesus offers. Love. Hope. Peace. Joy. In spite of circumstances, He will give your heart a deep, abiding sense of all of that if you let Him."

"My heart." She made a wry face. "Life seemed easier when I kept it a little on the chilly side."

Liv smiled. "Is it warming?"

"Oh, it's a slushy puddle. I can't find an ice cube anywhere." The tears began again.

Tasha appeared at Heidi's side. The child touched her shoulder and pressed a wad of bright orange napkins into her hand.

"Thanks, hon. I'm sorry."

Liv said, "No need to be sorry. Tears are never a problem. We're all family here. Aren't we, Tasha?"

"Yes, we are family." There was a smile on her lips and a question in her eyes.

Liv nodded.

Tasha grinned and hugged Heidi long and hard. Then she twirled in a circle and loudly began to sing to the *We Are Family* tune. "We are family!

I got all my Casa peeps with me." She waved her arms and danced away. "Stand up everybody. Come and dance around the courtyard with me."

Few could deny Tasha. Inez was the first to join in. Chadwick wiggled his hips over to a singing Coco and helped her stand. They swayed together. Déja joined hands with Louie and they kicked up their heels. Others soon followed until even Noah stomped a foot and sang. The musician in him was no doubt appalled, but community won him over.

Heidi stood. "I think I can still dance." She shuffled around and grinned. "Maybe not quite like I used to."

Maybe not, but Heidi Hathaway danced and her tears dried.

Liv followed suit, giving thanks the whole time for Heidi's slushy heart.

Fifty-Six

Adam knelt in the dirt, in the moonlight, at one end of two twenty-foot long trenches he had just dug. The Rose Finn Apple seed potatoes waited in a bushel basket beside him.

At times gardening was back-breaking work. At times it meant hours lost in research. At still other times, like tonight, it was more of a mental catch and release.

Any which way, it fed his soul like nothing else could.

The trenches were not deep, only about the length of his hands. The soil had already been tilled. The organic seed tubers were cut and had dried for twenty-four hours. They preferred not to wait any longer before being pressed into the earth, their eyes facing up.

The success of Adam's Garden surprised him every single day. He hadn't known the first thing about growing vegetables before he began working with the former owners of the farm. Those two were not particularly visionaries. They planted enough to eke out a living on just under ten acres. They were happy to take Syd Engstrom's money and later his son's willingness to give it a go.

Adam experimented like a mad scientist, following his passion and ignoring guidelines. Vegetables grew. He added sixteen acres. The rest was history.

Heirlooms and folklore intrigued him. *Plant potatoes at night so the eyes don't see the light.* Some said plant by the full moon. He went with those and disregarded the lateness of the season and the climate recommendations.

The Rose Finn Apple was a fingerling with skin the color of blush, a golden buttery flesh, and an earthy taste. His gourmet market would enjoy them. He placed a potato in the hole and sank his fingers into the dirt. Only then was he ready to begin to process the emotional junk that had been accumulating.

He had planned on going to the potluck at the Casa de Vida, the House of Life. The name suited Livvie. It suited his father. Adam regretted that he had missed out on their private wedding and their dozen years together. He regretted the loss deeply.

The topic remained a bone of contention between him and his sister, more so since Heidi's move into the Casa. That morning he had managed to elevate it to new heights by telling Val that he had, more or less, made up with their father's wife. There had been much toxic spewing from Val. He ducked behind his virtual shield, a trick he borrowed from a video game he'd been playing one day when she blew up. He was nine years old at the time. It served him well into adulthood.

That was not what kept him from attending the potluck, however. When he phoned Heidi to cancel, he blamed it on the hectic day and the unfinished chores. Life at the Garden sometimes preempted other aspects of life. Until February first of that year, that truth had not concerned him in the least.

The Garden allowed him to live out his passion. He hired staff of similar bent. He carried on some sort of relationship with Maisie. She was…comfortable. Her eyes were deep brown pools, she baked like a dream, and she displayed none of the extremes his sister and mother were famous for.

By now, most of their friends were married. They hesitated. Some unnamed matter had hung between them for years. Like the whiff of the scent of a plant growing out of sight, it came and went. He never grasped if it was flower or weed.

Maybe it was both.

Soon after Heidi's accident, he saw fear in Maisie's eyes. It turned to sadness. Today it had turned to stone.

"You love her, Adam. You always have. My assistant will be delivering the bread from now on."

And that was that.

For Maisie it had been a weed. For Adam, a flower. The trouble was, he had no idea how to cultivate the thing.

Dealing with the finality was what kept him away from the potluck.

Fifty-Seven

On the Tuesday morning after Memorial Day, Heidi sat in the lobby of SunView Property Management Agency. It was only six-thirty. Sam had dropped her off. They were both on the early track today.

She liked riding with Sam. She was an aggressive driver, but with a measure of defensiveness Heidi had lacked. Sam would make an excellent role model for her. If Heidi ever decided to get behind the wheel of a car again. If she could ever afford car payments and insurance. *If, if, if.* Given the current business situation, the imminent loss of her condo renters, and medical bills, affording anything seemed a horrendously iffy proposition.

"I miss driving. Oh, I miss it so much."

She did? Really? Since when?

Could it be she was getting on with life?

"Honestly, at the moment I'd rather keep up the ostrich role. My head in the sand feels exactly right. And why am I talking out loud to myself?"

Or was she talking to something, someone more?

Liv would say she was getting in touch with the Source, tapping into the life that flowed through her. In other words, praying. When Heidi had phoned Liv Saturday morning and told her about the mess, Liv said she would pray for them all to have wisdom to figure things out. Then she suggested, in that manner of hers that came within a hair's breadth of annoying, that Heidi might talk to God too.

"What do you mean?" Heidi had asked.

"Well, dear, I don't imagine God far away in the sky. I see God as always with us and within us, as close as the air we breathe. Always listening and ready for dialogue. Always the Source, ready to pour courage and insight into us. Sometimes it helps to speak out loud. For myself, that makes God seem more present."

"That's praying?"

"I believe so. An attitude of gratitude puts me in a receptive mood. I try to begin with a thank you, although that's not always possible in an emergency."

"Like my accident. I yelled 'help' when I flew off the freeway. Was I praying?"

"Most definitely. Heidi, I never asked, did you have a near-death experience?"

"No."

"Too bad. I enjoy those stories. I guess you were given down-to-earth medics who knew what they were doing."

Heidi smiled now. Yes, she had been given down-to-earth people who provided exactly what her body needed. "You know, God, I could do with a bit of ooey-gooey comfort and encouragement here."

So much for an attitude of gratitude. Whining came naturally as a default mode.

Heidi leaned back in the armchair and admired the office she and Val could no longer afford. "All right, I can do gratitude. Thank You for the years in this nice place."

The lobby was cozy with two distinct seating areas to either side, complete with coffee tables, lamps, and silk plants. Soft southwestern pastels dominated. A low wooden divider with an opening in the center separated it from the desks that Cynthia and Dawn used. Behind those were a glassed-in conference room and a small office. To the right, out of view, down a short hall, were her and Val's offices, a restroom, and a back door that led to an alley.

On the desk in the small office beside the conference room sat a name plaque. *Treena Smith.*

"Thank You for...? Hm. For removing her from our midst?"

Heidi squirmed in the chair. Developing an attitude of gratitude was turning into a tough assignment.

"Thank You for SunView. For its good reputation. For the good work we've been able to do. Thank You for all the people I've met through it. Thank You for my growth, personally and career-wise. Thank You for Val and our friendship. Thank You for Adam, even if he is a jerk at times."

Adam had not come to the potluck at the Casa. He phoned her and apologized. The day had been hectic with customers galore, he said. Although the Gardens closed early for the holiday, he needed to work. He sent regrets to Liv. His voice had been sincere. He truly had wanted to meet her neighbors and spend time with Liv. So why hadn't he made it happen? She suspected something else besides work was going on, something he didn't want to tell her.

That was the post-college, post-globetrotting Adam, reticent to a fault at times. He slipped into the camaraderie of the old days and then the next minute he communicated like a stranger.

"Huge letdown, God. Huge. For me and Liv. No way can I say thanks for that one. The hurt is too, too much." She hesitated as a new thought came to her.

That too-much hurt sprouted from deep inside. It wasn't from the place where feelings get ruffled because an old friend turned down an invitation.

No, this was crushed heart territory.

Well, she had enough going on in her life. She wasn't about to sign up for that too.

※

Heidi and Val canceled appointments, accepted the offers from Cynthia and Dawn to increase their workloads, and commiserated in Val's office.

Her friend was looking the worse for wear. No amount of coverup could mask the purple puffballs under her eyes. She'd forgotten to put on earrings and her wrinkled white silk blouse refused to stay tucked into the gray skirt. "Let's go over it again."

"You think something will change?"

"You never know."

Heidi couldn't decide if Val was optimistic or stupid. She simply went along and recited the story once more. "Christina Eggers, a.k.a. Treena Smith, played us for chumps and is in Rio with our money, which she started siphoning off some time ago. She holds dual citizenship with the U.S. and Brazil. According to the lawyer, extradition most likely will not happen even if we could prove enough to press charges. Christina/Treena also earned a degree from UCSD. She is one very smart, very mean, very icky person."

"'Allegedly' with our money, Heidi. You have to say 'allegedly.'"

Although investigators had learned Treena's real name and where she had flown to, they had not yet traced the money beyond the first two off-shore accounts.

Val said, "On the upside, insurance will help. Our receivables will help. We have a number of properties in escrow. We still have clients, buyers, and sellers. Craig's working on getting us a loan."

"All that adds up to paying Cynthia and Dawn and the rent for about two more weeks. That's a negative exaggeration, I know, but let's cut to the chase. Stop elongating this miserable process."

"We've been this low before. Almost."

"When we worked out of your house and did not have a staff." She clamped her mouth shut before adding that neither had they owned things like the Jimmy Choos peeking out from under Val's desk.

"At least we both have money in the bank this time."

Heidi's throat closed up. She hummed it clear. "Mm."

"You don't?"

"Once I subtract medical and mortgage payments, no. And I'll still owe on both. If I walked out the door and sold four mid-range houses today, I'd be a smidgen less in the hole."

"You can move back into your condo. That'll save you rent. How much do you pay for the quaint little cottage?"

Heidi told her.

"You are kidding me. That's dirt cheap." Val smirked. "Appropriate for a—"

"Val, please. Don't go there."

"Sorry." Her tone implied she was not the least bit sorry for attacking Liv's character. "If you move home, you'd have different options. Even if you went into foreclosure you might be able to stay for a while without making payments."

She shook her head. "The thought of stairs makes me nauseous. I'd have to buy a car and be able to drive. Or hire a chauffeur full-time. Like that's in the budget. And besides…" She shut her eyes as another new thought wriggled its way into her consciousness.

"Besides what?"

Heidi looked at her and whispered, "I like where I am."

They stared at each other for a long moment.

Val said, "My mother will disown you."

"What about you?"

"Jury's out. At least you've got Adam in your back pocket, but then you always have. What if you sell it? With what you owe and today's market, that would work. Right? You wouldn't make a bundle, but compared to a few months ago, you'd do well enough."

Heidi felt as if a rug had been yanked from under her feet and she landed hard. The sound of a branch snapping echoed over and over.

She caught the first sob in her arms atop the desk.

All she had ever wanted her whole life was to own a home and never ever have to move out of it.

Fifty-Eight

Piper hoped she was not a flibbertigibbet when she was sixty years old.

Stella, the sixty-year-old, was bent over an open drawer behind the counter, shuffling papers. Half-framed, funky styled glasses dangled from a pearl chain around her neck. She slid them onto her nose and tucked her long blonde hair behind an ear. "Now, where did I put that thing?"

The bell above the boutique's front door tinkled and an elderly woman walked in. Her hair was iron gray, cut in a no-nonsense chop. She wore creamy linen slacks and short-sleeved shirt, both crisply ironed, and a severe expression.

With a little stretch of her imagination, Piper decided the expression was her smile.

Stella turned and peered from the tops of her glasses. "Ingrid. Hello. I'll be right with you." She ducked back down.

Piper leaned over the counter. "Stella, may I?"

"Hm?" She looked up at her.

Piper tilted her head toward the customer.

"Oh." She seemed surprised. "Uh." Hesitant. "What an excellent idea!" She winked and called out, "Ingrid, this is Piper Keyes. She's going to be working here."

Piper approached Ingrid near a display of swimsuit cover-ups. "Hello."

"Piper is an unusual sort of name."

"Yes, it is. It was my grandmother's maiden name."

"Is that a fact? What a clever way to keep it going. Maiden names typically get lost in the dust. My grandchildren—not one of the three named after me in any fashion—are coming to visit. They'll want to get in the pool. I'll want to look as if I am interested."

Piper smiled and went to work helping the woman find a piece of clothing that made her feel good about herself and perfect for the occasion. As her dad would say, it was like a walk in the park for her.

Lately at Tellmann's, work resembled a trudge up a muddy hillside. It culminated in the five-day Memorial Day weekend sale, an insane marathon of straightening up after hordes of shoppers as they paraded through the department. Fitting rooms resembled the aftermath of a windstorm.

A short while ago, the moment she entered Stella's, she realized how she longed for a quiet atmosphere. But she had come to inform Stella that she had decided against buying the boutique.

Several red flags steered her to that decision, the latest one being Heidi's situation. First, the mere hint of owning a business and losing money, in whatever manner, still shook her up. Before that, her dad had advised her not to do it. Before that she fell in love with photography again. Before that, Gildy was being nice. Before that, she had met Hud.

Bottom line: if she bought it, she could not pop down to Baja at a moment's notice. Not even a week's notice.

That *twenty-four/seven, this is your life* scenario had begun to sink its sharp teeth into her psyche. The bite hurt.

Ingrid left the shop, clearly content with her purchase. Stella was ecstatic. "I knew you were good, Piper, but that…" She pointed at the door. "You just earned a PhD. Now." She laid a paper on the countertop, removed her glasses and smiled. "Here's my new plan."

When Piper had phoned earlier and said she'd like to stop in, Stella said perfect. She wanted to run an idea by her too. She had changed her mind about selling. Again.

If Piper were honest with herself, she'd admit that Stella's personality concerned her. Owning the shop and not knowing the ropes with the possibility of Stella flying the coop was another red flag.

"Piper, I want to travel. My family and my attorney say that is not a valid reason to quit altogether and sell the place. Sixty is the new forty, you know. I'm taking an Alaskan cruise in July, going to Europe in August, and taking an autumn tour on the East Coast. I have two summer part-timers who start back next week. They've worked here for years and know their way around. So, what do you think about working for me, full-time when I'm in town and managing on top of it while I travel?" She slid the paper over to her. "My attorney said I operate like I have a few loose screws. He advised me to put it in writing, or better yet, pay him to write it up. Here are all the financial details and how our working relationship will specifically play out."

Piper scanned the pertinent points, blinked, and slowed down. The offer was generous in pay and did not legally tie her down. If the woman changed her mind again, Piper could be looking for a job. But the thought of staying on at Tellmann's felt like suffocation. Worrying about the future with a flibbertigibbet paled in comparison.

"Stella, this is—uh, yeah. Yes." She laughed. "I'm not ready to buy. This is exactly what I am ready to do."

ᴓℓℓ

Tuesday evening, one thing led to another at the Casa as they sometimes did when two women squealed with delight in the courtyard.

It began with Piper telling Jasmyn about her new job and, more importantly, showing her what she had brought home from Stella's for Sam. Their laughter drew Liv and Tasha from the office where they had been doing the girl's homework. Heidi came in the front gate, driven home by one of the employees at her agency. Riley came from Coco's bungalow, saw the gathering, went back inside and pushed Coco out to join them. Inez scurried from her place, wearing an apron, her hands dusty with flour.

At last Sam walked down the path from the back gate with Chad, the two of them lost in conversation. They were funny together, like bickering siblings half the time.

As they approached, Piper ducked behind Heidi, hurriedly zipping up an opaque plastic hanging bag. Voices hushed and all eyes went to Sam.

She noticed. "What?"

Chad stomped a foot and pouted. "You girls never let me in on things."

Sam said, "What things?"

"That's the thing. Who knows?"

The giggles started again.

Tasha grabbed Chad's hand. "It's a girls-only thing, silly."

He tapped her nose. "You're silly."

Piper said over Heidi's shoulder, "Sammi, we have a gift for you."

Sam's eyes widened. "You're not supposed to do that. Beau and I don't need a thing. We're combining two complete households."

Chad elbowed her. "Just say thank you already."

Sam sighed. "Thank you already."

Piper said, "We've all been talking and this is what we decided to get for you. But if you don't like it, I'll take it back. No problem."

Inez said, "You are like a daughter to me and Liv, a sister to Piper. You know we wanted to take you shopping."

Piper said, "Exactly. Since you wouldn't let us drag you to the mall, this is what you get." She glanced at Jasmyn who was keeping an eye out for Beau. When she gave her the all-clear nod, Piper swung the bag out of hiding and held it up. "Sorry, Sam, but you can't wear a black business suit to your wedding."

Jasmyn added, "You simply can't." She unzipped the bag and spread open its front to reveal a dress.

Sam put a hand to her mouth.

Chad whistled in admiration.

Piper thought again how beautiful it was. If Stella had not sold it to her at cost, if all the Casa women were not chipping in to pay for it, she still would have bought it for her friend because it was so perfect.

It was a white sheath, covered in beads, and would be absolutely gorgeous on the tall, slender woman who avoided fancy like the plague. It was simple, subtle, and elegant.

Sam touched it. "This is too much. You're all too much."

Inez said, "But do you like it?"

"You think I'll look all right in it?"

Giggles went through the group.

Chad put an arm around Sam's shoulders. "Sammi, Beau's going to take one look at you and think he's died and gone to heaven."

Fifty-Nine

The women in the courtyard dispersed. Piper went to help Samantha try on the gorgeous dress. Liv was certain it would fit. Piper had a knack for sizing and for matching women with styles.

Riley and Tasha picked up the girl's schoolwork from the office and headed home. Liv enjoyed playing the grandmotherly role for them. Their extended family lived on the East Coast. For whatever reason, Riley had not wanted to move back after her divorce from Tasha's father.

"Liv." Jasmyn met her coming out of the office now. "Heidi hasn't had your mac and cheese yet. I'll cook the macaroni. Do you have truffle oil? And the three cheeses?"

"Are we having dinner together, dear?"

Jasmyn nodded, her eyes pleading. She whispered, "She needs a huge, huge dose of comfort tonight."

Of course the girl needed it. "Small group?"

"You, me, Piper. But we'll cook for the army, as usual."

Liv smiled. "Just in case."

A short time later, the four of them sat around Liv's kitchen table while the casserole baked. Heidi filled them in on the latest news.

"Without proof that Treena took the money, we can't do much to recover it or have her arrested. They haven't even found her yet. Investigators are working on it. In the meantime…" She gave them all a little smile. "Thank you for…for this."

Liv squeezed her hand. "It's what we do, dear. You were saying?"

"In the meantime, Val and I are figuring out if we can stay in business or not."

"You're under an enormous amount of stress. How are things otherwise? How is your body holding up?"

There was the briefest squint of her eyes. "My limp is permanent."

"Oh, sweetie."

"You're supposed to say you haven't noticed it." She winked. "I'm kidding. It's noticeable."

Jasmyn said, "I promise not to call you Hop-Along-Heidi."

Piper blurted, "Jasmyn!"

Heidi's smile carried resignation. "It's okay. Really. I figure this is just part of the new me."

Liv said, "It's going to take time for you to get to know that woman."

"Tell me about it. I don't recognize myself half the time. Every single thing has been turned upside down. I love playing the real estate game, but the thought of running SunView feels like a tournament that I'm ineligible for. That I'll always be ineligible for. And then there's my condo. I could use the money from a sale. But I could also keep it and live in it." She sighed loudly. "But I don't want to keep it and live in it."

Liv's mouth formed an O and she stared at the newcomer who had insisted not many months ago that she did not need a home.

Heidi nodded. "So can I stay in Number Three until whenever?"

Liv laughed and clapped her hands.

"I take it that's a yes." Heidi grinned.

⁂

They ate and chatted. Other news spilled from the girls and Liv soaked it all up.

Piper told them about her decision to change jobs. She planned to give her two-week notice tomorrow.

Heidi asked, "Did you tell Hud?" She turned to the others. "Usually I get my Piper updates from him."

Piper blushed. "We don't talk all the time. And no, I haven't told him."

"Well, when you do talk to him," Heidi said, "tell him I'm ready to drive."

Piper reddened further.

Jasmyn said, "That's wonderful. Um, how…who…?"

Piper said, "Hud will take you."

"Nah. He's close to a deadline. You haven't been through one of these yet. He basically goes dark for about a month. If there's an emergency, we contact his neighbor who knows two words in English, 'Get Hud.' At least my brother is not totally out of touch like he was when I had the accident. He was off somewhere in Ecuador. Seriously, when did you talk last?"

"Friday night."

"But who's counting, right?" Heidi smiled. "I'm sorry. I shouldn't tease you. My brother having a friend who is also my friend and a wonderful woman is like the only bright spot on my horizon at the moment."

Jasmyn said, "Piper, you are redder than a beet. I didn't think you ever got flustered."

"I...I..." She made a shooing motion. "Speaking of friends, Adam could take you driving."

It was Heidi's turn to appear rattled. "He's busy, too. My dad would, but he can't visit for a while. I was hoping one of you two wouldn't mind taking me. Once I get over the initial shock, I'll be fine."

Piper and Jasmyn exchanged a glance. Jasmyn cleared her throat. "It's the initial shock part that sounds a little much."

Piper added, "It's your reputation that sounds a *lot* much."

"What reputation? Besides the fact that I flew off the freeway."

"Hud told me about your racecar driving in Las Vegas."

"That's a controlled thing. It's not like I—okay, maybe I did generally drive fast. All the time."

"Too fast?" Piper winced.

"I really was a good driver. You're all giving me a funny look."

Jasmyn said, "Sean would do it. I'll ask him for you."

Liv agreed. "Yes, Keagan is the perfect choice. Nothing scares him. And he's pretty flexible with his schedule."

Jasmyn grinned. "Except he's busy from June twenty-fourth to July second."

"Oh?" Liv saw an extra sparkle in the woman's dark blue eyes. "What is he doing?"

"Getting married and going to Hawaii."

"Jasmyn!" They cried in unison.

"Yeah!" She let out a shriek of delight. "I know."

"When did you decide that?"

"The night he proposed. We didn't want to take attention away from Sam and Beau's wedding, but honestly. The end of July? She is such an engineer, isn't she? She's all about planning. Anyway, we can't wait. We have no reason to wait."

Liv chuckled. Jasmyn was a few years older than Samantha. Keagan was about the age she was when she and Syd had decided to marry. By then, there was no reason to linger. "Once you know, you know."

"The one thing I don't know is if I should change my last name. 'Jasmyn Keagan?' Seriously?"

Piper giggled. "Go with the hyphen. Jasmyn Albright-Keagan. It's a mouthful, but it sounds better."

"And besides," Liv said, "we won't let you drop the 'Albright.' *All bright* is too precious. It's your personality. Okay, tell us more. Are you eloping?"

"Sean would except we want to share the day with others. My Chicago friend Quinn can't make it but…" She paused to squeeze her hands into fists and shake them, like an excited little kid. "My half sister and her family will come and, I hope, all of you."

"We wouldn't miss it," Piper said. "Where?"

"Liv's church. I guess I can call it my church now. Maybe even *our* church. Sean likes it there too. Anyway, we talked to the pastor today."

"Nice." Liv knew that Jasmyn felt something special toward the elderly man. She had been attending services with Liv for several months. Pastor Ted seemed a perfect Jesus example for the woman who was still new to the life of faith in God.

"It'll be on a Friday evening. Afterwards, we'll head straight to the airport."

No party? Liv kept her mouth shut.

Piper shouted, "Woo-hoo!"

"Congratulations." Heidi smiled.

"Oh no!" Piper was still shouting. "You need a dress! Like yesterday!"

"I thought I'd go with the poodle skirt and Mary Janes. I'm sure my boss won't mind. It'd be free advertising."

Piper laughed. "No way. We'll shop at Stella's, okay?"

"Okay." Jasmyn's eyes brimmed with happy tears. "I'd like that."

Heidi said, "I have to say that living at the Casa is like being adopted into a family."

From the glow on Heidi's face, Liv assumed that the independent career woman was perfectly comfortable with that situation.

Thank You, Abba.

Sixty

Piper sat in her car in a far corner of the mall parking that employees used, stunned beyond words.

Twenty minutes ago, her boss Gildy had accepted her resignation, flinging out a few thunderbolts with her response. "You've done an adequate job here. You may leave now. Two weeks' notice is not a requirement. Drop your keys off at the office. Goodbye."

What? That was it? No hug. No *I'm so sorry to see you go*. No party?

"Well, Pipe," she said out loud to herself, "I am amazed you lasted as long as you did." She frowned. "Good riddance."

Now what? She had two free weeks. There were a couple of coworkers she wanted to see. At least they would say they were sorry to see her go. She would shop with Jasmyn for a wedding dress—definitely not at Tellmann's. Heidi might need some help moving out of her condo. She wondered if Zoey had had her baby yet. Maybe Stella would let her start the new job ahead of schedule.

She thought of what her dad said last night when she called to tell her parents her plans to quit. They had been gracious about her decision to leave Tellmann's. Solid as Stella's business appeared, it was not a nationwide department store backed by some huge conglomerate. He had said, "Honey, you work harder than anyone I know. You might consider simply taking some time off in between jobs. Work on your tan. Read a book. Just relax. And for goodness sake, stop the—what do you call it?"

"Whirligigging."

"Yeah, that. Give yourself a break from it, honey. Okay?"

Her dad's advice had surprised her coming from the ultimate doer.

The man must be mellowing in his old age. He even offered to send her money if she needed it. If Piper hadn't visited her family in January, she'd consider going to Wisconsin.

What about Baja?

No. Too soon for that. And besides, Hud was in another space, exactly like Heidi had said he would be. Last night, after talking with her mom and dad, Piper had roamed around the cottage, cell phone in hand, working up the nerve to call him. Before she did, he texted. *Crazy, brain-frying weeks ahead. The story consumes me. Apologies ahead of time if I don't catch up with you for a while. I will miss you.*

The last phrase helped. Sort of.

She couldn't imagine their friendship moving forward into any sort of relationship. It might have been love at first sight, but without a few more sightings, that would dwindle into a curious memory to tell her children.

Her children.

Piper waited. Nothing happened. Whew. She hoped the mommy hormone had buried itself until…Until? *If* was a better word. Although she had opened her heart to the possibility of loving someone else, its happening was not exactly a certainty.

"Miss you, Jared. And I always will."

She thought of her dad's advice again. Work on a tan? Not her thing. Read a book? She had a new biography on the nightstand—She smiled. "Okay, okay. Crack open that borrowed copy of *Silver Heart*." Just relax? Photography jumped into her thoughts.

Of course. She had the time now to edit those last pictures of Jared and take new photos of his favorite places and things. She would create a memento for herself.

Instead of pretending that the next anniversary was not happening, she would meet it head-on. When July ninth rolled around—the anniversary of when they would have been married—she would be ready this time. What better way to hold and let go than with a tangible keepsake, to reflect on with tears and smile, and to tuck away for the coming years?

It was a good plan.

Piper started the engine. "*Adios*, Tellmann's. It's been a trip. See you around."

Sixty-One

Two weeks passed before Heidi embraced her brave words about being ready to drive.

Now, seated behind a steering wheel, she adjusted the car's rearview mirror. She adjusted the one on the left door. The one on the right. She slid the seat forward and back and forward a little. She pulled at the seatbelt. She gripped the steering wheel. She adjusted the rearview mirror.

"Like falling off a log." From the passenger seat, Keagan murmured the not-so-helpful encouragement.

"I have no idea what falling off a log feels like, but it sounds incredibly painful."

"Sorry. How about easy peasey, lemon squeezy?"

"That's a little better." She checked the outside rearview mirrors again. "I'll get going here. Any minute now."

"Take your time. No pressure."

She touched the key in the ignition and then moved her hand back to her lap. "So why did you agree to do this?"

"It's Jasmyn's car. Newer model. Every safety feature imaginable is in this baby."

"We won't get hurt?"

"Not sitting at the curb." He slipped his seat belt on. "I can feel you're getting close."

"Really, why are you here?"

"Jasmyn thinks I'm a nice guy. I don't want to let her down. We're getting married, you know."

Heidi rolled her eyes. She wasn't going to get a straight answer out of him. Evidently he was simply a nice guy who would do anything for Jasmyn and Jasmyn would do anything for anybody. Except get in a car with Heidi at the wheel.

She turned the key. The car was a new model, small but comfortable enough. It should be a breeze to drive. Easy peasey…

Heidi pulled away from the curb in front of the Casa and crept down the street. Her muscles had been tight since she and Keagan had decided that morning to go at nine-thirty. It showed in the rough way she controlled the pedals. The car lurched. At the stop sign she braked and her seat belt cut into her chest. The car lurched into the intersection.

"Relax, Heidi. You're doing fine."

"I'll just go around the block."

"My eye, you'll just go around the block. Get on Coast Highway. We'll go down to Encinitas. I have to pick something up there."

"What?"

"Jasmyn's wedding band. You won't tell?"

Heidi shook her head and kept her eyes glued on the road. It was going to be a long, long thirty minutes. Or fifty or sixty, depending on how far below the speed limit she'd be going.

⁂

Heidi turned off the ignition and turned to slap Keagan's high five.

"Great job. You can borrow my motorcycle anytime."

"Thanks."

They climbed out of the car.

He said, "You sure you don't need me to stay?"

She glanced around the auto dealership, at all the glossy cars in the lot, and smelled the sun-kissed, rubbery-scented air. "I know which one I want. Make that, I know which one I can afford. I'll get my dad on the phone and grab the salesman we know over there. Then we'll do it."

"You've bought a car or two in your time."

She laughed. "Thanks, Keagan."

"You're welcome."

She watched him drive away, still amazed at what she had accomplished that morning. By the time she had driven rather slowly down

Coast Highway and parked near the jewelry shop, she was shaky but felt a renewed sense of confidence. While Keagan was in the store, she phoned her dad and ran her car-buying idea past him. He had hesitated about half a second, and then he said, "Go for it, princess."

They'd always bought cars together. He was waiting now for her phone call. She pulled her cell out of her shoulder bag, pressed his number, and put it on speaker.

"Heidi." Ethan's excited voice came through loud and clear. "Remember, we agreed. Not the red one. Red ones insist that you drive them fast."

She smiled. Long distance was better than nothing.

Late that afternoon, with a surer foot and a mind less filled with ghosts of experiences past, Heidi white-knuckled herself in her own car to the office. She avoided the freeway.

The SUV was American made, larger than her old car but not huge. It was last year's model, with a silver blue exterior with an off-white interior. She felt good about her purchase.

It also shored up her motive to make money. Looming car payments had that effect.

Val was out of the office. Cynthia and Dawn were holding down the fort. They congratulated her on her achievement. She thanked them for being such gems, for sticking with SunView and pitching in above and beyond the call of duty.

Heidi sat at her desk and studied the client database. It didn't take long. The profile nearly sang and danced across the monitor.

She had a fairly good memory when it came to remembering personalities and what they wanted in buying or selling a home. She knew that this woman was a complete stranger to her. Heidi checked the date of when she had first contacted SunView.

February first. The day of the accident. Seriously?

Heidi called her. At six o'clock they met at Heidi's condo. Her renters, the Thompsons, had graciously done as she asked and went out for the evening. They left behind a spotless home, a cute teapot on the stovetop, and the sweet scent of a dozen red roses on the dining table.

Evelyn Vogler was a friendly fifty-something, widowed pediatrician with short salt-and-pepper hair and a quick smile. "Heidi," she said as she stepped through the front door. "This is exactly what I want."

Apparently the woman bought condos like Heidi bought cars.

"Val never presented this one to me. Did it just go on the market?"

"About two hours ago. It's mine."

By seven o'clock, they had agreed upon a fair price. Heidi shut the door behind Evelyn.

It felt a little like trading a house for a car. She wasn't sure whether to mourn or to celebrate. If the Thompsons weren't coming back soon, she might have flopped on the couch and mourned a bit. Instead, she went…home.

ગૈહ

At the Casa, others made the choice for Heidi about how to respond to the sale of her condo. There would be no mourning, not when a hurdle had been leaped and there was a new car to be seen.

Jasmyn and Piper caught up with her as she reached her front door, ecstatic about her driving achievement. Keagan had told them about it and the fact that he'd left her at a dealership.

Heidi walked with them back to where she had parked, a few doors down from the Casa. After they admired it inside and out, she told them about selling the condo.

Piper said, "Wow, that was fast. What a bittersweet day for you."

"Unbelievably, on both counts." When her smile wouldn't stick, she knew she was exhausted.

Jasmyn took her arm and steered her down the sidewalk. "You've got way too much going on, girl. Is there anything we can do?"

"You already did it. You convinced Keagan to take me driving. And I have Liv's leftover comfort food in the freezer. What more could I want?"

"How about for Piper to call your brother to give him your news?"

Piper groaned.

Jasmyn said, "Piper's had her own bittersweet day."

Heidi looked at her. "What happened?"

"I gave my boss two weeks' notice and she said I was done, then and there, this morning."

"I'm sorry."

She shrugged. "I have leftover mac and cheese in my freezer too."

Heidi turned to Jasmyn. "How was your day?"

"It was a tough one. I spilled a strawberry malt all over the floor. The whole, entire thing. Icky, sticky."

"I suppose you'll be wanting mac and cheese too."

"Liv gave it all to you two and Chad."

"Boo-hoo," Piper said. "You're not getting any of mine."

"Nor mine," Heidi said.

They teased and giggled their way back to the Casa. By the time Heidi walked into her quaint little cottage, most of the bitter had fallen away from the sweet. By the time she showered, ate the yummy leftovers, and snuggled under the covers, she felt as if she'd melted into a sea of sweetness. By the time Adam surprised her with a phone call, she was too comfortable to dodge emotional darts.

She liked the guy. Pure and simple.

"Hi, Adam."

"Val just told me you sold your condo," he blurted, his tone upset.

"Hello to you too," she teased.

"Sorry. Hi. Are you all right?"

"I am. I really am. It needed to happen."

"But it's such a huge thing for you. I know how much it meant to you, owning your own home."

She knew that he knew, that he understood her more than anyone. "Thanks. Did she tell you I also drove today and I bought a car?"

"What?"

"I did. Isn't it amazing?"

He chuckled. "Heidi, you're amazing. You always have been. I, um, I should let you go. It's late. I just wanted to check in on you."

"I'm glad you did."

"What are old friends for? See you."

"See you."

Heidi turned off the phone and felt a stab of disappointment. What were old friends for? Apparently they were for making her want more and for messing with her sense of well-being.

That sounded like a first class whine.

She smiled. She could fix that. "Thank You for Adam. He can go away now."

Sixty-Two

If Liv had been wearing buttons, they would have popped. The swell of pride and joy just about burst her dress apart at the seams as it was.

From almost the moment she had met Jasmyn nearly ten months ago, Liv loved her like a daughter. Something about the young woman captured her heart in a big way. Holding the bride's hand now as they walked down the aisle, she felt like a surrogate parent, symbolically ushering Jasmyn from the covering of one home into another, the one she would share with Keagan.

Liv grinned from ear to ear and most likely looked a bit dotty.

The no-frills wedding reflected the couple's tastes. Jasmyn wore a sweet, white lacy dress and a wreath of fragrant tuber roses in her hair. Her bouquet was three long-stemmed yellow roses tied with ribbon. Keagan wore a long-sleeved white embroidered Latin style shirt and black pants.

Samantha and Beau stood up with them. Tasha scattered rose petals. Piper took photos. The pianist played Beethoven's "Ode to Joy." Early evening sunlight streamed through the stained glass windows, casting rainbow glows over them all.

The church was small and only a few pews were needed for the guests. All of the Casa family was there. Inez, Louie, Riley, Coco, Chadwick, Heidi, Noah, and Déja. Jasmyn's half sister was there with her husband and two young children. A handful of staff from Keagan's gym had joined them too.

Liv had hoped to see Adam and Hudson. After discreet inquiries, she began to get the picture. They were either both too busy with work or else Heidi and Piper had not bothered to invite them.

Well, it was none of her business.

Liv listened now as her pastor—such a dear old man—led Jasmyn and Keagan through their vows. They had chosen to write their own promises. The traditional words felt stale to them.

She smiled. They might not have known it, but their words echoed the spirit of the classic ones. Respecting and cherishing and hanging in there were not passé.

The newlyweds planned to leave the church immediately after the ceremony, sans any rice, and drive straight to the airport in time to catch a flight to Hawaii. There would be no dinner, no toasts, no dancing.

The rest of them, however, would dine and toast and dance, Casa de Vida style, at a nearby pizza restaurant. It was the best they could do on such short notice. And it would undoubtedly be a lovely event.

Sixty-Three

Hard feelings between Heidi and Val agitated their conversations like an off-balance washing machine jerking around its load. Still, though, Heidi turned to her friend for moral support.

They arrived at her condo the last day of the month, a Thursday, mid-morning. The Thompsons handed their keys to her, repeated yet again a string of gracious regrets and thanks. They left and Heidi shut the door behind them.

Val said, "You're not going to cry, are you?"

"I might."

Val gave her a small smile. "I'm sorry, sugar-pie."

"Thanks."

"You've been through worse."

Heidi sighed in reply, not sure if she agreed with that assessment. The accident, the hospital, and the injuries were beyond awful. They had taken a heavy toll and left her with a limp. But was all that worse than giving up her lifelong dream of the security of owning her own home? Of feeling the solidity of staying put, unlike anything she'd known growing up?

She rubbed her hands together. "Okay. Let's get to work."

The place was spotless, which helped big time. If the condo closed as scheduled, the new owner, Evelyn Vogler, planned to move in July fifteenth. Heidi had a couple of weeks to move her things out.

"Start here in the living room?" Val suggested. "It should be the easiest."

"Right. Most of this furniture won't fit in the bungalow. And since Evelyn wants to buy some of it…" Her voice trailed off. Furnishing her condo had been a blast. It was the first time she'd had enough money to purchase entire sets of anything. The living room, master bedroom, and guest room still looked brand new.

And yet horribly outdated. Not according to current styles, but according to Heidi Hathaway. Sleek, smooth, black, white, sharp corners…they all made her cringe.

Val handed her three pads of sticky paper, one red, one yellow, one green. They had an easy system. If an item stayed, stick on a red paper. Going? Use green. Unsure? Yellow.

Heidi said, "I'll take the bed, dresser, and kitchen table. Linens. Pots and pans, just in case I get a hankering to cook." She wondered if Liv would sell her the dishes she had been using. They were pretty, so colorful. "And desk." Working from home would soon be a necessity.

"You'll want a couch and chair, don't you think?"

She eyed the stiff leather couch and tried to imagine Hud bunking on it. "I'll pick up something cozier." She smiled at Val. "For the quaint little cottage."

"Oookay. Are televisions allowed in the quaint little cottages?"

"Yes. I'll take mine."

"Artwork?"

She made a face at the collection of splatters of colors on canvases. Little Tasha's watercolors were far prettier.

Val slapped a red sticky on the one behind the couch. "This won't take long at all."

No, it would not take long at all to dismantle what had already been removed from her desires and replaced by new ones when she wasn't paying attention.

⟡

Heidi and Val ate a late lunch at a funky, beachy restaurant that consisted of a few patio tables and a walkup window for ordering. They were in the heart of tourist heaven. Sidewalks and streets were crazy summertime busy.

Heidi set down her fork and swallowed the last of a delicious Asian salad with cabbage, mandarin oranges, wonton strips, and peanut dressing.

She'd scarfed down both her and Val's sourdough rolls using the whole pats of butter. Her appetite had returned. If she didn't start some sort of exercise regimen soon, her pre-accident weight would return with extra friends.

"Val, in the spirit of openness—"

"Returning the favor, are you? Giving what I always give you?" She smiled. Her smiles in recent days were strained, as was everything about her, but typical Val, she kept on going, head down and plowing ahead.

"You deserve nothing less than the favor returned."

"All right. What are you trying to say?"

"Look at what you're wearing. And then look around us."

Val shrugged.

"Heels. Pencil skirt. Dressy blouse. Great accessories." Heidi turned toward the sidewalk and then she looked back at her friend. "I see shorts. Swimsuits. Cover-ups. A lot of skin. A lot of tattoos. A lot of piercings."

"So? I have a career, unlike ninety-five percent of what you're looking at."

"Exactly. People with careers that require dress clothes do not live here. They do not even hang out here on workdays." Heidi glanced down at her own wrinkly linen slacks, casual shirt, and sandals. If clothes made the career, she better renew her interest in her wardrobe. "I'm sorry, Val. It's the whole beachy culture here. You don't do casual, but clothes are only one aspect. You hate crowds, noise, and clutter. This idea of yours to live here is just too bizarre. Are you absolutely sure about it? You know they say not to make major changes so soon after a crisis. Especially not during it."

"That's like the pot calling the kettle black. Did you not just sell your home?"

"Financially necessary. Nothing to do with the accident."

"Whatever. I am most definitely continuing with these bizarre plans." Sunglasses hid the hazel glare that would be aimed at Heidi right now. "I am divorcing Craig. There is nothing to work on in that department. I am selling the house. I want a brand new start. Like you. What makes you think you're the only one who gets to try something outrageous?"

Heidi opened her mouth and decided the protest wasn't worth it. "The truth is, you don't fit in here. I think you'd absolutely hate it."

"I'm sure I would have said the same thing about you and that place you're in."

No argument there.

"Give me a break, Heidi. Let me try. Maybe I need this wild environment to help me get through this mess."

"Why would wild help? Val, the Casa de Vida is a house of life. It's full of peace and laughter and—and family."

"Okay now seriously, give me a break from the rose-colored glasses view. I'll get worried that you all smoke something funny there."

And the off-balance washer agitated away.

Heidi held up her hands in surrender. "Fine."

"Fine. Let's go."

They went, slowly because high heels and sand-covered walkways did not work well together. After a couple of blocks, Val stopped and removed her shoes. "Barefoot is the culture here, even with business outfits."

"You're quicker than you appear sometimes."

"Shush. Ohmygosh." She pointed ahead. "That can't be it, can it?"

They neared the beach house. Julian's secret beach house. The one Cynthia and Dawn had mentioned was available for rent. For nine years it had been booked solid, but not this month or next.

They slowed their steps. It was a beautiful area with a low seawall to the right. The beach itself began on the other side of that, a long, wide stretch to the water. The ocean was one huge, uninterrupted expanse. On the left were houses upon houses fronted by tiny patios that met the wide boardwalk. There was everything from three-storied glass mini-palaces to small, old cottages like Faith Fontaine's.

They stopped at a low fence that bordered the flagstone patio at Thirty-Four Hundred Oceanfront Walk.

Heidi chuckled. "You know what, Val? This looks like one quaint little cottage." She stopped short of rubbing in how it was so not Val's style. Who knew? Maybe her friend would change as drastically as Heidi had. Before the accident, she never would have considered such a possibility.

"'Quaint little cottage.' I'll give you that. And it's almost as ugly as Cynthia and Dawn described it. Weathered East Coast shingles the color of marigolds with mud-colored trim."

"The white picket fence is sweet."

"That's me. Sweet as honey."

Heidi looked at the neighbor's house to her right, a beautiful, glassed design that towered over the cottage. Cynthia and Dawn had said Julian lived to the south. "Wow. I think that's Julian's."

"He always was showy."

Heidi's impression of the man had been anything but showy. Maybe he'd bought his house years ago and then he, too, changed drastically.

"Come on. Let's go inside." Val opened the low gate and strode to the front door where she punched in a code on the lockbox.

Heidi followed her inside, leery about her friend continuing the charade that Val was interested in moving here.

The front of the house was one open space. It combined living room and kitchen. She knew it had miniature-size bedrooms and two baths, enough to accommodate a small group of friends or a family. It was not the Taj Mahals that surrounded it, but it was…cozy. Comfortable. Unpretentious. Downright *quaint*.

The décor must have been Faith's, a woman from another generation. There were lace doilies, knickknacks that appeared to be mementos from around the world, built-in bookshelves stuffed with hardcover classics and paperback beach reads.

Perfect for sweet, unpretentious, beachy Val Laughlin. *Right*. What on earth were they doing there?

Heidi couldn't help but blurt, "Well, this doesn't have your name on it, does it? Remember those other listings? That one in La Jolla sounded promising. Cynthia thought we had some wiggle room on the rent—"

"I like it." Val disappeared down a hallway.

What did she like? Heidi would have liked it for a long weekend to surf with friends. Val wanted to live in it for ten weeks. In the summer, with noisy crowds literally right outside the front door. In the summer, the not-cheap season.

Val reappeared. "Plenty of closet space. Not all in the same room, but what the heck. All I need to bring are my clothes. I can live here and look for something more permanent. Craig has to get out of where he's staying with a friend. This way he can live at the house and get it in order. We'll sell it. Go from there."

Go from there, at the moment, meant divorce.

"Val, why would you like this place?"

"Why would you like your place?"

"I don't know. I was in an accident. Bumped my head."

"I'm losing my business. Bump on the head."

"But…" But Liv came with the Casa. And a host of new friends. What came with this cottage but sand and noise and—"Val. Are you after Julian?"

"What? Ew, no. He's like my uncle and way too much like my dad. Chalk it up to needing a drastic change. And stop worrying about me. I'm going to check out the parking space in back."

Heidi couldn't help but worry about her friend who was slowly falling apart before her very eyes.

Later that day, Heidi sought out Liv. She found her in the office and told her about Val's decision to move into Faith Fontaine's cottage. Julian's cottage.

"I don't understand it, Liv. Even from hearsay, you probably realize that she is not a beach culture kind of girl. I don't think she has ever been in the ocean. She called Adam and me weirdos because we were always surfing or playing volleyball. She hated to get sand in her toes."

"Julian next door must be an attraction. She had her issues with her dad, but a daughter always needs a dad. Or an uncle, as she said. A father figure to help her through this time, perhaps?"

"It doesn't seem that would be enough for her to put up with a house that is totally out of character for her. On another day, she would have made gagging noises the minute she stepped inside. If she even stepped inside."

"You sound upset, dear."

"I am. I'm concerned about…" Heidi paused. Mix a woman on the edge like Val with the nonstop partying environment and trouble was guaranteed. "I'm just afraid of her going off the deep end. It's such a wild place down there."

"It is. But it's also Faith's home and I think that's why it appeals to her when it seems it shouldn't. There is something about the place that draws people in."

"'Something?'"

Liv nodded, an enigmatic smile on her face. "Something."

"Care to elaborate?"

She shrugged. "There are no words."

Heidi blinked. There might not be words, but there was Liv who epit-omized the something. Ages ago, Faith Fontaine was probably of the same ilk. Julian could very well be a male version of whatever it was they had going.

Who was Heidi to argue? Val could be headed to her own Casa de Vida experience.

Sixty-Four

Liv shifted on the beach blanket and wondered how long she could keep up the act. Someone was bound to figure out that she was not twenty-nine. Probably that would happen tonight, about the time she tried to stand up. Her old creaky bones and muscles would protest loud enough for the others to hear and she would plop back down.

How she loved hanging out with the girls, though. It was a small group on this Fourth of July holiday. Coco was at her niece's home. Inez had gone with family as well, to a daughter's home. All the guys were busy. That left the young women. Well, the young ones and Liv.

Earlier in the day, everyone had been in and out of the Casa. Liv met friends—old ones, literally and figuratively—for lunch. That evening as she checked on a jade plant—growing like a weed and huge; she needed to trim it—Tasha said she and her mom were going to see fireworks down at the beach. One thing led to another until they all headed out the gate as twilight fell. Tasha, Riley, Piper, Jasmyn, Heidi, Samantha, and Liv now sat on blankets in the dark, waiting for the show along with hordes of other people.

Liv turned to Jasmyn seated beside her. "What is Keagan up to?"

"Gym catch-up stuff. A week was a long time for him to be away." She grinned. But then she hadn't stopped grinning since her return from Hawaii, nor had Keagan.

Liv grinned back at her. It was catchy, in spite of the discomfort of sitting on the hard sand in cool, moist air that dampened her clothes and hair. *At least I am closer to twenty-nine than either Inez or Coco.*

Tasha scooted next to Jasmyn and laid her head in her lap. "When will they start?"

"Soon." She stroked the little girl's hair and said to Piper, "Are we looking the right direction?"

She pointed north. "They'll come from Camp Pendleton. We should be good. Sam." She called out to the other blanket. "Is Beau coming? Tasha might need to sit on his shoulders."

"He said he'd be here in time."

Liv noted a trace of somberness in Piper's voice. "How are things at Stella's?"

"Fabulous." She smiled. "Stella left on Friday, so I've been in charge for all of two days and I absolutely love it. The customers and the whole atmosphere, the merchandise…it's just great."

"I'm glad for you, honey." Liv leaned close toward her ear. "I bet you and Jared watched these fireworks from the base."

"Yeah, we did. But we have a pretty good view here."

Liv studied her face, partially hidden in shadow. A vague thought nagged. She couldn't capture it. *Blame it on my mind, all preoccupied with aches and pains.*

Piper said, "Thursday will be the date of when we would have been married."

"Ohhh, Piper dear. Four years?"

"Mm-hmm. I'm okay." She rocked a hand back and forth. "You know."

"I know. Do you have plans for the day?"

"I have to work, of course. That'll be good, fill up the hours. Maybe I'll do some extra work at the shop. Come home and take a walk down here."

"Did you finish the photo journal?"

"Yes."

"Would you want to share it?" She gestured. "Between us girls?"

"You think they—yes. They would be interested, wouldn't they?"

"Yes, because we all love you, dear. How about Thursday evening, my place? Come for dinner. It's too soon for the macaroni and cheese again. Seafood linguine primavera?"

Piper laid her head briefly on Liv's shoulder. "Perfect. Thank you."

A loud boom exploded. Tasha giggled and sat up. "They're starting!" Everyone stood, except Liv.

A huge figure approached in the dark. "Where's my girl?"

Tasha squealed again and jumped into Beau's arms.

"Where's my guy?" Liv muttered to herself and pressed her palms on the blanket. More fireworks boomed and sizzled. Their lights splashed on the ground. If she timed the struggle to her feet, no one would notice. They'd still assume she was twenty-nine. Unless she tipped over.

"Liv." A strong arm came around her shoulders, a brick wall of a chest steadied her as she rose. Keagan, the Casa's knight, had arrived.

Too bad he was taken. Like she always said, if she were thirty years younger, he'd be starring in her daydreams. She laughed to herself, grateful for his discreet rescue.

✍

Tuesday morning, after the fireworks, Liv and Jasmyn directed traffic in the courtyard as Keagan, Beau, and Chadwick carried furniture out of Cottage One. Some of it went into Cottage Ten to complete Jasmyn's household. Some of it went to the alley and onto Chadwick's pickup truck, headed either to Goodwill or Keagan's gym. There wasn't a whole lot. The man was as Spartan as they came.

During a lull, Jasmyn said, "Are you all right, Liv?"

"Why wouldn't I be? You and Keagan are married. You're living at the Casa."

"But now we have an empty cottage."

"Child, you know the right person will come along at the right time."

"You sure you don't want to advertise? There's that bulletin board at Jitters for community notes."

"Jasmyn Albright-Keagan." She stifled a giggle. It had to do with Jasmyn's last name of *Keagan*. It was what everyone called Sean. It was what he had always gone by. It didn't fit as Jasmyn's last name yet. Liv should quit trying to use it.

"What?"

"You remember when Cottage Three was vacant. And you remember exactly how Heidi arrived to fill it. Out of the blue."

"Yes."

"I've never advertised."

"But would you if you had to?"

"How would I know if I had to?"

"By not being able to pay bills."

Liv smiled. "All right, yes. At that point I would advertise."

"Once Sam moves out and we move into her place, then we'll have two vacant cottages. And some days I worry about Coco. She seems so feeble."

"My goodness gracious!" She feigned shock. "If she had to leave, then we'd be up to three empties!"

"How can you tease about it?"

Liv laughed. "I've been at this a long, long time. Remember my father bought the Casa when I was in middle school. He was one smart cookie and taught me everything he knew. He advertised, by the way. When I took it over, I didn't advertise, as an experiment. I guess that experiment is still going on. Things have always worked out in the end."

"It seems a little unorthodox."

"That's why they call me an odd duck."

Jasmyn smiled. "Whose motto is 'out of the blue.'"

"You're catching on."

The guys came out, each carrying large boxes. Keagan said, "It's all yours, ladies." He paused long enough to plant a kiss on Jasmyn's mouth. "We're heading to the gym."

"Bye."

Liv and Jasmyn went into Cottage One, the first cottage inside the gate, to its left. Cottage Eleven, Coco's, was to its right, but her front door faced a different direction. Number One had been the sentinel's abode for almost six years.

Liv swallowed with difficulty.

Jasmyn headed to the kitchen. "We already cleaned inside the cupboards. There sure wasn't much to it. Marrying a military guy is like marrying a housekeeper. I'll wash the walls, get them ready for Beau to paint." She stopped at the sink and began filling a pail with water. "Is he starting today?"

"Um." Liv swallowed again. "The prep work, I think. We want it done by Saturday."

In the past, Liv had not furnished the bungalows. When Jasmyn showed up last year—out of the blue—everyone pitched in so that the girl who had no home or clothes was taken care of. Later, as Jasmyn began to buy her own things and the borrowed couch, tables, lamps, and chairs were moved out and no longer wanted by their owners, Liv decided to store them in Cottage Three.

One thing led to another. Liv added a new bed, new dishes, a new television. If another Jasmyn showed up, they would be ready for her.

Heidi had been a type of Jasmyn. As a temporary resident, she did not want to move her things. Now, because her condo had been sold, she had to bring her things. Liv decided to outfit Number One as she had Number Three. Just in case.

"Liv." Jasmyn stood in front of her. "You're rubbing your chest."

Liv lowered her arm. "Bad habit."

"I know it doesn't mean you're having a heart attack. It means your heart is having some sort of attack though."

She gazed around the bare cottage and felt at a loss. "Cottage One is special."

"The angel-slash-knight can work from Cottage Ten."

Liv's smiled wobbled. "It won't be the same. I think I might have a little cry."

Jasmyn hugged her.

Having a little cry with a loved one eased the distress like nothing else could.

Sixty-Five

The End.

Like a deep sea diver surfacing from the dark depths of the ocean, Hud looked up from his laptop. The walls and desktop swam in a haze.

From experience he knew that if he did not take things slowly, he would get the bends, so to speak, complete with vertigo and nausea. At snail speed he rose from the desk, walked across the room, and stepped through the open sliding door.

His eyes smarted in the sunlight. Colors came at him, pinging vision receptors like BBs shot from a gun. Every nerve ending on his skin prickled as if fresh air were tangible. He held on to the back of a chair, steadying himself for several moments. He breathed slow and deep, nearly reeling with the scent of ocean. The squawk of a seagull overhead deafened.

It was over.

The laughter began in his belly and worked its way up and down and out until his entire body tingled with pure, unadulterated joy. He tried to shout. Only a quiet "Yesss" emerged.

His eyes adjusted. Shapes took on dimension. Colors settled into place, richer and brighter than ever before. Turquoise sky. Turquoise ocean. Blond sand. Green palm. Beige stucco. Fuchsia bougainvillea, mounds and mounds of it falling over the patio wall.

Birds sang unfamiliar melodies. The ocean whooshed not many steps from the patio's edge.

It was over. The story he had lived and breathed for the past year, the story that totally severed his link with reality for the past six weeks, was done. Mystery solved. Perps brought to justice. Good guy gets the good girl.

The good girl.

Piper.

Hud smiled. In time.

In his current hypersensitive state, everything and everyone remained *out there*, in the future, in time. It took hours to reattach to life. He first needed to walk, to let the images recede from the inside of his eyelids, to let the characters stop talking.

He would fish. He would eat the fish. No, he would savor the fish. He would laugh and cry. Later he would check for messages.

Piper.

He went back into the house on the beach in Baja and blinked. What was he looking for? The phone. Where was it? He looked at the desk and shook his head. He didn't want to touch the desk nearly buried in papers.

He roamed around the small living room and kitchen, at last happening upon the phone. It was on the floor under the coffee table.

His eyes burning, he checked for messages. He scanned blearily through seventy-seven texts, looking for her name. He scanned through twenty-one missed calls, looking for her name. He scanned through fifty-eight emails, looking for her name.

What was it he had told her? Something about frying his brain on work. His sister most likely told her not to bother contacting him. At least, he hoped Heidi had told her that.

He began the process again. A text caught his eye. *Cubs!* It was from a friend who had awesome seats behind home plate at Petco Park. He opened the text. Cubs in town Saturday night. Want the seats?

Hud hit the speaker function, said "Yes," and sent it. Then he put the phone back under the table, went outside, and from a corner of the patio grabbed his fishing pole.

The rest could wait. It was over.

Sixty-Six

Saturday afternoon, there was a lull in the action at Stella's Boutique. The part-timer was gone on her lunch break. Piper rearranged a display of costume jewelry, happier than a loon, as her mother would say.

Stella had been gone for a week, the first of two. Piper thought working with the woman was ridiculously delightful, but being in charge was even better. She could imagine herself owning the shop. She wouldn't change much at all, except the name. *Pipe Dream* had been her first idea, but when she mentioned it to Jasmyn, Keagan was nearby and shook his head, muttering something about a reference to drugs.

The accessories could use a bit of updating. She might switch racks, put the casual outfits nearer the front. Nothing major. It was a lovely boutique overall. She would keep the music, soft rock from her mother's era. It appealed to most of the clientele and it did not put her teeth on edge.

The bell on the door jingled and Piper turned toward it with a smile. When she saw Hudson Hathaway enter, she grinned and walked over to meet him. "Hey, stranger."

He smiled. "Hey, yourself."

Then it struck, that school-girl crush reaction. Her throat quivered. Her thoughts froze. Her skin flushed. Words refused to form.

"Hi."

"Hi."

It was like a script they had to repeat every time they met.

"How have you been?"

"Uh, fine. How have you been?"

"Fine."

The guy intrigued her to no end. She adored his blue eyes, his height, his slender hands, the elegance of his movements.

"I'm sorry for being out of touch."

"You said you would be."

"I hope you don't mind me dropping in. I, uh, I don't know. I didn't want to talk on the phone." He shrugged.

She smiled. "How did you find me?"

"Heidi brought me up to speed on everyone. I missed out on a lot, didn't I? Let's see, a wedding, fireworks, her condo sale, her driving, the all-comfort-food dinner for her." He seemed to stop short.

She knew what it was. "And the comfort dinner for me?"

He nodded. "Seafood pasta primavera and brownies. You doing okay? That was a biggie."

"I'm okay. I'm better than okay." Now that he was there she was beyond loon-happy territory. Now that he was there she just might be able to fly. "This new job is great."

"The shop is nice. Not that I spend much time in women's boutiques." He glanced around. "There's a welcoming feel to it."

"I think so too."

"I feel so bad for Heidi. I haven't been much help to her lately. Is there something she'd like? Maybe the equivalent of Liv's mac-and-cheese dish?"

She laughed. "Come over here." She led him to a corner table laden with bath items. "How about a gift basket of soap, lotion, and candle?" She opened samples for him to smell.

"This one. What is it?"

"Plumeria. It's yummy. Let me put things in a basket. I'll gift wrap it too." She busied herself, gathering the items. "You're a good brother. Not one of my three would ever think of getting something like this for me." She led him over to the counter.

"They need a friend who runs a boutique."

"Even that might not get their attention." She worked on filling the basket, removing the tiny price stickers and arranging things just so. "It's fun to put this together for a friend. Did you finish your book?"

"Yes."

"I finished your book too. *Silver Heart*." She held the basket up for him to inspect.

"Nice." But he wasn't looking at the basket. "You won't hurt my feelings…"

"It's a great story. I can see why it's so popular." She began to ring up the prices on the cash register.

"I hear a 'but.'"

"There's no 'but.' It was good. It kept me up all night." She looked at him.

He stared at her for a moment. "You weren't reading all night."

She shook her head. "Scared the beebers out of me."

"What are beebers?"

"Scary things."

"You made that up."

"My sister did."

He laughed. "I'm sorry. Did you really finish it?"

"I did. I had to find out what happened."

"Please don't read any more."

"How do you come up with that stuff?"

He tapped his head. "I'm really not weird. Hey, how about those Cubs?"

Now she laughed and opened a narrow drawer full of sheets of tissue paper. Pink wasn't Heidi, but it was the prettiest pattern they had. She pulled some out.

"Piper, seriously. How about those Cubs?"

"What about them?"

"They beat the Padres last night."

"They did? I missed that." She gathered the paper around the basket.

"They're playing tonight too. Do you want to go?"

She looked up at him. "Tonight?"

"Yeah. A friend gave me his tickets."

She cocked her head. "Are they good ones?"

"Behind home plate."

She let the tissue paper fall open. "I was teasing."

"Is that a yes?" He smiled.

"I would have said yes if they were way out in leftfield, nosebleed section…"

Bases loaded, bottom of the ninth, two outs. Cubs down, three-zip. From the sixth row behind home plate, Piper saw the hit, saw the ball soar into the leftfield seats.

She whooped and turned to Hud. "We won!"

"You won." He gave her an exaggerated frown.

People around them rose, grumbling, collecting their things, and moving out into the aisles. Padres fans, blocking her view of those four runners coming home.

"I can't see."

He smiled.

She smiled.

He leaned toward her.

She leaned toward him.

When their lips met, she didn't mind missing the end of the game. She'd just discovered her own home plate.

Sixty-Seven

Heidi pulled the lever of her new recliner. With her legs elevated and her back stretched out, she finally relaxed. It had been a long ten days of moving from her condo and into Cottage Three, Casa de Vida, Seaside Village, San Diego County, California.

She sighed, glad that she had purchased the recliner with the couch rather than the armchair. Her body wasn't what it used to be.

She'd chosen tan microsuede. It was basic, comfortable, and the couch was long enough to accommodate Hud. The pieces were also dull enough, she was sure, for Piper to enjoy helping her add color.

Her bedroom set fit snugly. Her kitchen table looked great in front of the French doors. She found places for a few lamps and an end table. The desk crowded things in the living room, but she liked it next to the bay window. She liked the thought of working there, of being centered every time she viewed the courtyard.

Although the two new items were inexpensive, her bank account was taking a beating. She'd hired movers and a cleaning crew. She had a car payment and insurance. She had bought Liv's dishes. She owed doctors and the hospital. She had donated most of her things to Brother Benny's Thrift Shop—not so much out of the goodness of her heart, but out of its practicality. It was simply easier than trying to sell it.

At least she was working. She had sold one house and found another for the sellers, all in the past week. She held an open house that afternoon that resulted in potential business. And she had signed on a new client—Hud.

Who now must be the person rapping on her front door and pushing

291

it open. She had left it unlocked for him. He walked inside with the biggest grin on his face and dropped his backpack on the floor.

"The Padres must have won."

"No, but I did."

She laughed. "Let me guess. You won Piper's heart."

"That would appear to be the case."

"Nice going."

"You don't sound surprised." He handed her a package wrapped in pink and kissed her forehead. "I got this at Stella's Boutique. Piper apologizes for the pink. She says it's not your color."

"What is this?"

He sat on the couch. "My mac-and-cheese gift."

A gift of comfort. If she weren't so tired, she might cry. She untied the ribbon and the paper fell away. A white basket held luscious-smelling girly items. "Hud, this is…" Maybe she wasn't too tired to cry.

"You're welcome, Squirt."

She dried her eyes with her shirtsleeve. He lit the candle. She told him about Val and Treena, about closing the office door for the last time. He told her about finishing the book and fishing. The biggest bit of information involved him and Piper. The fact that they *were* involved. At least they were on page one of involved.

"Did you tell her you were thinking about relocating here?"

"Not yet."

"You are a chicken."

"I don't want to scare her off. Maybe she prefers long distance for now."

Heidi cackled like a hen.

He ignored her. "But I drove by the properties."

"And?"

He gave her a thumbs-up. "Let's make some appointments."

She smiled. He had phoned the other day, after he had finished his manuscript, his voice borderline delirious. She'd heard the tone before, at the end of a project, at the announcement of a movie deal, at the news of a bestseller list. She chalked it up to his work, but he had declared on the phone, "I'm done with my hermit writing days. I want to move back."

In her opinion, he wasn't completely done with the hermit part of his days. He asked her for a list of properties for sale that were surrounded by wilderness instead of people. She found possibilities and gave him the addresses to drive by.

"Which ones did you like?"

"All of them."

She laughed. "You just like the isolation."

"I do. I actually couldn't see most of the houses themselves. They're all gated, so probably too grand for me. But the canyons and avocado trees and eucalyptus were beautiful. Peaceful."

"It's not the ocean."

"No, but I don't want neighbors and the gazillion dollar coast price tags. Maybe next week. Okay with you if I stay here a few days?"

"While you court my neighbor?"

He grinned again.

She laughed. "Absolutely."

Sixty-Eight

Late Saturday night, Liv made her rounds with Tobi at her heels. The fountain still trickled. Solar lights on the ground and strings of patio lights in the trees and bushes created a soft glow. But her heart refused to accept the peace so generously offered.

She zigzagged about the courtyard, stumped as to where to begin. Number One was not number one tonight.

"Tobi, it's just one of those times. And no, I can't be more specific. Everything is jumbled."

She gave up numerical order and followed the path of least resistance.

At Cottage Ten she halted. "The newlyweds. Peace and joy to you, Jasmyn and Keagan. And since it's really all about me, I am grateful, Abba, that nothing has really changed." She smiled. "Except they're both a whole lot happier. Thank You for their kindnesses toward me. Especially today for Jasmyn's extra help arranging things in Keagan's—in Cottage One."

They had gone ahead with the plan to outfit the vacant cottage for any temporary resident who might pop in out of the blue. Beau had finished his painting the other day. Because Heidi had bought dishes and a few odds and ends, Jasmyn and Liv shopped to replace those.

Today Heidi had hired movers to bring her furniture from her condo and to also move the other furniture from her cottage into One. Like mother and daughter, Liv and Jasmyn had worked side by side, creating a homey environment with new dishes and leftover furnishings.

The thought of Heidi beckoned Liv over to Three. "Abba, thank You for bringing her into our midst. Give her rest tonight after her wearisome

294

day. I think Hudson is here now too. Let them enjoy and encourage one another."

Cottage Six drew her across the courtyard. "Riley and Tasha, two bright spots in our family of the heart here. Give them a good night's sleep."

Liv turned to Five. "Noah has been off lately. Grow him through whatever challenge he's in. He must feel alone, living separate from his family. If there is something we might do for him, clue us in."

She stepped over to Eight. "Dear, dear Inez and Louie. Blessings upon blessings to you old folks. Abba, give Inez strength and Louie the will not to quit too soon. He's more than a little testy these days."

Liv walked to Eleven. "Lord, have mercy. Christ, have mercy." That day, Coco had faded out more than she had faded in. She recognized Heidi but not Liv.

Liv turned, headed back over to Seven, and sighed. "The soon-to-be newlyweds. Blessings on your plans, dear Samantha and Beau." She sighed again. "Abba, it seems to me that a mother should be at her daughter's wedding."

Liv frowned and tried to imagine a relationship so messed up that it made her opinion about mothers at daughters' weddings invalid. Nothing came to her. "Maybe I can't imagine because my mother doted on me? Anyway, remind me that it's not my job to get Rosie Whitehorse Chee here." At one point she had thought it was her job, which was why she made it a point to learn the woman's name from Samantha. "Not my job. Whatever the woman decides, to come or not to come, protect Samantha's well-being."

Tobi had kept pace with Liv. She bent over and picked up the fluffy cat, hoping she was in the mood for a snuggle because Liv certainly was. There were two cottages left.

And one person who was an outsider.

Julian had phoned that morning to report that Valerie's first week living in the beach house next to his had been, as far as he could tell, uneventful. "She apparently leaves for work early every morning. She comes home late in the evenings. I haven't noticed anyone else with her. I haven't seen her take a walk."

"Julian, you needn't babysit."

"I feel responsible."

Liv had wanted to say he shouldn't, but he already knew that.

"We spoke for the first time last night. I was on the boardwalk and she came outside. She was friendly. Promised not to throw too many wild parties. Livvie, I simply cannot figure out what this is all about."

"I can't either. It's easy to imagine that Faith's house can work its wonder on her."

"Yes. Heal some soul wounds. But…"

"Yes, but."

There was no need to say it aloud. *But why had she come in the first place?*

The question had hung in the silence between them for a moment. Liv felt what he probably also felt, a fear that Valerie went there in the first place because she needed to fall apart. What better spot to fall apart than next door to the man whom her dad admired? It was either her cry for help from Julian, a father surrogate, or a bizarre way to heap hot coals on the memory of her dad, the man who had taught her how to succeed at business and fail in marriage.

Now, in the courtyard shadows, Liv spoke the old prayer because it covered everything she did not know about Valerie and her needs. "Lord, have mercy. Christ, have mercy. *Kyrie eleison.*"

What next? Piper…Or an empty cottage.

Liv walked past Piper's and went to Cottage One. "Abba, I trust You'll bring someone new who will benefit from living here, someone we might love on. Someone who might give us gifts as well. But good golly, here I am looking at this vacancy and doubting and yes, feeling unsettled because this was Keagan's. Cottage One is different. It's just *different.* So…so I don't know. I'll leave it at that."

You don't always have to have the answers, Liv.

She let the thought sink in. If it took root this time, that would be a good thing.

Liv inhaled deeply and turned back toward Piper's cottage. "Let's go."

Near Number Four, she stopped, still hugging Tobi. "What are we going to do?"

Tobi meowed. It was her blunt meow, the one that conveyed a message.

"All right, all right. I admit I am a news junkie. It would be best if I quit reading online news. But in this case, it's too late. I already read it."

Tobi jumped from her arms.

When Liv had first met Piper's mother, Darlene told her about Jared's death in the war. In subsequent talks, she mentioned that he deserved a medal, that several in his unit had said so. But there were complications, conflicting reports as to his actions.

Evidently, the issue hadn't ended years ago. That afternoon at Camp Pendleton, Jared Michael Oakes was posthumously awarded the Bronze Star Medal for valor in direct combat.

Piper should have been there. Liv knew for a fact that Piper had been at work. She also knew Piper would have told her about it. Darlene might have even phoned Liv to make sure she knew. No, Darlene and Piper's dad would have been there in person.

Which meant Piper didn't have a clue that her fiancé had been honored in front of many, many people not too far down the road.

"Abba, something isn't right here. Something is terribly, terribly wrong."

Lord, have mercy. Christ, have mercy.

Sixty-Nine

"A party in Hollywood." Piper giggled into the phone. "With movie people."

Her mother laughed. "Will I read about you in *People* magazine?"

"Maybe. Oh, Mom, I really, really like him."

"I can hear it in your voice. You'd like him anyway, wouldn't you, even without the bonuses like Hollywood and bestselling books?"

"Yep. Those are icing on the cake." *And it is one yummy cake.* She kept that thought to herself. Much as she shared with her mom, describing the first kisses and hugs of a new relationship remained off-limits.

"What are you going to wear to the party?"

"Ack! I've tried on four outfits. What do you think? Cute, sassy, Vogue ad, or hubba hubba?"

"Piper, you are none of those. You're beautiful inside and out."

"And you're no help. I gotta get ready."

"Love you, honey. Have fun. Don't go with the last one."

Piper laughed. "Love you. Bye."

She twirled and leapt through the cottage, trying to throw off some of the excess energy so she could focus on the task at hand: deciding what to wear to a party in Hollywood.

Or deciding how long she could wait before rushing next door to Heidi's where this guy she liked was probably drinking coffee.

She rummaged through her closet one more time. If Hud had invited her to today's party yesterday, she would have brought home the sea green sundress hanging in Stella's. If Jasmyn were standing there in need of a dress for a party in Hollywood, Piper would have found just the right out-fit in her closet in two shakes of a puppy's tail.

She groaned. How could she have it so bad already, this belief that he hung the moon in the sky?

Her cell rang and she picked it up from the bed, hoping it was him. It wasn't.

Her old friend Zoey was calling. Piper had visited her before start-ing at Stella's and met the brand new baby. Mommy hormones had had a field day. "Hi, Zoey."

"Hi, Piper. Do you have a sec?"

"Sure." She was dying to tell someone else about the Hollywood party with producers that she had been invited to by the bestselling author and screenwriter Hudson Hathaway.

"I'm sorry. You probably should sit down."

"What? What's wrong?"

"Are you sitting?"

Seriously? She sat on the bed. "Yes, I'm sitting."

"Remember the Bronze Star Medal the guys always said Jared should get? There was some controversy over what happened, but they petitioned for it for years."

"Some of the guys did."

"Most of the guys did. Piper, they awarded it to him."

"Ohhh." She shut her eyes, shocked at the news. "Oh, Jared, baby," she whispered.

"It takes some getting used to, huh?"

"Yeah." She laid back on the bed and looked at the ceiling. "After all this time. He was so deserving, wasn't he, Zoey? He was a good man."

"Yes, he was. I'm glad it happened."

"I remember—what was his name?—that funny guy with curly black hair. He said Jared earned a hero's medal every single day they were over there, just by being his regular self, taking care of others. Whew. I...I don't know how to process this. The whole posthumous thing is—strange. It feels like another funeral. But it's a good thing. Like a finality. His parents are going to be so proud."

"Piper, I'm sorry. The ceremony was yesterday."

The words made no sense.

"They gave it to his parents. I'm sorry. I am so sorry. There was rumor it was going down. Then the baby was born and Nicky and I got side-tracked. I didn't even know about the invitation. It slipped Nicky's mind until Johnson called a couple days ago. The two of them went yesterday. I just…just assumed you would be there. Nicky came home last night and said you weren't."

Piper blinked, her mind still not caught up to what Zoey was saying.

"Didn't anyone tell you?"

"N-no." It was her fault. She had cut herself off from Jared's old friends, her old friends. They were scattered around the country now. But the military knew where they were.

"Maybe because you weren't married, your name slipped through the cracks. But…my gosh. Jared's parents? Why didn't they…?"

Jared's parents. The people who had never accepted her as worthy enough to deserve their son's love.

"Zoey, I can't talk right now."

"Yeah." Her voice was thick with tears.

Piper feared she might drown in her own.

Seventy

Knowing she was about to set everything off, Liv phoned Piper's mother in Wisconsin with a prayer on her lips. She explained the troubling situation to Darlene.

"No, Liv. That can't be."

"I'm afraid so."

"His parents—Hold on, please." There was a distinct edge to the woman's tone.

Liv listened to muffled voices. Loud, angry muffled voices. She imagined Darlene was telling her husband, Bob. From what she had gathered in the past, Piper's parents adored Jared. They were having a meltdown of their own.

"Liv." Darlene was back on the phone. "I'm sorry. Piper should have been told. This is going to bring up his death all over again. His parents must be there. How could they do this to her? Exclude her from such a significant event? They have been unbelievably—oh! I won't go into that." She paused. When she spoke again, the tears had begun. "I just spoke to her. She was so happy about going on a date with that writer."

"Hudson Hathaway?"

"They went to a ball game last night. Today they're going to a party in Hollywood."

That was lovely news, but Liv shoved it to a back burner. "Darlene, I'm here for you. Whatever you need, let me know."

"Liv, I can't tell you how grateful I am for that. We'll call her. Would you mind being there when we talk? I don't want her to be alone."

They made a plan. Liv checked her kitchen clock and waited a few minutes. She didn't want to arrive too early and announce, "Your mom is calling." That would frighten her. She didn't need a dose of fear ahead of what she was going to be enduring.

Poor Piper. *Lord, have mercy.*

Liv slipped on her sandals and went into the courtyard. The mayhem had already begun.

Heidi and Hud stood in Piper's doorway. The girl was beside herself, pushing Hud away, crying loudly. Had she read the news online?

Liv hurried over.

Piper disappeared inside her cottage. The door was open, but Heidi and Hud did not enter.

"Liv." Tears wet Heidi's face. "A friend called her and said something about a posthumous medal for Jared? That they gave it to his parents yesterday. Which of course they would since she and Jared weren't married, but she didn't even know about the ceremony."

"I read about it." She told them what she knew and about talking to Piper's mom.

Hud looked ready to strangle someone. He paced in a tight circle, speechless.

Heidi wiped at her eyes. "She's such a kind person. This is awful."

"It is. Her mom's calling her in a few minutes. I better go inside."

Heidi nodded. "She didn't want to be with us. Can we do anything?"

"I'll let you know." Liv eyed Hud and saw such anguish on his face her own heart ached for him. After what Darlene had said about the two of them getting together, this was a setback. She caught his arm and he stopped pacing. "Whatever she said to you, Hudson, let it go. She'll get through this."

He shook his head. "And then there'll be something else. I can't compete with a dead guy." He walked off.

Liv mashed her lips shut and turned toward the door, where Heidi stood, still weeping. Probably for Hud as much as for Piper. She wrapped her arms around the girl.

Heidi whispered, "She told him to go away."

"Men take things so literally, don't they?"

Heidi snickered and cried at the same time.

Liv gave her one last squeeze and went inside.

ℒℓℯ

Piper cried her eyes out, talked to her mom and dad, cried some more, accepted Liv's hugs and cups of tea. She said things she did not mean, things that did not make sense, and probably a thing or two that she did believe.

"I hate war."

"I'm not supposed to move on. I'm just not."

"I hate his parents."

"They were right about me. I'm a fluff head from Wisconsin who likes to play dress-up all the time."

"Jared was just doing his job. He wouldn't have wanted a medal for getting blasted to kingdom come by a roadside bomb."

"Why wasn't I there? Why wasn't I there?"

"If he hadn't joined the Corps in the first place, he wouldn't be dead. We never would have met. I'd be living in New York City doing fluff head things."

"I'm going to move back home. There's nothing for me out here. There was only Jared."

"Who do I think I am, quitting Tellmann's and running a boutique in Rancho Sierra? I can't believe I actually considered buying it. What an idiot I am."

"And Hud. Another bigger-than-life guy, exactly like Jared that way. Out of my league. Too much trouble."

"What is wrong with me?"

"I'll never ever get over him."

"Stupid. Stupid. Stupid."

Liv let her ramble.

Suddenly Piper stood. "I want to read about it."

Liv hesitated.

"Please."

"All right. Maybe it will bring some closure."

"I should have been there in person for closure."

"Yes, dear."

They went to the office. Liv rolled a second chair to the desk and they both sat. She gently pushed aside Piper's shaking hands from the keyboard. After a few searches for the article she had read last night, she found another source.

With a photograph of Jared's mother and father receiving the Bronze Star.

Liv's heart hammered. She imagined Piper's did the same. They silently read the citation.

The President of the United States of America takes pleasure in presenting the Bronze Star Medal with Combat "V" to Sergeant Jared Michael Oakes, United States Marine Corps, for heroic achievement in connection with combat operations against the enemy...

A description of his actions followed. From what Liv gathered, he had done a whole lot more than get himself killed. He'd led others to safety and held back enemy forces—on his own, at one point—and that was just on his last day. There were more examples of how, where, and when he served with valor.

By his bold leadership, wise judgment, and complete dedication to duty, Sergeant Oakes reflected great credit upon himself and upheld the highest traditions of the Marine Corps...

Piper eyed the screen, a hand over her mouth. "This is a nightmare. Why am I awake?"

Liv put an arm around her shoulders. She had nothing else to offer.

Seventy-One

At some point during that never-ending day, Piper recognized that she had been in the same pit before.

It was a brief consolation, assuring her that footholds were embedded in pits. She would climb out. Eventually.

Now, though, she wondered if she was still in the pit she'd fallen into the day she learned of Jared's death. Had she grown so accustomed to living in the hole that she only imagined she'd made an exit?

She turned to Chad, seated on the couch beside her. The glow from the television lit his face. "I was getting better, wasn't I?"

He turned to her. "You were soaring like an eagle."

"For real?"

"For real. You just hit some space debris and got an owie. You'll get better."

She scooted closer to him, and he slipped an arm over her shoulders. The nightmarish fear that had haunted her all day was that if she stopped touching people, she would dry up and turn into a pile of ash.

Liv was her rock, but everyone else had jumped in with hugs and pats and squeezes. Her surrogate family hemmed her in with love while her mom and dad made plane reservations. They had a tendency to be over-protective, and had put their frequent flyer miles toward the trip. Piper had not tried to talk them out of coming.

When night fell, she couldn't bring herself to shut her cottage door. Who else to call but Chad? He came immediately with popcorn to micro-wave and silly movies to get lost in.

Hud faded from the scene. Piper knew she had said ugly things to him.

She had lashed out because he resembled Jared so much. Not in looks or demeanor, but in capturing her heart. And that—that business was over. She had nothing left to give.

Hud was not Casa family. His only role to play was to remind her of Jared, and Jared was all about surviving the pit. If Jared were there, if Hud were there, Piper's ability to survive was zilch.

She snuggled against Chad, the goofy but trustworthy guy. "You know you're like a brother to me."

He sighed dramatically. "Lucky me."

"Lucky me."

"There you go. If you think you're lucky on this appalling day, that owie must be healing already."

How she hoped that was true.

Seventy-Two

In the strip mall's parking lot, Heidi looped her arm through Val's and gazed at the storefront with the large sign up high. *SunView Properties.* The bold, block letters were a reddish purple hue, a blend of both of their favorite colors.

It seemed a silly thing now, but they had spent hours devising every detail of that sign until it was exactly what they wanted. Anybody could design a sign with a name on it. But a distinct and functional expression of who they were as women and professionals was a work of art.

Val held the smaller sign that had been in the window, the one that contained the entire mouthful. *SunView Coastal Property Management and Real Estate Agency.* Their names were printed below, next to their photographs along with cell phone numbers.

Heidi felt a twinge of regret and then of embarrassment because it was only a little regret. She should be feeling gobs and gobs of regret. The agency was no more, at least nowhere near what it had been. That was something to feel bad about. Instead she felt a truckload of relief.

Recovering from the accident and selling her condo had all but undone her. By now, leaving behind the agency that had come to represent a lot of heartache and nastiness did not begin to compare to them. She was a racehorse at the gate, her hoof stomping the ground, stirring up dirt. *Let's get going already.*

"Heidi. Heidi!"

It took a moment for Val's voice to register. "What?"

"I said come with me to my car. I've got your new business cards."

"Okay."

They walked across the parking lot in silence. In spite of her sense of relief, Heidi knew it was a solemn moment. They were leaving behind a lot of history.

But SunView would continue, virtually for a time, as a real estate agency. Cynthia and Dawn were in the process of purchasing the property management side of the business. Although it consistently provided an income, it wasn't enough to carry them all. Heidi and Val were not the least bit interested in running it, and so they let it go.

Finances were a complicated mess. Craig still worked on their behalf. Treena still had not been tracked down. Val still commuted from the beach house.

"How's Julian?"

Val gave her a funny look. "Fine, I guess. I've seen him like twice."

"I'm just glad he's next door. Right now, I need my neighbors."

Val ignored her comment, as she did all comments about the Casa. "Is Hud around?"

"He left yesterday." Poor Hud. Poor Piper.

"I thought he was going to hang out this week and look at some properties."

"Something came up." He'd skipped the Hollywood party and hightailed it back to Mexico. The chicken. "The houses weren't quite right, anyway. He wants small and basic."

"That's a challenge in the area he likes. Maybe he could build."

They reached Val's car. She unlocked it, ducked inside, retrieved a small cardboard box, and handed it to her. "Here you go. There are postcards and notepads too. No address, which seems weird."

"You didn't like my idea of using coffee shop addresses?" They had decided that when they needed to meet in person, coffee shops were their best choice of virtual office space. Val refused to come to the Casa. Heidi refused to do down to the beach house, a long haul even for someone who drove on the freeways.

When necessary, they would go to meet people in their homes. Most business was conducted via e-mail, even the signing of contracts. They envisioned making it work virtually. If push came to shove, they could use the conference room at Craig's office, he promised.

Val ignored her question about coffee shop addresses.

Heidi peeked inside the box and saw her old photo staring up from a notepad. Long blonde hair, no glasses. No sideways V scar on her cheek. The woman was a stranger.

"You're good to go, then?"

"Yep." Heidi had an appointment to show a few properties to an eager client. "How about you? I can take over showing your house. I only had to do my condo once. If I'd have had to show it again, I'd still be in a fetal position on the floor."

"I'll be fine. Craig has kept things in order and even done some packing."

Heidi eyed her friend. "Did you see him over the weekend?"

"No. We talked for five minutes on the phone. And no, we are not considering reconciliation. Get off my back." The words and tone were vintage Val.

Heidi felt tired. Even in full-on meltdown, Piper's demeanor nowhere near assaulted her senses like Val's could any day of the week.

Val blew a kiss toward the office and gave Heidi a quick hug. "Remember, sweetie, we are simply relocating. Go get 'em." She drove off.

Heidi limped to her car, carrying her shoulder bag and one lone cardboard box. She let out a very loud, very long sigh of…satisfaction. *Getting 'em* was the furthest thing from her mind.

Heidi rescheduled the appointment with the eager client. Given her precarious business situation, she should fire herself. But the man sounded as if tomorrow worked better for him anyway.

It definitely worked better for Heidi. The closing of the office impacted her like a flu shot, something she'd become rather acquainted with since her body had taken on its new susceptibility to every passing bug. It pricked, her arm ached, her stomach roiled, and she walked through crowds with courage. All in all, the positive-negative emotional pull rattled her. She needed the day to un-rattle.

She needed to attack it head-on. *It.* The monster of all monster emotions.

At a gas station within sight of the I-5 freeway signs and on-ramps, she pumped gas, washed the windshield, and then she sat behind the steering wheel. Excuses not to follow through with her plan whipped around her mind like flung darts. *This doesn't have to happen today. You just walked away from nine years of your life. It may be positive, but it hurts too. You know it does. Your brother is in the wind. Adam is in the wind. Piper is basically in the wind. You could lend a hand to all of them and tackle this issue another time. Set a goal, not do it spur of the moment. Say six months from the date of the accident. August. That's only a few weeks away. Or how about nine months, perfect incubation period.*

She debated calling someone. Her parents, Val, Liv, Jasmyn, Piper? No. She checked them off the list. Hud? He was too far away, probably headed to the Tijuana airport to catch a flight to Ecuador. Adam?

Adam.

Well…no. Not Adam. They had kept their distance, for whatever reason. Between the Val and Craig thing and the Liv thing with Val and Adam, feelings were too intense and not in a particularly good way. She and Adam seemed destined for a long-distance type of friendship, one based on old memories.

Nope. She would not call anyone. She had gotten herself into this without help from others. She could do it all by herself.

Except…except maybe for God?

Growing up, Heidi assumed that if some Other was out there, their paths did not cross. Then Adam had begun expressing his faith, sometimes more with actions than words, like when he gave silent thanks before eating. He described God as present everywhere in the mystery and beauty of His creation.

She had put all that on the back burner until she met Liv, whose path seemed not to be crossing with God's, but one and the same. The sense of God became palpable.

"God," she whispered. All right, she was going there, into the Presence that Liv promised was waiting for her. "This has to be done today. I can't ignore it any longer. I just cannot. But I can't do it alone." She smiled crookedly. "I've lost my bluster. Maybe You've noticed."

She waited, trying to calm her thumping heartbeat. What was that exercise Riley had taught her? She stretched out her arms and studied them until it came back to her. She crossed her wrists, clasped her hands, and folded her arms back in and against her chest. The gesture soothed her.

"Whew. Okay. Well, I don't feel You, God. But Liv says You're always everywhere and believe me, I tend to trust anything that woman with the invisible sandwich board says. So, I need—I need to do this, to get through this. With flying colors would be preferred, but…You know. Whatever."

Whatever came as a sense of well-being. It felt like a brief hug from arms she could not see or touch. Their imprint remained, though, deep inside where all gifts of love and courage lingered.

She was going to be okay.

Heidi drove the route that Hud had taken her on. In Oceanside, she turned onto the ramp and merged into the right hand lane of the freeway. She kept her foot steady and smoothly sped up to sixty-eight. She would not be going any faster nor changing lanes.

She was the kind of driver who five months ago she would have fussed at.

She managed a little smile.

A driver honked. Every other vehicle zoomed past. The car shook in the wake of a passing semi.

Twenty minutes later she exited in San Clemente, turned around in a gas station, and without stopping, proceeded to the southbound on-ramp.

Seventy-Three

"Piper, dear, where shall I put these?" Liv held up a lacy black bra and matching panties. She couldn't help but note the sizes and imagine that whoever wore them would present a nice package.

The retail of women's clothing was indeed a curious business.

Piper looked over from where she stood near a rack of tops. "Where on earth did you find those?"

"On the floor in the fitting room. Behind the chair."

"Whoops. I must have missed them when I closed up Saturday night. I was in a..." She frowned and swished hangers on the rack. "A hurry."

Liv caught on. The girl had been in a hurry to leave the shop that night and go to the Padres game with Hudson Hathaway. Whom she had not yet mentioned.

Piper waved a hand. "Just put them on the counter for now."

Liv did as she was told and then she sat on a stool. Stella's Boutique was a lovely, feminine shop. It smelled and looked and felt like a cloud, or what she imagined one would smell, look, and feel like. There were collections of basic black, of course, in lingerie and elsewhere, but overall it was a bright, airy, and pastel sort of place. It fit Piper like a glove.

Piper crossed the floor. She was a beautiful girl in spite of the obvious exhaustion. "I'm sorry, Liv."

"For what, dear?"

"For snapping."

Liv chuckled. "You don't know the meaning of the word."

"Whatever. Thank you for coming."

"My pleasure. If you don't work me too hard, I may shop. Stella has a good selection of styles and sizes for my age."

"Mondays are typically slow. You don't need to stay all day."

"Business is not why I insisted on joining you."

Piper nodded and straightened things on the countertop. "If you hadn't, I might still be home in bed. Or at least curled up in a corner here. If I'd had the part-time ladies take over, I'm sure I wouldn't have a job once Stella came back."

"You'll be fine."

"I'll be fine."

"So how was the Padres game?"

Piper gave her a startled look. The corners of her mouth twitched. "Did my mom tell you?"

"Yes."

"I almost got to go to a Hollywood party too, with movie producers."

"You'll have another chance."

She shook her head.

"Yesterday threw a curve ball at you."

"Yep. I swung and I missed by a mile."

"I think you hit a foul ball. You're left standing at the plate, dealing with the stages of grief all over again."

"The stages of grief. Been there, done that. Haven't I? I was moving on. I was into the acceptance stage. I know it's not a 'once and you're done' thing, but after four years of up and down, back and forth, I had both feet right there this time. Otherwise, how could I have fallen so hard and so fast for Hud?"

Liv felt her brows rise. She let Piper's slip of the tongue pass without comment. "Perhaps what you're feeling now is more about your relationship with Jared's parents. That seemed to be an open-ended situation. Their actions sealed it shut. This will sound harsh, honey, but they made it clear that they don't consider you part of their family."

"But they were my link to him."

"Yes, they were. And that's why it hurts so much."

"Are you saying I need to deny all that and be angry and bargain for their affection and feel depressed over their rejection and then accept it?"

"DABDA. Denial, anger, bargaining, depression, and acceptance.

You've got those stages down pat." She paused. "Yes, that's about it in a nutshell. One more time for the parents."

Her shoulders sagged. "Is it worth it?"

"You know it is, child. Pretending this was not a grievous event won't get you to a Hollywood party with movie producers."

"Liv." Pink tinged her cheeks.

It was a good sign. Liv stood. "Well, put me to work. I can shop at the same time. Do I get the employees discount?"

Piper laughed.

Another good sign.

Seventy-Four

Heidi exited at the rest stop. The whoop and the holler and the fist pump could not wait until she drove into the city.

She parked, slid from the car, and whooped, hollered, and pumped her fist into the air. "Yess! Yess! Yess!" She gyrated around the car. "I did it. I did it. Yess! Whew! Hallelujah!"

It took a while for her excitement to taper off to a low gurgle. Only the ocean witnessed her kooky behavior.

She had driven past the site. She had not crashed. She had not cried. She had fought her fear and won. Next time she could change lanes. She could drive a little faster and keep up with the flow of traffic. She knew she could.

But not today. Today was for celebration.

She leaned against her car and gazed out over coastal wilderness and at the vast expanse of sky and ocean. Today was also for admitting that she loved Adam Engstrom. That being a long-distance friend who shared an outdated past and moments here and there was totally unacceptable. She was in a new season. And she wasn't going to go through life alone.

What if he still loved Maisie?

That was his problem. He'd have to tell her and then he'd have to explain why he bought a super expensive kayak to take her out one time.

She reached into the car and picked up her cell phone.

He answered on the seventh ring. "Hello."

"Adam, it's me."

"Hey, you." He spoke to someone who must have been with him. "Sorry, Heidi. In the middle of a delivery here. What's up?"

"I drove it."

A few seconds passed and then he whistled a note of disbelief. "No kidding."

"No kidding. Just now."

"And you're walking and talking."

"I am."

He laughed loudly. "Way to go, Hathaway! How was it?"

"Scary. Amazing. Healing. I'm a little shaky."

"You did it alone?"

"Yes."

"I would have gone with you."

Really? "I had to do it by myself. But I would like to celebrate with a friend."

"Did you have one in mind?" The grin was obvious in his voice.

She chuckled. "Pizza at my place tonight?"

"No swing through the Gaslamp District or fancy dinner at Mr. A's? I'd take you. Or a spin out on the ocean?"

"Honestly, I'm wiped out. I've had enough excitement for one day. Some quiet time with you in my quaint little cottage sounds perfect."

"Who are you and what have you done with my wild and crazy Heidi?"

"Sorry. She took off about five months ago. Just bailed on me along the side of the freeway without saying goodbye."

"Don't be sorry." There was a catch in his voice. "Seven o'clock work?"

"It works fine." And then some. She smiled.

Adam arrived with a pizza box, a grin, and a bear hug. "Congratulations, Ms. Road Queen."

"Thanks." She shut the door behind him.

"Look at this place. You've moved in. I like it."

"Me too. What is this?" She took the box from him. "I was going to order delivery."

"I have a new guy in the kitchen, Jésus Gonzales. He's easily bored with the menu. I swear he's more artist than cook. He creates daily specials that are a little weird and off-the-charts amazing. When I told him what I was doing tonight, he whipped this up for us. We need to bake it."

While the pizza baked, they worked together on a salad and setting the table. A comfortable familiarity spilled into her kitchen. They had shared countless meals through the years. Now that she thought about it, they'd shared everything...

Well, not *every*thing.

And why had that thought popped into her head?

Because he looked good, smelled good, and he added a distinct air of masculinity to her cottage. He wore blue jeans, flip-flops, and a pale green shirt with a message. A wide canopy of branches was filled with letters: *Green is not just a color.* She sniffed again. A minty soap. His hair was damp. Its reddish tint shone in the light.

Standing beside him at the counter, she elbowed his arm. "Thanks for this."

He elbowed her back. "Sure." He chopped cucumbers and yellow peppers, adding them to the lettuce in a bowl. "I talked to Val this afternoon. She told me about the office. It seems that you, Heidi Hathaway, have had a red-letter day." He glanced down at her. "How'd you get from saying goodbye to the office to slaying the freeway dragon?"

"I was in a mood."

He chuckled. "I imagine closing the office was a sort of dragon too. You doing okay with that?"

"As Val says, we are simply relocating. Juggling things there and worrying about the cash flow was getting to be too much. I'm fine with taking a step back from the rat race." She barked a laugh. "That doesn't sound like me, does it?"

"Nope."

"Is it a good thing that the wild, crazy, competitive rat died alongside the freeway?"

"You said she bailed on you."

Heidi remembered the appointment she had canceled and took her silliness down a few notches. "No. She died."

Adam moved to the sink, rinsed his hands, and carefully dried them on a towel. "The question is, do you think it's a good thing?" He looked at her.

"It scares me to death."

"Beginnings are notorious for that." He stepped before her, cupped her face in his hands, and gently kissed her scarred cheek. "I've been wanting to do that since I first saw it covered in stitches."

She blinked.

He slid off her glasses, set them on the counter, and kissed the other cheek.

"Why?"

His face was very close, his eyes intent on hers. "Why what?"

"The, uh, scar."

"It's a long story."

"I'm not going anywhere."

"I hope not." He smiled. "It puts a chink in your armor."

"Armor."

"Mm-hmm. The shield that served you well in sports and business. I always read it as an 'I can do it myself, thank you very much' sign. And of course you could and you can. You're an amazing woman. Look at how you've taken on these dragons and reordered your life, even with the chink."

She frowned, not following, not really caring that she wasn't because there was a new light in his eyes. She wondered what it was.

He traced the scar, from her hairline to the dimple to the spot right beneath her earlobe. "It's a lopsided V. Like a symbol of victory knocked over by vulnerability." He kissed it again. "Just enough to make me think you're okay with me telling you how much I love you."

She smiled, but had no voice to reply.

"And to say that I don't want to go through life without you beside me, being a whole lot more than just an old friend."

He kissed her on the lips then.

They ignored the oven timer, and the pizza burned.

Seventy-Five

"We ate burnt pizza." Heidi grinned from ear to ear.

Liv set her tea cup on the table between their Adirondack chairs outside her cottage door. "Oh, dear. I hope the oven isn't on the fritz."

"Operator error." Her grin stayed put.

Liv felt a smile growing on her own face. Heidi had just told her about closing the doors to SunView Properties yesterday, driving on the freeway past the accident site, and about Adam Engstrom coming over for dinner. She sensed there was more to the story than the girl revealed. Something personal? With Syd's son? That was an extremely pleasant thought.

"Anyway." Heidi stood, her coffee mug in hand. "I have to go to work. In my home. In my sweats." She laughed. "Although I do have an appointment later that will require a wardrobe change."

Liv chuckled. The girl was already jumping into her new routine and it wasn't even six a.m. The courtyard still lay in grayness. The June gloom had seeped into July, its moisture capturing floral fragrances. It was a morning for lingering.

She said, "Do you mind if I ask about SunView?"

"Not at all. You've been there and done that, haven't you?" She sat back down, apparently not yet ready to start work. "I mean, you closed your real estate agency."

"Years ago. My father started it before I was born. It was extremely difficult to let it go, but Syd and I wanted more time together. As it turned out, he died five years after. I'm grateful I didn't wait."

"I wish I'd known Syd better."

319

"Adam and Valerie both resemble him in different ways." Liv smiled. "How are you handling the end of SunView?"

"It was sad to shut the door for the last time. But at the same time it feels incredibly good to move ahead. Between you and me—Do you get that phrase a lot?"

Liv winked. "Why, what on earth do you mean?"

"You're so easy to talk to and trustworthy and wise. I bet everyone…" She made a sweeping gesture. "Every one of these people have sat in this chair and said, 'between you and me,' and then shared a secret or a problem."

"Joys too." She leaned toward Heidi and whispered, "Noah hasn't."

"Not yet anyway." Heidi smiled. "Anyway, between you and me, I've been talking to Craig behind Val's back. He tells me more than he tells her because she tunes him out and won't listen. Our finances are a mess. A horrendous mess. Obviously. Neither Val nor I have any savings left." She grimaced. "For now I'm living on the sale of my condo."

Liv reached over and touched her arm. "Stop paying me rent for as long as you need."

"No, no. Thanks, I'm fine. And Craig says we can be fine. Or at least I can be fine. When things slow down from what I have pending, I might want to consider joining another firm. Solo marketing and networking can be overwhelming."

"But Val won't be fine?"

"He's concerned. With her spending habits, their divorce, her refusal to consider joining another firm, and the fact that they're upside down on their house…" She shrugged.

"He has a solid job, though."

"He does. Craig really is a good guy who made a huge mistake. He'll spend his life trying to make up for it. He will take care of her, as far as he can."

"I'm glad to hear that. Syd left her a trust fund. Adam inherited the farm and Valerie inherited enough money to keep a real estate company going for a long time, through fat and lean years."

Heidi leaned back in her chair as if she'd been shoved. Clearly this was news to her.

"Oh my. Now I should be the one to say 'between you and me.'"

"I won't mention it. Val and I started the agency from what I thought was her inheritance, a good lump sum, that we easily earned back within a few years. Nothing like you're describing. Craig never even met Syd. He was gone before they got together. I wonder if he knows."

"Well, perhaps she has something tucked away then."

"That would be good for her. And she probably would do that." She stood again. "In the meantime, I have a desk to go to. Did I mention it's in my cottage? And that's where I'm working today and tomorrow and the day after…"

Liv smiled and watched her walk across the courtyard. *Lord, have mercy. And thank You for that freeway ride. Woohoo!*

After Heidi left, Liv went inside to make another pot of tea. When she returned, a sleepyhead Tobi on her heels, Jasmyn was seated in the chair. They exchanged greetings and Liv—who always had an extra cup on the table—poured tea for both of them.

"I hope I don't make a mistake at Stella's today."

Liv smiled. "I made several yesterday, hon. Piper didn't care. She just straightened up behind me. It gave her something to do when there weren't customers in the shop."

"I'm all thumbs when it comes to fashion." She seemed nervous.

Tobi must have sensed it. She jumped onto Jasmyn's lap, turned three times, and snuggled down for a nap. Jasmyn rewarded her with soft strokes.

Liv said, "Fashion isn't something I spend much time on. Let me tell you, if it weren't for L.L. Bean's senior catalog, I'd be wearing the same skirts and tops I bought when Syd and I were married."

"If it weren't for Piper, I'd have worn blue jeans to my wedding."

"We would have sewn on some lace." She smiled. "You're not there to work."

"I know. She just needs company."

"Right. And you're the best kind of company for her."

"How was she last night?"

"Much, much better than she'd been when we left in the morning. By the time we came home last night, she was in a better place than she'd been at eight a.m. I imagine she'll be ready to be on her own tomorrow with one of the part-time ladies."

They chatted a bit about Piper's parents' upcoming visit.

"Liv, what do you think about offering Cottage One to them?"

"Ooh, I like it."

"Don't you want to think about—You already did, didn't you?"

She smiled. "It's all ready for guests. I see no reason not to share it with family of family."

"I mentioned it to Keagan and he got all serious and said, 'The Casa is not a motel.' I reminded him that neither is his gym a homeless shelter in the wintertime. He saw my point."

Liv laughed. "You're the best kind of company for that man too."

Seventy-Six

Piper heard a knock on her open front door and went out from her bed-room, hairbrush in hand, to see who else was up at dawn.

Heidi greeted her from the doorway, a coffee mug in hand.

"Good morning. Come on inside."

"Did you know your door was open?" Heidi stepped through it.

She shrugged. "Yeah. It makes everyone seem closer and that makes me feel safer. It sounds silly."

"Whatever works. Do we have critters in the courtyard?"

"Yes."

"Ick. You didn't leave it open all night, did you?"

"No." Piper smiled. "I'm making coffee. Do you want some in your mug?"

"No, thanks." Heidi followed her into the kitchen. "How are you?"

"Okay." She filled the carafe with water.

"What is 'okay' on a scale of one to ten? One being 'so-so' and ten being 'I can imagine putting the dance shoes on again.'"

"Four."

"I'm sorry." She sat at the table. "Do you mind hearing news from a 'twelve'?"

Piper's stomach churned. Her chest muscles still ached from sobbing again last night. She switched on the coffeemaker and sat down. "I'd love to hear news from a twelve."

"Are you sure? If I were a four, I'd tell me to get lost."

"Go ahead."

"You're a good person, Piper. Thank you for befriending me and bringing me to the Casa. You're the one and only person I can talk to about this." Her expression resembled a balloon, stretched to its limits with a face painted on it.

"You look like you're going to pop."

"I am." She exhaled, a sound of a balloon whistling air. "Adam came over last night and the pizza burned in the oven because he kissed me and then we kissed some more."

Piper grinned. "Wow."

"Wow." She stood. "That's it. I have to get to work." She sat back down. "Do you have any suggestions for the way I look?"

"Huh?"

"Cosmetics. Hair. Glasses. I'm feeling out of touch with pretty."

"And yet Adam has begun this kissing relationship with you."

"Go figure." She tilted her head. "He likes my scar."

Piper studied her happy friend. She'd grown accustomed to her hair, now about two inches long, cut in a style suitable for messy or spiky. Heidi had not yet replaced her contact lenses and still wore the black-rimmed square glasses. The jagged scar most likely appeared as a neon light to Heidi, but to no one else. She wore sloppy sweats, but she'd brought her nice clothes to the Casa now.

"Heidi, you look like you."

"And that means…"

"Real. You look real."

"You used to help me look not real."

"No, I used to help you enhance the real because real doesn't look good billboard size. That's just the way it is in our culture."

She groaned. "Maisie was real, but it was attractive on her. Billboard size would have flattered her looks."

"Maisie. The girlfriend?"

"Ex."

"Whew."

"Tell me about it." Her smile returned. "I'm the reason they never got together for good. She told him he always loved me, and now she's not hanging out at the Garden anymore."

"Guys can be slow."

"And chicken. Hud is both."

"Heidi—"

"Sorry. We won't go there. But FYI—and then I promise to shut up—Hud wants to buy a house in San Diego County. He especially likes the rural area east of Rancho Sierra."

Hope rose and fell, a whirling Ferris wheel ride that made her dizzy and nauseous. A healthy person would not buy a ticket for such a ridiculous ride.

"I'm checking out some properties today."

"Is he going with you?"

"I have no idea where the chicken is."

The Ferris wheel stopped. "Why don't you swing by Stella's? She has some cosmetics, a hairdresser next door, and an optometrist down the block."

Heidi laughed.

Piper laughed with her. She might have scooted from a four up to a five.

Seventy-Seven

Nothing could knock the dippy grin off Adam's face...or so he thought the day after kissing Heidi.

That she loved him too—and not solely in the platonic fashion they'd known since college—had not completely surprised him. It had, however, put the dippy grin on his face. Staff began to question, guess, and tease. His privacy was history.

The situation also made him miss his father. He missed Syd every single day, but the uncanny resemblance of his relationship with Livvie McAlister and Adam's with Heidi deepened the ache.

Not that he and Maisie had been anywhere near married like his parents had been. Not that he had children like them. But falling in love with his best friend was something he longed to tell his dad.

It wasn't the same with his sister and mother, the ones who knocked the grin off his face.

Less than a day home from a months-long stay in Europe, Cathy Moseley sought out her children. Why invite the kids to stop by the house some evening when she and her husband, Gunther, could regale them with European adventure stories and photos? Better to leave Gunther at home, interrupt his and Val's workdays—spur of the moment, naturally— and hang with them at the café.

Adam admitted that he had mother issues. He loved, respected, and appreciated Cathy. He always had. But she pushed buttons that made him squirm. He would recognize what was going on, explain to her what was happening, and set boundaries. She would agree until she forgot. And her memory was very, very short.

The main reason for the twist in his gut today was because he loved Heidi, who lived at Cathy's ex's widow's complex. On top of that, he liked that widow very much. If he talked about his wonderful news, her response would press his whole set of buttons. His grin faded.

Val had her own news. She lived next door to the guy Cathy blamed nearly as much as she did Livvie for pulling Syd away from her.

Poor Cathy was about to eat lunch with two mute children or be blindsided in public.

Now, seated at one of the tables in his café, his mother studied the décor she had designed. She was an attractive woman, her chestnut hair gone to white, simply styled. Her seventy-year-old body had plumped some, but was still healthy from a devotion to walking and organic food. She was his best spokeswoman. "I'd love to spruce this place up."

Val exchanged a glance with Adam and put a finger over her lips, holding back a smile.

Adam said, "Have at it, Mom. I bet you have a ton of new ideas from Europe."

Her eyes lit up. "Whatnots from Venice and Geneva are being shipped even as we speak." She picked up her fork. "This is a fabulous quiche. I must get the recipe from Jesus."

"Jésus. Hey-soos."

"Where's Maisie?"

"Um, she's not here much anymore." He berated himself for the half-truth. "She's not here at all. Her baked goods are, though."

"Adam, I thought you two were, you know, hooked up."

Thirty-five years old and two words from his mother made him blush and stammer. "We've, uh, gone our separate ways. Actually, she loathed the farm."

"How could she loathe the farm? It's so beautiful and so successful. It's so you. What's a little drive from the city?"

He shrugged.

Val's eyes were wide open. "Really?"

He shrugged again. He preferred muteness.

Apparently, Val did not. "He bought a kayak, Mom. Took Heidi out on it."

"That sounds lovely. She's a nice girl."

Val snickered.

Adam shot arrows at her. "Yes, she is. We…" He paused. Why prolong the agony? "We're sort of seeing each other. We are seeing each other."

Val nearly jumped out of her seat. "Since when?"

"Last night."

"News to me."

"Me too."

"Now how can that be news to you?"

"Well, let's see. I figured we were just friends. She figured we were just friends." His voice rose. "Duh. We *were* just friends. For years and years. And then." He snapped his fingers. "Poof. I want to wake up every morning for the rest of my life looking at her."

Across the room, behind the serving counter, Jésus caught his attention. His arms, covered in a white chef's jacket, were raised, palms up. He mouthed, *What gives, Boss?*

Adam swallowed and decided to lower his voice.

Cathy reached over and patted his cheeks. "Adam, that's wonderful, wonderful news! I am so happy for you both. I always liked Heidi. Except for a while when you two were flunking college. She was not a good influence at that time. Will there be grandchildren?"

He smiled crookedly and shrugged again.

She gasped. "Ohmygoodness. Her brother! Hudson Hathaway."

Val said, "Yeah, yeah. We won't be related to her brother, Mom."

"Close is close, honey. The man is famous. We saw his books in Paris!"

Val glared at Adam with her snake eyes. "Well?"

Well…He went for it. "Mom, you know about Heidi's accident. With her leg injury, she couldn't live in her condo with the steps. She stayed with her folks and then she found a bungalow to rent in a complex."

"Poor dear. Is there permanent damage?"

"To her leg. Um, the place she lives is owned by, uh, um." He wanted to smack his own head. "By Olivia McAlister."

Cathy stared at him, speechless.

"Heidi didn't know until after she had moved in who it was."

"Hm." It was a grunt.

"By then, she liked the place. She liked the owner."

Cathy gave a terse nod.

"And, the truth is, I talked to her. To Livvie. And, well, we got along."

"You met Livvie." She spoke the statement without expression.

Adam had no more to say.

"Well, Adam, it's about time you met that woman. Your father loved her very much. She's smart. Ran a highly successful business. They had a solid marriage."

Adam thought he might slide off his chair.

"Just don't expect me to have dinner at your fiancée's—what'd you call it? Bungalow. We'll get together here or at my house. Heidi will understand." Cathy turned to Val. "What's your bombshell?"

"What do you mean?"

She laughed. "I mean, you two are open books to me. I've seen those same expressions a time or two. Let's see, there was the football thrown through the grandfather clock when you played in the house. The lost jewelry and broken high heels, Val, from playing dress-up. The bike Adam put behind the car so that I'd run over it and you'd have to get a new one. So come on. Fess up."

"I'm living temporarily in a beach house. Next to Julian."

In a split second, Cathy's face went from amused to raging.

"Mom, it's temporary. SunView runs it. He doesn't."

"Listen, both of you. Olivia made sense. Julian never made sense." She scraped her chair backwards. "I'm going home."

They followed her, but she refused to acknowledge their presence. They watched her drive away.

Adam clung to the encouragement that his mom accepted Livvie, but the hurt expression on Val's face struck a chord of fear in him.

"Val, she'll get over it."

"Doesn't matter. I won't. Say hey to Heidi. I am glad for you two, really." She strode away through the parking lot.

Adam let her go. He'd had enough family time for one day. Maybe he'd go pull a patch of weeds…find the dippy grin again.

Seventy-Eight

Heidi parked near Stella's Boutique on a side street lined with flowerbeds and understated storefronts. The temperature was much warmer than at the coast, but who would mind in such a pretty area? Eucalyptus and other trees shaded the quiet village. There was no freeway noise. No crowds.

Hud would like it.

She phoned his number yet again, vowing not to leave one more huffy message about how she'd viewed the perfect property and—

"Heidi." His real-life voice came through the phone. "Sorry."

"For finally answering?"

"Been busy. How are you doing?"

She rolled her eyes. He hadn't listened to one of her messages. "Hud, I checked out one of those properties, the one that seemed the best fit for you. It's a writer's paradise. Three private acres. The house is not fancy. It's not huge. It's not outrageously priced. It's full of windows with views. The owner is eager to sell. He's recently widowed and is moving up north to be with his kids. I'll send you the link."

"I'll think about it."

"You need to come see it."

"I mean, I'll think about moving back."

"You've thought about that."

"And I rethought it. I'm not so sure now."

"I suppose that was on Sunday, when Piper was upset. Before that—"

"We're into after that. I don't see us going anywhere. If I relocate—"

"Why don't you see the two of you going anywhere?"

"Because she's not over Jared."

"Hold on. You thought she would get over him?"

Hud went quiet.

"She's not getting over him. She is who she is because he's a part of her. He comes with the package. It's not a competition."

"It's too…messy."

Heidi guffawed. "Honestly, Hud. You've been in your fantasy world way too long. Life is messy."

"I don't do messy well."

"None of us do. That's why we need each other. Messes put chinks in our armor and that's how we let people in and then we can help each other."

"Chinks in our armor?"

She smiled and touched her scar. "That's what Adam says. He said that before the accident, I was so independent, he didn't know how to get close to me."

"I thought you guys were always close."

"Well, not this kind of close."

"And what kind of close is this?"

"Oh, you know."

He chuckled. "Didn't I just see you on Sunday? What happened in forty-eight hours?"

"I drove on the freeway yesterday all by myself. And then I called Adam because I wanted to celebrate with a good friend and you were too far away. So he brought pizza over last night and ta-da." In a silly, singsong voice, she said, "We're going steady."

Hud laughed loudly. "That's great news."

"You too could have this sort of great news. Shall I make an offer on the house? At least we can get you into the neighborhood."

"Anyone ever tell you that you're pushy? I want to hear more about Adam."

She could take a hint. Her buyer needed some space. And she didn't mind talking about Adam, not in the least.

Stella's Boutique impressed Heidi as much as it had the first time she visited. She roamed around the shop now, chatting with Piper and Jasmyn. "Piper, you look at home here. More so than at Tellmann's, I think."

"Thanks. I feel totally at home here." She smiled. It didn't completely erase the tension that lingered on her face.

Yep, Hud, life is messy.

Jasmyn said, "How's your first day working from home, Heidi?"

"Super. I made a to-do list, which I hadn't done in five months. I met a client and he bought a house."

Jasmyn laughed. "Wow. Just like that. Congratulations. You're off to a roaring start."

"Yes. I also checked into a property for my brother, east of town here."

Piper turned her back to them, but not quick enough for Heidi to miss an expression full of everything sad.

Heidi could be pushy with Hud all day long, but that probably wasn't the best approach with Piper.

Jasmyn said, "Is he moving?"

"Considering it. Anyway, I'm here for a makeover. Did Piper ever tell you how she made me over a few years ago?" Heidi grabbed at her short hair with both hands and made a funny face. "It's going to be a tougher job this time."

They laughed. Piper showed her makeup, accessories, and clothes. Heidi went next door and had her hair trimmed and styled. She made an appointment with her eye doctor. Maybe she would get contact lenses again, maybe not. She would definitely change the eyeglass frames.

In the end, she decided against buying the heavy-duty makeup. She wanted the reminder every time she looked in the mirror of a chink in her armor.

By the time Heidi headed home to the Casa, she felt pleased with her first day of working on her own. She'd crossed every item off her to-do list…except convince Hud and Piper that they should give each other a chance.

Seventy-Nine

Liv opened the courtyard front gate and welcomed Julian inside. They hugged.

"I haven't been here for quite some time. It's lovelier than I remember it, Livvie. Is that the jacaranda Syd planted?"

They walked over to it. A few tenacious purple flowers dangled behind the slender leaves. "It's my favorite gorgeously messy tree. This whole area has been a purple carpet. Would you like some tea?"

"Thank you, no. I'm on my way to a meeting in the area, so I only have a few minutes. I wanted to catch you up on Val."

At his somber tone, Liv's spirits sank. "Shall we sit outside?"

They sat in the chairs outside her cottage.

"I'll get right to the heart of the matter," he said. "Val remains a mystery. I am concerned about her. It's none of my business, but I can't help but notice that unsavory people hang about her patio all hours of the day and night."

"Are they loud?"

"Yes, but it is typical of the neighborhood, especially during summer and spring breaks. None of it falls under the category of disturbing the peace. I'm not sure what they're up to. No, actually, I probably am sure."

"Should you call the police?"

"They're not overtly breaking the law."

"Do they go inside the cottage?"

"Thankfully, no." He cocked his head and shrugged. "What can I say? It's Faith's home and it simply is never disturbed."

Liv nodded. "I hope it stays that way."

"As do I. Val is looking the worse for wear. We have talked four or five times now. She seeks me out, always to discuss business. She asks about her dad's way of doing business and about how the two of us worked together. She asks for my advice about investments and about real estate."

"She's picking your brain."

"Precisely. I'm quite all right with that. I feel perhaps I'm relaying information Syd would have had he lived longer."

"And yet she's deteriorating?"

"In my opinion, yes. She informed me this morning that she is moving out next week, much earlier than expected. She told me she's found a condo to lease nearer where she and Heidi conduct most of their business. It seems another spur-of-the-moment decision, like the beach house was. Like I said, I am concerned. There is a darkness about her."

"You've done what you can, Julian. As least she approached you for help. I wish she would trust me. Not that I could save her, but she is Syd's child. I so want to love her."

"She has Heidi in her life and she has her brother, who both happen to be in your life. Correct?"

She smiled. "That makes a connection?"

"I think you know the answer to that."

"Speaking of Heidi and Adam, I have a bit of news." She paused for effect. "They've developed a fondness for each other."

He chuckled. "That's marvelous news. I told you Adam was fine."

"Yes, you did."

Syd would be happy for his son, for his success, his contentment, and now for his new love…with the old friend.

Well, that story had been told once before with Syd and Liv in starring roles. She only wished she could tell Syd a good story about his daughter.

Eighty

Heidi peered over her shoulder at Adam. His sunglasses glowed orange with the reflection of the setting sun. The kayak rocked gently as they sat out beyond the surf, waiting for the end of day.

She grinned. "We've been seeing each other for one week tomorrow."

Laughing, he flipped his paddle and sprinkled water on her arm. "Turn around. You're missing the main event."

"I don't think so."

"I love you too."

She faced the horizon again. He said that often. Every time she heard it, fireworks boomed inside of her.

In less than a week they had become each other's main event. She had never imagined such a glorious thing. What she had felt in the past when dating others could not compare. She must have been attracted to the mere idea of having a boyfriend, not to the guy himself.

The other day she phoned her mom and dad with the happy news, which told her how serious she was. She never shared such things with them. Her armor had probably been in the way.

Of course it was easy to tell them about Adam. From the day Ethan and Rita first met him years ago, they thought he was, quote, the best thing since the Colonel started frying chicken.

"Adam, did I tell you what my mom said? She said that I've always sub-consciously compared other potential boyfriends to you and they never measured up."

Behind her, he chuckled. "Rita is an artist. She sees more than we do."

"I'm beginning to realize that."

"Did I tell you what my mom said?"

He had told her too much of what his mom said. It still ruffled her feathers to think of Cathy's hurtful reaction to Val's living next to Julian. At least she was fine with Adam reconciling with Liv. "What did she say?"

"That I did the same thing."

"She did not."

"No, she didn't. But it's true. I can't believe how dense I was not to see it sooner."

"You were incredibly slow-witted," she teased.

"I want to make up for lost time." His hand touched her back. "What do you think about spending Mondays together? We both work on the weekends."

"Mondays?"

"Aren't they slower for you too? We could just play. Take time to get reacquainted."

Heidi's muscles tensed. Take Mondays off? There was always work to do, especially now when she had to focus on building her business. Val would never agree. Mondays were a good day for them to meet. There was always work to do! People to talk to. Properties to see and to list. Realtors to network with. Research to do. Papers to sign—

"There it goes."

She watched the sun disappear over the horizon. The ocean's edge lit up like a river of gold. It was almost as beautiful as the dazzle that filled her when she thought of loving Adam…of being loved by him.

The obvious smacked her like a volleyball to the head when she wasn't paying attention. Rejoin the old rat race or live at a different pace? Fill in that chink and hit the streets full on or stay connected to the guy sitting behind her?

She reached back and felt his hand take hers. "Spending Mondays together is hereby officially on the calendar."

Eighty-One

Piper lingered with her parents inside the airport. They were early for their flight and the security line was short. None of them wanted to rush through a goodbye.

Darlene and Bob were teachers, on summer break, practical, down-to-earth, and parents of five. Slight of build with light brown hair turning even lighter with gray, they had begun to resemble each other. They were also two of Piper's favorite people in the whole world.

"I love you guys." Piper easily spoke the words.

"Oh, honey." Her mother hugged her. "It's been wonderful."

"Wonderful?" Her dad frowned. "Dar, it was dreadful. It was like we buried Jared all over again."

"Yes. I meant other than that."

Piper said, "I know what you mean. And, Dad, it was wonderful to be with you. You helped like you always have. I wouldn't have wanted to go through these past few days without you."

"And," Darlene added, "it was wonderful seeing Liv and all the others again. And wasn't it a treat to stay in the Casa this time? I adored Cottage One. I adored Stella and her boutique."

Her parents had arrived the same day Stella returned to the shop. Piper was taking a few days off, but after Darlene told Stella the situation, the few days turned into a week with pay.

They chatted a few more minutes and hugged a few more times. They waved and walked toward the end of the line.

Then her dad turned and marched back to her. "Go get him, honey." He flicked a hand. "All that waiting for the knight to come to you, hogwash.

Sometimes guys just don't catch on. I know you'd be just fine without him, but I think you like him. And sometimes lonely is not a good thing." He kissed her cheek and left before she had a chance to say anything.

Go get him, honey.

She stood for a long time, glimpsing her folks here and there as they made their way through security.

Go get him, honey.

But…but…

She had told her parents about Hud, about her feelings, about her fears, about her decision to let things settle on their own. Their paths might cross again, if he visited Heidi or if he moved to the Rancho Sierra area. Maybe they'd see a ball game together or go out for coffee. It didn't much matter at this point—

Go get him, honey.

Piper always carried her passport with her. She had gotten into the habit when Jared went overseas, in case he would need her in the blink of an eye at a hospital in Germany or somewhere.

She always carried a change of clothes in the car with her. Another habit, this one prompted by a job that sometimes required twelve-hour days and a new outfit depending on the activity.

There was no need to backtrack to the Casa after leaving her parents at the airport. She drove straight to Tijuana.

The drive took less than thirty minutes. Although she had been across the border a couple of times years before with friends, the area felt unfamiliar. The city was busy, colorful, and confusing. The Spanish signage was so different in appearance from American ones, they made no sense to her. In the back of her mind she was remembering reports of violence not far from the border.

She was quite certain her father had not meant for her to enter Mexico, but she was running on adrenaline. Sanity had nothing to do with her decision to *go get him.*

Hud lived further south. She had a vague notion about traveling to him. There was one highway that led down through Baja. If she stayed on it she would be safe. She would recognize the name of his town when she saw it. Did he say he drove about an hour from the border? Hour and a half?

She had called Heidi for directions but her friend had not answered. Piper left a message.

Now as she crept through traffic on a narrow side street, she wondered if she had taken a wrong turn. She thought the one obvious sign with the word Baja and a number on it would have led her to the right place.

The adrenaline rush fizzled. She wanted to cry. "Nuts, nuts, nuts."

She pulled into the first empty space alongside the curb that she could find. So much for surprising Hud. She had to call him. Would he cut her off? Would he nip whatever she hoped for in the bud by saying don't bother to come?

He answered on the second ring. "Piper."

At the sound of his voice, her heart thumped in her throat.

"Piper, are you there?"

"Hi. It's me. Um…"

"Yeah. Um…"

She laughed nervously. "So anyway, I'm in Tijuana and I'm probably lost—"

"What? You're here?"

"I wanted to surprise—Hud, I'm so sorry. I'm sorry I'm such a nutcase. I'm sorry I told you to go away. I'm—"

"Shh, shh. Calm down. I'm sorry for all of the above too. Listen, where exactly are you?"

"I have no idea. I think I saw a sign for the highway. I followed that and here I am. Nowhere."

"Piper, I'm in a line to cross back into the U.S."

At least an hour passed before they were able to find each other. They stayed in contact on the phone and maneuvered their way through blocks that had no familiarity about them. They parked within sight of each other.

His expression was a mix of panic and relief and…and something else. It was the something else that carried her down the sidewalk and into his arms.

Several hours later they sat in a fast-food restaurant. Piper had followed Hud to it not long after crossing the border. They ate fish tacos and tortilla chips and salsa.

They also smiled often and a little bit crazily. They held hands often.

She said, "So tell me again. You were coming to see me?"

He chuckled. "I was coming to see you."

"And you bought a house?"

"I bought a house. At least my agent put in an offer this morning."

She smiled.

He smiled.

"Hud, I'm sorry I'm so fragile."

"Fragile? You were going to drive down through Baja and you had no idea where you were going."

"I knew where I was going. I was going to wherever you were."

He took her hand and stroked it with his thumb. "Piper, you're the most beautiful woman I've ever met and the strongest. You've been through some of the worst life has to offer, yet I think it has only made you shine brighter. I see what you've done for my sister. I see your independence and creativity in your work and your photography. I am so surprised that you want to spend time with me, you could knock me over with a feather. Sorry about the cliché."

She smiled.

He smiled. Then he stood, leaned over their messy table, and kissed her.

Eighty-Two

Friday evening, long after darkness fell and the men had helped set up tables and chairs, Heidi lingered in the courtyard with only the women. Tasha had informed Beau it was a girls' thing. He could go.

Sam and Beau's short rehearsal had consisted of the pastor talking them through the ceremony. Riley practiced with Tasha, who by now was an old hand at being flower girl. There was no rehearsal dinner, only girl time under the twinkle lights, time to anticipate together the coming celebration.

They covered the rented folding chairs with plastic to keep them clear of debris that the trees would shed overnight. A short aisle had been created between two small groupings of the chairs that faced the fountain. A makeshift altar sat in front of that. Jasmyn, worried that the pastor would trip and fall backward into the water, rearranged the table a few times.

Patio tables and chairs had been moved to one corner where caterers would serve the food. Centerpieces were a variety of flowers in large vases. Liv and her friends—all of whom had gardens—had cut and arranged them.

"It's perfect," Liv declared.

Sam agreed. "If I'd been one of those little girls who plan their future wedding, this is what I would have come up with."

Coco said, "This reminds me of my third wedding venue. Beautiful. Just beautiful. That was the one that Bing Crosby attended."

There was an exchange of glances. Piper whispered to Heidi, "We've only heard of two weddings."

Déja offered to take Tasha inside while Riley pushed Coco toward her cottage. Riley's voice carried, "What was your third husband's name, Coco?"

"Benjamin."

"I thought Benjamin was your first husband."

"We married two times. Before and after Roger. Was that his name? That doesn't sound right."

Heidi stifled a giggle.

Piper muffled her laugh behind a hand.

Inez hugged everyone goodnight. "I must get home to Louie before he forgets my name. Night-night, all."

Sam said, "I'm going to miss this."

Jasmyn said, "I promise to call whenever there's a gathering. And you'll be close enough to stop in often."

"What about the impromptu times?"

"I'll call then too, and you can put on your running shoes and get over here as fast as you can."

Liv said, "Whenever you come by, Samantha, you'll be the impromptu spark."

Sam put her arm around Liv's shoulder. She was the only one tall enough to do so without making Liv stoop. "Thank you, Mama Liv."

The women grew quiet.

Heidi noticed Jasmyn and Sam put fingers to the corners of their eyes just like she was doing. Sam's mother had canceled her plans to attend the wedding. From what Heidi gathered, the two were not close and the woman was not in good health. Still, though...

A wave of gratitude swept through her, for her own mother. Oddness aside, Rita was always on Heidi's side. She felt thankful, too, for Adam's mother, her first greeting aside. Cathy had thrown her arms around her and announced, *You are the ideal woman for my Adam. Maisie never even came close.*

Heidi also felt grateful for Mama Liv, the surrogate mother to them all. It spilled over into a gush of words. "Liv, this is the most special place I've ever known."

"Oh, thank you, dear." She paused. "Are you quite sure it's *the* most special place?"

She thought of the myriad of homes she'd grown up in and the great disruption they represented to her psyche because her family was always leaving them. She thought of the fun times in college dorms and apartments and how their temporariness also muddled her well-being. She thought of how much she adored her two condos, how she had been so adamant about owning them only to lose the last one.

An essential key had been missing from each and every one of her homes except the Casa de Vida. It was what its name implied, the house of life. There was a spirit about it, a presence that was absent in all the others.

"Yes, it's definitely the most special place."

"Well, girls, let's keep this between us. I thought for sure her most special place would be in Adam's arms. At least that's the way it was for me and Syd. I wouldn't want to hurt the boy's feelings."

"Not fair, Liv! That is so not fair. I was talking houses."

Laughter drowned Heidi's protests and she joined in.

Eighty-Three

The bride wore the white, bead-covered sheath the women had given her and a simple gardenia in her short dark hair. The groom wore a black suit and green tie.

Again Liv sat in the place of honor reserved for the mother of the bride. She wore a new dress from Stella's Boutique, a muted floral that reminded her of a Monet painting. When she had put it on that morning, Liv checked herself in the mirror and sensed the pride meter veer toward the *Mm-hmm, I am something else* end.

It wasn't the dress so much as the special mother's seat. Samantha and Beau had insisted, as had Jasmyn and Keagan. She reveled in the attention, she truly did.

It's okay to revel in the attention, Livvie. Syd's voice. *You are something else.*

He had told her that all the time, that she was special.

These people love you and this is their gift to you. Accept and enjoy it. And, by the way, you do look beautiful.

He would have liked the dress.

I seriously doubt you'll get a big head over it.

I might this time, Syd. I just might.

His laughter echoed in her heart. She missed him every day of her life. The imaginary conversations helped.

She turned her attention to the ceremony in front of the fountain. Beau and Samantha held hands, looked into each other's eyes, and made promises of love. Jasmyn and Tasha stood to one side, wearing pretty green dresses. Wearing his embroidered shirt, Keagan stood on the other. Beside

Liv sat a very nice man named Randy. Samantha's boss had escorted her down the aisle and seemed to pay close attention to the service, as if the girl were important to him.

The pastor pronounced a blessing.

Liv silently prayed her own. *Abba, give them wisdom and devotion in the ordering of their common life, that each may be to the other a strength in need, a counselor in perplexity, a comfort in sorrow, and a companion in joy.*

The small crowd included friends of Beau as well as Randy and his family, a wife and two young boys. There were also, of course, the newest members of the Casa family. At least Liv thought of them as family. Hudson and Adam had been around enough in recent days to qualify.

She smiled. The two men multiplied the joy around the place a hundredfold.

Seafood from Jojo's Catering was a hit. The two-tiered cake was elegant. Chadwick had done a fine job providing music on some sort of high-end contraption. He claimed he had once been a DJ. "Once" probably referred to a specific number. People enjoyed it, although it was a bit loud. Liv hoped neighbors would not complain before things wound down.

As guests came and went, she had left the front gate open. Every now and then, passersby peered inside and smiled at the obviously festive occasion. A few acquaintances from around the neighborhood stepped inside to say hello and offer congratulations.

And then, as twilight deepened and the solar lamps winked on, a stranger who was not a stranger walked through the gate. She passed the first few cottages and paused near the large bird-of-paradise that grew at the corner where Cottages Three and Four met, away from the crowd still lingering at the tables or dancing near the fountain.

She had long chestnut hair. She wore high heels, a black dress, and an attitude. Her eyes, Liv was sure, would be the same brown-flecked hazel as Syd's.

At Liv's elbow, Piper breathed, "Uh-oh."

Applesauce.

Adam darted across the courtyard and greeted his sister with words Liv could not hear. Something in the girl's face shifted. Her attitude seemed to lessen.

Lord, have mercy.

Did Valerie want to see Liv? Liv wavered and then she straightened her shoulders. If she were anyone else, Liv wouldn't ask. She would walk right over there and say, "Welcome."

All right.

Liv walked over to Syd's daughter who eyed her from around Adam's shoulder. She nudged her brother aside and waited for Liv to reach her.

"Hello, Valerie." Liv put out her hand. "Welcome."

The girl glanced at Adam who shrugged at her, turned to Liv and winked. He walked away.

Valerie put out her hand. "Thank you."

"You're more beautiful than the real estate ad photos."

"You don't have to schmooze me."

Liv chuckled. "I wouldn't do that."

Val gazed back at her and seemed to size her up.

Liv waited.

At last Val said, "I always hated the name 'Valerie.' It reminds me of that old Alpine hiking song. 'Val-da-ree, val-da-rah, val-da-ha-ha-ha-ha.'"

Message received. "Like your father. He disliked 'Sydney' immensely." She waited, not wanting to tell Valer—*Val*—something she already knew.

"Why was that?"

"He didn't want people to associate him with a city in Australia."

"I didn't know that. You could probably tell me all kinds of things about him."

"Maybe. Maybe not. He adored you. And I'm not schmoozing."

"I guess you're just *nice*. Mom said you were. Guess she got a change of heart in her old age."

"This happens. We mellow."

"I'm too young for mellowing. Just so you know, I'm not here for any big reconciliation. I was only curious since my business partner and brother seemed to spend a lot of time at your place."

"You're welcome to look around. I'm sure Heidi would be glad to show you her cottage."

She glanced here and there. "Mm, not quite into that yet."

Yet. Liv felt a dose of hope far too large for such a throwaway word.

Music blasted across the courtyard. Chadwick had increased the volume. Liv turned. "What on earth—Oh." She smiled at the sight of Tasha scurrying over to her. The familiar tune caught her attention.

"Miss Liv! Miss Liv! We are family!" The little girl spotted Val and halted in her tracks several yards short. "It's time to dance!" She spun on her heel and rushed off. Her reaction was un-Tasha-like. Typically people were magnets for her hugs, even strangers.

Liv watched Samantha and Beau each take one of her hands. She saw Adam and Hudson kick up their heels and swing their arms as if they'd done it countless times before. She heard the words ring out from a choir of Casa folks and guests. "I got all my Casa peeps with me. Come and dance around the courtyard with me."

She turned to Val. "Come join us."

Syd's daughter shook her head adamantly. "I just wanted to say hello." Without another word or glance, she strode to the gate and disappeared into the dark beyond it.

Abba. Please. The two-word prayer was all she could squeeze through her aching heart.

"Liv, Liv, Liv!" The chant came as the song faded away. Chadwick restarted it and the group began to sing again. "We are family." They beckoned to her.

Despite Val's denial, she had taken the first step toward reconciliation. Perhaps she would take another, perhaps not. Liv could not force her. She could only hope and, most likely, grieve.

But that was for tomorrow. For now, on the evening of Samantha and Beau's wedding, joy would reign, not heaviness.

With a smile and her voice lifted high singing about Casa peeps, Liv sashayed on over to her family and joined in the dance already in progress.

Discussion Questions

1. Both Heidi and Piper experience events that might be referred to as traumatic "Before and After" moments: After the incident, their lives will not be what they were before. What were the events for each of the women?

2. How were they each affected? What were some positive and negative effects on them?

3. Have you experienced a life-changing Before and After event? How did it affect you? Were you changed?

4. Until she meets Heidi, Liv has buried her painful past. So deep is this, she has not even told those closest to her at the Casa. Now, the past hits her with an onslaught of fear and doubt. She has two stepchildren who despise her. Why does she hesitate to share this information with others?

5. Have you struggled with past situations or decisions that you can't change or control? How do you deal with it? How do you let go? Have you been labeled a scapegoat?

6. If you've read The Beach House series, Julian is a familiar character to you. What truth about God does he remind Liv of? (Jason Gray sings a lovely song about this entitled "Remind Me Who I Am.")

7. Like Piper, do you have difficult anniversaries? How do you deal with them?

8. Heidi, Piper, and Liv must give up things—literally and/or figuratively—in order to mature and grow wiser. Discuss what these things are. Do you relate to the women's stories?

9. The Casa residents are a family of the heart—unrelated people living in community, offering love and support. How

do Liv, Jasmyn, Keagan, and Chad play roles in Heidi's journey? In Piper's?

10. Like these fictional people, do you have a family of the heart? Who are they? What makes them family?

Thank you, dear reader, for spending time at the Casa de Vida in Seaside Village. Neither are real places, but real bits of Southern California flow through them in sights, sounds, smells, and sometimes in the name of a location. I hope you've enjoyed your time here.

Peace be with you.
Sally John

To learn more about Harvest House books and
to read sample chapters, visit our website:

www.harvesthousepublishers.com

HARVEST HOUSE PUBLISHERS
EUGENE, OREGON